THE SPA DECAMERON

THE SPA DECAMERON

Fay Weldon

Quercus

First published in Great Britain in 2007 by

Quercus
21 Bloomsbury Square
London
WC1A 2NS

A CIP catalogue record for this book is
available from the British Library

ISBN (HB) 1 84724 092 5
ISBN-13 978 1 84724 092 7
ISBN (TPB) 1 84724 093 3
ISBN-13 978 1 84724 093 4

10 9 8 7 6 5 4 3 2 1

Printed and bound in Great Britain by
Clays Ltd, St Ives plc.

THE SPA DECAMERON

1

Yuletide Break
Special Offer For High Achievers
Ten days of peace and tranquility at world-famous Castle Spa.
Join us in scenic Cumbria on Christmas Eve, leave on
January 2nd.
Special Bargain Price £5000. All treatments inclusive.
Join Lady Caroline Evercreech and others of like mind for
a low calorie Xmas lunch. Women only.
Recoup from the past year. Face the adventure of the
new one inspired and refreshed…

The advertisement was in November's *Vogue*. Finding myself dis-astrously homeless and partnerless, I read it with attention. An out-of-date *Vogue* – we were three days before Christmas – is not my usual reading, but I was at the hairdresser. My name is Phoebe Fox, I am a woman of a certain age, and blondish. My roots needed doing and I wanted extra streaks. I had to have somewhere to go, as a matter of urgency. And wherever I was going I had to get there with good hair.

'Call up Castle Spa, then,' said Pauline of the Hair Salon. 'Find out if they have a space. Book yourself in. Treat yourself. You work hard enough, God knows.' It was pleasant to have this from someone who has been working on their feet five days a week for more than twenty years. I am a writer: at least I can sit down while I work. She can't. She must stand and bend, and it is hard on the feet, and the back. I have known Pauline for years. She is my guide and my confessor; she is buoyant, strong, hard-working and noble, and usually right.

I called Castle Spa on my mobile while I waited for the colour to take. The receptionist took my name and number and said she'd call back in five minutes.

'Perhaps she's checking you out to see if you're enough of a high achiever,' said Pauline. 'But I daresay you are.' I thought I would be too. Last time I looked I had 523,000 hits on Google. I write literary novels which get studied in US universities: it is not exactly fame but it is attention. Pauline's next appointment had failed to turn up. We had the place to ourselves, and poured ourselves some wine.

Castle Spa's receptionist, who introduced herself as Beverley, Bev to her friends, got back to me in four and a half minutes. Yes, they had one vacancy left for the special-offer ten-day break: someone had just dropped out. Yule was a magical time at Castle Spa: only sixteen guests instead of the normal forty, to allow staff time off with their families – the work/life balance being so important at Yuletide – but the very best world-class beauticians in attendance, and a brilliant White House chef as locum –

'Yes, yes,' I said, 'anything. Just book me in.'

The day before, our kitchen ceiling had come down, the bath having been left to overflow. The bath came down too. By 'having been left' I mean my husband Julian had left the tap on and gone away, but I am not one to apportion blame. I have done worse myself. Electricity throughout the house had shorted. There was no heating. I could not use my computer, and worried in case the 'save' facility had failed when the power went off. It was with mixed feelings that I cancelled the Christmas Dinner for twenty-two – family and friends – and with pleasure that I booked with Pauline for the next morning, knowing that at least with her I would find comfort, warmth and sympathy.

Even as Julian and I had tried to find plumbers, builders and electricians and failed, Julian's stepfather called from Wichita, Kansas, to say that his mother had had a nasty fall and broken a hip; it wasn't looking good and Julian should go at once. Flights at this peak time were full – there was a place for Julian though not for me. He had an hour to get to the airport. We were parted: a rare, terrible but rather exciting event.

I cried a little. Friends were away, or busy. Neighbours were indifferent. I spent that night with my head under the duvet, cold without Julian. The house peeped electronically for hours, warning me that the power was off and stand-by batteries were running low. I was conscious of food rotting in the freezer, milk souring in the fridge. A miserable night might be no more than I deserved – my first reaction, when the Wichita phone call came, having been to hope that my mother-in-law had died: a mean and wretched thought, if fleeting – but I could not put up with another.

I had thought I would have to push my way through seething crowds to get to the Hair Salon in St John's Wood High Street but the streets were quiet. The group soul of the consumer crowd around Christmas is unpredictable. A mass of spending humanity will surge through the street and then suddenly withdraw, like the tide before a tsunami. It had withdrawn now and the pebbles were showing, unnaturally bare and dry, and my instinct was to turn and run – but where, nowadays can one run to? Other than, for the likes of me, at least, Pauline's Hair Salon.

I gave Pauline my house key so she could go and empty fridge and freezer and take what she wanted. Waste not, want not. I confessed my evil thoughts about my mother-in-law, my relief at not having to cook Christmas lunch for twenty-two – I have three grown sons, Julian has three grown girls, and most are partnered, and some have children – and the sense of mixed panic and joy at the thought of days on my own, with nowhere to go, and no roof over my head. She absolved me. I read the advertisement while she mixed the bleach, and she gave me permission to go to Castle Spa and indulge myself.

Thus it was that Bev booked me in for the ten days of Yuletide. I was to be expected late Christmas Eve. I would miss a few treatments by arriving after the others but I must understand this was my responsibility and there would be no discounts. She asked me if I wanted to sign up for the nature ramble on Friday. It booked out quickly and was all inclusive. I said no, appalled. I am not good with nature, preferring indoors to out at the best of times, and it was midwinter. What kind of indulgence was this going to be? All lentils, health, no discounts and chakras? And I had envisaged high achievers as sophisticates from the world of business, high finance and fashion. People who competed to ramble in the middle of winter were not my kind of people. And I knew those White House chefs: there is a rapid turnover: they get fired for incompetence. What had I done? The days ahead would be desperate, bleak, hungry, and lonelier than if I had stayed home. But it was too late now. Bev had my credit card number, and as I held the line the bill was validated.

Bev waited until it was done to tell me that since the break was all about perfect peace and relaxation, ladies were asked not to bring in phones or laptops during their stay.

'Of course,' I said. 'Of course. Anything.' They would hardly do a body search. So that, for good or bad, was settled.

Pauline washed my hair and then set about the business of turning my head into a porcupine of silver foil spikes. That was when I asked her for the latest in the Nisha/Eleanor/Billy saga and got more than I bargained for.

The next ten days were to be full of stories. My real life being on hold, other lives seemed to rush in to fill the void. This, the terrible tale of the Bitch Witch, had revealed itself little by little over the last six months, instalment by instalment, a new one every time I visited Pauline. The drama had been safely distant in time and space – today it was to become alarmingly close, horribly real.

The Tale of the Bitch Witch

Nisha was one of Pauline's favourite clients, and Eleanor the least favoured of all. Nisha was a sweet, domesticated, dark-eyed heiress from Bollywood, married to Billy, a bluff Northerner, financial director of a media conglomerate. Eleanor, the bitch witch, was a lean, pale, bloodless, feminist set designer, and she was having a torrid affair with Billy. She worked from home.

Eleanor would tell Pauline all about it over the wash basin every Monday morning. Billy was most likely to stop by early in the week, so she always came in on Mondays. Nisha would come in on Fridays, to look good for Billy during the weekend. Nisha had no idea about the role Eleanor played in Billy's life. Though many of Pauline's other clients did. Word got round and Eleanor seemed happy enough that it did.

Pauline's clients tended to be in the media: her salon was in NW1. She was popular: she could get customers in and out while the taxi waited on the way to a meeting. Twelve minutes for a wash and blow-dry was her record. She could make you look as if you'd come straight from Harrods, or were just off to Crufts, depending on the image you wished to present.

Nisha stayed home and looked after her home and her husband Billy. She had a sweet face, a soft voice, and thick, long, dark, glossy Asian hair with a tendency to greasiness. It took a long time to blow-dry. Nisha never complained. Eleanor's hair, by contrast, was so fair, soft and fine it was dry almost before it was out of the basin. The problem was giving it volume, and shape. Eleanor sometimes asked Pauline to start again from the beginning, even if she had other clients waiting. Eleanor, in other words, could be a real pain.

And then every second Wednesday Billy would come in for a cut. Pauline confided in me that he was immensely vain: but then, she said, men who go to their partners' hairdressers often are. They like to compete. Pauline would squirm as Billy would boast to her about the two women in his life, and how they adored him. She would remonstrate with him, as she wielded the clippers, but could make no impression.

'My wife doesn't know. She's a sweet girl but frankly not very bright,' Billy would confide. Or, 'I have the most amazing sex with Eleanor, she'll do anything.' Or he'd complain about his wife. 'Nisha put my shirt through the wash and now it's a rag. And at night she just lies there, and I keep thinking how much shorter her legs are compared to Eleanor's.' Or, in favour of the mistress, 'Eleanor's so creative. She's making quite a name for herself in the industry. Frankly, the trouble with Nisha is that she has no brain. We're not right for each other.' It would go first one way and then another. 'But Nisha adores me; she'd be heartbroken if I left. I don't want to hurt her. What am I to do?' And then he'd talk about how a man had to be practical: his wife's father was a power in the international media, and would probably send a hit man after him if he ditched Nisha. 'You have to be careful with these Indian moguls. At the same time a man has to be authentic to his feelings. You're a woman of the world, Pauline, what am I to do?'

But he didn't really expect a reply, or want a solution. He just wanted to talk about himself.

My friend Annie, also a client of Pauline's – short chestnut curls – had been to parties at Billy and Nisha's, and had reported back. They were wealthy, and the house a triumph of Harrods' taste. Nisha would insist on preparing the nibbles herself – which was seen by some as cute and by others as eccentric – and drift through rooms full of hard-bitten media folk like an angel of grace in a pink sari, smiling and obliging. Eleanor would be there, posing as Nisha's dearest friend. Annie said she once overheard her advising Nisha on what underwear to wear to make her legs seem longer. And everyone knew what was going on, and no one had the courage to tell Nisha. Eleanor would tell everyone how before Billy she never knew what love was meant to be: she was the veritable queen of the land of Orgasma. Billy would fondle Eleanor in public when Nisha was out of the room. On one occasion they sloped off together for a ten-minute shag in a cloakroom before turning up again, Billy smirking, Eleanor licking her lips like a cat after cream, just before Nisha returned from the kitchen with a tray of quail eggs and avocado dip. And when Nisha came back into the room and saw Billy, her whole face would light up with joy. She really loved him: could never get over the pleasure of being married to him, away from a stultifying home life, living in London.

I had met Eleanor; I often came in on Monday mornings after a hard weekend. She lived just around the corner from the Salon. When she ran round from home to the salon, she'd often throw on a long brown knitted coat with wide sleeves and appliquéd yellow flowers. I quite liked it and asked her once where she got it from, and I forgot, and then felt I couldn't ask again. In summer she'd wear long denim dresses which no one could get away with who didn't have a model's figure, which she did, and a model's face, which she didn't. Her chin receded and her teeth were bad. She would be against cosmetic surgery.

'You have to say something to Nisha,' I'd say to Pauline. 'Someone just has to.'

'Me? I'm only the hairdresser!' she would say. 'I'm not going to be the one to make her unhappy, break the spell.' Pauline feels she has the duty of the priest or the doctor to hear but not to intervene, and besides, getting personal is the way to lose clients. Any unpleasantness and they're off. Pauline doesn't mind much if she loses Billy – and he'll never leave anyway: he loves talking about himself too much. She'd be happy to lose Eleanor. But she wouldn't want to lose Nisha. She likes her too much, and loves the feel of that heavy, happy hair. And Nisha was happy, you could tell by her hair, Pauline said. It was glossy and shiny. Unhappy women get rough, starey hair – the way dogs' coats go when they're ill. Mine, I am glad to say, is in reasonable condition.

'Who cares about truth?' Pauline would say. 'Relationships are sustained by lies!' Which I always found somehow shocking.

But it couldn't last. One Friday Nisha came in for her appointment distraught, tearful and wailing, tearing at her beautiful hair. Billy came back from having a haircut, packed a suitcase, said Nisha would be hearing from his lawyer, and left to go and live with his mistress. Eleanor, her best friend. It had been going on for months: everyone had known, except Nisha. She had thought people were her friends and they weren't. She was humiliated, betrayed on all sides. Her life was over.

'I expect you knew too,' said Nisha to Pauline, and when

Pauline had nodded apologetically, had gone for Pauline tooth and nail there and then, in the salon, in front of clients. Pauline's trainee had called Nisha's sister, who came round in a taxi and took her away to the doctor.

'And then on the Monday,' Pauline had said, 'just three days later, Eleanor came in, bright as a button and cheerful; and not even wearing that awful brown coat. She'd lost the kind of sly look, and I thought well at least someone's happy. But then she said, "You know what? I've booted Billy out. Living with men sucks. I cut up his suits and threw all his bags out the window. Five days and I was going mad. When he wasn't trying to drag me into bed he was trying to get me to make chapattis. What do I want with her leftovers anyway? I can get my own man, if I so choose."'

'You should have thrown the bitch out there and then,' I said, when I heard.

'I am not my sister's keeper,' Pauline observed. 'I am only the hairdresser. And I have the scratches to prove it.'

'It's appalling,' I'd said. 'Eleanor's a bitch witch. She was never interested in Billy, just in trampling Nisha. It's a type. In love with Daddy, wanting to usurp Mummy: when she succeeds she feels so guilty she throws Daddy out.'

Then it was Billy's turn to come in. He could hardly look at himself in the mirror for misery. Pauline had known kicked dogs look better. He'd been asked to resign because of his 'inappropriate behaviour'. He'd thought he was top dog, pack leader, and could do what he liked, but he'd found out he couldn't. People had closed ranks behind Nisha. There were bigger dogs than him out there, and they didn't like how he'd behaved, and had found his cloakroom behaviour distasteful. So it was out of the door with his belongings in a black plastic bag, and nowhere to go, because Daddy's lawyers were already in the house and the locks had been changed. And it was no good going to Eleanor because she had changed her mind and thrown him out. 'Gone insane,' as Billy put it, 'kicked me out of bed as soon as I tried to get into it.'

Pauline was opening up the basement area of her salon for

treatments: manicures, eyebrow shaping and Botox, and had taken on two assistants to run it. There was a juice bar too. It was as busy as can be.

'Nothing like a good scandal for encouraging trade,' I said to Pauline.

'It's an ill wind,' she said. They were all talking about it. Poor Nisha, bad Billy, stylish Eleanor. The latter was in great form, in and out all the time chattering, reborn as a feminist only with a 1930s air: a waved bob-cut (platinum, which her fine hair wouldn't stand forever), bosomless (which was easy), and a red red lipsticked mouth, talking about the villainies of men, getting to go to a whole new set of glam parties.

'She came in for an eyebrow dye,' said Pauline, 'and all she could talk about was how she'd met Sam Klines, the film producer.'

I knew Sam Klines – I'd worked with him once – and was friends with his wife, a nice girl called Belinda. Very thick red hair. I laughed and told Pauline Eleanor wouldn't stand a chance. Sam and Belinda as good as went round hand in hand. We remarked on how the tables had turned: once women got the blame when things like this happened, were ostracized for failing to keep their man: now men got the social spurning, and the victorious woman approbation.

Then Nisha's sister – an elegant, taller and slimmer version of Nisha, who ran her own business and didn't look as if she'd ever cooked a chapatti in her life – had came by to say she'd just put Nisha on the flight to Mumbai, complete with an attendant. Nisha was unbalanced: tended to be violent and aggressive to other women, and was being sent home to live with her mother and sisters. That put up the sales of cranberry and pomegranate juice no end. Then everything quietened down.

But next time I was in, for a quick blow-dry before lunching with my agent, Pauline said that Sam Klines' wife Belinda had just been in. 'Eleanor recommended her so I fitted her in. Lovely chestnut hair. I gave it a good cut: it needed it.' Belinda confided that she'd asked Eleanor, albeit a little reluctantly, to stay with her and

Sam for a week or two to help her get over the debacle with Billy.
Eleanor had been feeling depressed. Nisha had hanged herself
and she felt people were blaming her, unfairly. Nisha had always
been unstable and it was all Billy's doing, anyway. 'He as good as
stalked me,' she'd said. 'Why did she have such crap taste in men?
Why was it she couldn't sustain a relationship? Was there something wrong with her?'

'What could I do but take her in?' Belinda had said to Pauline.
'She kept saying she just wanted to be part of something secure
and cosy and for a bit: a loving household. And I like to help.
What are friends for?'

At that I'd picked up my mobile and phoned Belinda, in spite of
Pauline's warning that I would merely look stupid if I did. I told
Belinda she should on no account let Eleanor over the threshold.
Eleanor was bad news. Look what had happened to poor Nisha.
'Eleanor is a bitch witch and her evil eye is on Sam and that is why
she is so suddenly your best friend. She was Nisha's once.'

Belinda was polite but cautious. She said I misjudged Eleanor,
who was seeing lawyers about a possible sexual harassment suit
against Billy, and she'd be glad if I would put the record straight
wherever I could. Eleanor was a good and generous friend.
Presumably I had got the gossip from Pauline: she, Belinda,
wouldn't be going to that hotbed of gossip again! A good cut was
worth a lot, but not that much. Belinda thanked me for the
warning, and appreciated that my motives were of the best. In
other words I was an interfering bitch, go away. We exchanged a
few pleasantries and I put the phone down.

'Told you so,' said Pauline. 'That didn't go too well, did it!
Now she's insulted because you're suggesting Sam's seducible.
And I'll bet you've lost me a client. My general experience is that
if people can take things the wrong way they will. So least said,
soonest mended.'

'You're a fine one to talk,' I said. And then the story had gone
quiet and two months had gone by, during the course of which
Belinda failed to ask me to her birthday party, and failed to return

to Pauline for a booked henna rinse, Eleanor kept away from the salon, poor Nisha was no more, and the trail had apparently run its painful course. And here I was, just before Christmas with no Christmas in sight, homeless, husbandless, just booked into a Spa in the distant north where high-achieving women line up to get to go on nature rambles.

My head was in the basin, when Pauline's phone went. She excused herself and answered it. Fortunately it was the last rinse and I could grab a towel.

Pauline turned pale: she sat down. Eventually she put away the phone and spoke to me. Her voice trembled.

'Eleanor is dead,' she said. 'Murdered while she was asleep, lying next to Sam Klines in the marital bed. Knifed to death by Belinda. She didn't touch Sam.'

'She wouldn't,' I said. 'She loved him.'

'Then Belinda turned the knife on herself,' Paula said. 'Died on the way to the hospital.'

The life of the world must go on. My hair was wet: Pauline blow-dried it. We said very little.

'Sam's in hospital with shock,' she said.

'Must have been a blood bath,' I agreed.

'The paparazzi are already there. Ghouls,' she said, and brought me the mirror so I could look at the back of my hair.

'Very nice,' I said.

It is strange how other people's deaths affect us. A close colleague dies, and for some reason we feel nothing. A distant aunt is no more, and we are devastated. There are no observable rules. I had never met Nisha, knew Eleanor only to be irritated by her; the tragedy could remain a story; fair enough. But Belinda? My erstwhile friend? Why did I feel so little? Perhaps the unfortunate phone call and her rejection had humiliated me more than I thought. Perhaps being left off her party list had hurt more than I pretended. I felt shocked, and flat, but I could not grieve for poor Belinda, silenced and quiet forever, and was ashamed of myself for this reason.

2

I stayed the night on my son Alec's lumpy sofa, but slept well enough. His wife Miranda insisted on checking out Castle Spa on the internet. It had a five-star rating and mixed write-ups from its customers. Five thousand pounds for ten days was such a snip Miranda wondered over decaffeinated coffee what was going wrong up there. I did not care, I said. I was tired, and looking forward to a rest, a holiday, a massage and a manicure. And I was still in a degree of shock about the murder and suicide as who would not be? It was all over the newspapers the next morning. 'Tragedy hits London's la-la land', one columnist wrote. 'Knife crime spreads its social base', wrote another. Eleanor had come to stay. It had taken her only two weeks to get Sam to the marital bed. Belinda had come home unexpectedly to find them both in it. She had walked out, taking nothing. Came back the next day to find the locks changed. Sam and she were not legally married: there had been a ceremony in Barbados but they had not bothered with the civil one. The house was in his name. She had no rights, only Sam Klines' love and that was gone. Eleanor had looked out the window and laughed. The next week Belinda had broken into the house with the knife.

But I had my own troubles. Miranda said she would try and find me an agency which would restore the house to health over the holiday, while warning me it would cost a lot. But if I could afford Castle Spa presumably I could afford anything. She didn't have to add that £5000 would have paid for quite a number of non-lumpy new sofas. I knew what she was thinking. I have the novelist's gift for hearing other people's thoughts. It's fine on the page but horrible in real life.

But she forgave me and said she hoped I wasn't too upset by what had happened to my friends. Murder and suicide! I said I only knew about it by hearsay: they were not friends anyway, just colleagues, not close to me. And in that moment I denied them – shut them out of my thoughts. I knew I shouldn't but I did. And then Miranda conceded that I could probably do with a rest and a change, everyone could. She was a teacher and a mother of two, she should know. I hugged her; I am not given to physical demonstration, and I think she was rather surprised, but I am very fond of her.

It was a four-hour train journey from London to Carlisle. Alec drove me to Euston to catch the early train. As we turned into Camden Road my mobile rang. It was Julian in Wichita, saying his mother was looking good: there had been a fright but in the end no broken hip, just a nasty bruise. Wichita, he said, was now six feet deep in snow: getting home might be a problem. No worries, I said, I'd booked myself in to a spa until after the New Year and wouldn't be home anyway. There was a short silence from Julian. He seemed slightly shocked.

'That being the case,' he said, 'I might as well take my time coming home.'

His mother, he said, would be happy for him to stay; he was getting on with his stepfather okay. He might even take a couple of days in New York meeting up with old friends. The phone beeped a warning and went dead. We had hit a patch where the buildings are tall and there is no network coverage. And then when the signal returned I couldn't get back to him. This time the fault was his end – like leaving the bath running and going away.

The streets were quiet this morning too: there were few early shoppers about. I didn't mention my tsunami parallel to Alec because he and Miranda and the children had been in Sri Lanka on that Boxing Day morning, 2004, and had had to run for their lives. It would be tactless to remind him. I just remarked on the emptiness of the streets and he looked at me curiously and said hadn't I been keeping up with the news? I said frankly, what with one thing and another, no.

Alec, who works in computers, said YouTube and other internet video sites were spreading rumours of a flu epidemic. Sumatra flu was a variant of bird flu and a distant relative of the plague. It was said to attack the young rather than the old, and had a five percent mortality rate. There was official denial but blogs were advising people to stay home and avoid contact with others. On the Marylebone Road a cyclist wearing a mask crossed the lights at red and narrowly missed death by bendy bus. I gasped, and took in a breath of hot exhaust air. The grim reaper could come at any time, I said, not bothering with Sumatra flu. Pollution would get you, if a bus didn't.

At the station Alec opened the glove box and sweet papers and crayons fell out – the children are four and three. He picked out a slightly grubby surgical mask and suggested I wore it on the train if I was scared. I handed it back to him, haughtily. I was not chicken, and too old to die anyway. He did not get the joke.

I said again I was sorry about there being no family get together this Christmas, and Alec said actually the children were rather pleased. They would get to open their presents at home. I tried not to feel offended.

The train to the north was standing room only so I pushed my way to first class through festive and good-humoured crowds. As Miranda said, if I could afford Castle Spa I could afford anything. Empty lager cans already bounced on the floor: beautifully wrapped Christmas gifts overflowed from the laps of pretty girls. Everyone liked going home for Christmas except, apparently, my grandchildren. The weather was unseasonably warm but the rail company had been told it was winter and the heating was full on. One or two people were wearing surgical masks, but they were of the cycling kind, lank-haired and serious, and probably fearful of the common crowd at the best of times. Nothing to do with Sumatra flu.

I eventually found the one seat left in first class. I averted my eyes from headlines about the Eleanor/Belinda horror. I would put it from my mind: I would live in the present. Something had happened that could not be undone: the press would forget about it soon enough, so must I. I must concentrate on having a rest and polishing up my chakras. I had not had time at the station to buy a paperback. Four hours without reading matter! What was I to do? I studied the woman opposite. She was staring out of the window and took no notice of me. Why should she? She was strikingly handsome: around forty-ish, I supposed, with a toughened skin which suggested cigarette smoking, hard living and tropical climes rather than the passage of time. Her hair was short and sun-bleached; she wore a denim skirt, a slightly grubby white shirt and a blue and white spotted scarf, and carried it off with style. I felt hopelessly bourgeois by comparison, in my neat taupe coat and discreet gold jewellery. I tried to guess her occupation. It would be glamorous and involve travelling. She had the look of a Kate Adie, a male competence allied to a female attractiveness: just too busy to get her shirt to the dry-cleaners. She was brooding about something, and muttered to herself; she saw me watching and firmed her lips together.

Then a tear actually appeared on her cheek. She brushed it away and sniffed, and tried to swallow the sniff, and gulped. Women who cry on public transport are usually women in love, overcome by self-pity. I changed my mind about her. No exotic foreign correspondent she – more like a farmer's daughter going back home for Christmas, having been dumped by her boyfriend. I was disappointed.

My upgrade cost £213. I argued in vain with the guard: the women opposite got involved and egged me on in protest. Her voice was husky, as with whisky, cigarettes and hard, hard living. By the time we were finished I was £213 poorer but at least well disposed towards my neighbour. When she took out her ticket a leaflet fell out of her wallet. It was a flyer for the Yuletide break at Castle Spa. Was she going there too? She was. We had a four-hour journey ahead of us. To chat or not to chat? I had no book. She was upset. We chatted.

Her name was Mira Miller, she said. She was a journalist. The name was familiar, I said, truthfully enough.

'I used to be a foreign correspondent,' she said. 'A war journalist.' And she named a popular daily newspaper with a right-wing bias and a taste for scandal. 'Now I am relegated to features. The cost of insuring me abroad is too high. Or that's the official version.'

I told her my name was Phoebe Fox. She said I looked familiar. I said it was true I did occasional late night cultural programmes for TV but had the kind of face shared by many. She accepted that, rather to my chagrin. People have only a fitful memory for those who appear on TV, unless they are newsreaders or weather girls.

She offered me a swig from her water bottle. I accepted. We settled in to talk. I asked her if there was any truth in the rumours about Sumatra flu – she should know, if anyone did – and she laughed and said none. Emergency services and doctors surgeries were running as normal. Coughs and sneezes, nothing worse, to all accounts.

'Mind you,' she added, 'journalists tend to report what their editor wants them to report, and if the internet says one thing, Alistair' – her editor, I assumed – 'will want to hear the opposite, on principle. So I imagine we'll be feeding the panic.'

Something about the way she said 'Alistair', with a kind of appreciative lingering, made me think he was responsible for the tears when she thought no one was looking. Thirty years of feminism, and this?

'Isn't it kind of sad,' she lamented, 'going to spend these particular ten days in a health spa? What does that suggest about someone's life?'

I said briskly it could suggest all kinds of things. It could mean your bathroom floor had fallen through into the kitchen just before everything closed down for the holidays. It could mean you were a business woman and liked to fill in your time constructively: party time being over, and offices closed for deals and counter-deals, and you having had enough of people and friends and just wanting to relax, you might well want a dose of Castle Spa. Then you could rejoin the fray in the New Year, half a stone lighter and with your tattered chakras robustly restored. Or perhaps people just liked a bargain – £5000 for ten days sounded a lot, but it was nothing by the standards of the rich.

'It could mean,' she said bitterly, 'that your editor gave you this assignment, ten days of Christmas manicures, because he knew you had no one and nowhere else to go and he pitied you.'

I thought I was probably right about this Alistair. More, that it wasn't so much that he pitied her as he wanted some peace over the holiday. He would have a wife and children tucked away and be playing happy families and the last thing he'd want was his mistress calling to offer seasonal greetings.

'Or there could be people running away from stalkers, serial killers or the supernatural,' I said, 'or women just divorced, or recuperating after release from prison, or worn out by importunate lovers and just plain tired, or girls who have won the prize in a charity auction of wishes. Who knows? We will see.'

And see we did.

3

Castle Spa, for all its magnificence, is to the architectural eye way over the top. Based round the foundations of what had once been a Roman bathhouse, then a convent, then a fortified mansion, it had been renovated in the mid-nineteenth century by William Burges, he of the extravagances of Cardiff Castle. He had added a moat, a working drawbridge with heavy chains, turrets, gargoyles, cannons, a couple of Landseer lions and an excellent orangery. The place stood in isolation. Its nearest village was Limmus – little more than a crossroads in the valley set between craggy, unrounded hills, with a general store and a cluster of mostly new houses – a mile walk from the castle across fields, marshes and streams, three miles if you went by road.

Mira and I shared the taxi from Carlisle, a ten-mile run and only fifteen pounds. Just when the eye had got accustomed to the damp greens and pale browns of the Lake District in winter, and the dramatic swooping shapes of hills and craggy rock, we rounded a bend and the elaborate man-made structure of Castle Spa loomed in front of us. It seemed something of an affront: one feared draughts at best, rats at worst.

But once inside the great oak doors it became apparent that we were safe. Someone had spent millions, and quite recently at that, to bring the interior up to what Mira's brochure described as 'the most eloquent standards of contemporary taste'. In other words the baronial hall which we expected to enter was no different from the lobby of a new hotel in any cosmopolitan city.

Bev was there to welcome us. She had her best face on, as we were to find out. She swiftly persuaded us that her entire ambition in life was to greet special and important guests to Castle Spa. Meeting interesting people made her job worthwhile. She was tall, slim, neat, colourless and sexless. Euan the spotty boy porter would take our bags to our rooms: she would show us round. So we had met on the train: how nice; shared a taxi: how sensible. We were the last guests to arrive: too late for any treatments today, she was sorry, but in good time for the welcome dinner with Lady Caroline, who was running late but due in at any minute. Even as she spoke there was a sudden roaring, beating noise from the back of the castle which made us jump. The last rays of the evening sun were blotted out, as if some giant bird was hovering overhead.

'No worries,' said Beverley. 'Lady Caroline likes to take the helicopter, not the train.' And if her determined smile suddenly seemed a little thin-lipped and rictus, it was not our place to notice it. I didn't quite hear her add *'that fucking fat cow and her carbon footprints!'* I pretended it had not been heard, or said. Lady Caroline swept through the lobby almost before the rotors had stopped: a cool grunt to Beverley, a nod to Mira and me, and she vanished inside a door marked PRIVATE, slamming it behind her. One had no time to pick up details – just had the impression of a large, rather blowsy, bad-tempered Madame of a suburban brothel, annoyed because business was bad. She wore hoop earrings.

Beverley – I had decided I could not think of her as Bev, she was too major a player – recomposed herself and wanted to be certain that we had not brought laptops or mobile phones with us, and we reassured her.

'There's no network coverage here anyway,' she said. 'During our time at Castle Spa we focus on our chakras and our spiritual balance sheets, no nasty electronics to disturb us. If we don't learn to live at one with nature, the planet will soon find ways of taking her revenge.'

She went ahead and Mira and I tried not to giggle behind her back. The New Age blanket had grown wider and heavier since last I looked. Lift its edge and more things than ever peeped out at you: not just chakras, crystals and meditation, but organic food, work/life balance, global warming and a vengeful Gaia herself. E-mail, computers and all things digital: bad; spiritual balance, whatever that was: good.

She told us there was a Christmas tree in the Banqueting Hall in the south wing, if we liked that kind of thing, but out of respect for other faith groups the rest of the Spa had been left undecorated. And if I heard her say under her breath '*One way for the fat cunt to save money*,' I surely imagined it. But when I am tired or stressed I do have a way of hearing, not quite with my ears but registering in some other part of me, loud and clear, what others would like to say and don't.

I took this problem to a psychiatrist once and he asked if I was a writer of fiction. When I said yes, he said he had known other novelists complain of the same thing, and he could only suggest one looked after one's general health and immune system, and stopped bringing imaginary characters to life, if one wanted it to stop – and treated it as good for business and put up with it if one had the rent to pay. There was no cure, he said, for a propensity to let the dividing line between what one invented and what was 'real' become blurred. Electrical synapses leapt between the left and right brain barrier, and that was that. I could try sleeping pills. I left and he sent me a bill for £220.

It still happens on occasion. And it can be disconcerting, indeed really upsetting, to sit at a dinner party and hear what people think as well as what they say: you wait for uproar to erupt around the table and when it doesn't, realize you are the only person who heard what was said across the table to another guest – '*What fucking rubbish you talk*,' or '*God, you're boring*.' I could see, hearing Beverley's words or non-words, that I could do with a ten-day break in a Spa, communing with Gaia, erasing carbon footprints, massaged into peace of mind.

The Oriental Room was the Spa's *pièce de resistance*. Mira and I gasped obligingly and almost sincerely. The original Burges features had been kept and restored: a vast vaulted room, a ceiling which featured pre-Raphaelite paintings of nubile, veil-draped, well-breasted women, and which was supported by four stone Evangelistic beasts with massive paws, clawed and dangerous. Medieval tapestries lined the walls. In the foreground stood, incongruously but impressively, a great heart-shaped marble Jacuzzi, which hissed and steamed gently, and sent waves of scented vapours drifting into long low-pillared corridors which led off the central space, and which surely could not be good for the tapestries. Unless of course they were nylon fakes. The pillars looked like malachite and green obsidian. Perhaps they only looked like the real thing, perhaps it was only a Las Vegas version of original splendour: but it would do.

'Actually this room gives me quite a headache,' confided Beverley. 'I'm a minimalist myself. But the ladies love it. Sometimes we let it out for film productions. But they always manage to break or spoil something.'

'But then you can claim on the insurance,' I said, mindful of the destruction at home. I would have to call Alec and make sure the builders were on board.

'Too right we can,' she said.

Would my insurance company countenance overflowing baths? I realized I had no idea.

The Oriental Room was not enough. I wanted a bed, a bath and dinner. Failing a shot of vodka and some bread and cheese on our arrival, a glass of sherry and a peanut would have done. What was I doing here? It had been madness. Ten days out of my life on a whim? I am a size fourteen. Would they seize me and diet me and turn me out into the world a twelve? Please no. I need padding: my nerve endings are too near my surface for comfort as it is.

I am not, by the way, an alcoholic. The drink-driving conviction was exceptional. Julian and I had been out to a Valentine's Day dinner. I had thought he was the one not drinking, he had thought I was. By the time we realized it was too late.

Nothing would now do but Beverley took us round the treatment rooms – pale green, conventional, soft lighting, what Mira referred to in my ear as crematorium music – music to die to. She read my mind: she slipped me a junk chocolate bar from her large and trendy bag when Beverley wasn't looking. I had a friend.

Guests who had arrived at the time most desired by Beverley drifted around the treatment area, in a silent, trance-like state, bulky in white towelling gowns, faces denuded of make-up, hair damp, stunned by the shock of a sudden change in their life and times, in the transit lounge of their lives which was Castle Spa. The girls who were paid to massage them, oil them, exfoliate them, stick needles into them, and who flickered in and out of the treatments rooms – *'I'm ready for my lady now'* – seemed a special twittering race bred for the care and comfort of stronger, wilder, richer women than themselves. Lightly boned little things, with pale, delicate, indoor faces and big, startled eyes. But I knew their hands would be like iron as they kneaded and pressed reluctant flesh: they sought revenge, and why should they not?

Our bedrooms, when Beverley finally allowed us to reach them, were standard hotel rooms, executive grade, but without television, radio, clock or telephone, off a long carpeted corridor on the ground floor of the west wing. Mine faced the moat: green algae covered the water. There was indeed no signal for my mobile. Fortunately I had a watch. Beverley said the castle's one telephone was in her office at the top of the East Tower and would be available in emergencies. Dinner would be in fifty minutes. Most ladies liked to dress for this special occasion. Did I know anything about computers because hers kept crashing? No, I said. It was not strictly true. She went away and I fell upon my bed. The search for tranquility can be exhausting.

4

Lady Caroline presided over the soup course. Dinner, elaborately staged and served, complete with place names, was set out along the long table in the Banqueting Hall. It was an all-women event. I couldn't find my place name, and hunger and tiredness making me paranoiac, at first suspected Beverley of omitting my name on purpose because I had assumed she was Australian when she was a Kiwi and I hadn't helped her with her computer. Thus guilt works upon one.

But then I found my name. I was seated between a Jane Jones and a Mary Smith, both pseudonyms so obvious they longed to be asked who they really were. I refrained. Mira's shirt was now white silk rather than white cotton, and the spotted scarf was now long and green. I had changed into the boring blue lace dress I wore for literary readings; the others for the most part were in the simple, expensive, little black pack-and-go dresses they took for the end-of-conference party, plus minimal gold jewellery. We would all, I guessed, have rather stayed in our rooms and eaten off trays, but it was not to be.

Lady Caroline, overdressed in low-cut green velvet and diamonds, with hard eyes, big bosom, tight blonde curls, a small mean mouth, and an impenetrable background – she was no lady of the county kind, but might I suppose have married an elderly peer for his money – welcomed us and exhorted us to polish up our chakras and avoid electronic communications, which were sapping the vitality of the planet. She was, I thought, slightly mad. She was with us only for the soup course, low calorie lobster bisque with a rather too strong flavour – and made her apologies and left the table. Beverley followed her out. Lady Caroline and she had an altercation outside the door, but it was brief and we could not make out what was being said. A sharp, strong jab from Beverley's shoe pushed the heavy door shut and there was no telling what had happened next. No one around the table commented. Conversation remained stilted. During the steamed sole and broccoli course we heard the helicopter come to life and clatter off into the night sky, and watched search beams sweeping the fields and cliffs around. After that we all relaxed, the more so when Beverley appeared after the chicken course was cleared by spotty Euan, unlocked a cupboard and set bottles of champagne at intervals down the table.

'It is fucking Christmas Eve,' she said, or certainly thought. Then she went away, pink with rage, and left us to it.

We drank champagne with our lemon mousse, flavoured with honey, served with tiny almond biscuits, speculated to no conclusion as to what went on behind the green baize door, and decided it hardly mattered. Beverley would look after us. There were twelve of us and we got through six bottles. Someone, who I was later to know as the Trophy Wife, produced grappa. Those of us with strong constitutions soon finished it off. We found a second and then a third wind. Someone rolled a joint and passed it round. When the Trophy Wife suggested we repaired to the Jacuzzi and saw in Christmas Day by telling each other stories it felt like a good idea.

We trooped into the Oriental Room, where it was warm, steamy and dim, and sat round the marble edge, legs dangling. A few stripped and got right in, but it was pleasant just sitting in gentle wafts of steam beneath the threats of the Evangelistic Beasts and the promises of the pre-Raphaelite maidens, dangling our legs in gentle bubbles.

Someone found chocolate and we told ourselves the ten days didn't really begin until the next day, and though some argued that point, all agreed that since none of us had so far been asked to weigh in, the fatter we were in the morning the more pounds we would have lost when we left. That is the way the minds of dieters work.

Our conversation that evening of the first day led us into games of truth and dare. We would tell each other the truth: things which had happened which we normally kept secret, even sometimes from ourselves. Chatham House Rules applied: what we found out in the room would never be attributed outside it. But I am a writer – and so you have this book. It is for the Higher Good. And I have of course changed names to protect the innocent.

The Trophy Wife went first. She felt the need to talk. She had let herself go of late. That is to say her frizzy, reddish hair had been allowed to grow too long and thick and the ends were split. She bit her nails. She seemed skinny and bony, rather than lissome and slender – though mind you that can be a matter of presentation – how one carries oneself, sees oneself. The muscles in her arms were slack; she did not work out. I even fancied I caught a glimpse of dark hair beneath her armpits, and her feet and elbows needed attending to with pumice stone and exfoliator. But perhaps she was here at Castle Spa to have exactly these things seen to. She had only been here a few hours. She was reluctant to wear one of the swimsuits provided and brought her own down from her room. It was the one-piece black and white kind cut low on the thighs, which had been fashionable enough two years back, but no one wore any more. The cut had not proved popular.

In her favour was her thin, intelligent face, creamy skin, bright if hooded eyes, long aristocratic nose, and a slightly haughty demeanour, so it seemed slightly out of order for me to have noticed her imperfections. She enunciated beautifully, but not quite naturally, as if she had spent time at elocution lessons. One of these onion people I thought: peel away the layers and there will always be another one beneath. That was fine by me, and one should not judge people by their appearances.

5

The Tale of the Trophy Wife

'I had intended to keep quiet,' said the Trophy Wife, 'about my two years in prison, but I feel confident in this company and can see I need not. Women of achievement, courage and given to independent thought, as you lot obviously are, will not be easily discommoded. Now, knowing that I was inside for murder, will you be frightened of me? I hope not. I am not in the least likely to murder you. You will, I am sure, be sympathetic – on my side, indeed, if sides are to be taken. That the Athens court gave me a mere two-year sentence demonstrates their understanding of my predicament. The Greek authorities may take English bird-watchers very seriously, convinced that as they scan the skies they can only be spying on Greek Air Force activity. They cannot conceive of such a degree of nerdishness – but they do understand crimes of passion. They understand jealousy. I would have been out six months ago but for the small part I played in a prison riot. I tried to warn the authorities that a riot was building, but they would not listen. Signs of impending riot are the same the world over: inmates start stocking up on food supplies; more prisoners than usual in the lock-ups; more demands for transfers; more staff requiring sick leave; an increased level of outside agitation from lawyers and activists – the signs are obvious if you know what to look out for. Just as in any collapsing marriage – the collapse practically announces itself – the warning signs are overlooked. It is as if, unconsciously, in our search for event, for drama, we actively prefer to discount warnings. Thanatos, Freud's death wish, is alive and well in all of us.

'I know more about prisons than most because once there was a real possibility of Lucas being arrested for fraud in the US, and I needed to brief him. Lucas is – was – my husband. I am – was – his Trophy Wife. Trophy wives are no longer bimbos, they are either women of distinction with careers in their own right, or they are efficient PAs who add bed to the their job description, and are rewarded with a marriage ceremony.

'Little did I think that I, not Lucas, was the one who would end up in prison. Lucas had me sent there.

'One thing I have noticed as I go through life is that goodness is its own reward. No good deed but goes unpunished. For warning the authorities about the pending riot in Korydallos, Athens' premier prison, I was at once suspected and then accused of instigating it. They could not conceive that a prisoner might act for the greater good of all. Just as I could not conceive that Lucas would treat me as he did after so many years of what I had seen as real affection between us. But men are different from women. Once they have decided to put you away as a wife that is the end of it. They forget all that has gone between you before: the sacrifices you have made, the pleasures you shared. Their acknowledgement is only to the woman currently filling the bed, currently at the stove, providing wifely benefits. If there is no one to fulfil this role, they quickly find someone who will. Women are not so rational. Let them find themselves a good lawyer at the first sign of trouble.'

'I'm really glad I don't know as much as you do,' observed the pale, fragile little thing who shivered on the edge of the marble slab, wearing a negligible pale pink bikini. 'I'd get so depressed.' She was all of twenty-two. We were to know her as the week went on as the Manicurist. She had an awesomely massive bodyguard in attendance, one Kimberley – armed, broad-shouldered and firm-jawed, but with a surprisingly sweet expression – who from time to time would come out from the wings to place what looked to me like a mink wrap around her charge's shoulders, only to take it away on the nod.

'Don't worry about it,' replied the Trophy Wife. 'With experience come the tools to deal with it. When I was finally released from Korydallos in Athens ten days ago, she went on, I made my way here to Castle Spa as soon as I could. When I studied History of Art, my special field of study was Burges and the Pre-Raphaelite movement, and I knew of this castle by repute, but had never in the past had the opportunity to visit it. We trophy wives are always in the same double bind – we must learn so much, so fast. We must never show ignorance in whatever world a new marriage takes us to – whether it be Hollywood, banking, horse racing, computing, the further reaches of the art world or Arctic exploration – we seldom get a chance just to sit back and enjoy. Even now I cannot afford to waste time. Time is a woman's enemy and I have a living to make. But ten days, I thought, just ten days, after all that has gone before, all that is yet to come – surely this is justifiable!

'Tomorrow I will begin on my body, which so badly needs professional attention. I will have my hair coloured and cut for a start. A pedicure, most of all a pedicure. At Korydallos cockroaches would run over one's feet. Such a pleasure to be here at last – where there is air and space, and rest and good food of a kind, and quiet. One of the worst thing about prisons – for those of you who do not know them – is the continual noise: shouts and shrieks in echoey corridors; TV and radio blaring out from individual cells, all set to different programmes. The stink of urine; dreary and barely edible food shovelled out onto plastic plates; and most depressing of all, the ugliness of the all-pervasive concrete. Stone has surface, depth, difference, and aesthetic quality: concrete has none. Nature cannot help being beautiful: man in a bad and punitive mood prefers to make things ugly.

'A few artists in every generation rise up to fight back the tide of depression and squalor with which mankind chooses to surround itself. This place, for example, this Burges' hall of rare delights! This marble pool, the oriental tiles which line the walls, the obsidian pillars, those four ceiling beasts looming over us as we chatter on: marvel at the balance thus created between the geometry of the hall and the rocking, thrusting beasts. This is very different from what met the eyes at Korydallos. Oh, the magnificence, the absurdity of it! And we such little fleshly creatures, soft and vulnerable, yet holding so much within our comprehension; from the vastness of outer space to the intricacies of the microcosm by way of William Burges. But I am carried away. Do I bore you? Embarrass you? Even now I can feel Lucas's eyes upon me, warning me to shut up. Sometimes at dinner parties I would get carried away, and racehorse dealers and their wives, or casino chiefs and their floozies – whatever the field be in which Lucas was currently operating – would look at me curiously and I would fall silent and smile apologetically. I should have been more careful. We might still be together.'

There were reassuring murmurs from around the pool, but some did look a little startled. I am a William Burges devotee myself, but can moderate my enthusiasm. Hers could seem a little desperate. But I took back my earlier opinion. She looked pretty good for someone just out of prison.

'Two years in Korydallos, talking mostly to hapless victims of slave trafficking, arrested because their kidnappers had abandoned them in a strange land without papers, gives one little opportunity to talk about what one loves. There were a few English-speakers inside, true, but one was limited largely to the exchange of information, not ideas. Though I quickly learned enough Romanian, Albanian and Bulgarian to get by, and my Greek has always been adequate, I found the same to be true of the majority of the prison population. Information, not ideas. Language itself is not the difficulty; it is the mindset of others. And yet wherever one goes in the world, I have found, there will always be one or two people of like mind. Stranded in a strange place, as is too often a woman's lot in life – they will insist on falling in love and following that love – she should not despair. There will always be someone in the same boat as herself. The dreariest suburb hides a free thinker or so: one of the flat-earthers will turn out to be a Darwinist; the pub landlord turns out to be a Schopenhauer enthusiast.'

'I found that,' said the Vicar's Ex-wife. 'Even in this little village I was landed in, I found a couple of friends. We started a book club and others came and soon it was a place I rather loved, before it all went wrong.'

The Trophy Wife smiled her support and continued.

'Inside prison it is bad form to ask why other inmates are inside: best to wait until the information is volunteered, adapted to circumstance as the teller sees fit. I told no one I was in prison for murder: I told them I had been incarcerated for the sin of hatred, fuelled by jealousy. They accepted that. Most Mediterranean peoples understand the concept of sin. It is only in the northern lands of the Reformation that it's gone out of fashion.

'And as for hatred, as for jealousy – I should not have succumbed to them. I deserved to be in prison, though perhaps not for so long: that was what kept me going when I was inside. Trophy Wife was my vocation, the way of life I had trained for from an early age: it was a job, albeit a 24/7 job, which many these days refuse to put up with – and I should have gritted my teeth, stiffened my chin, and put up with the indignities piled upon me by Lucas and the abominable Lithuanian, Vera Meirovitz. Trophy wives should keep their emotions under control, especially in sexual matters. They are meant to manage their men, not be swept away by passion.

'But some women are just insufferable. Vera Meirovitz was one such. She had no taste, and she was fat, stupid and dull. She had a penchant for embroidered peasant blouses and dirndl skirts. Can you imagine? She worked in Lucas's office as a book-keeper. Lucas, say what you will, normally had good taste in women. I do not understand what the attraction was.

'Vera was not known for her visual taste. She even carried a little bright blue knitted woollen bag around with her for good luck, slung over her wrist. It had bright red felt flowers sewn to it. Peasant art, a tribute to her Eastern Europe beginnings. In this hideous little bag she kept three decorated eggs – an old religious art form in the East known as *pysanky*. I expect the walls of her house are covered with cuckoo clocks and painted virgins. I still have no idea why Lucas said she was such a relief after me.

'What I *do* is relief. I am relief. I am the shelter from the storm, in Dylan's words: *"Come in," she said, "I'll give you shelter from the storm."* Why couldn't Lucas see it? It's not that I loved him – trophy wives don't go in for love – but I had a very, very clear sense of duty towards him. Having said that, I do wonder. My reaction to being put away as a wife is more than being put away by a boss after years of faithful service. Perhaps I did love him.'

'You were a victim of Stockholm Syndrome, that's all,' interjected the Lady Surgeon, briskly. 'You fell in love with your captor. So many women do that. Ask any woman in an arranged marriage. Love is the least stressful way out.'

'Sex sends up some hormonal response in the woman,' said the Judge. 'She needs to feel good about the man: she adopts his political views; she lies for him. I see it in court all the time.'

'Thank you,' said the Trophy Wife. 'I just need time, I suppose, to recover. Only ten days ago I was still in prison. Culture shock makes one so vulnerable. Many of the women in there were in thrall to the most horrible men, who landed them in prison in the first place and then abandoned them. That was what Lucas did to me and I must not lose sight of it. Oh, I have tried so hard all my life to be sensible, and where has it got me?'

'It's got you here,' said the Weather Girl. 'There could hardly be a better place than here.' At which the Trophy Wife cheered up, talked a little about how she should have her hair cut – and then went on with her tale.

'Many women like to define themselves by what they dislike – can't stand her; loathe him; hate yellow shoes; lobster soup? yuk! – it makes them better able to separate themselves out from the crowd. A few descend to actual hate. With women it's usually some rival in love, someone they once saw as an inferior – older, perhaps, or fatter – who has nonetheless managed to steal their man. With men it can be some low-grade business rival or a dullard bank manager who once had the nerve to stop them making the millions they deserved. Someone they felt superior to in the rightful pecking order who has managed to outsmart them. If status is involved the slight can niggle and outrage for decades. But while hate is reserved for the inferior, all tend to bow down to the leader of the pack, men and women too. I've known men happy to hand their wife over to the big boss for the night, and bear no grudge. A size-sixteen woman will bow gracefully out of the mating contest when a size ten comes along. To those that hath shall be given, as the Bible says. It's the reversal of the proper order of things that so upsets.

'Lucas was my husband. I was his fourth wife. Four times and a wealthy, ambitious and effective man will usually get it right. The first wife will be the girl next door, who didn't have the class or energy to keep up as he went up-market. She will pine for the rest of her life wondering what went wrong, why the happy ending promised in the books didn't happen. The second will be posh totty: have a title perhaps, ride to hounds, have the class but not the brain. Once the thrill of ownership has worn off he will be bored and, a couple of children in, will be easy prey to the sexual wiles of some accomplished bimbo, on the lookout for one such as he. There will be a very expensive divorce and a remarriage for him that he believes to be made in heaven. But the long, entwining legs, the startling emerald-green eyes which become grey when the contact lenses come out, the bounciness of the young silicone breasts over the dinner plate become an embarrassment as lust wears off, and the deal becomes more and more major, and involves governments and potentates: and taste becomes important as well as wealth, and a man has to have art on the walls and a wife who can tell the difference between a Monet and a Manet and not think it okay to serve Cristal at tea time.

'Enter the Trophy Wife. She will have the qualities of the other three: she will be fresh and sweet as the girl next door, posh-enough totty, bimbo with real breasts, all in one. And she will

---

have much more – she will be intelligent, discreet and elegant and have excellent secretarial skills. She will know whom to seat next to whom, understand the finer points of his business, will be sexually attractive to his rivals but never succumb to their advances. She will understand the art market, have read the entire Booker Prize shortlist, know her opera and her Burges, and will never herself watch television, unless he wants to relax in front of *Match of the Day*, when she will keep him company. And this, friends, was the woman I was. After I have had my hair done and my nails, and a drop of Botox and exfoliated myself from top to toe you will see it.

'My marriage to Lucas was my fourth as well. I too had had a chance to get it right. The first was in the days of my naivety, to a Rastafarian pub singer. He became world-famous and wealthy within the year, singing about white hos and bitches. Dumped by him, and sorrowing, I claimed my heritage. As one-time head girl of a leading girls' public school, and a fine horsewoman, I was able to marry suitably, this time to a young politician in need of a bit of class. He moved on to Cabinet level, and needing me no more, put me away and married a B-list celebrity. It was a humiliation, I admit it, and after that I went rather wild. I ran lap-dancing contests in Texas. I didn't have the legs for it myself, not really, not by US standards, but you can get away with a lot if you walk the walk. And people over there don't expect you to be genuine about anything. Suited me.

'Put that escapade down to pre-third-wife blues. In retrospect I am ashamed of myself. Do you think there is something wrong with me? Is defining oneself by one's husband so strange? Women have always done it: it's just these days the husbands change so fast, one might be in a kind of psychic shock. Or perhaps it is that both my parents died when I was small. I was brought up by trustees, like Shirley Temple in *Poor Little Rich Girl*. Did you ever see that film? A classic weepie? 1930s? No? Her mother died and she was sent to a boarding school while her wealthy father went abroad. When the money stopped coming through, she was made to sleep in the attic and treated as a servant. Everyone was nasty to her. Then her father turned up and it had all been a misunderstanding. She was reinstated as a proper person and everyone was nice to her.

'I always identified with poor little Shirley, never mind that the money always came through on the dot from the trustees. Never mind that my father, let alone my mother, never turned up.

'Next I married this really old guy, an oil billionaire, a Texan, and waited for him to die. Typical third-wife behaviour. I didn't marry him for his money exactly, though of course people said that I had. I just wanted to know that for once I could be married until death did us part. Or perhaps I just wanted to be holding someone's hand when they died, and set about organizing it in a rather complicated way. My parents both died at a distance: nobody's hand to hold. One moment they were flying to Aspen in a private plane and the next they flew into a mountain. My father didn't have bad-weather equipment: he shouldn't have gone up in the first place.

'The oilman's family said I fucked him to death on purpose but believe me that kind of thing takes two. He wouldn't have wanted it any other way. I handed all the money back to the effing family as soon as I had it. Well, nearly all of it. I didn't need it. Now I had my pride to keep me warm.

'After the old man died I really worked at myself. I wanted to put the lap-dancing past behind me. Determined never to be at a loss for conversation at a dinner party, I took courses in art history, politics, philosophy and economics. I developed quite a talent for portrait painting, and even had a show or two in Cork Street. I'd always dabbled about with paints, but now, more expert than most in the ways of the world, I seemed able to sum people up and get them on canvas pretty well. Through a lover in the royal household I was asked to paint the heirs to the throne, and after that my name was made: that casual, lanky diffidence, that blonde shock of hair, made an excellent composition. I was ready to be a fourth wife.

34

'And then Lucas came to me to have his portrait done. I managed to get onto the canvas the charisma of the man, the sense of easy power that emanated from every pore. He was flattered: I made sure he was. Poor Little Rich Girl's daddy had finally come home. We were just right for each other. Fourth-spouse types. I had my connection with royalty, a degree of artistic celebrity but not too much; I was well-dressed, well-educated, moderately submissive, and apparently stable. I was truly appropriate fourth-wife material, as he was fourth-husband material for me. The bimbo was quickly relegated. I became a Trophy Wife. I gave up painting. It seemed only fair. Being Lucas's wife was a full-time job.

'With my help Lucas had made a successful bid for a vast new sports stadium in East London. He had friends in government, a few of them quite well known to me over the years. Work on the structure had been abandoned a couple of years back when levels of ground contamination – including chromium, lead, cadmium, mercury and other minor metalloids – were declared unsafe by the unions. Lucas moved in and bought the land. In the interval those initial reports had not only been proved biased and unreliable, but new, more economical methods of remedial land clearance had been developed. Now work could go ahead. Lucas, who had bought cheap, could sell dear. He was in two minds – he could go for the millions or, more excitingly, he could develop the site. It was a risk, but the nation could do with another Lords cricket ground, a new sports and concert stadium, a new casino. He could do with a knighthood. Either way, he was elated, and also popping blood-pressure pills like sweets. He did not tire, but his people were, frankly, exhausted. Working for tycoons can take it out of you. So can being married to one, now that Viagra is available and the same energy was released in the bedroom as it was in the office, and I was four years into wedlock. We could all do with a holiday.

'I murmured as much in Lucas's ear. I had witnessed an outburst of temper when some junior brought him the wrong document. It was a simple error, such as anyone could make, but Lucas had

shouted and stamped, in the hearing of the whole office. I knew
the importance of keeping the staff sweet, especially these days
when no one can be hired and fired at will, when equality is the
watchword and teamwork is the rage. It was a mistake, and mistakes happen when you are tired. As with the junior, so with
Lucas. Disgruntled employees, and today they are so easily disgruntled, can do an enterprise a lot of harm. I did not know – it is
better not to know, let me say I suspected – that a certain amount
of shuffling had gone on around the early high-contamination
reports. There had been much wining and dining with the unions
at the time: then the withdrawal of labour – but it was not my
place to draw conclusions. In the end the public are the ones who
benefit from the activity of entrepreneurs. Buildings stand where
no building otherwise would: businesses flourish, where otherwise
there would be stagnation and entropy.

'"My dear," I said. "Let's take the staff on an outing. Let's take
out the *Minni*. Let's all have a week in the Aegean."

'The *Minni* was our yacht, over 85 meters long, sleek Japanese
lines, costing quite a few million dollars, and accommodating up
to 36 guests. It had all the features such boats do: a business centre
and conference space; health and fitness gym; a spa on the lower
deck – more Philippe Starck than William Burges, true, but at
least it could survive salt water. The same could probably not be
said for the Lempicka originals which lined the premier state
room, and I had told Lucas so, and now at least they were stored
on land when we were not at sea. There was too much plump
orange upholstery around for my taste, but to a certain class of
people it represents the ultimate in luxury, and I put up with it.
Most of the year we let the *Minni* out for corporate entertaining
at a good profit, but this summer someone with a spectacular
bankruptcy had dropped out, and the boat was just sitting there
in the Dodecanese with a full crew twiddling its thumbs – not to
mention chefs, catering staff, fitness trainers and so on. It would
be an outing for the staff to remember all their lives, and off-
settable against tax too.

'"Fine by me," said Lucas. "A works outing ends up cheaper than a bonus. They'll expect something now the stadium deal is done." The rich stay rich, or such is my experience, because they are mean. "But is the *Minni* available? If she is she shouldn't be."

'"She's holed up in the new Leros marina," I said, "ready and waiting." He gave me a little peck beneath my ear. He loved it when I knew things he did not. "Her last cruise was aborted, but we're suing the client's receivers, so it's a win-win situation." He gave me another little peck. The *Minni* had been the *Debbi* after the last wife, the bimbo, but he had renamed her, as good manners required, as a wedding present. He hadn't, however, given me the boat. And the pre-nup agreement had been on the stingy side, my lawyer said – but never mind, I lived and dressed well, and had a life I loved. Lucas had been badly stung financially over Debbi – I understood his feelings well enough. Life is a matter of reciprocal rights and duties. Lucas provided money, security, and the sexual charisma of power. I provided beauty, charm, entertainment, aesthetic competence. It seemed to me to be a more than satisfactory arrangement and, I had assumed, a permanent one.

'"We can fly everyone down in the Lear," I suggested.

'"You know the cost of aviation fuel these days? She only takes eight. I'm not forking out for three or four trips! We'll take six with us: the rest can go easyJet and take the ferry from Athens."

'And so it was arranged. The six we took with us in the Lear included Vera Meirovitz and her husband Timmy, a dweeby young environmentalist with an earnest manner and no sense of humour. The requirements of social responsibility required that we had such people in senior positions on the staff, though we paid them very little. I had nothing against Vera at the time, other than a general sense of boredom when I saw her, which was seldom – she was one of the three girls in Lucas's anteroom at work – and a dislike of her embroidered pull-string peasant blouses. She was not Lucas's taste and to date I had considered her no threat; rather heavy and lumbering, with black hair plastered round a porky face. Her wide hips seemed too big for the aircraft, which is designed for lean, quick people. She had a knitted bag dangling from her wrist and in it a painted egg, which she insisted on showing us.

'"Look everyone!" she cried. "St Christopher will protect us! He's the patron saint of travel back home. I painted this especially for the trip. See, the child on his shoulder? Nothing can go wrong now."

'At which no doubt we were all meant to ask her where home was, and she would tell us, and we would all take notice of cute little Vera because she came from Lithuania, and congratulate her on her trip, and at her skill in pricking traditional designs onto eggshells. She was over-bright and over-familiar and determined not to be in awe of Lucas or me, the Lear jet, the *Minni*, a trip in the Aegean, anyone, anything, simply because we had money, which was even more irritating than if she had been dumb-struck and intimidated, as most people are. She had been born into a communist society, but it was no excuse. Still, I gritted my teeth and said nothing. The whole outing was an exercise in teeth-gritting anyway: it had just started rather early.

'Ocean cruising has never been my idea of fun: people who like lying about on decks covered with sun oil seldom have much conversation. The women are routinely narcissistic, the men routinely lecherous and the conversation is more about cosmetic surgery or how many tentacles an octopus has than Rilke or Kierkegarde. But if Lucas felt it was good for business to own one of the more expensive ocean-going yachts in the world, then I'd go along with it and not complain, and make sure it did at least something to earn its keep when resting.

'As to sex, there was some token activity between us, but for the most part we went our own ways. Lucas spent an illicit night here and there, with one beauty or another. What rich and powerful man does not? Surely that is why he has become what he is, to be top dog, to have first sexual pickings? As for me I'd choose a personal trainer here, a film star there, young muscled men, but more for form's sake than any real passion. Lucas liked to feel I was appreciated by the pick of the crop. The notion fed his vanity. And I kept well out of the way of his colleagues, other than a minor flirtation or so, certainly not enough to upset wives – there must be no great emotional drama to influence a deal one way or another. That too was part of the unspoken contract.

'The stars glittered in a navy sky as the yacht slithered through the Aegean waters. Lucas's office staff, I am sorry to say, are not a particularly glamorous lot. He is not a lavish payer, he doesn't have to be: having worked for Lucas looks good on anyone's CV. If you can survive three years with Lucas you can survive any-thing. Nor does an easyJet flight and a ferry trip bring out the suavely casual in anyone. Hastily bought M&S yacht wear is okay but the crew were used to better and tended to be off-hand with those who wore it. We also had the usual free-loaders, celebrities and fashion designers who, on hearing the *Minni* was having an outing, remembered they knew us and came down for the sea air, and of course the photo opportunities with the paparazzi who tracked her round the world. I did not bother as much as usual with guest lists: celebrities, fashionistas and arms dealers would just have to sit next to website designers, secre-taries, accountants and earth environmentalists and put up with it. It really was just an office party. Lucas needed to relax, and so, frankly, did I.

'All went well until, on the second night out when we were off the island of Kos, we moored and ate dinner on deck, al fresco: long tables placed round the upper deck with paper tablecloths, deliberately casual. (Not inexpensive, either. It is often cheaper to have real linen laundered on shore than buy logo-ed table sta-tionery but never mind: the effect's the thing.) It was the usual menu for a casual meal: asparagus, fresh lobsters, fresh bread, French butter, champagne – Cristal, which I would never serve normally, but the celebrities liked it and Lucas had acquired a few hundred crates of the stuff in pursuit of the Stadium deal and this was left over. Personally I prefer a simple Meursault – the Clos St

Felix is serviceable and unostentatious – with my lobster, but never mind. The scent of flowers drifted across the ocean.

'It was unfortunate that a consignment of blooms brought on board just before we left Leros was found to be swarming with tiny spiders. Since a noisy proportion of the lesser guests were Buddhists or environmentalists of some kind, and could not bear to see little creatures squashed or sprayed, the spiders were allowed to run riot. The rich, left to their own devices, are not so squeamish: nor indeed were the Greek and Australian sailors who crewed us. But I prevailed upon them not to terminate the spiders: I asked them to wash every single bloom free of them instead. One does have to be careful, and the last thing one wanted was some angered animal activist on board turning whistle-blower.

'The matter of the environmental reports had surfaced again in the form of a question in the house, and though the Stadium deal had been signed and put to bed – there is such a thing these days as retrospective legislation, and one can never be totally in the clear. The bedclothes can still be pulled back and the pillow snatched from under one's head. We still had to be careful; I had been worried somewhat about the advisability of throwing forty baby lobsters alive into boiling water – but no one had chosen to object to that. I daresay they tasted too good, slightly marinated in raspberry vinegar and strewn with red peppercorns.

'Now I had seated the abominable Vera Meirovitz and her husband Timmy Black on the top table. Timmy had a degree from the University of Strathclyde in sustainability issues and the economics of the environment, and his report, published before we took him on the staff, had been instrumental in the early stages of the positive Stadium decision. He was sound enough, but had the in-born innocence of the do-gooder. We all tend to believe that other people are like ourselves, and those who wish no ill find it hard to believe in the more complicated intentions of others. Also, he looked rather good in an open-necked shirt: far less dweeby than when he wore a tie, and in the candlelight under the starry sky he looked young, virile and positively desirable.

His hair was red and curly and reminded me of my second husband.

'I had imagined Vera had married him for his nationality; now I could see that it might have been for more than that. The marriage was legal: she was entitled to work in our country – I had checked. I rather despise women who insist on keeping their own name while married, don't you? It's such a halfway house. Married is married, and that's that. What was the matter with being Vera Black? But no, she must cling to Meirovitz and her ethnic roots, peasant blouses, *pysanky*, little felt flowers and all. Tonight she was wearing a wholly unsuitable and very low-cut crimson red velvet dress, but at least it was not embroidered. Sailing in the Aegean seas simply does not call for crimson velvet. Her skin was very white, opaque and waxy like some rather unhealthy jungle orchid, she had a stupid little red mouth with too much lipstick and her little black eyes crumpled up like Renée Zelwegger's when she smiled. She had let her hair down and fluffed it up so it flowed rather untidily over what I had to admit were splendid shoulders. She reminded one of some hefty opera singer, like Callas before finally she found a diet that worked. She was not fat but she looked fat, like so many people who have only come to a state of slenderness through excessive dieting. Personally I was born thin.

'Lucas sat in the middle of the top table and I sat on his right. Unusually, I had not done individual place names for the top table: rashly thinking "let them look after themselves for once". Vera had seated herself on Lucas's left. Timmy found a place further down. You have to be quick if you're working a room, and Timmy was not quick. Vera had annoyed me during the asparagus course by looking up at Lucas with a trusting devotion which better suited a Trophy Wife than a jumped-up secretary with a higher salary than she deserved. Then over the lobster she helped him crack open claws which he could perfectly well have done for himself and then hooked out some of the flesh for him as if he were a child. How I wished then that I had bothered to do place cards. If I had I might still be Lucas's wife. Not in a thousand years would I have sat them next to each other. Bad enough, I now realized, that she was in and out of Lucas's office all the time. The bosom in its inappropriate red velvet was really quite magnificent.

'My husband had a silly smile on his face and smacked his lips together as, using a prong, she slipped a piece of lobster between his teeth. The boat took one of those lurches boats sometimes do and the waiter stumbled and the hem of the tablecloth was swept up and I could see my husband's hand creeping up between his secretary's cellulosed thighs. Had Vera Meirovitz been beautiful, elegant, or titled, I could have forgiven the offence: had she been Orlanda the famous shoe designer with her pretty charming ways, and elegant little feet, or the appalling but appealing Bambi, the arms-dealer's bit of wide-eyed totty, both present on board that night, I could have endured it. But Vera Meirovitz from the office!

'How badly it reflected upon me! His hand was equidistant between Vera's thighs and mine and he had chosen Vera's. The tablecloth fell again, but I had seen what I had seen, and felt a fury and upset far beyond anything this dull and tawdry situation demanded. That creeping hand of Lucas's was mine by rights, not hers; she was not worthy of it.

'And then something even worse happened, something unforgettable, unforgivable, even after two years in Korydallos. Even as a I tried to calm my breathing, what I can only describe as a spider invasion occurred: a whole host of these tiny little red things swarmed out, like ghosts from the enchanter fleeing from a delicately scented melon – part of the table decoration, not intended for eating – the skin of which suddenly ruptured, no doubt because of the teeming agitation inside and the warmth of the candles – setting free the hordes of tiny creatures. I coped, even as I seethed. No spider was harmed as waiters clustered, cloths were whisked away, changed, replaced, and the dinner party settled down again.

'But one guest had eaten a spider, mistaking it for a peppercorn. She blamed herself and not the spider, in the modern manner. And the guest was, of course, Vera Meirovitz.

'"I must have startled it or it would never have bitten!" she actually said. "Poor little thing. I think it bit the roof of my mouth on the way down," she said. "It's feeling quite sparkly!"

'Even as she complained she had been bitten she forgave the spider, the silly bitch.

'"Show me your mouth," said Lucas. "Open wide. Sparkly, you say!"

'She opened her silly little mouth, with its tiny white teeth, opened it wide, and Lucas bent over and put his tongue up to the roof of her mouth. "You're right," he said, withdrawing it. "'Sparkly' is the word."

'Now a Trophy Wife cannot afford to show her jealousy. It is beneath her dignity. But I could not let this incident go unmarked, I could not. I did what I could. I rolled the menu into a spill which I then lit in the flame of a candle. As if by accident I brushed the lighted spill past Vera's long untidy hair before setting it to the edge of the tablecloth. The weather had been hot and dry. The tablecloth flared up and flames raced down the table between plates and glasses, to little cries of alarm and surprise from the guests. It was all most satisfactory. Timmy, I was sorry to say, rushed to Vera's side all too soon to put out the flames in her hair. The crew very soon had the fire under control, but some damage was done to the deck, and in some places nasty black smoke lines stained *Minni*'s paintwork.

'"What the fuck did you do that for?" asked Lucas, when the guests had dispersed around the boat, to enjoy the en-cruise entertainment in the comfort of the grossly over-orange upholstery, and the fire-fighting equipment had been put away, and the Kos coastguard – ever hopeful of a salvage claim – had gone back to base.

'"Such a dull evening, darling," I said. "I thought your staff deserved a little entertainment."

'"You've done at least $100,000 worth of damage," he complained, though what was $100,000 to a man like Lucas? I was upset and hurt, for all the careless tossing of my head, and I said so. To get involved with a member of staff was folly: it laid one open to harassment claims and other blackmail. Besides, it humiliated me.

'"A spider had run up her leg," he said. "And my hand was following it to catch it and get rid of it. I was trying to help you out."

'That was so absurd it might even have been true.

'"Your tongue in her mouth," I said, "in front of everyone!"

'"When did you last care what other people thought?" he asked. "I just wanted to test out sparkly. Such an unusual word."

'I said things I never thought I would say, never have said since I was the girl next door, in my first marriage, and suffering. "You love your fucking boat more than me," I said, "and you fuck your loving Vera when I'm not around and you don't care who knows it."

'I, who had never used the word before now wanted him to say it, but of course if you want something too much things just don't pan out your way. Love, love, love, I should have said. Tell me you love me. He might have been so taken aback he would realize it was true. He just stared at me. Had he fucked her? I don't know. Possibly not. What difference does it make?

'"See that she's fired," I said, and she was. I sent a fax down to her cabin on headed paper.

'She came to me the next day as I lay in my deckchair by the pool, with the Aegean isles drifting by, and begged to keep her job. Something about length of service and insurance, and visas and being pregnant, but I didn't listen. Beyond thinking, oh, pregnant, that's why she looks so fat. I had her put off at the next island to make her own way home. I even organized three consecutive ferry tickets for her to island-hop back to Athens. After that she could go stand-by on easyJet. I explained her husband couldn't go with her – under the terms of his contract he must stay on board in case something came up in relation to the Stadium project.

'"Anyway," I added, "if you can't even be bothered to take his name he can't be very important to you." It was a cheap shot, but I hated her.

'I stood at the gangway and examined her bags as she left. I felt entitled. She was, after all, an ex-employee and might be stealing trade secrets. I found her absurd decorated egg in its horrid little woollen bag. "Ugh, spiders!" I said. I shouldn't have done that. It was pure malice. Malice can rebound.

'Then, holding the bag at a safe distance, I dropped the lot overboard, St Christopher, the child on his shoulder, felt flowers and all. I have never allowed a baby to come to term, so on the whole I am out of sympathy with pregnant women.

'"Now you've taken my luck as well," she wailed. And so I banished her from my sight that morning. She was gone before Lucas had even crawled out of bed, while Timmy banged on the bedroom door to rouse him and get him to talk some sense into me. I think it was my luck that went, as it happens, along with her *pysanky*.

'I could see as she went that she was quite pregnant: she waddled. People in that stage of pregnancy are unsightly and should stay home, unless they are a Grade One celebrity and can get away with it. She should not have opened her mouth for my husband to stick in his tongue.

'I refused to speak to Lucas all day and in the afternoon summoned Timmy to talk about the environmental report he had signed when perhaps he wasn't properly qualified so to do. I told him he needed my protection, if he wasn't to end up the fall guy for a whole lot of things that had gone wrong recently. He stammered and protested his innocence: I explained innocence was nothing to do with it; power politics beyond his ken were being played out. He was quite a sweet lad, really, all horrified, wide blue eyes and this rather nice red hair which stuck up on end. I took him into bed with me if only to prove to myself that Vera wasn't the only one who could play that game. Bed with the boss. He was too dazzled by the honour of my invitation to refuse. Or perhaps he was just too terrified. But I don't know. Men only go where they want, don't they. Not like women. I reckon he wanted to well enough. He acquitted himself nobly.

'Lucas came into the cabin, looking for me, as I knew he would, and found us together. He dragged me out of bed. I thought I was safe enough: trophy wives cannot be seen with bruises. I assumed, in any case, that the full blast of his rage would be directed not towards me but towards Timmy, the office hand. That was the way things worked. I was right. Lucas sent the environmental scientist reeling with a swift blow. Timmy regained his balance, looking helpless and confused. A whole race of young men has grown up lately who seriously believe force is no way to solve a problem, and he was one of them. Besides, he was obviously in the wrong. I was another man's wife. Lucas looked at me as if he hated and despised me, and left the cabin. But I thought he would get over it. I had overlooked his indiscretions often enough. Heaven knows how much illicit fornication took place on the *Minni* that weekend.

'"You'd better be careful from now on," I said to Timmy as he dressed. "Lucas won't take this lightly. He'll get his own back one way or another. He's like that. Check your brake cables before getting into your car, don't stand too near the edge in the underground, or fat Vera will be a widow." And he fled. I said he was not to leave the *Minni*, until the business of the lost report had been solved. His look of desperation quite entertained me. I don't know what was the matter with me. I am not usually either so vicious or uninhibited. But I think the trouble is that those to whom damage has been done do damage in return.

'And of course the same could be said of Lucas. It was his turn to surprise me. I was not to get off so lightly. We were alone on deck. How beautifully the sea glimmered in the moonlight.

'"You threw her egg in the sea," he said. "Her precious lucky *pysanky*. What a bitch you are."

'"You were having an affair with her," I said.

'"No I wasn't," he said. "I just always rather liked her turn of phrase. She learned English so well it came out quaint. She was quite a relief after you."

'"I hadn't realized 'quaint' was on the job description," I said bitterly. What does one have to do to please a man?

'He said he supposed I'd gone with Vera's husband just to get my own back. I was Circe, who turned men into pigs, but I was the pig, and no doubt I would tell her.

'I said I wouldn't stoop to telling her but I would certainly make sure she found out.

'He said he was giving Vera Meirovitz her job back and I said no he wasn't. He said there was no way of stopping him and then I did something very stupid. Even as I spoke I could almost hear and see the bubbles as the little embroidered bag went glug, glug, glug down into the clear Aegean Sea. I said if he wasn't careful there might be another question in the House because supposing the missing documents turned up. Those clever enough to hide them in the first place might very well find them again in the second. In other words I knew where the bodies were hidden. And supposing I had hidden them in the safe behind the Lempickas in the state room.

'He looked at me for a long time, as if finding out who I was. I didn't like it. I should have been more careful, less trusting about the pre-nuptial agreement. I should have made him give me the yacht, not just named it after me. I should have had my own diamonds, not just borrowed his sister's. She had married well, into the Romanovs, and had Russian imperial jewellery – including marvels by Fabergé, Sazikov, Khlebnikov, Ovchinnikov – at her disposal. They were wonderful but they were not mine. Well, I could always go back to portrait painting.

'"You know who you remind me of?" he said at last. "My mother. You are turning into my mother. You are spiteful, vicious, and full of hate. You will destroy me if you can."

'I remembered then what I had forgotten, that Lucas hated his mother. Now when a man hates his mother he hates the source of life itself, and no normal rules apply. He marries you because you are not like his mother, sets about turning you into his mother, and when he's succeeded he leaves you, and tries again with someone else. Before I married Lucas I was a perfectly nice person, and now I was not; he was right: I was horrid.

'Fire is a cleansing thing. It propitiates the Gods. In the night Lucas laid a trail of fuel and set fire to the *Minni*. The guests were brought screaming from their beds and had to take to the life-boats. At first I rejoiced. I had not realized how much I hated them. A fire at sea is a spectacular sight. A funeral pyre for everyone's fine hopes. The Kos coastguards were delighted. We watched from lifeboats as the flaming *Minni* dipped, bow first, sighed, and went to the bottom. As she gurgled down I caught a glimpse of Lucas's face, and he was smiling.

'"How did this happen?" asked the policeman in Athens, when finally we hit dry and comparatively civilized land, still wrapped in blankets and with seaweed between our toes.

'"Lucas did it," I said. "He burned his own boat to burn some documents and collect the insurance. If you investigate you will find the fire started in the state room, where the safe is."

'"I am sorry to have to report," said Lucas, "that my wife is unbalanced. She is an arsonist. She's disturbed, obsessively jealous. She has a history of this kind of thing."

'And of course I did have such a history: everyone had seen my first impulsive act of hate, setting fire to the tablecloths, and to Vera's hair. Poor pregnant Vera! Everyone had seen me drop her St Christopher egg into the sea. Everyone had watched her limp away down the gangplank with me watching and laughing. Who was going to believe me? What, Lucas, now up for a peerage, guilty? Impossible! Because now the Stadium development was roaring ahead.

'The newspapers loved my disgrace. I, who'd once painted an English prince, nothing but a murderous arsonist! I was a mad woman, vicious. Why, once on the *Minni* I'd released poisonous spiders amongst my own guests. Now I'd done it – burned my own luxury yacht, sent her to the bottom, just out of spite. I'd destroyed original art, worth millions, that was another thing. There had been a lot of stuff in the papers about the increasing gap between rich and poor, and I was now held personally responsible. I was an affront to decent hard-working people. The

marriage to the Texan and the manner of his death were resur-
rected. How everyone loved to hate me.'

'I remember all that,' said Mira, the Journalist. 'Yes, it was
quite a stir. We called you the *Minni* Medea. Perhaps now you're
out of prison you could do a piece for us? We could have it ghost
written if you preferred.'

'I don't think so,' said the Trophy Wife. 'I think it's safest if I
just stay quiet and leave town as soon as I'm through at Castle
Spa. I will try my luck in Australia. At the trial I did not even try
to defend myself. It would have been hopeless. I had no proof.
Even if they'd retrieved the safe from the seabed and found it still
intact, they would have found it empty. There were no documents.
Rumours that the ground glowed greenly in the night around the
stadium site were posted on the internet, but were ignored. There
were no more questions in the House. The roof went on in the
stadium, to public acclaim: the seating came in. Timmy was pro-
moted, Vera got her job back. Lucas had effectively silenced me.

'I elected to stand my trial in Greece, where crimes of passion
are treated less harshly than in England. I had been motivated by
jealousy. The attempted murder charge was dropped. But I hadn't
realized that in a seriously maritime country it's also better not to
burn boats. I went to prison for arson, for two whole years, and
was lucky not to get twelve. I served my term in Korydallos.
Moussaka, often mouldy, became my lot in life. I suppose I was
lucky not have gone down with the *pysanky*, glug, glug, glug into
uncharted depths.

'Lucas divorced me in my absence. The pre-nuptial agreement,
pathetic thing that it was, was nullified because I now had a criminal record. Once some men turn, they turn. Once you are put
away, you are put away. He claimed on the fire insurance for the
yacht and got his near billion back: also $100,000 for damage to
the tablecloth on the night of the al fresco lobster dinner. You
had to hand it to him. I heard that Vera's babies – twins – had
been DNA-ed and declared to be Timmy's. I don't know what that
was about. Perhaps something insisted on by Orlanda the shoe

designer? She was to be Lucas's fifth wife, the second in his trophy series. From the sound of it she would be better than I ever was at looking after her own interests. I find I wish them both well. I wore malice out in Korydallos. It's difficult enough for people to get by in life without adding to their troubles. I try to forgive Vera, but I find that hard. Swallow a spider and say it was sparkly! Invite a man's tongue down your throat!

'That is enough for today. Thank you all for listening. Do they lock the kitchens at night or do you suppose we could raid the fridge? I am so hungry!'

6

I slept soundly that night and was relieved. It's possible to sleep in a strange bed and find that the nights are restless, full of ghosts, demons and a kind of mental flutter of unfinished business. And I was to be ten whole nights here, if I stood the course. But Castle Spa breathed a kind of solid contentment: the minute I lay my head upon my pillow I slept, dreamlessly, and when I pulled the curtains it was a bright day. It was, moreover, Christmas Day, and I was both sorry and glad not to be with my children. I could not remember a year when I had not fallen asleep on Christmas Eve worn out by exhaustion, or woken on Christmas Day not burdened by the prospect of tasks to be accomplished. But here at Castle Spa it seemed it was to be treated as a day like any other, with just a few Christmas touches; which was both a relief and a disappointment. A relief because there was nothing to be done, no weighty obligations towards one's nearest and dearest, and a disappointment for the same reason. And yet there was lightness in the air: it was Christmas Day – *unto us a child is born* – take it literally or metaphorically – look, good things happen! The promise is that all will be well, and all will yet be well.

I opened the window. I looked out over the moat and drawbridge: to my left I could see the castle wall, to the right a magnolia tree, bare of leaves, its branches oriental, curved and supplicant. A bird arrived on one of its branches and began to sing – are birds meant to sing in midwinter? Aren't they meant to be huddling against rain and snow? Come to that, should one be able to throw open a window on Christmas Day and breathe in warm air? Had the spring come too early, or winter come too late? How little we city dwellers know about the natural world. I could not even name the bird, except to be pretty sure it was not a robin. One has read that the seasons are out of kilter: that the trees keep their leaves too long, that the ice caps are drip-drip-dripping away, but one seldom has direct experience of it. The bird flew off. It seemed unworried. I resolved to be the same.

I tried to call Julian in Wichita but couldn't get through: too early to ring the children. I slept some more.

A slip under my door told me that breakfast was between eight and ten and that my first appointment, a massage with Heather, was at eleven. Hydrotherapy was at four. It being Christmas Day treatments were limited to two per client: to allow staff to spend time with their families. Guests were advised that robes were acceptable throughout the day and reminded that contact with the outside world should be kept to a minimum. The outside line (sic: what only one? and no mobile signal? This place was still in the Dark Ages) was available for guests in the office, situated in the north wing (map attached), as a special Christmas Day concession. And remember – no laptops or mobiles. 'Tranquility is all.' It was signed 'Your friend, Lady Caroline.'

Hunger drove me downstairs. I had my mobile in my gown pocket. I would probably find a signal outside the castle walls. There was fruit, plain yoghurt and oats, for those on a weight loss programme. For those on R and R – Rest and Recuperation – there was bacon and eggs, kippers – date bread, fig bread, olive bread, you name it – rolls, croissants, butter, preserves, fruit juices, though everything in tiny portions, as if to tempt anorexics, which no doubt was how it worked. I decided, naturally, that I was on the R and R plan, and encountered Mira, stoically munching raw oats. But then, I had decided, she was unhappily in love with her Alistair. I was more fortunate: Julian did not seem to mind what weight or shape I was, and so I could choose to please myself.

I did not point out to Mira that the difference of a few pounds here or there was unlikely to induce a man to leave his wife and cleave to his mistress. It would have been unkind. Let her live in hope. Men usually like to maintain the status quo: and the status quo for Alistair, having both a docile and trusting wife and a heartbroken mistress, could only be pleasant enough. To alter it would be pointless, and expensive. Nor did I say that I had known men in Alistair's situation resolve their guilt by running off with a third party altogether. On the other hand I did not suppose he was particularly sensitive to guilt. As a newspaper editor, he would be too busy. Mira might as well eat. She seemed to read my thoughts and compromised by slicing a banana onto her oats.

We agreed over decaffeinated coffee – there was no other kind – that we were in the hands of control freaks: we also agreed it was no bad option. That to surrender the will to others was indeed rest and relaxation. Just go with the flow.

The Trophy Wife came in for coffee, dressed as we all were in a white towelling gown but with her hair sprouting a mass of silver foil. She looked happy. She said the Jacuzzi was to be switched on at two, and she for one would be there, and she was looking forward to someone else's confession. She could not be the only one to bare her soul. Others must take their turn. Mira asked if she could be the one: she had something she wanted to get off her chest: it wasn't exactly a confession, but she would like a moral verdict.

'You're not the only one,' said the Public Speaker. 'I've been lying awake all night working myself up into a state. People think I'm so in control but I'm not. The thing is I've no one to talk to. I live with a man but he hardly speaks any English at all. Which is good in one way, but not in another. I'm too busy to have friends. And I'm on the lecture circuit and talk and talk to people from a platform, and they listen, and even clap, but it's not like a proper conversation. Let me speak, please, let me speak.'

And she seemed so distressed of course we let her. Some had to go off to appointments, but most stayed. She was in her mid-thirties, I supposed, blonde and attractive, her movements normally quick and confident, with a brisk manner and an air of knowing better than anyone else, her proper place on a platform, holding forth and dismissing doubts. It was strange to see her thus: pathetic and reduced to pleading.

7

The Public Speaker's Tale

'Other people have friends they know well. I just have hospitals. Mostly these hospital friends are good to me, but occasionally they let me down, throw me out before I want to go because others are already knocking on the door, saying 'what about me? what about me?' I've known one or two who seem only to want to chew you up and spit you out. They can gobble up your taxes and break your back, send you out with MRSA. But mostly you can trust a hospital to be good to you, loyal to you and welcome you back when they see you. Better than friends, better than lovers.

'All hospitals have a different feeling tone. You have to learn them, the same way other people learn lovers. Some like to keep you, some like to hurry you out. Some like you to be brave and not complain, in others they prefer you to weep and be dependent. In some it's all rush and hurry, in others even the crash team dawdle. Pick and choose, pick and choose. I have been to dozens of A&Es in my time, all over the world.

'I have been to Bellevue in New York where the beds are patrolled by women with machine guns; to Sarajevo where the electro-cardiac leads hang from a butcher's hook in the ceiling; to Rouen where they experiment with new drugs, and watch your near death with interest; to Moscow where they drive vast needles into your buttocks to render you insensible. In San Francisco they would rather you died than took an antibiotic.

'In my job I get about the world – I lecture in the history of occultism, morphic resonance, that kind of thing. Spiritualist societies like to know about their history and I am happy to provide it. I have an excellent PowerPoint presentation at my fingertips relating to the Victorian mediums, Slade, Foster and Davenport. Are any of you acquainted with their work? No? They were denounced as fraudsters at the time but I have sound recordings of some of their séances which suggest otherwise. Wherever I go in the world, these lectures of mine attract capacity audiences. I am paid surprisingly well for them, and I live well, albeit, until recently, alone.

'In short I live a busy and stressful life. I also have a heart condition, supra-ventral tachycardia, or SVT, which can be triggered by travel, emotion of one kind or another, or a general superfluity of adrenalin. Shortly after my arrival in a foreign country I will have to take my racing pulse – 200 is nothing – in a taxi to Casualty. SVT patients are rare, but welcomed, because the ailment is both dramatic and curable, and the patients, being high achievers, are seldom violent, and are usually clean and respectable. Tony Blair is one such.

'Sometimes the heartbeat reverts to normal for no known reason. I normally leave it three or four hours before finding a hospital. During that time it is just about possible to carry on as normal. I have spoken from platforms and given interviews while it beats away – the beat is at least regular; just very, very fast – and seems to sharpen the mind no end. But then you tire, your blood pressure drops wildly: you feel faint: you do faint: it is time to go. In the hospital there is no hanging about. They lie you down and wire you up and inject a drug called adenosine into a vein. Staff gather to watch the monitors. When the drug reaches the heart it stops it beating altogether. The patient flat-lines. Then the drug wears off and the heart starts up again in its normal rhythm, and the watchers drift away. It's like switching off the computer and when you switch it on again all problems have disappeared. The drug has worked so far, certainly on me, and no final deaths, only temporary ones, have been reported.

'Since I started sharing my bed on a regular basis with a man I haven't had a single attack. It is very disappointing. I miss my visits to hospital. I like the drama, the welcome, being the centre of skill and attention, being looked after. Certainly, the spasms of dying are not pleasant – as the heart stops the whole body panics – but you get used to it. I can see I might almost be hooked on it. But I don't suppose many studies have been done on adenosine addiction.

'Few high-earning women ever have time to form proper domestic relationships. That, I imagine, is why they keep so busy. It was certainly my plan for my own future. Something about me seemed to suggest to men that I was mistress, not wife, material, and that suited me very well. I enjoyed weekends with married men very much, knowing I was safe from commitment, but was always pleased to get home to my neat and ordered house. I hate kissing; I like to go straight to the real thing, and never in my house thank you. My hours are too anti-social: early flights, late flights, leaping out of bed when the alarm goes. If there's a man in there with you it's difficult; they are so slow to get their act together, to come to life and get their clothes on. I leap out of bed. I cannot bear moony-eyed men: that sad reproachful look they give you when you ask them to leave. Lingering over romantic dinners is not my style; there is always something to be done, organized, money to be made. Men do like one's undivided attention, I find, and I am always thinking of something else, not concentrating on the matter in hand.'

'As the bishop complained to the actress,' said someone, lewdly. The Public Speaker looked daggers.

'And then what happens? One day you break your own rules and you're sunk. Lumbered. Look at me now. Weak and muddled in the head and full of unreasonable emotions. Once proud and free – no pets, no partners, no line manager, no children: just me, answerable to no one; and as a weekly tonic, or twice or even three times weekly, a dose of applause. And then I weakened, and now I don't care about the applause: I'd rather have sex with the one man, once, twice, or even three times weekly. My work is suffering. I am meant to be in Stuttgart tomorrow for a lecture on

Marley's Ghost: Dickens and the Supernatural, but I messed up the bookings: I was no longer concentrating, I was washing a shirt.

'I booked in here just to show I can get away, I can break the addictions.

'The last time I had an attack of SVT was in my own home town: a good six months ago. I was giving a talk at my old school. I am the only famous old girl they can muster so you can tell what kind of a dump it was. It was the tenth anniversary of my mother's death. That may have had something to do with it. My mother was like me in temperament. She never wanted to settle but had been somehow pinned to the ground by my father, like a butterfly. She had been married three times before she met him, had three times as many lovers, and had no domestic skills. I arrived in the world, in spite of all her efforts to prevent it, when she was forty-one. She did not like me very much. She saw me as a rival, and hated the way that as I grew into beauty she grew out of it. I left home as soon as I could to save my parents the tension of living with me. When she died of cancer, I scarcely mourned her, made sure I would be out of the country for her funeral, and shed not a tear. But little by little her memory has crept up on me. The occasional kindnesses, the way she taught me to read, the smile which followed through when I'd been witty and managed to make her laugh. Before I turned up at the school I visited her grave in St Pancras cemetery, and found myself weeping a little. I was weak, yes, I was weak. I shouldn't have gone. I'd just finished what I had to say to the girls – my general theme is "if in doubt, do" when my heart started to beat its triple rate and presently I had to take a taxi to one of my favourite hospitals, which as it happens is in Huntley Street off Gower Street, midway between the school of my youth, in south London, and my present home in north London. One can wait for an ambulance but a taxi is quicker, and I am only walking wounded.

'"What you again," said the hospital, in its kindly, caring voice, "only three times so far this year. It's a record! Welcome! We'll have you right in no time," as they whisked me in. I declined their wheelchairs and walked myself into the crash unit, and briskly undressed, refusing their offers of help, and clambered with a relief I tried not to show onto one of their hard, high, narrow beds. And I refrained from telling them about the hospitals in Oslo and Stockholm, Canberra and Auckland, Portland and Seattle, where I had been taken in over the past year and healed. It seemed vaguely impolite to suggest that they were only one of many.

'Now perhaps because I was feeling low – an internet date which looked promising had disappointed badly – and was missing my mother, that for once I wished I had a family, a father, a sister, a partner, a husband even, anyone to come to the hospital, make sure I was okay, and help me find a taxi home. I realized there was no one, that I had no one. On one occasion I had a temporary PA and she came with me, but when she saw me flat-line she fainted. I was the one who had to be sorry for her.

'That day the hospital was busy – there had been a multiple pile-up locally – and after they'd got my heart back to normal, and taken a last EEG, there was no lingering. No lying down back in admittance and resting up and eating the free sandwiches and listening to the life and death dramas happening on the other side of the flowered pink curtains. No, no. I was briskly discharged and told to go home and rest. And as I went out the automatic doors – how they slid open without human help, as if humanity itself was unneeded – I admit I wept a little.

'It was dark and drizzling. The black taxis that passed were all occupied. It was five in the morning. When a battered minicab stopped and asked if I wanted to go anywhere I said yes, and got in the back – there were papers and old cans on the front passenger seat: no welcome there. I usually stick to black cabs. Minicabs are cheaper but the drivers do have a reputation as rapists and serial killers. But tonight I was past caring. Instead of rejoicing at my own victory – had I not just turned the tables on death itself? – I just wanted to go home and cry.

'The driver was an asylum seeker, for thus these days anyone with swarthy looks, inadequate English and a dejected air is described. Actual citizenship status is irrelevant. His shoulders hunched over the wheel. His hair was long, not sleek, hippy-ish long, but no-money-for-a-haircut long, and no money to waste on shampoo either. The back of his neck was dirty. I gave him my address in Muswell Hill. He said he knew the street. I hoped he was not lying, but at least he started out in the right direction.

'It was a hair-raising drive. Perhaps I'd thwarted death once too often and this time the grey, grim figure, whom I'd seen so often out of the corner of my eye, was really determined to get me? The driver certainly drove as if he sensed he was after us, choosing the back streets whenever he could, slamming his taxi round corners, not slowing down at the approach, as driving instructors like to think people do, but speeding up instead. But then he had probably never had a driving lesson in his life, let alone insured or licensed his vehicle. Why should a man on the wrong side of society bother? He enjoyed the squeal of tyres well enough, especially down quiet suburban roads, and waking people up. He wanted conversation. I did not. He asked if I was a bad girl, out in the streets so late and alone? Piqued, I said I was not, and he nodded and took my word for it.

'"Not good for women alone, your city," he said. "Pristina better."

'I bristled: I said at least in my country I didn't have to wear a veil. He said women in Kosovo often went unveiled and that was bad for men because then they had to look at so many ugly women. This was a monstrous statement whichever way you took it. I said so. He said he didn't mind me not wearing a veil. I took that as flirtatious and changed the subject fast, asking him how long he'd been in the country. Seven years, he said. I asked him if he was married and he said no. I didn't like to ask him if he were Muslim or Christian; how could I understand the complexities of whichever answer he gave? He might see the question as an impertinence in the same way I took his asking me if I were a whore.

'I told him the reason I was out late and alone was because I had been in hospital. Again, the cry for sympathy. I despised myself. And he drove slowly now, and carefully, almost tenderly, as if I were delicate. I asked him about himself.

'"I live like a dog, alone," he said. "No family, nothing." Like a dog? In our country, I pointed out, dogs always lived with families. Loneliness was not their problem. But perhaps the poor beasts he was accustomed to in Kosovo skulked in sheds at the end of a chain, or were street dogs, and stoned by children?

'"My country good country," he agreed. "But not for dogs."

'I suggested he tried another analogy. An eagle, perhaps? *"Live alone, like an eagle?"* In its mountain eyrie, proud, triumphant, lord of all it surveyed. He grunted. I wondered what he looked like. One seldom actually looks at cab drivers. Now I had only the back of his neck to go by, and the shaggy hair. Early thirties, I supposed: a dreadful shapeless thick sweater in grey knitted nylon. A sad, sulky voice, a broken accent. Then I noticed the single, casual, long-fingered hand on the wheel; one hand, as if he would not accord these empty city streets the privilege of his full attention. At the Camden intersection he turned and looked at me, and I saw he had the strong face of a mountain tribesman, a hooked nose, and bright, bright eyes. He went through a red light. I fastened my seat belt, taking care to be quiet about it. I did not want to offend his feelings by the click, the suggestion that I did not trust him to get me home safely.

'"But every eagle has a mate," he said, not at all persuaded by my simile. "A family, a nest, eggs. I have no one, Miriam. You have to believe me. I am no better than a dog."

'How did he know my name? I realized I was still wearing my name badge from the prize-giving.

'"Okay then, not an eagle," I conceded. Lions had prides, he would know that. A tiger?

'"Live like a tiger, alone," I quickly amended. No one knew much about the social life of tigers: or at any rate I didn't. There was something tiger-ish about him, beautiful but sinister. My mouth was dry. He seemed to have forgotten to drive carefully, he had picked up speed and verve again. We screamed round the Camden intersection, veering off towards Kentish Town. There were two ways to go – round the Heath was minimally better, but perhaps the Parliament Hill way there were fewer police around. My house is in a good part of Muswell Hill, and rather elegant, as he would soon discover. For once I felt bad. I had all this wealth to myself and he lived like a dog, alone. Weren't people meant to share?

'He said that tigers lived in prides, like lions. A tiger was only alone when stalking his prey. I asked why had I never seen a film of it, then, and he said perhaps tigers were more dangerous to get near than lions. He asked me if I lived alone, and I panicked, and said no, I lived with my husband. "He'll be waiting up for me," I added.

"And I have no one."

'He could be a madman, fresh out of a psychiatric ward. I said I was tired and had to be up at eight and he sounded surprised and asked if I was still working. I knew that trick. Make a woman feel as if she's past it and she'll be grateful for your attentions, and the more likely to come across. He might be the driver and I the driven, I the citizen and he the immigrant, but in basic life terms I was older than he was and I was only a woman, and he did the picking and choosing. He stopped at the next red light, if only to be able to turn his head and smile at me. The dirt behind his ears could have been nothing but shadow misinterpreted. He took his identity tag from round his neck, and laid it on the seat next to him. I doubted that it meant anything anyway. You could buy them in any pub and who was going to check? He turned off the meter. We continued on our way.

'"No creature in nature lives alone," he said, firmly, "except a dog."

'"What about moles?" I asked. Moles live underground in single-person households, and hate other moles. Their young dig themselves in on their own the moment they can. Males reluctantly make a single annual excursion, paddling away through earth with human-like hands, to find a female. They meet, they mate, they fight savagely and quickly return to their own quarters, licking their wounds and hating the other. They heave up people's lawns just for the hell of it. I said as much to the driver, but my heart wasn't in it. I knew what was going to happen. He said he did not believe me. He said I lived like a dog, alone, like him. He could tell.

'We turned into my street. "Nice houses," he said. I could see how it would go. I would ask him in, there would be sex, we would end up married, thus he would stop being an illegal and get citizenship. He would use up my capital and turn himself into an arms dealer or some such and then run off with a girl from his own country of his own age.

'"Shall I come in for a cup of coffee?" he asked. "I expect your husband's still asleep."

'So I asked him in, and he searched the house for a husband and found none. I asked him to bath and shave but he wouldn't. Dogs in a shed, eagles in a nest, tigers in a cave, moles underground, driver and driven – rank and sweaty and moved by the same need.

'In the morning I gave him a house key, and that was six months ago. I told myself that next time I had an attack and had to go to hospital he would take me and I would tell him he had to go and he would. I would give him and myself so long and then normal life would resume. But I have not had an attack since he moved in. I have flown about the world and been here and been there, I have been stressed in Utah and had an adrenalin rush in Nova Scotia and a hostile audience of born-again Christians in Newcastle who told me I was dealing in witchcraft. And my heart has beaten steadily on. When I get home my bed is filled. In my drive, next to my 4x4, is a battered old taxi. He has applied for asylum, he is taking driving lessons, his mother and sister want to visit from Pristina. Soon they will be living with me too. What do I do? Please tell me, what do I do?'

We considered. Did he go or did he stay? Her heart was telling her one thing: keep him – and health, we agreed, is certainly important, especially when it comes to hearts. But perhaps she should ignore her heart and use her common sense? That she was right; that he was using her. He would indeed move in his family, marry her, get citizenship, spend her money and when he had drained her dry, leave her. He might be good for her heart now, but in the end he would break it. She should throw him out now.

'If you don't get involved, you don't get hurt,' said the Trophy Wife. 'Look what happened to me when I started to care. Two years in prison.'

But there were other views too. Better to care, better to hurt, than to have a steely heart. A man of your own in the bed was worth multiple affairs that didn't last. Vice versa, said the Vicar's Ex-wife, surprisingly. Someone said rough trade always ended in tears but who cared. Someone else said men were a diversion, the career was the only important thing, she should focus on that and if she really wanted sex – and what was wrong with dildos – go back to weekends with married men. The Manicurist said she thought he sounded really sweet and she was lucky to have him. Mira agreed and said if the Public Speaker really wanted conversation she could always learn Serbo-Croat. The Company Director said she should build on what she had: fund him to start a taxi company of his own.

'I think it's wonderful,' said the Screenwriter dreamily. 'So romantic. In the film you'd live happily ever after.' She'd made quite a fuss the night before, demanding breakfast in her room, saying she'd only come to Castle Spa to write a script, not to be with others. Yet here she was.

'What's the matter with living alone?' asked the hard, sharp, brisk woman who turned out to be a mortgage broker. 'What did all those feminists fight for? Women can live perfectly well without men. All one needs are friends. And our friend here uses hospitals as other women use friends: now she's in danger of losing them, and all because of a man. He has to go!'

We were quite noisy. The Public Speaker said she was not accustomed to everyone talking at once. She was feeling dizzy and confused. Indeed, she had gone rather pale. She put her hand to her chest. We all fell silent and stared.

'It's started,' she said. She felt her pulse. 'Around 190,' she said. 'Oh, thank God! It's all right. I can have my friends as well! I can have my man, I can have my heart, I can have it all!'

The Brain Surgeon insisted on driving her in to Carlisle hospital herself. The Public Speaker needed to get to A&E at once. There was to be no hanging about to see what might or might not happen. The sooner she had adenosine the less she would need. The surgeon had known adenosine end in permanent cardiac arrest for the patient. It was rare but it happened. In her opinion the Public Speaker should most certainly keep the minicab driver in situ if it stopped her heart slipping into SVT.

The Public Speaker seemed pleased to hear this, and spoken with such authority. She looked cheerful, if pale, as she went. We could see the pulse fluttering wildly in her neck. She said goodbye to us with affection, speaking of us as her friends. Perhaps she could indeed have it all, though she had to risk death to achieve it.

8

After the Public Speaker's story I went outdoors and wandered round on the green sward between the castle walls and the moat looking for a signal for my mobile. I found none. It was very bright, still and quiet. I was rather glad there was no signal. Conversation with unseen people would have seemed unnatural: something out of a future that was not quite right. I could hear the sound of running water and realized that a stream had been diverted to feed into the moat, which was why the water in it was so clear and pleasant. Grasses and ferns ran down to the water's edge in the places where original brickwork had fallen away. In the ferns was what I realized was a dead bird, its once bright feathers sodden and dull. I had a vague memory that one was meant to report dead birds, and stop other animals eating them, and though surely that scare was long behind us, I went inside, and following the instructions on the map, made my way through vast and vaulted rooms, up half flights, down others, to Castle Spa 'offices'.

I was reminded of Castle Leslie in County Monaghan, where a similar peace was imposed upon its guests. No telephone in the rooms, no TV, no radio: just a very expensive isolation and an office phone tucked away in a turret room accessible only through the kitchens. Faced with this lengthy excursion, the importance of the phone call diminished with every step required, and it seemed wiser just to give in and go trout fishing or pheasant shooting. One turned back upon the stair.

But it was Christmas Day, and though in Ireland the will is easily sapped – in the north of England the opposite is the case.

My family would expect greetings and be put out if I did not get in contact. I realized that without a telephone connection in my room I couldn't use my laptop to e-mail. I didn't suppose for one minute Castle Spa would have a Wi-Fi link. Anyway, the sound of the human voice is nice. I followed the map and eventually – it felt like quarter of a mile of long, chilly, uncarpeted corridors and unexpected stairs – found Beverley in the office wrestling with her computer. A half-eaten sandwich lay on her desk. She didn't eat her crusts.

'I don't know what the matter is,' she said. 'I've got hundreds and hundreds of Happy Christmas e-mails coming up on the screen, all from the same six people, none of them I know, but I can't be sure. I've been deleting them for hours.'

'Sounds like a virus to me,' I said, resolving to keep my laptop away from anything that might infect it. So one reacted when the children were small and there was a chicken pox outbreak at the school. 'Can I make a phone call?'

'Lady Caroline doesn't like guests using the office phone. You won't get the full benefit of the treatments if you do. It's for your own good. The whole point of being here is to be away from everything.' She spoke automatically. She wasn't concentrating. She was too busy deleting. I reminded her that it was Christmas Day and we had been given special dispensation, and she shoved over the phone, without noticeable grace.

The trouble with taking up bargain offers is that no one gives you the respect you believe you deserve. You're seen as cheap. Five hundred pounds a day is a lot of money – especially if you're only going to get two treatments on one of the days instead of the normal five – but in peak season it would be at least eight hundred. So it goes. Well, what did one expect? The stand-by passenger gets herded and shoved: only the full-price passenger gets civility.

I got through on the Spa landline to Julian in Wichita. I woke him but he didn't seem to mind. There had been a ferocious ice-storm the evening before: this morning it was beautiful to look at, but eight people had been killed, the roads were bad and the airport would be closed for days. New York was out. God alone knew when he could get home.

'I hope this isn't a long distance call,' interjected Beverley.

Annoyed, I put my hand over the receiver and told her she was out of order, and she'd better stop deleting like a maniac or she'd get a repetitive strain injury. She should just turn the thing off. It was paranoiac to think I had detected an undercurrent to Julian's voice which meant to he was glad of the snow, glad to be trapped. He was staying with his mother, who was elderly and poorly: he was hardly likely to be having it off with the maid. It was just that at Castle Spa one got the feeling the real world was going on somewhere else. One had been moved sideways, deliberately. I left Julian to sleep on and keep warm, having sent my mother-in-law and her husband Christmas greetings. They'd met each other on an internet dating site. He had an auto concession in Wichita, and she went out there to meet him and now they seemed very happy, to everyone's astonishment, and lately had appeared much fonder of me than she had in the early days of our acquaintance.

'Sorry,' said Beverley. 'But it's for your own good. I'm a Kiwi. I know what overseas calls cost. Castle Spa charges the special hotel rate, and double on public holidays and Sundays. Why else do you think you got a special concession? These places make more out of phone calls and bottled water then anything else.' And she said there's been a move to put up a mast but the old bitch soon put an end to that. I thought that then she may have said '*fat mean cunt*' but perhaps not.

I forgave Beverley, who was obviously stressed by her job, and ventured calls to the children in London. All lamented that we would not be together this Christmas, and that was fine and left a warm feeling. Son Alec asked me if I had seen the news and I said there was no TV or radio, and my laptop was useless up here. He said that was probably just as well. I was to close it down properly if I hadn't already – he knew what I was like – and disable the Wi-Fi. The government was asking people to shut down new generation mobiles and personal computers for twenty-four hours while the servers coped with a hacker attack – no, not a virus, more a worm, a time bomb, linked to a Happy Christmas message. I said it had already travelled this far.

He said people weren't being too co-operative. Most thought the warning was a government ploy to censor the internet and bury news about Sumatra flu. And who could stop children using their mobiles anyway? It was now too much part of their lives. I said I had it from the horse's mouth that there was no such thing as Sumatra flu, just the normal seasonal burst of sniffles and wheezes, and he said be careful of the horse's mouth while I was about it: Sumatra flu could be carried by all mammals. I asked which was worse, the biological virus or the technological one and he said it was much of a muchness. It was all just bloody inconvenient.

I told Beverley her computer had a virus and she should close it down, restart it and do a Systems Restore which would take her back to the previous day. She did. But once she had disconnected from the internet she couldn't get back on it. Everything just said 'page not available'.

I said by the by there's a dead duck in the moat and she said, 'Shit, I'm meant to report that, but now I've no e-mail and no one at DEFRA will thank me for phoning them on Christmas Day. It'll just have to wait.' She added, or didn't add, 'Thanks to you,' but it didn't make much difference because that was obviously what she thought.

So I left her to it and had a massage with Heather, who was a tiny little thing with big brown eyes and the strength in her hands of a gorilla.

And after that I went down to hear Mira Miller's confession.

9

The Journalist's Tale

'Another place, another spa,' she told us. 'Two years back it was at Hillfont Spa in Wiltshire, a less eccentric and more puritanical place than this, where calories are counted seriously and chakras and champagne do not enter the equation, and colonic irrigation is the high point. I lay on a high couch on a white sheet while the girl gave me a facial. Her name was Zelda. I knew that from her name tag: otherwise there was nothing significant to remember about her at all. Her face bent over mine and I kept my eyes closed. Why would I want to have so clear a view of a stranger? When a heavy, hot tear from her eye fell upon my bare chest – my gown had been well pushed back from my shoulders – I was rather annoyed. I was the one with the problems; I was the one who needed soothing and cosseting, not the beauty therapist. I was the one who way paying. It was not fair. I lifted my arm from where it hung, until now so pleasantly relaxed, and still with my eyes closed, wiped away the tear, as one would brush away a fly. I made no comment. If I forgot about this lapse of etiquette I hoped she would too. I could sense the face move away and it was safe to open my eyes. I continued to lie on my back, eyes open and staring at the blank ceiling, as she coated my neck and the slope down to my breasts with a strange black mud allegedly from the Black Sea. There was a snivel, which I hoped came from grief, rather than the common cold. I determined that I would not, would not, ask her what the matter was. She'd only tell me.

'Now I do not often frequent spas. I am not obsessional about my looks, I am too busy and too easily bored. The first massage is fine, the second is pleasant, the third is okay, and the fourth is a real bore. I know I am here today but this is mostly for work. I am researching the place for a feature I am writing for Alistair. He's my editor. Ours is a family newspaper – up to a point – but 45 percent of our female readers when asked if they'd rather spend Christmas at a spa or at home voted for the spa. So I've been sent up here to check it out.

'But at the time I encountered Zelda I was just back from two years globetrotting – much of it in Iraq, following Hans Blick's WMD team, culminating in a nasty three-day stint as a kidnap hostage. It turned out to be a matter of money not politics, and Alistair came out in person to secure my release. It cost the paper ten thousand pounds. Be that as it may, hot sands and dry winds, not to mention the fierce air conditioning in the five-star hotels we foreign correspondents inhabit can wreak havoc with the complexion. My mother, meeting me off the aircraft, offered to pay for a week's stay in Hillfont, saying my skin looked older than hers did. She complained I must have been using water to wash my face. I said that in the factory warehouse where I had been kept shackled to a wall, blindfolded, I didn't think there had been a tap, let alone any soap. She just said, "Nonsense, if you'd have looked properly there was bound to have been a tap."'

'I know the feeling,' said the Trophy Wife. 'You come back from these unspeakable places and no one has any conception at all of how bad things can be. It's wilful. They don't want to know.'

Already the Trophy Wife was looking better. Her hair was short, shiny and reddish, lightened by blonde streaks. It had taken the whole morning to get even to this stage. Her legs were wrapped from thigh to ankle in silver foil beneath which some herbal potion would be working its soothing, rejuvenating magic. She would emerge from her ten days fit, literally, to marry a millionaire.

'Go on about Zelda,' I said.

'The snivelling subsided,' Mira continued, 'and still I said nothing. She bent over my face again so her eyes were now only inches from mine. I was obliged to look at her. She was one of the older girls and one of the least pretty. I remembered I had noticed her legs as I came in: they were bowed, as if from carrying too many weights as a child. A lock of her mousy hair fell into my face and I brushed that away too, irritated.

'"Many of my ladies like a lash and brow dye," this Zelda said, "so everything matches. Shall we do this next?"

'I said yes, because inasmuch as in the country of the Romans it is only sensible to do as the Romans do. If Hillfont Spa ladies thought in a perfect world hair, eyelashes and eyebrows should match that was okay by me. She coated the area around my eyebrows and under my lashes with a protective oil and then brushed a thick yellowish cream on to my brows. It stung a little.

'"We leave this on for ten minutes for it to take," she said. "Don't get any on your fingers. It's strong bleach and it can burn. Close your eyes, please."

'And I had, automatically, before I could say to her, "In that case forget about the lashes," because she was already coating them with the cream, in thick dollops, first the right eye, then the left. Top lashes, bottom lashes.

'"Don't squeeze your eyes together because if you do it might find its way in," she said. "And we don't want that. And don't open your eyes whatever you do. We don't want you to go blind."

'Now I am used to desert warfare. I know when I am under attack. There's a kind of metallic edge to the air, almost of electricity: you get a sniff of it, a whiff, someone nearby wishes you ill, and is about to spring with the knife, hurl the mortar, whatever. You dodge or you freeze or you run and hope to God you've chosen the right one. I got a whiff of it now. I also knew that people who say they hope you don't go blind rather wish you would. And that I was lying on my back, helpless. I chose the freezing option, perforce, and lay very still and very quiet. Nor did I open my eyes, nor did I squeeze them. I am terrified of blindness.

'She moved to the chair I'd left my slippers under and sat down. I could hear the rustle of her overall and caught a whiff of dandruff shampoo as she passed me.

'"Are you there?" I asked. "Are you all right?"

'"Fat lot you care," she said. "I'm just the girl and you're the client, and so far as you're concerned I'm a piece of shit."

'"I'm sorry you feel like that," I said, after I'd assimilated this. Perhaps she'd been fired?

'"Oh shut your face," she said. So I did.

'I lay, she sat. I needed her to get the stuff off my eyes. As I lay I heard a click. I knew that click. It was a revolver. A Colt 22?

'"Saved!" she said. And a little bitter laugh. Another click. "Saved again!" This time a snivel. I tried to make sense of it. The only option I came up with was that she was playing Russian roulette. She was clearly mad. Only beauty therapists who are mentally unbalanced call their ladies pieces of shit. The question was, was the barrel of the gun pointing at her head or at mine? I had done nothing to offend her, unless she was attributing to me some kind of group guilt because of her situation in the world and my own. Which was of course possible, just unexpected.

'"Zelda," I said – thank God I remembered the name – "Zelda, please, it's not like the Lottery. Every time you do it the odds don't return to normal, they shorten. What sort of gun is it?"

'"If you open your eyes," she said, meanly, "you'll go blind. How do you know it's a gun, anyway? It could have been me clicking my nails, or closing a compact, anything."

'"A Colt 22, isn't it," I said. An old-fashioned single-action revolver, favoured by ladies.

'"Trust you to know a thing like that," she said. "Bitch! You fancy women are all the same. I could die beneath your nose and you wouldn't give a fuck."

'"True," I said, and shouldn't have, just because it was. But I'll do most anything for a smart answer. Even, it seemed, risk an armed response from a murderous and/or suicidal maniac posing as a beautician.

'At this there was sharp intake of breath from Zelda: and then there was another click. I was still alive. But I'd made her angry. The revolver was pointed at me all right, even if it hadn't been before. I had been a fool. Worse, this was not the kind of conversation she believed I would survive. No longer "my lady this and my lady that" but shit, bitch, fuck. Had she planned this from the beginning? I thought fast.

'Three down and three to go. The thing about Russian roulette is that the you're safe – well, safer – until the sixth bullet, because the weight of it makes the barrel fall back at each firing so that it stays in the bottom position. But who knew how many bullets she had placed in the chamber? I could still cut and run and made a dive for the door but I didn't seem able to move. My mind was willing but my body had decided to paralyse me. All it cared about was my eyes.

'"Clive gave me the gun," she said. "You're right, it's a Colt 22. Stupid little thing. He said it belonged to his mother. I could have done with an automatic. I was in the house on my own and there'd been break-ins in the locality. Another good reason for him to leave me alone. Off with his fancy friends."

'"Tell me about Clive," I said. The ire currently directed towards me might get diverted to its proper place, presumably Clive. Then I'd have a chance. I remembered now that a few Colts have a five-bullet chamber, not even a six, in which case it would be only two to go. But surely fate would not be cruel? But I could see luck was not at all on my side – crossing my path with Zelda in the first place, giving me a lunchtime appointment when the clinic was deserted, allowing her to shed a tear which I had callously brushed away. I felt a glimmer of remorse. It must be hard to spend a life pounding away at other women's flesh in service of their vanity when your own life is in pieces.

'"That pig," said Zelda, "that bastard. He stole the best years of my life. And you don't even remember me, do you. You deserve to die." Her words came out in a cold hiss. She really meant it.

'I waited for nemesis. But there was no next click: no sound of the hammer going down on an empty chamber. She had stayed her hand: she was allowing me time: she wanted a witness to the life. She wanted to tell me about Clive. But in the meanwhile she wanted my apologies. When and where could I have possibly met her?

'"I'm sorry," I said. "I'm very short-sighted. Have we met? You must remind me."

'"You came to this place once," said Zelda. "I was up a ladder."

'"Good God," I said. "Not *that* Clive!" And I remembered. Four years back, when Sir Clive Hillfont, old Etonian and man-about-town, was single-handedly bringing the ancient family home into life, Alistair sent me to interview him. I'd been to this very place: Sir Clive Hillfont drove me up in his red open-topped sports car in the late summer evening, whizzing me up the M1, all verve and charm: even I had been impressed. He was good-looking, persuasive, square-chinned, energetic. We'd met the photographer here, had strolled round the splendid rooms, admired the gold leaf on the pillars, murmured our astonishment at the comparison between the before and the after: the snapshots of peeling paper, damp plaster and exposed lathes. And all his own work. The shooting, hunting, fishing, partying playboy now turned his hand as builder, plasterer, plumber, painter, to restore the family fortune, return the family home to its original glory.

'"And really, truly all your own work?" I asked. His hands had seemed rather smooth, the nails rather well manicured, better fitted to shuffling cards than mixing cement.

'There'd been a slight hesitation, I remembered that. And then he nodded upwards and I saw there was a ladder behind a pair of half-open, lofty, gold-embossed doors, and up the ladder was a girl with a paintbrush, and at the most awkward angle, touching up some kind of Austrian eagle with cobalt blue. It was Zelda. Of course it was Zelda. I remembered the short and stubby legs.

'"I've had help from the treasure in my life," said Clive. "The one who's always there for me."

'And he blew her a kiss, and I remembered the long-legged classy broad we'd left behind when we left South Ken for Hillfont, and the complicit look they'd exchanged, as if in "hurry back to bed, darling", and I thought this poor cow up the ladder, she's in love with him, much good may it do her, he's using her, she probably doesn't even get paid.

"'So that was you," I said to Zelda. "The girl up the ladder. You did a good job on that eagle."

"'That eagle," she said, "was nothing. That was frills. That eagle was the treat after four of the best years of my life as a builder's labourer. I tore down walls, I put them up. I plumbed, I wired, I plastered. My hair was hard and dry from lime dust. My hands were cracked and rough. All the summer daylight hours I worked and in the winter by arc light and on Friday nights he took me out for fish and chips and Wednesdays he spent the night with me in the attic on the mattress on the floor. But I loved him, how I loved him. Little me, little Zelda Florence, beloved of Sir Clive Hillfont the great playboy and gambler, whose name was in the gossip columns. I worked for love, not money. We were restoring the family home – it was to be our home when it was done – the great surprise for his family who, because of his wild past, were having to live in his Aunt Irene's dingy dower house. When it was finished he would bring them back to Hillfont House, now restored to its original grandeur, and they would forgive him. He had gambled the family fortune away but he was now reformed – he went to Gam-Anon: there were meetings nearly every night which was why he had to stay most of the time with his gay friend David in town, and couldn't be with me as he longed to be. And I, Zelda, was to be the greatest and best part of the surprise. They would be so proud and pleased to find he had found the right girl to settle down with – and then we'd be married."

"'Are you sure he said married?" I asked.

"'I thought about that a lot," she said. "No. He never said exactly married. He said become part of the family."

"'That figures," I said. "Old Etonians seldom tell direct lies. Tell you what" – I was pushing my luck again – "surely this stuff has taken by now, surely my eyebrows and eyelashes are the exact shade of my hair and if it stays on any longer they may get overbleached. Shouldn't it come off now?"

'Another sharp intake of breath and a whimper. But at least no click. No end of life itself.

'"You don't care," she wailed. "You just don't care. You only think about yourself. All I am to you is shit to wipe off your shoes. But I have feelings like anyone else, I have a youth that can be wasted on a no-good, toe-rag, cheating bastard, and it counts as much to someone like me as to someone like you. I'm not less than you are just because I do this stinking rotten job and you just lie there with your leaking body fluids and your bodily stenches expecting me to put up with it."

'I didn't say what was fairly obvious: that if this was the way she thought of her clients she was in the wrong job and perhaps she should try her hand at something else. Though I was tempted. I hadn't leaked or farted while on her table, so far as I knew, though a lesser client, threatened with death, might well not be able to control all bodily functions. I chose to overlook the insult and did what I could to soothe her down. Even by old Etonian standards Sir Clive seemed pretty much of a rotten egg.

'"You're not the only one, girl," I said. "Believe me, I know what you're talking about." And I told her my theory about how some vulnerable women could become addicted to a particular man's sperm. "See it in how abused women keep going back to their abusers, in the face of all common sense," I said, "for another fix of the very thing that's destroying them. See it when a woman spends her life worshipping a man not observably worthy of the worshipping and when she gets thrown out thinks it's the worst thing that ever happened to her rather than the best."

'"Then you do understand," she said. "You've got some heart. All right. If I was addicted that makes me feel better about it. It's just the cold turkey nearly kills you. I'll go on. But I'm not going to take that stuff off. You stay exactly where you are with your eyes closed in case you go blind, wondering if I'm going to shoot you. Which I still might."

'Ah, in a nutshell.

'I told her it was just a misfortune if you happened to run into a man to whom your body reacted in this way, and why it was just as well so many women these days made men wear condoms. The more condoms in circulation the less unrequited love.

'She told me she thought I was disgusting.

'"Sorry," I said. True love and romance and all that. "Anyway there you were, up a ladder in the middle of the night painting an eagle."

'"I'd gone to bed at eight," she said. "I normally did, I was so tired by then. It was a Tuesday so I wasn't expecting Clive back. Tuesday was a Gam-Anon night. They all were except Wednesdays. I woke up and realized I hadn't finished the eagle's eye. It needed a cobalt-blue iris and a touch of glitter on the pupil and I got out of bed and did it. I wanted it to be right. I loved being up close to that eagle. It reminded me of Clive. It had that kind of powerful, haughty look. I wanted it to take me in its soft wings and carry me off to a place where we'd be happy ever after. And then I heard the car and you came in with him, and looked at me as if I wasn't there. I expect you went to bed with him that night."

'"Believe me, I didn't," I said, taken aback. "I was a journalist. I had other fish to fry. It was a work assignment, nothing more."

'"But you thought he was attractive," she said.

'"I did," I said. "True, there was a certain amount of white powder on the way down and we were quite excitable, I suppose. But nothing happened."

'"What scum you all are," she said. "Scum deserve to die.'

'"I don't do that stuff any more," I said, hastily. Nor did I. It's good for the complexion for a time but you start getting pimples and your voice can get nasal and people suspect.

'She seemed to believe me because she continued her life story. I like life stories though one would prefer to listen to them under more easy circumstances. I had to shift my position every now and then without startling her because my back hurt from lying in one position for too long.

'"My mother left home when my baby brother was born. She took the baby but left me, which was strange, because her husband, a jobbing builder, was the baby's father but not mine. I was seven. Or perhaps it was not so strange, because no one ever seemed to like me very much. She didn't even say goodbye, let alone give me the name of my father. The builder said I could stay but I would have to earn my keep working for him after school and in the holidays. So I went with him to work when I could and soon picked up the various trades. I had a real gift for plumbing. He never liked me but I was a good worker and I think I earned his respect. But when I was fifteen he started to come into my room at night when he thought I was asleep. He never did anything; he just stood and watched, and listened. But it was frightening, so I ran away from home, and lived on the streets for a while. The police picked me up and I was put in a foster home. I was lucky; they sent me to art classes and presently I got a scholarship to art school. It was all right, but everyone drank, drugged and forni-cated, and nobody seemed to have any idea of what hard work was. All the girls had boyfriends except me. I just didn't seem to have been born a sexual prospect. My father abandoned me, my mother gave me away, the builder looked but didn't touch, even the pimps and the white slavers left me alone; presumably they didn't see me as a money-making prospect. You can imagine what that kind of thing does for a girl's self-esteem. So I decided to give up any thought of marriage or sex and be a loner and concentrate on picture restoring, which I loved."

'"Making good what time has made bad," I said, sympatheti-cally.

"Yeah, except that I was bad to begin with. Time had nothing to do with it."

'"So how did you come to meet Clive?" I managed to shove an elbow into the small of my back to ease the pressure. That was better.

'"I'm coming to that," she said. "My final year – I got a starred first, by the way – we students were hanging the end of year show. Correction, I was hanging the end of year show. The others were off bonking or ironing their hair or whatever it was they did.

I was trying to get the Vermeer up on the wall single-handed. It was a great big thing with a heavy frame. I'd rigged up a contraption with some pulleys, a couple of tables and a chair, so I could do it on my own."

'"A Vermeer? At a student show?" She was a fantasist: why was I letting myself be taken in?

'"I'd been doing work experience at a studio where they restored old masters and this was one of them. That was their story and they were sticking to it. They were certainly planning to sell it for a couple of million. They let me put it in the show since I'd done all the work on it. Work experience is a con. All those hours and not a penny do you get paid."

'"But wasn't that risky? Supposing it got lost or stolen?"

'"Exactly," she said. "Then they could claim on the insurance. That was the general idea, I suppose. Safer than going for verification. Look, I'm not blonde and pretty: they could hardly have been doing me a good turn, you stupid cow."

'I could see why people had trouble liking her, even when she wasn't mad and carrying a gun.

'"I wish you wouldn't interrupt," she went on. "Things like this probably happen to you all the time – or did – but not to me. I was balancing on a chair when someone spoke behind me. 'That's a good painting,' the voice said. It was a man's voice, a bit gravelly and croaky and with a good education behind it – you know the posh kind which sounds as if it's strangling itself? I knew my fate had come along. Somehow the future was pushing forward into the present to let me know he had arrived. This voice would ring in my ears forever.

'"'I know,' I said. 'It's mine. I did it.'

'"And I looked round wondering what fate had in mind for me. A dwarf, a leper, a Cyclops? But he was the kind of man the ironed blondes had in tow – tall, good looking, well dressed; he even looked as if there was a flicker of intelligence behind the eyes. I nearly fell off the chair – just as well I'd wedged the pulleys.

'"'Looks more like a Vermeer to me,' he said.

""'Bits of it are. About one percent. The spoon in the foreground was there when I began. But more likely school of Vermeer, anyway.'

""'Could have fooled me,' he said.

""'That's the general idea,' I said. And I told him to stand back and I loosed the clips so the pulleys ran and the bottom of the painting leaned out towards me and I manoeuvred it so it fell half a centimetre onto the six waiting hooks. It settled nicely.

""'Who rigged this thing up?' he asked, pointing at the contraption I stood upon.

""'I did,' I said, truly pleased with myself, and I hopped down and stood before him boldly and said, 'Look at me! Genuine inventor, all-purpose builder, fine plumber, good plasterer, okay electrician, Vermeer forger, starred first. Short legs, plain face, greasy hair, sorry about that. You can't have everything.'

"'He stretched out his long, elegant hand and touched my hair and the side of my face and said to me, 'Your hair is full of gold dust.' And so it was. When the painting settled loose motes of the gold leaf I'd applied to the frame had drifted and fallen on my hair and made it glitter. At that moment I fell in love with him.

"'And he looked at the finger where he'd touched my hair and said, 'Now there's gold on my ring finger, what are we to make of that?'

"'From which I deduced he had fallen in love with me. Though when I think about it now I think the finger he spoke of was on the right hand not the left, and isn't the ring finger the third one on the left? But I guess it was a genuine mistake on his part, otherwise he would have had to have thought very, very fast. But what do I know of men, or marriage, or wedding fingers and who men marry and who they don't?"

'Mostly, I could have told her, if men have titles they do not marry the short-legged, illegitimate daughters of unknown fathers, no matter how full of gold dust their hair is. But for once I didn't say so. I wanted her to get on. My eyelashes were going to fall out unless she did something soon.

'"He took me home to my dingy student flat," said Zelda, warming to the recollection, "and washed my hair and rubbed it dry with an old towel and smoothed it with the breath from his mouth. He looked through my mingy wardrobe and seemed un-shocked by what he saw, and picked out an old grey dress, so flimsy with wear it seemed altogether unsubstantial. I felt like a wraith but a beautiful wraith, the kind that haunts men's dreams. He took me out to dinner and told me which knife and fork to use, and before the night was over he was in bed with me and before the week was over I was installed in the attic room of the ruin that was Hillfont House, and his mother's ring was on my finger. Not that I met her, and it was only an opal. My potential job with the Vermeer people was abandoned. I, little Zelda Florence who was once nobody, overnight had a lover, a fiancé, a room of my own – though at first I had to carry water up from the stables and the loo was out-of-doors – and one of the great houses of England to restore.

'"Clive would have been with me all the time but he had a gambling problem and had to go to a Gam-Anon meeting in London nearly every day. It made sense for him to stay with his gay friend David five days a week. He would come down on Tuesdays with materials, and occasionally a labourer if the work was heavier than I could cope with. I am strong but not all that strong. I can heave a Vermeer about with the aid of a couple of pulleys but I can't hold up an RSJ with one hand and knock away an oak beam with another. Though sometimes it seemed as if he thought I should. Occasionally he'd bring an architect friend with him, but I loved it when it was just him and me. On Tuesday after-noons he'd take me to the shops – I don't drive: I have this thing about driving into large objects instead of going round them, so they won't give me a licence – and we'd buy everything I needed for the coming week; he was so extravagant: anything I wanted! In the evenings I'd cook for him, and we'd eat up in the attic and then we'd go to bed together, and wake up together. Wednesday morning he'd inspect the work and suggest improvements and changes, and on Wednesday afternoon he'd go away again, back to fight his habit.

'"Three years! This went on for three years! I was happy," she said. "And this beautiful, beautiful house was rising up around me, and once the heavy building work was done and I could start on the mouldings and the pargetting and so on, it was heaven. Sometimes I'd feel I wasn't significantly consulted in the decision-making process. Once I asked why we had to spoil the grand state rooms by converting them into lots of little en-suite bedrooms, and he said because the family was so large and he wanted everyone to be able to come and stay whenever they liked and they would learn to love me as he did, and once I asked why the stable block was to be divided into cubicles which needed so much plumbing, and he said because he was going to have lots of horses and these horses expected all mod cons and he would teach me how to ride. I was so thrilled! We're in the old stable block now. I did all this plumbing. Now I just work here. Sometimes I'd feel restive and ask to meet his mother, or David, or even the therapists at Gam-Anon in case I could help – but he hated me asking questions, and would shout and throw things. I didn't like to annoy him. He said things were just perfect as they were and my day would come."

'Nothing like a female masochist to bring out the sadist in every man, but I was prudent enough not to say so. "And the sex was so good," she said, by way of further explanation, "and I had everything I wanted. And if he didn't want me who would? Do you understand?"

'"Yes," I said, and I did. She was no murderer; she was just another sister flailing about trying to ease the pain.

'"I'll take the stuff off now," she said, and I heard the swoosh of her dress as she moved towards me and gently smoothed layer upon layer of cream across my forehead and eyes, and then lifted it off with certain, delicate movements.

'"Don't open them yet," she said. I didn't. "The eyebrows are certainly a bit pale," she said, "but I can dye them back to match the hair."

"'Oh, it'll be okay," I said. "Don't let's bother."

"'And you've lost an eyelash or two, but not too many. I know how to transplant eyelashes: it's tricky but I went on a course and got a certificate of merit."

"'Bet you did," I said.

"'I'll do it for you half price," she said. "I should have got it off a bit earlier."

"'Honestly," I said. "It's okay. Don't worry about it." I opened my eyes. It was some time before I could make sense of what I saw. She was back sitting on her chair and the gun was pointing at me. She was fatter and plainer than I remembered. As I watched, the barrel drooped and she rested it in her lap. Now's my chance to cut and run, I thought, but I wanted to hear the rest of the story.

"'So what happened?" I asked. "How did the story end?"

"'It ended just after you came down," she said. "You were the first shot in a publicity campaign."

'Of course. I'd been sent abroad just after I'd written up the interview with Clive and been out of touch with the gossip for some months. Developments in the Hillfont saga had passed me by.

"'The house was finally ready for the family to arrive and Clive to win back his place in their hearts. Down to the last beautifully restored cornice, gold tap, slab of under-floor heating gently vibrating, the great marital bed, carved by Zelda, hangings embroidered by Zelda, dominating the master bedroom, where Clive and Zelda were to start a new dynasty – all was finally in place. The last brushstroke had been made to the Austrian eagles with the glittering eyes which guarded the great hall. The land-scape gardeners had gone – the interior decorators too: though how there was suddenly money for them while Clive and Zelda still ate pork and beans she could not be sure. Clive had achieved his ambition. His demon was defeated. He was finally free of Gam-Anon. The love of his life had stuck with him through bad times and good."

'"Oh don't," I said. "Oh don't, I can't bear it."

'"I can bear it," she said. "Lots of women have to bear it. I am just rather an extreme example."

'He dumped her by fax. Zelda was sitting in the great hall wondering why the office equipment people had just moved in a reception desk and were wiring it up with a communication system and why her beloved house suddenly felt less like a family home than an hotel, and why the messenger was waiting for an approval on a glossy invitation to the opening of Hillfont Spa on the day she thought his mother was coming, when the new fax burst into life. It was in Clive's handwriting.

Dearest Zelda, Let me get this over with. I have fallen in love with someone else and am to be married and I must ask you to pack and leave Hillfont at once. The press are on their way – she has royal connections – and for everyone's sake it's best that you're not in-house. Thank you for all your help in the restoration of Hillfont, which I much appreciate. I will be forwarding a cheque for £5000 in recognition of your services, and if you give me your new address I will forward it forthwith.

'"Bastard!" I said, and worse. "Wanker!" and variations.

'She raised the barrel of the gun and pointed it at me. "I don't like swearing," she said.

'"Sorry" I said. "Really sorry." She was not above bad language herself, but it didn't fit in with her vision of herself and she was armed and I was not.

'She lowered the gun.

'"It can be very difficult for men to express their feelings. I expect he had been putting off telling me for ages."

'"I expect he had," I said. "Did the cheque arrive?"

'"Yes. He wrote he knew he had been generous but he thought I deserved it, and hoped I would accept. It was quite a nice letter. Men always think work in the home should be free, don't they?"

'"The way they see it, it's what you do in return for sex," I said.

'"I had nowhere to go except home to my father – he offered to marry me, because we weren't blood relations – but I said no. I used the cheque to train as a beauty therapist and got a job here. I like to be in the house. I know it so well. The girls here say the plumbing is really good: none of the troubles you get in other places with water pressure and running too hot or too cold. Clive married his princess. He was always ambitious. I found he'd opened two other spas before Hillfont. I expect I was just one of a train of girls he thought he loved until the work was done."

'"I expect so," I said.

'"I hope I didn't frighten you just now," she said, and smiled, and suddenly looked much prettier and almost attractive.

'"Think nothing of it," I said.

'"The thing was I'd just realized he's lying by the pool with the princess drinking gin and tonic. He must have booked in. I walked up and down once or twice and he didn't even recognize me. That upset me."

'"Take the gun and go and kill him," I said. "Kill him now."

'But she seemed quite shocked by the idea.

'"I don't think so," she said. "It would be so messy. The marble by the pool is quite soft and might get stained. If it was in here it would be different. I could sluice everything out. So I'm afraid it's not to be, not this time. I'm ready for my next lady now, so if you let me take the gown and you could just find your shoes…"

Mira put her head in her hands.

'I believe eyelashes do grow back in,' said the Trophy Wife, 'but only if you're lucky. Are they okay now?'

'Yes,' said Mira. 'Luckily. I left early the next morning, I couldn't face any more. I suppose I should have told management but I didn't. I just tried to forget the whole thing. The worst thing was that a week later Sir Clive and his wife were both found dead in their bed in Nice, shot by a Colt 22. They never found out who did it. Was it Zelda? Was it my fault? I can't get it out of my head. I told her to kill him.'

The ladies round the pool considered.

'He deserved to die,' said one. There was a chorus of agreement.

'Yes, but not his wife,' said someone.

'She probably knew what went on and chose to ignore it,' said another. 'She has to share some of the guilt.'

I said if we all took moral responsibility for our partners' pasts we'd be so crippled with guilt we'd be unable to leave the house, and we agreed to leave the subject, but of course didn't. We sat with our toes curling in the sparkling water and contemplated the men we'd dumped and the sisters we'd betrayed by making them dump others for our sake. And then –

'But a Colt 22!' added the Trophy Wife. 'That's pretty specific.'

'Not necessarily. It's the gun of choice for the vengeful woman,' said the brisk young woman who turned out to be a leading mortgage broker. 'Small, but perfectly formed, and if you know what you're doing you can get them on the internet.'

'And there were probably lots of women who wanted him dead,' said another. 'It's not fair to blame Zelda, and of course it's not your responsibility, Mira. If it was her, she did it, not you. Anyone can give bad advice.'

The oldest amongst us, the Company Director, finally spoke up. When she did it was to say that dead was very satisfactory. When she heard that the men who had spited her, or left her, or embarrassed her, or broken her heart finally died, there was a great sense of rest, and peace. She hoped one day to have outlived them all, every one, and so could look back on her life with equanimity. She said it was one of the few mercies left to women, that on the whole they outlived men, and that included every man they'd ever fucked.

Age did not make her mince her words and we were all a little shocked, I think.

And then she said, 'And actually, I went to Hillfont Spa once, to get over a face lift, and I'm sure it was your girl Zelda who did it.

87

She was a very good masseuse but rather plain. I don't remember much about her legs. I do remember she told me a long story about her early youth – she was going to be a concert pianist but was kidnapped by an admirer and kept in an attic room for four years and made to play the piano for him every day until rescued by the police. She had been so traumatized she could no longer play which was why she was now working as a masseuse. I didn't believe a word of it. I also happened to know Clive Hillfont – not a very nice man: charming, but greedy, ambitious and selfish: she got that right – though the new wife was sweet. It was generally assumed that the murderer was her first husband, who threw himself off a cliff the next day. I also happen to know the builders who restored Hillfont House – they did some work for me once. They were very proud of the Austrian eagles and had commissioned an artist to do them. So I don't think you have much to worry about, Mira.'

10

It was nearly time for my Hydrotherapy appointment. I walked with Mira to the treatment wing. She was making for the Snooze Zone, where she was to be wrapped in some kind of exfoliating foil prepared from herbs which grew only in the Ural mountains.

'It's all very well,' said Mira, 'but just because Zelda told the Company Director a pack of lies doesn't mean she wasn't telling me the truth. And what about the gun? That was real enough. And the builders could be making it up about the eagles and the artist. Or perhaps she was the artist—'

'Mira,' I said, 'give over. Just because you want to murder Alistair and his wife doesn't mean Zelda took the EuroStar and did Clive and his wife in. You're projecting.'

I thought perhaps that was going to be the end of a beautiful friendship, she looked at me so coldly – but then her face relaxed and she laughed and said yes, I was probably right. Should we leave it at that?

When I got to the Hydrotherapy room there was a handwritten notice on the door saying, 'Sorry, everyone. The pool is closed until further notice.' I was not altogether sorry. They direct water jets at your surplus fat and it can make you quite sore. But it made the £5000 even less of a bargain if it was going to go on like this during the entire stay. If you're going to stay open over Christmas the least you can do is ensure that the staff understand the concept. Mira came and found me and said that the Snooze Zone was deserted, and looked rather like the *Marie Celeste*. Towels were left where they'd fallen and potions mixed but hardening unused: she couldn't be bothered hanging about for someone to turn up, and she was going back to her room to have a proper sleep: 'snooze' was a revolting word anyway. She'd see me at supper time; and if she slept through that I was to be sure to come and collect her in time for the Surgeon's story, in the Jacuzzi at eight o'clock. She didn't want to miss it. The Surgeon was back from A&E. The Public Speaker's heart had reverted to normal: the Surgeon had taken her to the station and she had caught the train back home to the battered taxi in the drive. She promised to have a good rest when she got back and to let the minicab driver look after her, bring tea and banana smoothies, rich in potassium. He was good at those; the Surgeon thought the extra potassium might just be saving her from the SVT attacks.

Mira had taken a look at the appointments book in the Snooze Zone and seen that the Surgeon was booked in for three pedicures and two reflexology sessions during the ten days. She obviously cared about her feet. She was a tall, well-built woman with a pleasant demeanour, broad shoulders, a square jaw and long, steady, competent hands – which considering her profession, was just as well. Brain surgery is the high risk end of the profession. Her eyes were wide and her voice was deep. She wore her fair hair wound up around her head. Her legs were long and strong – and made four of the Manicurist's two – I had remarked upon it during the Trophy Wife's Tale – but they were shapely and the skin white and smooth. I looked forward to hearing her tale.

11

The Brain Surgeon's Tale

This tale is as Shimmer told it to us, written up by me from the tape I made on my mini recorder – with her permission – the noise of the Jacuzzi bubbles making direct reportage impractical.

She was named Shimmer, she had a twin sister named Sparkle. The parents were hippies, as one might have guessed, not quite attuned to the realities of the world, and wishing the same for their baby daughters. The little girls spent their early lives sticky-mouthed and straggle-haired, in a cow-hide tepee outside St Ives in Cornwall, one of a cluster owned by the PPP, the Peace and Perception People. The community had lived frugally, off the land, and on benefits, their enemy being the state and something vaguely called the bourgeoisie. Neither parent could bear to live in regular houses: there was 'too much gravity', 'too many right angles to stifle the free spirit'. Tent fabric stretched between bowing staves, deep, deep brown from the rising smoke of innu-merable spliffs, was a tolerable compromise. Both parents had university degrees, the father in anthropology and the mother in chemistry, and had started life with normal preoccupations and obsessions, but the over-strong LSD of the Seventies had short-circuited too many synapses in their brains and turned them into what Shimmer described as brain-dead visionaries, and Sparkle as mud-people.

The girls were not without affection for their parents, far from it, but lying shivering in their pallet beds, while the cowhide above them beat and flapped in an icy wind, or sweltering in the sweaty pong of summer nights, they had trained themselves in the art of seeing clearly, of distinguishing between what their parents took to be the real world, and what actually it was, and increasingly felt a certain disappointment in the way they had been reared.

The twins were, frankly, a disappointment to their parents: their craving for education, for passing exams, for getting on, for buildings with solid walls, was upsetting. The parents had hoped to create and mould free spirits and instead had produced two censorious little intellects with a craving for order. But one's children are the luck of the draw: it was karma, best to go with the flow. So when the State suggested boarding school and scholarships to Roedean the parents did not fight back. Now Shimmer was a brain surgeon working in Newcastle West General Hospital, she had the lowest vegetation rate in the north. (Success in brain surgery is reckoned thus: that you kill, you cure, or you leave in a vegetable state forever: the one with the lowest vegetation rate wins.) Sparkle was a leading gender academic, a professor at Sussex, head of its Institute for Interdisciplinary Gender Studies, already with eighteen publications to her name.

Some identical twins grow more distinguishable with age: Shimmer and Sparkle remained remarkably as one in looks, habits and personality, even though they now lived at a distance to one another. Perhaps their childhood practice in resisting parental influences contributed to this fact: they had clung together for sanity and merged yet the more. Now, in their mid-thirties, both enjoying the esteem of colleagues and good incomes, unmarried and with no time to waste on boyfriends, writing papers for learned journals in their spare time, they seldom saw each other, but spoke to one another on Skype a good deal, computer cameras switched to 'on', feeding mirror-images back to one another as they spoke.

One Saturday night, while Shimmer was on call, during a little extra study in front of her computer in her small uncomfortable flat in West Jesmond, Skype summoned her. It was her twin, calling from her equally small and equally uncomfortable flat in

Brighton. Neither sister was good at looking after her creature comforts. Both lived in their heads, as their parents complained, not in their senses.

'Shimmer,' said Sparkle, 'it is Saturday night. What are you doing?'

'Reading a rather good book on cranial mononeuropathy, type 3.'

'Doesn't that strike you as sad, for a Saturday night?'

'Not really,' said Shimmer. 'It's very interesting.'

'I'm reading Sedgwick's *Epistemology of the Closet*, but it isn't enough,' said Sparkle. 'Other women go to parties, dress up, have boyfriends.'

'I know they do,' said Shimmer, 'but that's other women, not us. Is that a glass of Belgian beer you have by your computer?'

'Yes, it is,' said Sparkle, and Shimmer moved her bottle into her webcam's field of vision.

They had a discussion as to the nature of coincidence and the inheritability of aesthetic perception, and decided it was more to do with a similar arrangement of taste buds on their tongues than any shared mystical bond which led them, as so often, to be doing the same thing at the same time. Shimmer admitted with some reluctance that she too had been feeling restless: perhaps they needed boyfriends. You couldn't deny the effect of hormones on the female body. Facts were facts, although inconvenient.

'You don't mean we want babies,' exclaimed Sparkle, in horror. 'You mean we are as primitive as that, in spite of our best efforts?'

Shimmer said it was a long time since the culture had made any close connection between procreation and sex: it was perfectly possible to want sex but not babies, and she saw Sparkle exhale in relief. They agreed that it was one thing to want boyfriends but another to find them. They agreed they were perfectly good-looking, not deformed in any way, and if they put on make-up and frilly clothes might even be regarded as quite sexy. It did have to be acknowledged, though, that men did not seek them out. They discussed pheromones and whether or not a lack of them was to blame, and whether or not the condition could be treated med-ically, and Shimmer finally came out with the fact that both hesitated to recognize – their brains got in the way of true love. Simply, they frightened men off.

'If I get into conversation with a man I don't know, and they ask me what I do, and I say I'm a brain surgeon, at first they don't believe me and once I have convinced them they smile politely and move away.'

'The same thing with me,' said Sparkle. '"What a lovely name," they say, "Sparkle!" And then they ask me what I do and I say I am a professor of gender studies and they're gone. It's true; men are terrified of brainy women.'

'Then supposing we found men brainier than ourselves,' sug-gested Shimmer.

'There aren't enough around to create a critical mass in which choices can be made,' said Sparkle. 'Or else they have Asperger's and few social skills.' They agreed they liked men with social skills, broad shoulders, taller than themselves with slim taut bellies and firm neat buttocks. They agreed that perhaps shared intellect and interests were not as basic to a relationship as many supposed.

Sparkle would come up and stay the following weekend when Shimmer was not on call, and they would go out and look for boyfriends. They would go to a pub. Sparkle would say she was a teacher, and Shimmer would say she was a nurse. They would shop during the week for fuck-me clothes. It was difficult for them to go shopping together: both would want the same thing and it was the nearest they got to quarrelling if there was only one in the shop in the right size and colour. Besides, people stared.

So the next weekend Shimmer unfolded the Put-U-Up in her little living room – she had the ground floor of a terraced Victorian villa, near the shops and transport and easy to maintain – and Sparkle unpacked her bags and put her nightie under the nylon-cased pillow – a long-sleeved cream flannelette, decorated with the occasional sprig of some enigmatic blue flower: Shimmer had recently bought one similar only with a pink flower. Then she spread out her other purchases on the navy uncut Moquette sofa which Shimmer had found on a tip – almost new and perfectly clean and comfortable. They had a good deal of money saved between them: not that they were in any sense mean: they just saw no point in spending money unnecessarily.

Shimmer had made a conscious effort to choose items which would be unlike anything Sparkle was likely to choose, but of course Sparkle had made a similar resolution and both came up with pale green flimsy undies embroidered with gold thread, the bra slightly padded – both were 34-24-38 – very short, white, pleated skirts and expensive pink cashmere sweaters of the same shade and make, far skimpier than they would normally wear, and black shoes with stacked heels. Both had thick, straight, bobbed blonde hair, of the wash-and-go kind, pudding-basin cut, but since this was fashionable at the time it seemed that quite a lot of artifice had been employed in creating the look. Both agreed that what men seemed to find attractive in women was artifice.

They dressed for their outing and crowded together in front of the one wardrobe mirror to see how they looked. How they looked, of course, was alike, and a source of confusion to potential suitors, and indeed, looking in the mirror, to themselves. So Shimmer, trained in such matters, precise and certain in her movements, tie-dyed the pink cashmere fabric of her sweater with a concoction of turmeric which she used for the egg curries she favoured, mixed with olive oil. Now at least they could be told apart. The fabric moved under pressure much as did brain tissue, she affirmed to Sparkle. It was true the sweater now left marks upon the skin but they were attractive enough: her white torso was marked agreeably with orange streaks as if she had taken part in some native ritual. By and large they were pleased with themselves and one another as they left the house, giggling with the unaccustomed effort of balancing on high heels. They drank gin and tonic before they left, and shared an Ecstasy tab Sparkle had lately confiscated from a girl student.

They hailed a cab and went to a pub near the Newcastle West General, much patronized by doctors and nurses and the hangers-on who liked to keep them company. Shimmer was sure enough that she would not be recognized – people would see a pair of identical twins out on a date, not a respected professional – and the doubling-up effect, as they had come to call it, would interfere with any concerted attempt at recall. People would think '*look at those twins*' not '*haven't I seen her somewhere before?*'.

There was a hush as they came into the bar, but it was an approving one – two identical, well-built, smiling girls, unaccompanied, very long legs, blonde hair in the latest style, short white skirts and one with a tight pink sweater and one in pink with arty brown streaks. No one would have thought they had a brain in their heads.

They sat near the fruit machine, on the grounds that the ones who played it would have money to spare, and downed gin and tonics. They had rather hoped someone would treat them but no one did.

'Look as if you've come to get laid,' said Sparkle.

Shimmer said she was trying to look like someone who was hoping to have dinner before she got laid.

'That may be rather too up-market,' said Sparkle. 'Aspire to no more than fish and chips.'

'Fish and chips!' said Shimmer. 'The grease, the ammonia batter, the slime between fish skin and crust—!'

'That expression on your face,' said Sparkle, 'is why neither of us has a boyfriend.'

'Sorry,' said Shimmer.

'I do it too, I suppose,' said Sparkle. 'It's the look of one whose aesthetic values are being assaulted, but a simple man might not know that. They might think it was personal.'

'That time I lost my virginity,' said Shimmer, 'it's true I was revolted by the sight of the contents of the condom, and said "yuk!". But the foaming slime between squashed and flattened rubber – it fascinated me even when it repelled me. There are times in a brain op when you're releasing a build-up of fluid – I never like that – I couldn't understand why he didn't call me back the next day. He was a nice-looking guy who came to deliver a pizza.'

'People don't necessarily believe you when you say you're a brain surgeon. They think you're joking,' said her sister. 'We just have to learn to shut up. I think I say I'm a professor and a virgin too early on in the mating game, and that's why I still am one. In less developed parts of the world virgins are at a premium, but here it just seems to put men off. There is an interesting thesis to be developed here. Why? Fear of disease or spiritual pollution? Shifting power relations between the genders? Virginity loss reduced to a rite of passage?'

But two young men were approaching so they fell silent and smiled blankly and amiably into space, trying to look as if they were ready for anything and disapproved of nothing. The Ecstasy might as well have been aspirin for all the good it was doing them, or perhaps it took longer to cut in than Sparkle had assumed. Just because a student believed a pill was illegal didn't mean that it was. Anything could be anything.

The two young men were brothers: Dave and Pete. Their parents also had had high hopes for them, and had also been disappointed. Dave was a plumber and Pete was a plasterer. They worked for others, and did not have their own businesses. Had they worked harder and passed their exams they might well have gone to college, as their parents kept telling them. (Derek, their father, was a lab technician up at the hospital; the mother, Lynn, worked at the local Labour Party headquarters – both would have earned more had they had degrees.) Perhaps as parents they were too insistent? At any rate both had hoped the family would rise in the world, not descend to artisan level, and been disappointed. There was only a year between the boys, from the start a good-looking, noisy, boisterous pair, so boisterous indeed that Attention Deficiency Syndrome was suspected, though not confirmed, owing to cuts in the local NHS child assessment unit.

Now Dave was twenty-four and Pete was twenty-three. They'd left school the moment they could: they made good employees – enough parental genes and example fed through to make them honest and hard-working – and were strong and healthy, earned well, spent well, drank well and fornicated whenever they could. One day some girl, growing out of her own hard-drinking, hard-fucking, half-naked-down-the-alley, drug-fuelled stage, would trap them into marriage, or one of the halfway stages currently popular, but the brothers would avoid it as long as they could, in the time-honoured way. If only the hippies had given birth to Dave and Pete, if only Derek and Lynn had produced the twins – how happy both families would have been. But it was not to be. But perhaps what one generation fails to provide, the next will?

Dave and Pete eyed up Shimmer and Sparkle from across a crowded bar. The karaoke had begun. They'll do, they thought. A bit old but new in town and the stranger is always attractive. And twins were always a turn-on. They themselves were sometimes mistaken for twins – same stocky build, same bright blue eyes, and same curly dark hair when the No. 2 cut was growing out. Certainly one was often muddled up with the other, even by their own parents. The thought occurred to the four of them at the same time – perhaps a foursome?

And Shimmer and Sparkle both thought, but neither said, because the idea of the two splitting, becoming three – or even four, a tendency to twins being hereditary – was to them so revolutionary it could not be easily expressed. But it went thus: 'If I had a baby I wouldn't mind one of them being the father.' Also, since it is possible for twins to be conceived by two different fathers – more than one egg descending, and different sperm available – both of them being the father.

The boys went to the fruit machine first and pretended not to have noticed the girls. The twins pretended not to have noticed the boys, though Sparkle pinched Shimmer as they passed by and Shimmer squealed. Well, a squeal is good. This much they knew. The men fed coins into the machine: apples, pears and plums whirred and failed to line up. They kicked and swore and thumped but still it would not disgorge money.

'Interesting,' said Shimmer, 'the theory of the probable. The odds of winning return to normal no matter how many times you spin the wheels. The fact that three airliners have crashed in one week does not make it less likely that one will crash the following week.'

'That is not a good example,' said Sparkle. 'Terrorist activity could intervene and make it the more likely.'

Shimmer refrained from offering another example. That her sister had tried and failed to lose her virginity did not make it more likely that eventually she would succeed. She resolved to do her best to shift the odds that evening. It did not seem right that one was a virgin and the other not. She could see that because it had happened to her she assumed it had happened to her twin, and that was absurd. She gave a little laugh.

'I suppose you two cunts think this is fucking funny,' said Dave.

'Only one of us was laughing,' retorted Shimmer, smartly.

Sparkle leant into her and whispered in her ear, 'No. Too pedantic. Repartee is not our strong point.' Shimmer smiled and licked her lips invitingly and the lads relaxed. Unpleasantness was avoided; ice had been broken.

The boys kicked and swore on. The fruit machine was firmly bolted to the floor and built for attack, but the ludicrous sound that accompanied the revolving wheels, the trills of triumph and belches of failure, combined with the sound of foot against metal were more than the girls could stand, accustomed as they were to the reverential hush of surgery and library. It became obvious the next move had to come from the twins.

'Let's have a smoke,' said Sparkle, loudly, and they drifted outside. It was a no-smoking establishment. The twins were quite active non-smokers, crusaders almost, but had bought cigarettes and lighters for the occasion. They knew that the most sociable and easy-going of the pub's customers would tend to gather outside its doors for a smoke. One of Sparkle's students had done her thesis on the impact of anti-smoking legislation on courtship rituals and had found that 'just outside the office' was more often cited than 'in the office' when it came to 'where we met'. Fortunately the twins were saved from inhaling, though they lit up bravely, for sure enough, after a decent few minutes, Dave and Pete followed them out, with gin and tonics for the girls and beer for themselves: by then they all felt secure enough in each others' interests. It was a warm evening and Dave and Pete took off their sweaters to reveal vest, biceps, and tattoos. The boys suggested the girls did the same and the girls giggled and whispered in one another's ears – which the boys were getting used to and rather liked – and declined.

Dave said he was a plumber; Pete said he was a plasterer; Shimmer said her name was Lucy and she was a nurse; Sparkle said she was Lola and a teacher.

'Posh then, eh,' said Pete. 'A couple of classy twins,' or words to that effect, leaving out an emphatic adjective or two. Lola refrained from pointing out that a 'couple of twins' was a tautology and Lucy from adding that a conclusion could not be equal to its premise. Pete and Dave lit up and the twins tried not to shudder, their own cigarettes had gone out from lack of attention. Forgettable pleasantries were exchanged. Safe in their new identities the girls joined the great majority of the human race in its humbler social and sexual aspirations and a good time was had by all.

'Mum would approve of this,' said Sparkle to Shimmer, while the boys went off for yet more drinks. 'It's so mindless!'

'Dad always wanted tattoos,' said Shimmer, 'but he thought the dye might be toxic.'

'Should I tell him I'm a virgin?' asked Sparkle.

'Certainly not,' said Shimmer. 'Which one do you want?'

'I can't really tell the difference,' said Sparkle. 'I'm easy.'

Shimmer said she preferred Pete the plasterer: there was just something about him.

'This is just sex,' said Sparkle, a little nervously. 'We're not going to get involved.'

'Of course not,' said Shimmer but before the night was out she was in love with Pete. The Surgeon and the Plasterer. Both are skilled jobs, both require a steady hand and a good eye and a faith in the future and their own competence. Shimmer had the lowest vegetation rate in the north; Pete's walls were smooth and flawless. They had more in common than they knew.

This is how the evening went. They staggered to the chippie for fish and chips. The lads were always hungry, and the drink needed to be absorbed. The twins outfaced fear of indigestion and ate valiantly. Pete finished Lucy's chips, and Dave finished Lola's. Thus preferences were confirmed. The four of them went back to Dave's flat, up side stairs above a sex shop. There were no books: but a copy of *Builder's World Weekly* and *AutoCar* on the coffee table, along with old coffee mugs, squashed lager cans and a general accumulation of male debris. But at least he had cleaned the loo and nothing smelt. A savage ginger tomcat had to be moved from the sofa before they could sit.

'What's its name?' asked Shimmer.

'Guess,' said Pete.

'Ginger,' said Shimmer.

'Right,' said Pete. 'On the brainy side, you lasses, out of our class, but who's worrying?' Or words to that effect.

Sparkle snuggled into Dave on the sofa, as if she were used to doing this kind of thing, and Pete pulled Shimmer down on top of him. Various items of clothing were discarded or removed. Dave's hand investigated underneath Sparkle's thong and Sparkle let out a little yell and excused herself and went to the loo; she stayed away a little time so Shimmer extricated herself from beneath Pete and went to see if Sparkle was okay. People have been known to choke on their own vomit and she had eaten too much fish in batter. Sparkle was fine, just cleaning off a little blood and removing her knickers.

'I just lost my virginity,' she said to Shimmer. 'The membrane must have been worn very thin. His finger just went right through. We could go home now.'

But Shimmer wanted to stay so Sparkle stayed too. Shimmer felt at home entwined with Pete, as if it was the right place to be. Dave said they could go into the bedroom if Lola wanted: he didn't mind about the other two but teachers could be strait-laced. Lola said it was okay with her: she and her sister were not like two people but one person divided into two so privacy was not an issue. Pete looked puzzled and said but surely that was the same thing, and Lola apologized for being airy-fairy.

'Fucking think so,' said Pete.

It was abundantly clear to both girls that the last thing the brothers wanted in women was to hear anything they didn't understand or required any effort to work out. If energy was to be preserved for sexual congress, it seemed, brains must be left wilfully uncultivated. It seemed a good enough path to follow, at least for the time being. The girls did their best to follow suit – that way orgasm lay – helped and disinhibited by the fact that they were now Lucy and Lola, not Shimmer and Sparkle. Lucy fell on her knees and wrapped her mouth round Pete's engorged member as he lay back in the armchair. Lola bent over Dave on the sofa and followed Shimmer's example – she did not want to be seen as completely ignorant. Lucy bent over the armchair with her bare bum in the air and Pete went at her from behind. Dave preferred the missionary position with Lola but with one of her legs over the back of the sofa to make penetration especially deep. The girls squealed and panted, and genuinely enough: surprise got the better of them. Finally satiated, the girls thought that was enough, but the brothers thought otherwise. Dave took his turn with Lucy, Pete with Lola.

'Comparisons are odious,' said Shimmer to Sparkle, as the boys headed off to the kitchen for more beer, 'but I prefer Pete to Dave.'

Dave, returning earlier than expected, overheard.

'Swallowed a dictionary then?' he asked. Shimmer realized he had not come across the word 'odious' before. The thought made her tremendously fond of him, protective and maternal. He was so young: he had so much to learn! Neither man had used condoms. She wondered if it was the flood of testosterone into her system playing havoc with her hormonal balance, which left her loving, not despising. She would get Sparkle to investigate the effect of the condom on gender relationships: perhaps nature had endowed women with a need for regular injections of male hormones via semen: perhaps there was a positive correlation between higher levels of PMT and condom use? Perhaps the current growing estrangement – as President Putin put it – between the genders in Russia was down to the increased use of condoms, now that abortion was no longer the nation's main contraceptive method? Sparkle would reject the idea as biologism but there was no denying this overwhelming feeling, this excitement in simply being, projected into the man who was staring at her with these bright eyes, this male being that she needed inside her, so she could be part of him, he could be part of her – sex the means to the end, not. The end itself – oh my God, thought Shimmer, I am falling in love. I had not bargained for this.

'Fucking cat got your fucking tongue?' asked Dave. He was obviously wholly unsuitable.

The brothers called a taxi for the twins at about five in the morning and they went home escorted only by each other.

Now that was the end of it for Sparkle. She went back to Sussex and her students and the Institute for Advanced Gender Relations fundamentally unchanged (having explained to Shimmer that she would never get funding for any research project which suggested men and women could benefit from close association with one another). However, having had a pleasant evening out, and feeling more in tune with the rest of the world, took to going out with her students, soon had a battery of suitors to pick amongst of a Saturday night.

But for Shimmer things never got quite back to normal, and a year later times and events had worked upon her to such an extent that now you could easily tell the difference between her and her twin. She had a less placid, more vulnerable look. She had become a prey to the doubt and anxiety that seize most women when they are in love – as well as the elation and joy that goes with it – *is it real, will it last, does he mean it, am I mad?* Such little, transient emotions had put their mark upon the tiny muscles of the face, and made its owner seem softer, a little anxious – more, frankly, female. It was not good for her work: she lost a spark of the blind self-confidence which suggests everything will work out all right, and her vegetation rate, though still admirable, was no longer quite the lowest in the north.

Or perhaps it just was that she was no longer concentrating on her work: she would keep thinking about Pete, Pete, Pete, and the brain tissue she stared at seemed all much of a muchness; and though she felt it better not to operate while menstruating anyway, since period pain affected the steadiness of hand and eye – it was not a reason any hospital board could accept.

In the tepee days her parents had kept rescue hens, saved from an untimely death in the battery farms where they had spent their lives. Once released from captivity, and become accustomed to the light of day and the ability to walk and move and search for food, they turned from quivering wretches into assertive, independent, beady-eyed creatures. But then her mother insisted on bringing a cock into the hen-run so they could live more 'natural' lives – whereupon they turned overnight, or so it seemed to Shimmer, into silly bustling, clucking things with no individuality. Now she herself had invited the cock into the walk, and he crowed upon his dung-heap, and she was lost and helpless, and back in a different kind of captivity.

As for Pete, when he had woken from his drunken stupor and staggered off to work – washing first of course – the sweat and scent of Shimmer, or the girl he knew as Lucy, stayed with him. It caught him by surprise as he mixed water into putty-based Venetian plaster, creating a creamy, lump-free, slightly elastic, highly satisfying effect. It enflamed his senses and engorged his penis as he waited for the architect to turn up and check his colour matching – tapping his foot until the cunts took the trouble to turn up. The clients were wealthy: they wanted a Marmorino finish, tinted to the 'Old Rose 3' of a 1950 colour chart they had unfortunately come across in a drawer. It occurred to him that it was the delicate rose of the skin behind Lucy's ear. He would like to check. He would need to see her again. He had not taken her number. She had vanished into the night. He thought perhaps Dave had put the number in his mobile – he seemed to remember something of the sort. He called Dave.

'That bird last night,' said Pete.

'Which one?' asked Dave. 'There were two of them.'

'Mine,' said Dave. 'The nurse,' and even as he said it, the scent and the feel of her came wafting over him from some unknown, unseen source.

'She was mine as well,' said Dave, and Pete warned him off ever referring to that again if he wanted to live, quite startling his brother with his vehemence.

It was, indeed, love at first one-night-stand, for both of them. But the course of true love did not run smooth – how could it? – for was it not founded on lies? Shimmer was a brain surgeon, not a nurse. If she had told Pete the truth on the very first coupling, he might perhaps have adjusted to it, but she had not: and just as other women are tied into more ordinary lies, and have to hide their passports in case their true age is revealed, and cut the size 16 label out of their new clothes, or keep the dental plate where other women hide letters from secret lovers, now Shimmer had to hide the true nature of her occupation, and indeed her salary, from Pete.

She did try to tell him on three occasions: once during their initial courtship, on their first outing to a Balti Bar in the city centre.

'I'm not really a theatre nurse,' she said. 'I'm the surgeon.'

He laughed and said, 'Pull the fucking other one; what are you trying to prove? That you're smarter than me? We know that. Don't overdo it. But I can plaster a wall and you can't.'

Two consecutive thoughts in one speech were rare for Pete so she took it the more seriously, and as a warning. She did not like to tell him that her manual skills too were of the highest order. She would just have to accept that truth and true love do not sit comfortably together. She did not want to lose him. She was addicted to his presence in her bed as heroin addict is to the needle.

She tried again when he moved in with her.

'I've been feeding you a story,' she said, one early morning after sex when they were lying cuddled, putting off the time when they would have to get up and go to work.

'I know that,' he said, and she was overwhelmingly relieved, but all he had noticed was that the initial on the utility bills was S not L. She confessed that her real name was Shimmer not Lucy. He said she must have nutty parents – well, he already knew that: she had told him and he had pitied her and she had wept out of self-pity and gratitude mixed. At last, someone who cared, who was interested, who understood at some level other than strictly rational: her life had been so hard and sharp, and now suddenly all the edges were being softened and smoothed. He'd never liked Lucy, he admitted, to tell the truth: it was too posh. He would call her Shimmy. So there she was, Shimmy: but somehow now when she looked into the pulsing brain tissue of her patients it felt more daunting than it had been when her name was Shimmer. Shimmer was without doubt: Shimmy was a diminutive: yet how she loved being Shimmy. Shimmy, Shimmy, Shimmy, theatre nurse, waiting for instructions. If others in the theatre noticed a certain new hesitancy in how she handled the operations, as if she was looking to some higher power to guide her – they did not like to say anything. The two unexpected cerebral vegetations were probably a statistical anomaly. She would bounce back. And she was still better than anyone else. Just about.

But keeping up the lie took concentration and ingenuity. The modern world makes dual identity difficult. She opened another secret bank account, and paid in the surplus above that of a theatre nurse's salary. A theatre nurse could expect to get £25 an hour, as compared with Pete's £12: as Shimmer she could expect

£500 an hour and if she went into private practice – which was against her principles – she could expect to die a millionaire. She explained away her lack of mortgage by saying she had been left the property by a great-aunt – she and Pete shared all living expenses – and she developed a taste for fish and chips and the gift of bulimia.

The funds in the secret account grew and grew: just occasionally she would buy some very expensive article of clothing and say she had found it in the charity shop. She instructed Sparkle, if she phoned, not to let her secret out, and Sparkle obliged, although she was horrified at this turn of events – to have a twin so enslaved to her sexual passions was alarming. Sparkle had no wish to see Dave ever again: he had served her purpose well enough during the course of that one evening.

But of course it could not last forever. Guilty secrets will out: class war erupts. Yesterday's happy ethnic mix turns into today's mayhem and machete. Pete found out. The deceit was too much for him. And besides, a man likes to advise, instruct and help a woman, and how can he, if she is a brain surgeon and he is a plasterer. But it was more than that.

It was Dave that did it. Dave had been having a hard time. Dave had been most upset by his young brother's desertion. Once they went gaily out on the town as a pair of likely lads, assets to pub, town and community: now that Pete had shacked up with a nurse, they were no longer the Magnificent Two, but Dave was seen as almost a loner, than which there can be nothing more derogatory said, with half the social skills he once possessed. He no longer strode into pubs but sidled up to bars and seemed unable to get the attention of the barman – once girls get a whiff of no confidence they seem to shrink away. Diffident in company suggests diffident in bed. As Pete flourished and grew muscular and benign, so Dave's shoulders seemed to narrow and hunch: he grunted instead of grinned; his parents worried about him, and wondered where they had gone wrong in his upbringing, when once they had scarcely given him or his brother a thought. He no longer played or assaulted the fruit machine: there is no point in doing it on your own. It's just throwing money away, as everyone sensible knows.

More, his boss Alan had fallen ill, and had asked Dave to take over the running of the business until he was better. Alan was famous in the plumbing world for his moroseness, the bad cooking of his wife, and now for the headaches which would strike out of the blue from time to time. The GP diagnosed migraine, but the headaches were now accompanied by a propensity to hit nails through copper pipes and fit UVPC pipes where he shouldn't, from sheer forgetfulness. He had taken to his bed, and now Dave was left with paperwork, employment tax, VAT returns and so on, as well as a day's work, and not even a girlfriend to help him out. Dave was now in love with plumbing, he thrilled to the sound and feel of water rushing through pipes, pursuing its own stubborn, sometimes enthusiastic, sometimes reluctant way in accordance with the inexorable laws of the universe, as Pete was with the textures, the feel and mastery of the substances he mixed, considered, applied. Paperwork was simply not the brothers' style: they were artisans and that was that. Nevertheless Dave wanted to help Alan out, and did his best. He bedded Alan's wife too, on occasion – mercy fucks – but Alan did not know that.

Dave took advantage of Alan's absence, in the nick of time before moroseness closed in to exclude all spirit of enterprise, to have a new logo painted on the side of the firm's three white vans. *Alan Hargreaves and Son, Plumbers since 1965*, was replaced with *Plumbers Plus, Plumbing for the Community, Hands-on Water Services*, and was rewarded when the NHS gave Plumbers Plus a contract to do occasional emergency work, as required, up at the hospital.

Picture the scene that Sunday morning in Theatre Number One at Newcastle West General. Eight o'clock in the morning. Theatre staff scrubbing up. Shimmer's bleeper buzzing as she crouches naked on top of Pete: firm, now muscular bottom bouncing as he gives her what he refers to as a good seeing-to. She stretches out a hand to answer it. He stretches out his to catch her wrist. He hates interruption: he hates the idea that her nursing duties can occasionally take precedence over the full attention and admiration he requires of her.

'You women and your fucking multi-tasking,' he says. 'Tell those boneheaded cunts at the hospital to fuck off.'

And he flips her over and goes in from behind to make her yelp and really concentrate. Which indeed she does: but she has her tricks and can make him bring the session to an end fast, so she can call the hospital back within three or four minutes. The message from the other end – as what else is a call at eight in the morning going to be? – is coded, but requires her immediate presence in the operating theatre. She punches in the numbers that say she is on her way. She dresses fast – but does not wash, believing in the almost magical testosteronic power of sperm to steady eye and firm resolve – and is quickly on her way. Pete has fallen back to sleep and gropes for her but finds her gone and is annoyed. Why can't she be a teacher, like her sister, and have a job with proper social hours and long holidays?

Alan is being prepared for theatre. He was brought into hospital by his wife in the early hours, fumbling and bumbling and falling over undone shoelaces and a brain tumour swiftly diagnosed. The experts have no truck with the GP's view that the man is depressed and malingering, and a brain scan proves them right. The size of a tomato, it's rumoured, though whether a cherry or a beef tomato is not made clear. But the sooner it's gone the better. The patient is beyond caring.

Dave is meanwhile up early on double time working in the operating theatre on a blocked S-bend in one of the sinks, combined with a loose washer that not only drips and irritates surgeons, but has made the sink overflow with waste. So many antibiotics have gone down it lately, in the attempt to stem drug resistant infections, that staff choose to overlook the regulations that say Dave cannot be working in the room while an operation is in progress, let alone have hysterics that there are pools of dirty water on the floor. Dave has already caught a glimpse of the white face of his boss on the gurney and wants to be in there at the kill, cure, or vegetation.

Dave, although he sees his brother rarely – Shimmer's little house seems to him cramped and suburban – and the episode of the shared fuck between the four of them is the elephant in the room when it comes to conversation, deadening sound and meaning – knows that Lucy, now Shimmy, works as a theatre nurse. He looks round for her but does not recognize her. He assumes she is safely at home with Pete, and is glad Pete has this much control over his girlfriend. Sundays are for cooking a roast lunch, not earning. Then all of a sudden there Shimmy is – green-coated, as he is, for hospital work – eager and from the body language of all those around, in charge. Indeed, they are practically bowing and scraping. No doubt about it. She is the surgeon, not the nurse. He doubts that Alan will make it now: he is receiving second-rate care from a woman. Surgeons are by definition male.

Dave is filled with rage at Shimmer for deceiving his brother, for pretending to be what she is not. And Sparkle, a teacher? He doubts it. Something more, something worse: the twins from hell. He and Pete have been taken for a ride, made fools of, mocked, ridiculed, seen as rough trade, used as sex objects, dildos. He escaped but Pete did not. Dave feels a surge of protective love for his little brother.

The surgeon's assistants cluster round: TV screens leap into life, pulses and beeps begin: how can anyone make sense of them? Dave kneels beneath the sink unseen and unnoticed: all eyes concentrate upon the victim on the table. The surgeon gestures and music starts up at her command: Bach's fucking poncy Brandenburg Concerto – he was made to listen to it at school. Alan's head is shaved and bare: the she-devil has him at her mercy. Dave trembles for him; surely she will have her revenge now on the entire male race. The drill whirrs, its tip against the skull, and now there are bone splinters everywhere, and a nurse wielding a little mini-vacuum sucking them up, on her knees, and nice little bum in the air – that's more like it. Will he tell Pete or will he not? That his Shimmer is a mirage, an illusion? Dave is in two minds. The bearer of bad news gets little thanks. Perhaps he should just shut up and let Pete find out in his own good time? Shimmer cannot keep up the deceit indefinitely.

There's a fifteen-minute break after forty minutes for all staff who can be spared: others take over temporarily for some routine part of the procedure. The rest-break is announced over the sound system as might be the interval at a boxing match. Shimmer comes out of the theatre wiping her forehead and making for the doctor's recreation room. Dave, who has anticipated her movements, is waiting for her in Sluice Room 1: now he opens the door and drags her inside. No one sees, other than Junior Nurse Valerie, the one who was vacuuming up skull dust and shards. She wonders briefly why Surgeon Shimmer has vanished into the sluice, but supposes she has her reasons. It's been tense in there. For a few minutes it had been touch and go, but then the patient had stabilized.

At least the patient is still breathing, his heart is still beating: his eyes flickering beneath their lids, his brain cells open to visual inspection. If he is like this six hours from now, all will be well; the patient will be restored to health and vigour. He will live to take Dave's message off the side of his vans, and restore the original. If there is an end to breathing, beating, flickering and pulsing, he will be gone from this world. If his eyelids no longer flicker, the other parts can heave and beat and pulse away all they like, Alan will be without will, or real consciousness, and Shimmer will have truly failed. Mind you, if she had done nothing, he would have died anyway.

'Pete!' says Shimmer. 'Darling!' as what seem to her familiar arms enfold her.

It's understandable. The brothers are alike: she does not expect to see Dave. That Pete has followed her to the hospital and lain in wait is not altogether surprising. If she is a theatre nurse, and has been paged in for an emergency op, and there is only one theatre functioning that morning, it being a Sunday, he will find her. He does not like being denied what he sees as his natural rights during a Sunday morning's lie-in. Nor does she like denying them. But she has her duty to her employer, to the hospital, to her honed, expensively gained and very rare skills, not to mention mankind and the future of medicine to consider.

She scarcely gets to see his face: Dave bends her over the sluice, hikes up her skirts, pulls down her black, pure silk panties, offers a prayer to the family gods that Pete will understand this necessity, and drives in. She squeals agreeably and giggles: what kind of brain surgeon is this? And poor Alan just lying there, his brain exposed for all the world to see? Pete may be angry for a while, thinks Dave, but this way he will see Shimmer for the lying slut she is, deceiving him with his own brother – of course she will deny it but then she would, wouldn't she, and who will believe her? – and soon get over it. Normal times for the brothers will resume; once again they will be a pair, blessed by the cheerful abandon of the young male in the first flush of his mating behaviour. Once again the two will operate as one. Depression will be at an end. Besides, he has never felt so urgent or determined, or his cock seemed so large, so imperious, or so much in charge of his being as now. This will take the bitch down a peg or two. And she is certainly not in the least unwilling. He thrusts, she bucks. It seems she cannot tell the difference, sight unseen, between him and his brother: the thought gratifies him and multiplies his pleasure: all that is Pete's is his, all that is Dave's – not that it's been much lately – is Pete's. For Pete the novelty will be wearing thin. Pete will be tired of her by now, these passages too well worn by a single instrument: after three months he will be looking for ways out. Yes, Pete will be grateful. Dave can see he might want to do this again, the pleasure is so intense. Thump, thump, and thump again. Perhaps this could run and run: perhaps Pete will not be averse to sharing: Shimmer aware of it or not as the case might be. All kinds of things can happen in the dark. Or perhaps there will be room in Shimmer's house for three? Perhaps Shimmer could get her sister in and they could live as a foursome? Stranger things have happened. Then sensation overwhelms him and rational thought is abandoned.

Meanwhile out in the corridor Pete, as Shimmer had suspected, had indeed come looking for his rightful oats, and was not going to let the mere matter of her formal employment get in his way. The self-employed often lack understanding of the nervousness of those who have bosses. Nurse Valerie, returning from the nurse's washroom, conscious that strangers are not meant to stride these half-deserted corridors – it is a Sunday – flinging open doors to see what they hide – sees him, challenges him. She is a brave, pert girl and he is a very handsome man in a Beckham kind of way. And the tension of the theatre makes her randy, as it has him. Operations are a kind of performance, a stage play built around matters of life and death, and just as actors, dancers, musicians seem to need frequent sexual release in order to make them function properly, Nurse Valerie is far from exempt.

'I am looking for a nurse,' says Pete.

'What does she look like? asks Valerie, her plump bosom brushing his tattooed arm.

Pete tells her and Valerie says, 'That's no nurse, that's Surgeon Shimmer, Newcastle's pride.' Oh, she's a pert thing.

And for Pete everything falls into place. The odd feeling that everything is not what it seems to be: the mysterious phone calls, the secrecy about money, family, friends. He has been lied to, deceived, taken for a ride, used as a sex object. All she wants is his body, to use and abuse. She is a liar and a fraud. All women are the same.

'But I'm a real nurse,' says Valerie, 'nothing fancy, if that's what you prefer,' and before she has time to work out what is happening, she too is bending over the sluice, Pete has her panties down – red nylon – and he is driving into her from behind, and she thinks the day well spent, and that this is worth even more than double time.

The transaction between Dave and Shimmer is not protracted, fired as it is by both their urgency, Shimmer to get back to her patient, Dave to get his own back. Shimmer straightens up and turns to face Dave and realization dawns. This is not Pete. Dave smirks, Shimmer pales, but she is well trained in emergencies: she does not squawk or protest, but wriggles her panties back on and smoothes down her gown in a most composed and aggravating way.

'Think yourself so clever,' she says. 'You've been there before, so I don't see why you think you're so special!' But actually she is extremely taken aback.

The transaction between Pete and Valerie is also brief but intense. The two couples, emerging pink and breathless from the sluice rooms at the same time, come face to face.

From this point I am able to report the Brain Surgeon's report verbatim. Someone realized the bubble feature was turned to full and switched it to low, so we could hear better. Someone else handed chocolate bars around.

'I know what you're thinking, but no,' Shimmer said, 'I did not. Prudence triumphed over lust. I had to get back to my patient. The brothers went into Sluice Room 2 with Nurse Valerie but without me. There is a time and a place for everything.

'The surgical team was one short for the rest of the morning, but I did not report Nurse Valerie. If nothing else she had deflected the brothers' fire: they no longer occupied the moral high ground. We were overstaffed anyway. Everyone likes to work on a Sunday morning because of the loaded pay scale. By the time I got home in the evening, Pete had moved his possessions out. I believe the three of them set up home together. And yes, the operation was a success. My hand was steady and true. There are now five Plumbers Plus vans in the Newcastle area.'

'And you?' I asked, on everyone's behalf. 'What about your sex life now?'

It was a crude question, crudely asked. Shimmer frowned, and stretched her long, elegant, if slightly hefty, legs and admired her large but shapely feet.

There was a pause. In the suspense one of the ladies dropped her chocolate nut bar into the bubbling water and did not fish it out. Still we did not move. Then Shimmer said she was now suitably engaged to a cardiac specialist. Indeed, she was at the Spa to lose weight and freshen up before the wedding. It was to be a double ceremony – herself and Sparkle – but Sparkle had up and married an ornithologist and gone with her new husband to live in a yurt in Mongolia where he was to film birds of prey and horses. Love made one do the strangest things, she said – or perhaps the influence of the family was harder to shake off than one supposed. Those early starry nights, for both Shimmer and Sparkle, had meant a lot. But she was glad she had told her tale, and relived a few of those important moments. Everyone, she said, should enjoy the experience of rough trade at least once in their life. To be mindless is to be free, but it cannot be expected to last. One has a living to earn and a duty to the community.

Silence fell. The Mortgage Broker looked at the fur round the Manicurist's flimsy shoulders and said, 'I hope that isn't real mink,' and the Manicurist swore it was just a fun fur, bought in a charity shop. The Mortgage Broker raised her eyebrows in understandable disbelief, but no one came to her aid, so she just sniffed and gave up. The general feeling was this was not the time or place to bring up such matters. We were in the business of bonding.

The waters frothed up chocolate brown and sticky around us and we clambered out of the pool, shrieking, and fled to the showers, divesting our bikinis as we ran, bosoms bouncing in our haste to be clean again, but not before agreeing to return at eleven and bring in Boxing Day by listening to the Judge's tale. We would gather in the Orangery: it was generally agreed that we were Jacuzzied out.

12

But first I dragged myself all the way to the office in the west wing to make it clear to Beverley that it was not okay just to pull appointments like this. I'd been promised a minimum of three appointments every day and already it seemed I was down to one. Fair enough, it was Christmas Day, but why make promises if you couldn't keep them? It smacked of false pretences.

Beverley waited patiently until I had finished ranting and then said, 'Christ, you Poms. If the world was coming to an end all you'd do is stand about and demand your rights.'

I was used to Beverley by now and didn't take offence. She made me laugh. She was just one of those people who, in my mother's terms, didn't know how to behave.

'All I want you to do,' I said, 'is make a note that there was no one in Hydrotherapy when I turned up and I don't want to be charged.'

'You didn't bother to read the small print,' she said. 'It says all our staff are self-employed, so any discussion regarding fees or services should be directed to the member of staff concerned.'

'That's just criminal,' I said.

She shrugged. 'I just work here,' she said. 'You chose to come here. More fool you.' And she observed that if there was no one in Hydrotherapy or the Snooze Zone that meant Silvana and Regina had both walked out. 'Well, that figures.' I asked why and she said there was a threatened rail strike locally and perhaps they were frightened of being stranded. Or else it was the Sumatra flu. Pommies were such wimps. In New Zealand if there wasn't a train you got on a bicycle, if there was flu you went to bed and sneezed until it was over. But over here people were saying germs were coming in to the country on dried fruit and throwing their Christmas puddings away, and anyone who had eaten a mince pie over the season was running home to be with their families.

'There's no such thing as Sumatra flu,' I said.

'I know, you know,' she said, 'but all the same the flights to New Zealand are fully booked. And I'd be on one too; just to get out of this little haven of hysteria you call Great Britain.'

I felt defensive of my country and vaguely insulted. I asked her stiffly if she'd managed to get her e-mail under control, and she said yes, thank you, no thanks to anyone. I asked her if there was anything on the news about Sumatra flu, and she said no, but that didn't mean anything one way or another, did it. And the rail strike? She said it wasn't affecting main lines, so far, only local lines. What was it about? The union was demanding a return to little brown wage packets, because electronic payments were un- reliable. Out of the Ark! As if little brown envelopes couldn't be unreliable too, as she knew to her cost.

I felt too exhausted to try and wring another phone call out of her, made sure she had at least taken a note of the missed appoint- ment and went back to my room and fell asleep until it was time for the Judge's tale.

The Orangery, whither we were summoned, was a fabulous place and Castle Spa's glory – a long, high hall made almost entirely of glass and mirrors, with art nouveau paintings set in stucco between each of twelve tiled arcades, an arts and crafts grotto and fountain in each one. Furniture was made of some metal resembling silver, so that everything glittered and gleamed: bare- bosomed sylphs entwined themselves around slim, shiny, freestanding pillars which supported nothing in particular but just looked nice. Once every arcade had featured row upon row of orange and lemon trees: the orangeries so popular in the great houses of the past were nothing but long, lofty glass houses from whence trees in tubs, lovingly imported from warmer climes, could be wheeled out in the summer and wheeled back in the winter. This year the couple of token orange trees were still out of doors in December – yet another indication of climate change though not necessarily statistically valid. The light in here, by day, was rather eerie, watery and melancholy; a green mould was beginning to crawl up some of the windows and needed attending to. But here at night, with rows of candles which the night porter had rather unwillingly lit for us – *'most ladies are in their beds this time of night'* – the place seemed warm and cheerful, suffused by a friendly, flattering glow.

The Judge's title belied her presence. She was a slinky, elegant creature, tall, flat-bellied and narrow-hipped. She had arresting almond eyes which took up a great deal of her face, a trim little nose, a sweetly dimpled chin, a brow which slanted away quite strikingly, and perfectly round breasts. We had all agreed they were most likely silicone – nature does not normally give women of this build such leanness here, and then such roundness there. Also all agreed that we would not want to come across her if we were in the dock. We would rather have some bumbling, dusty man to judge us. She would expect her pound of flesh: she would coolly carve it from the living body of her enemy, smiling sweetly the while.

And this is what she told us, as we sat in the candlelight and drank champagne or sparkling water, according to taste and aspiration for a new, improved future. My mind drifted from time to time as to where exactly Julian might be, and what he was doing, but at least I was freed from visions of my children and grand-children coughing and groaning with Sumatra flu. Sometimes I cursed Lady Caroline for her refusal to have a mobile mast to bring the real world to Castle Spa; sometimes I blessed her for her wisdom.

13

The Judge's Tale

'I sit before you here as a woman but once I was a man. Or was taken to be one. You will ask me – people always ask me – who has the better pleasure in sex, the woman or the man. But I cannot really speak for men, I am sorry to disappoint you; I was never really one in the first place, just a woman cursed with a penis and a superfluity of testosterone.

'I was born transsexual: a woman short of oestrogen, wretchedly play-acting male. Perhaps the great pleasure I now have as a female depends upon the skill of the surgeon? Mine certainly did well enough by me. Yes, to answer your unspoken question, I have orgasms.

'The climax of the man I almost was, I remember as short and urgent and over fast, a matter of grabbing and thrusting and gone: with a voice in my head all the time telling me this is all wrong, all wrong, shaming. The climax of the woman I am, is a long, suffusing, rosy glow, dawning and blossoming like a new day from somewhere in the depths of space, and returning like sunset on a turning world, red at night, shepherdess's delight. Let the male shepherd look after himself.

'This afternoon in the Jacuzzi, did you notice my toes, my little pink toes, not knobbly, hairy or gross? I curled my feet in the bubbling water, and looked at your toes and yours and yours, and mine were best of all, though the Surgeon's came a close second. Mine most beautiful of all. My feet are narrow and not too big, and they slip into shoes with heels with ease, and I neither wobble, stumble nor trip: I glide. Mirror, mirror on the wall, I am most lovely of you all. I have been made, I was not born, and mine was the perfect surgeon's knife: if nature bungles, man perfects.

'Have you heard of Dr Sydney Nail? He is my surgeon, my hero, my idol. He is world-famous. He is not young, but working on it: he made Marylyn Monroe the girl she became, Michael Jackson rashly chose another for his treatment. I am proud that Dr Nail chose me for his patient: he saw my potential and took me on. I claim him as my doctor, my surgeon, my saviour, my delight.

'Yes, I am truly female now. Are these breasts not full and rounded, my shoulders nicely sloped: do you see any sign of Adam's apple or bony protuberances on my brow? All have been shaved away. I lay in pain for a year and a day and then I arose a true woman. My hair is glossy and my own; my skin is smooth and pale; my expression is sweet, my demeanour modest. My body pulses with oestrogen that gentle, life-enhancing stuff, that friendly essence of all things womanly: it is not muscle-bound by nasty, bad-tempered testosterone.

'My early life was tragedy, before I encountered Dr Nail. A fairy godfather flew out of hell at my birth, and sprinkled me with the dreaded T: my mother the Emperess did nothing to stop it. So I grew testicles and a penis: I, who started out in the womb as all do, female. And I daresay my father didn't care one way or another: eaten up by the foul hormone as he was. He loved only my mother: he never loved me.

'If God gave us oestrogen, why then the Devil gave us testosterone. Blame wars on it and global warming: man's focused ingenuity will be the end of us. Testosterone-ridden man, prone to paranoia, is an unreconstructed creature of the tribe. He'll live at peace for a time with his friends over the hill, then nothing will do but that he races over it on some imagined slight, murders his erstwhile male friends and rapes their women. From the War of Jenkins' Ear to the Hutus and the Tutsis, to the Sunnis and the Shiites, so it goes. War runs in the very blood of man: he-dogs the lot of them, creatures of the pack, snarling and fighting. The ladies set up institutes for peace, but they might as well stick to embroidery. Men love war too much to ever give it up.

'The War of Jenkins' Ear? No? You don't know about that? Well, you are women, why would you? These things interested me in the old days, when I was a she-man, before I knew better, when I courted masculinity, when the loathed hormone-pulsing piece of flesh between my legs dictated all my actions. In that long ago, troubled, male life I studied history, studied law: I was the most Aspergery, fact-conscious, litigious of men.

'But this I remember. Under the Treaty of Seville, 1729, between Britain and Spain the British had agreed not to trade with the Spanish colonies. To verify the treaty the Spanish were permitted to board British ships. In 1731 Robert Jenkins, captain of the ship *Rebecca*, claimed that the Spanish coastguard had boarded his ship forcibly and severed his ear. In 1738 he exhibited his pickled ear to the House of Commons, and the Prime Minister, to cheers, declared war against Spain. For nine glorious years, men were entitled to rape, pillage, and slaughter. And just when the excuses for war were drying up, there was the whole business of the Spanish succession to fight about, and after that Napoleon came on to the scene, riding his white horse, waving his sword: a small man with a withered arm, he had to wave something about. His piece of manly flesh, pickled like Jenkins' ear, went to auction recently, and sold for $3000, it is said, to a Dr Latimer, having failed to reach its reserve price at Christie's.

'I'm sorry. Some old habits die hard, especially the one to instruct and inform the unwilling. You'd rather I talked about me, lovely me? Well, so would I. You are right to cry 'deviation'! Jenkins' pickled ear can hardly be of interest to any of us sitting round in this beautiful place, with the smoke of Acapulco Gold drifting in the candlelight, and my voice so soft and low and tempting. Dr Nail has a colleague who specializes in vocal cords: a little stretch and a twang and they go slack and the harshest, most male voice turns gentle and loving. It is all so simple; the mind follows where the body leads: to change the mind, first change the body. But the habit of history, the habit of the questing mind, has been the hardest thing to break. As I say, I'm sorry.

'Dr Nail says our pasts are irrelevant; we must live in the now. We think too much: words longer than three syllables are suspect: it is a male tendency – to deal in abstracts is to succumb to the power of four-syllable testosterone. I was an early victim to it. Pitiful. Adolescence came early. I was a pretty blonde child until my knees grew bony, and hairs sprouted where no hair should be.

'When my mother was angry with me – which was often – I would be sent as a punishment to stand in the dark of her walk-in closet. In fact quite a glimmer of light came through the ill-fitting door. I would sit amongst her shoes and the dresses and furs which had slipped from their hangers, and wrap myself in silks and satins. I did not become a transvestite through exposure to female clothing under stress, oh no: it was because I was essentially female that I so loved the forbidden clothes. My mother had over fifty pairs of shoes: it was her habit simply to fling them in when she took them off, so they were never in pairs, let alone with shoe trees, breathing and stretching as leather should, but lay about in unassorted mounds. My mother had the littlest feet. I would pass my time in the closet by sorting them into pairs, trying them on, but by the time I was eleven they became too small for me.

'I was stricken with sorrow when I realized this and what it augured for the future, as an anorexic girl will be horrified when her breasts begin to grow and her destiny can no longer be denied: if she does nothing she will grow, she will swell, she will wither and perish, and die like anyone else. Childhood saves her from death so she risks death to avoid growth. Me, I longed for the breasts which would never come; my lengthening toes seemed to be as gross as the man-wolf's in the film *An American Werewolf in Paris*. But I also realized then that I could never rival my mother in my father's affections: I had grown too male, large and clumsy. I had better try to be like him rather than like her. I would opt for the male rather than the female inside me. Perhaps then my mother would love me.

'My shoes? They are a size eight. Many women these days have size eight feet. The human race is getting bigger. Jerry Hall wears size elevens. My mother took a size four. She told me once the more breeding a woman has, the smaller her feet. Just as well, she said to me once, that I was not a girl. Oh, she was a bitch! My poor father.

'In pursuit of the macho I developed my muscles: I affected a loud and clumsy manner, and a reluctance to take baths, which seemed to me symptomatic of the young males by whom I was surrounded. I failed examinations on purpose, though I could never, when IQ tested, quite resist demonstrating my superiority over the clumsy, smelly, hormonal cretins who shared my schooling. I was investigated by the authorities on suspicion of Asperger's, but cleared of the charge. I hung about on street corners with associates I despised. I, who had always hated sport, joined the school boxing team. I was successful enough with the girls. My body operated as if it were a man, but – how can I explain this – where the body went the soul did not follow. I fathered a child when I was fourteen: the girl's parents took her away, to my relief. No, I have never met the child nor want to.

'But for all my efforts the lad who looked back out of the mirror seemed to have nothing to do with me: I was like no one else. I remained a one-off. As for my parents, they did not even come to the boxing match where I was declared regional champion: they had eyes only for one another. The children of dedicated heterosexuals are orphans. Or perhaps they sensed I was some kind of sport.

'When I was fourteen I saw a TV documentary about transsexuals and realized what I was. A victim to my hormones. But the realization at that time brought only shame. I was a failed man. There was nothing I could do about it. Only transsexuals feel the true impact of that single, terrible word: shame. Fifty percent of us die of it – by our own hand, for the most part, because of it; or at the hands of others, yobbos, who beat us to death, horrified by our oddity. Or perhaps, if one is to control outrage, because they see it in themselves: once put on their girlfriend's knickers and can't get over it. I decided then to give my body a rest, avoid all sexual and emotional attachment and simply develop my intellect. I took refuge in my studies – I was to be a lawyer, like my father. I would do what I could to be male.

'Then I met Dr Nail. I was nineteen. I was at law school. I was doing a course on gender law. I remember seeing the poster. He was giving a lecture on the principles underlying surgical gender reassignment. It was a new field in those days. Now we are all acquainted with the terms – we can refer knowingly to pre-op, post-op transsexuals, bisexuals, transitioning, and can tell a cross-dresser from a transvestite, but in those days we were ignorant. Male or female were we born, and all else was perverse or crimi-nal. And I, I had decided, was male.

'I saw his face on the poster. The calm, kind eyes called to me: the silky white hair, the air of wisdom, of tranquility. I could not stay away. All through the lecture I stared: I did not hear a thing. Afterwards I went up to him – he was signing books – and stood tongue-tied.

'"What's the matter, young man?" he asked, and there was a smile in his voice. "Or perhaps young woman? Do you think you need my services?"

'I shook my head. Who, me? A woman trapped in a man's body? I had trained myself in denial. I just wanted to be near him. It was love at first sight. No way that he was not male. Yet I knew I was not gay. The hanging piece of meat still engorged itself all too readily at the glimpse of a bared breast, the curve of the female buttock. That I could be lesbian had not occurred to me. Or indeed merely bisexual. I gawped. I was struck dumb. He knew what I was feeling. I blushed: is there anything more ridicu-lous than a blush rising on unshaven cheeks?

'"Give it time," was all he said. "And when finally you know you need me, come to me. I will be waiting." And then he went back to California, and that was all, except his hand – so lean, so dex-terous, so full of pure creation, the maker of women into men,

men into women, and all stages in between, brushed against mine, and the touch stayed with me for ten more years. Perhaps I related to the woman, as I was to discover later, he too once had been.

'I denied him: I denied my saint, my saviour, my God. I would be a man, I would be. I looked like a man, I was called by a man's name, no doctor had ever doubted my right so to describe myself, and just because I never felt at ease with my raucous, noisy, foul-mouthed, brutish, stupid fellow man did not mean I was not one of them: I could be just one of rarer clay. And to be a woman – fleshy, bulbous, mincing, shrieking, so often coarse-grained, coarse-skinned, given to leaking blood and juices – what kind of ambition was it to be one of these? No, I would be male.

'I tried hard. I lived the life of a man about town: I leapt ahead in my career. I appeared in the celebrity columns, the most eligible bachelor in the heterosexual ranks (if anyone thought of the pos-sibility of there being an inner girl in there somewhere they did not say – though it's often the sergeant major Bill who turns up one day as Belinda. Transsexuals try hard, before they give in.). I made money. I wore good clothes. I took anabolic steroids and body built. I was into cocaine, clubs and bad girls, but never to the degree that I endangered my career.

'I was called to the bar. A barrister needs to have his wits about him and I always did. In fact I made sure I had no time for reflec-tion. I presented myself as certain, positive, arrogant. A few nice girls of good family pursued me but soon I was known as being one of the non-committal ilk, and today's girls know better than to waste their time. "Relationships" did not last, and I was relieved when they did not. My parents died in an accident. I went to the funeral but was bored by the arrangements, which I left to an uncle to do. I was a man, but a man without gender, a man without family, without attribution even to that one great sweep-ing traditional division, the male here, the female there. And though I buried it, I knew it.

'Eight years passed. One night Dr Nail appeared to me in a dream. He beckoned me and said, "The time is ready. Come."

I rose from my bed and stepped out a woman; I looked down and saw tip-tilted breasts, I saw my dainty feet as I walked towards my lover: long blonde hair fell down around my face.

'I woke: I looked at the strange girl still asleep in the bed beside me – she was young and silly and very pretty – with her sweet, neat shaven pubic mound, and I stood naked in the mirror and saw the truth and loathed what I saw: the hairy angularity, the swollen, purpled, exhausted shaft hanging between the legs; I could not let this thing define me. I was more like her – neat, contained, and small – than I was me. I paid off the girl – I always paid if they would let me – it kept the relationship clean and uncomplicated. I faced myself and the hard road ahead. Dr Nail was right. The time had come.

'But I fought myself. I put difficulties in my own path. I would not go abroad. I would have my own society's approval. I went through the free health service – my own doctor was less surprised than I thought he would be – to a gender reassignment clinic. Loathsome, loathsome, if not so loathsome now as my male state. Such power freaks, the staff you find in these places! Once the disagreeable doctors clustered in obstetrics: now they cluster in gender reassignment. You must live like a woman for a year, they say, before we will touch you with the knife. More, you must dress like a woman as we see her: a woman through an old man's eyes – short skirts, high heels, practically fishnet tights – vulgar and obvious, without aesthetic sensibility, not a woman as she sees herself. Personally I was more the T-shirt, jeans and ballet pumps model of woman than the one they insisted I be. I fled. I found Dr Nail on Google. I found his website. I saw his image on the screen. The eyes spoke to me, with the same force now as once they had. They called me, and I went. And he remembered me, and the touch of his hand was as familiar as if we had been hand in hand since first we met. And this time we did not part.

'Dr Nail has made me what I am today. He is a saint, beyond all sexuality. No, no, you insist on clinging to your misunderstanding.

He is not gay; he is beyond gayness. Let me just say that we found closeness, intimacy; but that the cloak of my maleness stood in his way. The penis must find the vagina, the vagina the penis: we were stymied. And I was obviously the one who must change: the excess must be banished from my body, before we two could be made one.'

'Did he charge you for the operations?' interposed the Mortgage Broker. 'I hear they're very expensive.' There was a faint murmur of disapproval, not just at the interruption but at the crudeness of the question. Though of course we all wanted to know the answer. 'I mean, it's a good way of making money, isn't it? People like you must be very vulnerable.'

'Of course he did not charge me,' replied the Judge. Midnight struck. We were out of Christmas Day. The worst of the season, for those who had no families, or wanted none, or chose not to have them at this particular time, or like me were deprived of them perforce, or like Mira had been dispatched to be out of the way, or were otherwise oppressed by the nation's holiday, was now over. Boxing Day. Anyone can do anything without regret or sorrow on a Boxing Day. A breath of relief seemed to tremble through the Orangery. A few stood and released the tension in their shoulders. Others dived for the loos in the treatment block. Someone brought coffee. The comfort break over, we returned refreshed to the Judge's tale.

'You must understand,' said the Lady Judge, 'that Dr Nail worked for love; I suffered for love. He is even paying for my stay here: the totally outrageous fees for substandard service. The place is hopelessly understaffed. Then why am I here without him? you ask. How can I bear to be without him? I assure you he has not lost interest in me, just because he has had his way with me. I am not some silly girl: he is not some seducing villain. He has created me, he is Pygmalion: I who was Galateus, am now Galatea. He gave me my heterosexual libido back. Yes, there have been others for him, of course there have. Many semi-female others he has made truly female, but very few, I believe, that he has loved. Indeed, though many say there have been four loving Galateas for Dr Nail during his working life, I know I am the only one who really counts.

'Dr Nail is not here with us at Castle Spa because he can't be here. He would be if he could be. He is undergoing rejuvenation treatment at a clinic in California: they plan genetic transfer of certain selected stem cells into his bone marrow, cells stripped of the ageing gene. It works on newts, why not on Dr Nail? Science these days is so ingenious. They say we can live forever; there is no need after all for living organisms to fade and die. A genetic tweak here, a genetic tweak there, a single cell becomes immortal, and can infect all humankind! Or at any rate those who can afford the treatment. He will be returned to me young, and beautiful, and male, I daresay, but that cannot be helped. I will put up with it.

'In the meanwhile Dr Nail is a generous man. He is happy to share me. Of course, he wants me to experience the full joys of female sexuality: what has his life's work been about if not this? He fully understands a woman who was once a she-man must be test-run: I am here at Castle Spa for the final oiling, as it were; when I leave here, yes, I daresay I will look around. My perfect body, my perfect breasts... every tingle of sensation a tribute to the skill of Dr Nail. One falls in love, and that is that. Yes, I will wait for him to return rejuvenated, just perhaps not forever.'

'Are you still a fucking judge?' asked the Manicurist. 'I mean if you qualified as a man, do they make you requalify as a woman? In case you go peculiar and bring back hanging, or something?' She came from Liverpool, and had a Liverpudlian directness and vocabulary too. The diamonds on her tiny hand glittered in the candlelight.

'Of course, young lady, as you put it, I am still a fucking judge. Anti-discrimination laws make sure of that. And intellect is barely affected by gender. If anything, women impose harsher sentences than men. True, I find that these days I do tend to go for the longest sentence, the heaviest fine. But it is my job to administer justice. In the male view the quality of mercy may be expected from the Portias of this world, but I, an ex-female transsexual, now post-op and fully female, renounce the Portia inside, no more feeling the need to crush my balls in softest silk, since I now have none. No soft-headed carer-sharer me, no, vengeance is mine, sayeth the judge, and genderless. I am no fool. I know villainy when I see it, and I know it must be ground beneath the foot, or better still stamped with a stiletto heel. Not for me the doctrine of reformation and repentance: I am of the retribution school. To punish not to cure must be the aim: society must claim its due revenge. Without the hanging piece of flesh I move as spirit not as flesh.'

'Sorry I fucking spoke,' said the Manicurist, and a movement from the shadows had Kimberley on her feet in an instant, hand at her shoulder holster. But it was only the Spa cat, a great fat black thing, slouching across the tiled arcade.

'I hope you have a licence for that weapon,' said the Judge idly, once more in her soft, pretty voice. When she was excited her voice tended to be less modulated, revert to old male habits. But now she was in control again. Kimberley nodded, and the Judge looked at her appreciatively, almost flirtatiously, before continuing.

'Softest silk!' she went on. 'High Court Judges in full regalia wear silk stockings and, it is rumoured, tight silk panties under-neath their fur-trimmed gowns. I certainly did. Agent Provocateur has a nice ladies' line in scarlet silk which, when worn the wrong way round, confine the balls and focus the male mind quite nicely. Though all that's in the past for me. High Court wigs are horse-hair, heavy and hard to clean: many members of the bar would like them abolished: it is the lowlife who want them kept. Criminals are suckers for ceremonial.

'No, young lady, I would not bring back hanging, why do you think that? Execution is too short, too simple, the pain of exis-tence too soon over. Let life mean life and castration be the penalty for the sex offender. It did me no harm.

'Shimmer, I see you open your mouth to protest. You have been trained in the care of the body; it is understandable. Your job is to be popular, mine is to be unpopular. I was noticing you in the Jacuzzi. Your splendid, firm thighs flattened on the marble shelf, scented water rippling all around! You a surgeon, me a judge! I have quite a thing for surgeons. And your soft hip touching my soft hip: did you realize that? We were sharing bubbles! How often do you have to shave your legs? These days I can go a whole week without, and the hairs are so soft and fine. Dr Nail is a truly wonderful man: I owe him so much. I suppose he is famous in the surgical profession? No? Not quite your field? I suppose not.

'Am I embarrassing you all? I am sorry. Everyone, delete, delete! No one should feel nervous, I am not that way inclined. I am no lesbian. It's just that sometimes habit reasserts itself and when I look at a woman I remember what it was to be a man.'

'This Dr Nail is something else,' said the Surgeon, askance. 'What has he created?'

'Yes, you are right, dear lady,' said the Judge. 'This Dr Nail is something else. Not gay, not simply gay; there is no simple gay, any more than I am gay, just because his and my hands touched and the current of desire flowed. We live in a new world. "His" is a misnomer. "My" is a misnomer. "I" am just one life-choice amongst the myriad sexual life-choices available to us today. True, if I had not seen Dr Nail's face on a poster all those years ago I might still be a man. True, if he had not spoken to me as he did, and touched my hand, I might have never known the sensual pleasures that lay the other side of pain. I might be richer than I am now.

'But if you must have a definition, and people do crave definitions where gender is concerned, I reckon Dr Nail is a non-heterosexual with sadistic leanings whose sexual orientation is to transsexual females who have undergone a sex change. There are not so many of us around. So perhaps it is true: Dr Nail needs to create the likes of us just to satisfy his own personal needs. It's like writing the book you want to read because no one else has written it.

'Well, too late now, and I prefer to have ladies' toes with no black hairs sprouting up in a nasty line from stem to nail, thank you very much! I like to have these perfect breasts peeking out from under my gown. I like to have my nice soft voice and my smooth neck and pretty hands and to be able to sit here amongst women as just another one of them. I am satisfied. If Dr Nail was here we wouldn't be able to talk as we now are, would we? I love it like this. Just girl chat.'

14

We took ourselves off to our beds and our sleeping pills. Sleeping that night was difficult. Everyone complained of it the next day. True life stories can be more disturbing than fiction. Nothing is ever quite resolved: narrators are too unreliable for comfort.

The moon was just past full and the night was bright and restless, and unseasonably warm. It had been another one of the unnatural winters, with not so much as a touch of frost – which played into the hands of those who thought the season of plagues was upon us. While Julian shivered in his ice storm on the other side of the Atlantic – at least I hoped he did, and had not found some new source of warmth – we did not even bother to turn on the central heating.

Outside the castle owls hooted and foxes yelped. A coven of cats howled their mating calls, or whatever it was that was going on in their lives. The tomcat has a barbed penis, which hurts the female and it's the hurting which brings on ovulation, so that mating results in kittens. The cries of the assaulted female alert all neighbouring toms to its presence, so they assemble to make sure she gets what's coming to her. If she doesn't get what's coming to her she seems to be in a worse state of distress than if she does. All the females in the area of all species pay attention and are disturbed as the cat howls for them all. Whoever thought nature was benign is seriously bats.

Eventually it was over and I pulled the curtains tight and finally slept and dreamed that I was in the house where I lived when the children were small and I had a different husband than Julian. I dreamed of furniture I had long forgotten and pots and pans long since thrown away, and woke to the feeling that nothing is truly over: all things run parallel, I am as much myself then as I am now. It is an exhausting thought. But soon the dreams seemed far away in the past and the morning was fine and very clear, and at last, properly and seasonably cold. I hopped out of bed to turn on the central heating and stayed to gaze out of the window in amazement.

The fields around were palest, greyish green, and the latticed windows in the Gothic turrets caught the early sun and rebroad-cast light over drawbridge and moat, so that stone and water seemed almost alive. The central heating, thank God, was still working. It is all very well to be living in a large establishment whence all but a few have fled – but systems break down: wind blows the gas pilot out and no one knows how to relight it; a mouse nibbles through the deep-freeze wiring, and frozen goodies deliquesce. Worms get into the internet. The modern world needs constant guarding, upkeep and attention.

Most of us, I imagined, had smuggled laptops in: ladies who lunch may do what they're told; high fliers do not. They were unreliable. Batteries run out and there were no power points in the bedrooms. You had to sneak in to the public rooms to power up. The longer you were at the Spa, anyway, the more irrelevant the outside world seemed. Only Mira and I remained obsessed.

This morning's news gave a soothing portrait of the world outside – empty streets, but that was normal for now: the sales would not begin until tomorrow. There was no mention of Sumatra flu. The worm attack on the internet had been resolved, beaten back by the web's well-established defence systems, every-thing in the virtual world was back to normal and the culprits, a couple of north London schoolboys, were being questioned by the police. And then my screen went blank. The battery had run out and I had, of course, forgotten to bring my lead with me. Well, that was that. I shouldn't have bothered to lug the thing all the way up here.

I would just have to face this unreasonable new anxiety about

Julian, triggered by Shimmer's tale about love amongst social and financial unequals, and saving that, worry about the state of the ceiling back home, to which I had barely given a thought since I arrived. Anxiety had to find a home somewhere, and there's nothing like a strange bed for setting off a nasty bout of the free-floating stuff. Well, I would outface Beverley later in the day and wring a phone call to Alec out of her, and perhaps the noble linemen of Wichita would have the lines humming again and I could get through to Julian. I could see I took him for granted. Glenn Campbell. 'The Wichita Lineman'. '*And I need you more than want you, and I want you for all time.*'

The note under my door said that due to the holidays the Snooze Zone would not be available to guests and those who had booked in for pedicures and manicures were entitled to a free Reiki session, courtesy of the Castle Spa. My massage was at eleven, my Dead Sea mud at twelve and aqua aerobics at four. A little map accompanied the note. It was nice to be told when and where to go. It was like being back at school again.

The Weather Girl offered to tell her story in the Jacuzzi at ten past one, to give clients time to get the mud off their faces or the cling film off their knees, or recover from the tingling left by over-enthusiastic administration of electrolysis pads, whatever, and even grab a salad lunch. It was more like half past before we were all assembled, back in the familiar bubbles, and this seemed to irritate her. She was easily irritated. She kept consulting her ladies' Rolex – one of the new ones with the diamond bracelet, and I for one thought this was over the top in a Jacuzzi. Then she'd hiss a little through the big, unnaturally white teeth. I hoped it was waterproof, for her sake, but I don't think they waterproof the ladies' models. I may be wrong.

She had one of those narrow faces that look better on TV than they do in real life, bouncy, short-cropped fair hair and rather large teeth showing between lips which were born to be thin but were now plumped up by silicone. Her smile was startling and sudden and without warmth: her mouth moved but her eyes were unaffected. Her ribs showed through the skin too prominently: she was borderline anorexic. I thought she lacked eroticism – which is a kind of still, contemplative quality: a held memory of couplings past and hope of others still to come – her mind and her movements were too fast: memory and expectation both fell off her like shower water on an oiled skin – she was rather like a captain of hockey on speed. She would make a man come to suit her purposes, and then take his money and run. Worse. No, I confess I didn't like her, and her story made me like her rather less.

15

The Weather Girl's Tale

'You have to look after yourself. No one else will. There is no good or bad except as it affects oneself. I have given some thought to the nature of God and have come to the conclusion that He does not exist. Not on the grounds so many people give "there can't be a God because children die of lung cancer" – it is wishful thinking to believe God is necessarily *nice* – but because in life the "good" are not rewarded and the "bad" are not punished but flourish like a green bay tree. Look at me. I am flourishing. And according to my parents I am "bad". And where has being "good" ever got them?

'I am a weather girl on a prime TV channel, have a fan club, a top publicity agent, a personal trainer and a lover high up in the BBC who will presently move me out of weather – which is a little limiting, and the hours are anti-social – into the arts. He will have to, otherwise his wife will find out about me and though he is not interested in his wife he loves his children and doesn't want them upset. Which is stupid of him, because I don't suppose they will be in the least upset, they will hardly notice: he is seldom there at bath-time. There is always some crisis or other which keeps him from going home. He's in News. I am not interested in breaking up his marriage – he is more than welcome to it – I just don't want to be stuck in Weather for too long. Rafe – that's my PR man – says Weather is essentially B list – though a really good step on the road to A.

'The Newsman is hopelessly in love with me: he gets this stupid look on his face when he sees me. His jaw goes slack: there's something horrible about it. I really do despise him when he's like this. It's as if there's something on my shoe I have to get rid of and can't: some sort of wet slimy coat hanging off my shoulders. He's at least fifty-five: it's pathetic. He married again and his new lot of children are four and five. I think he's just sad: too old to be a father. His first lot don't speak to him, and he says he's learning again with this batch, but so far doesn't seem to be doing too well, does he. He's always turning up in the Club or some Green Room or other where I happen to be. I do a news quiz every couple of weeks and he finds out the questions for me and then briefs me, and if he begs hard enough I occasionally give him a blow job to keep him on side, and tell him one day, one day we'll go away for a weekend and do it properly. Yuk! Men are so stupid, aren't they.'

'He sees the questions and tells you the answers?' asked the Journalist. She sounded a little dazed.

'Yes.'

'But that's a hanging offence,' I said.

'What do you mean?' she asked. 'We don't have capital punishment in this country any more. Or do we? Oh, I see what you mean. Yeah, I expect he'd lose his job, if anyone knew. But they don't know, do they, and won't unless I tell them, and that's his lookout, not mine. But as I was saying before I was interrupted—'

She looked at her absurd Rolex. It glittered almost as brightly as the Manicurist's earrings.

'I have an eyebrow shaping at two and I like to be on time. Punctuality is one of the keys to success, especially in TV. If I've decided to tell the story of my life that's what I'm doing. Interruptions are not appropriate. It's different from a conversation which can drag on.'

'Sorry we spoke,' said the Journalist, with heavy irony.

'That's all right,' said the Weather Girl, benignly. 'It's just that it breaks my flow. I hate it when the producer starts talking into my earpiece mid-show, especially if we're going live. It's like that. But as I was saying, don't think my life has been easy. I've had a real struggle to get where I am. I seriously think I was switched at birth – and have asked my parents to have their DNA tested, but they won't co-operate. I've explained again and again that taking a smear from inside your mouth for a DNA test hardly counts as a transfusion, but they are so stupid they can't even see that. They've told me time and time again that I'm no child of theirs but when I take them up on it they won't see it through. I certainly don't look like them. They're Jehovah's Witnesses: as a child there was no TV, no holidays, no Christmas, just dreary, dreary, God-fearing misery. My mother's fat and lumpy and my father lives with his head always to one side because he's got some kind of twisted nerve in his neck. Imagine being picked up from school by people like that. My two elder sisters were lumps of lard. Thinking of their conception sickens me. I just do not believe I can have been the result of the union of those two sub-humans. I have looks, charm and intelligence, and they have none. No, I was switched at birth: my real parents are A list, I just know it. One day the truth will emerge. My alleged mother pretends to be upset when I don't go home at this time of year but since she refuses to celebrate Christmas she can hardly complain. When I explain that there is no God she looks at me with these stricken eyes.

'Believing in God and being virtuous has done them no good at all. They face a poverty-stricken old age, and I am not going to help them. They made my early life a misery: why should I look after them now?'

She looked around at us for affirmation, but since she had forbidden us to speak no one did so.

'As I say, a hard life. My father worked in the dispatch department of a shoe factory and my mother in a bakery, overseeing the production line of a range of white sliced breads. Between them they earned quite well, and believing that frugality was a virtue, and the end of times was coming any time now, must have accumulated a fair bit of wealth over the decades while they waited. I saw none of it. I shivered in the cold for lack of a good winter coat and suffered the humiliation of not just being poor, but of having the kind of parents who would let one die rather than receive proper medical treatment. Other girls had luxuries beyond compare – TV in their rooms, pocket money to spend, holidays to look forward to – not me. I was scorned at best, derided and bullied at worst. Unfortunately in their bid for heaven my parents preferred to give great chunks of my inheritance away to charitable causes rather than investing in pension schemes. God will provide, they said. Well, He did not and I am not going to come between God and his plans for their future. They had it coming to them.

'When my father had me disfellowshipped at fourteen – cast out from the family and set on the path to hell, deprived of all hope of salvation – my mother continued to see me secretly, but refused to divorce him, which annoyed me. She could choose between him and me and she chose him. Yet never was a man more pig-headed and stupid – not even born stupid, as she was, but imposing stupidity upon himself. If you train yourself in casting out all doubt and spirit of enquiry because of a religious belief this is how you end up. Stupid. My father presently relented – when he reached sixty, and his own father, my grandfather, turned ninety-three – he realized the second coming was unlikely to occur within his lifetime, and softened enough to have me in the house again, though he would still not address me directly, but only through my mother.

'But from the beginning I was ambitious: one way or another I would escape from the grim, suffocating background that had been thrust upon me by a cruel accident of fate. But how? As a child one is helpless. I realized early the power of the smile – a rarity in my home – and used it as a weapon. I remember smiling at every person who approached my cot when I was barely able to stand up in it, the better to get my way. I did not cry; it worked better if you smiled.

'Education, I could see was the other way out for me: but getting one wasn't easy. I had no trouble with exams, but was only grudgingly allowed to school at all and certainly not allowed out to "play" with non-Witnesses. Being top of the class was dangerous.

One was "*striving after wind*". Ecclesiastes 1:14. Worldly ambition was frowned upon. I once rashly let out that I intended to work in television when I grew up. But television was the Devil's work: they were horrified to find out it was in the classroom. I got a beating for that. Witnesses are hot on family discipline. Rather than urging me to pursue recognition and prosperity, my parents would quote the Apostle John – "Do not be loving either the world or the things in the world. If anyone loves the world, the love of the Father is not in him; because everything in the world – the desire of the flesh and the desire of the eyes and the showy display of one's means of life – does not originate with the Father, but originates with the world. Furthermore, the world is passing away and so is its desire, but he that does the will of God remains forever."

'That has a certain beauty, I daresay, but could lull one forever into mental sleep. Dozens and dozens of quotations from the Good Book, instilled into me when I was very small, stay with me as a kind of poison in my mind, which has to be endlessly struggled against in case I slip back into belief.

'When I was fourteen my mother was already taking me with her to work in the hot, yeasty bakery, where vast vats of dough were set to rise ceiling-high to be whacked down again by mechanical paddles, and rose again, only to be whacked down once more, and again, and again, like giant lingams that would not be stopped, finally defeated, and shipped off to the enormous ovens and baked, and cooled, and sliced with razor-sharp blades under my mother's watchful eyes; quality control, forever searching for error, at work as well as home. Her skin and mine would become hot and oily to the touch, slippery, should her bare fat arm touch my thin one by mistake – how I hated that – as the hours dragged by. One evening I said to her, as I watched the metal knives cut through crisp crust into the softer consistency of the crumb below, that there was no God. She went home and told my father, and I repeated it to him.

'"Yes, there is no God. I have worked it out." I forgot to smile, and not much smiling was done for the next week, not much joyousness, while I was hauled before the elders and disfellow-shipped. "No *discipline seems for the present to be joyous, but grievous; yet afterward to those who have been trained by it, it yields peaceable fruit, namely, righteousness.*" In other words in the fullness of time one repents and is accepted back. But what have I got to repent for? I will not, cannot – unlike my father, who started out as an Oxford graduate, before having the misfortune to meet, fall in love with, and be converted by, my fat, idiotic mother – I cannot deny my reason: there is no God. And without God, there is no reason why one should not act solely in self-interest, which I now do.

'At the age of fourteen, cast out, literally by my parents, disfel-lowshipped, I was put into one foster home after another by the State. Bright children tend to have a hard time if placed with fam-ilies of lower intellect than themselves. They are seen to be argumentative, troublesome, and ungrateful. Their siblings dislike them. It was easy enough to change homes. All I needed to do was be seen to flirt with the husbands, or walk around the house with no clothes on in front of the wives, or tell the younger siblings graphic tales of child abuse amongst the witnesses – which was real enough. I was skinny but had good tits and a nice bum. And so I managed scarcely ever to stay in one place for more than a month or so – and was passed from home to home and school to school. I think I had a vague hope that one day I would find myself in some posh house and meet up with my rightful parents and live happily ever after where I belonged. But no such luck. Indeed, I found I tended to go socially downhill as transfer succeeded trans-fer, and I'd end up in the kind of school where the teachers knew less grammar than I did, and didn't respond well to my pointing it out to them. One or two even hit me, which if one put one's mind to it one could usually achieve. I lost one woman her job a week before retirement. Men teachers liked me, and I encouraged their inappropriate behaviour whenever I could. I ended up with a kind of job-warning which went ahead of me – *this one spells trouble* – which made me popular with the other kids. In my

A-level year I had two special friends, Velicette and Gretchen, and between us, in one year, we got three teachers put on the sex register. Dirty beasts.

'The trouble was how was I to pay for college? By now no one in Care was bending over backwards to help me get there. I had a bit of a drug problem and had been trying to get through my exams on Ecstasy, which, frankly, had been stupid, and my academic record hadn't been looking too good. Many girls in my situation simply go on the streets or into the massage parlours. But I didn't want that for me, though it would have been easy. I might have been tempted if offered some posh place in a high class brothel but I was realistic enough to know that wasn't likely to happen. Frankly, I was by now low on class, education and culture. And if you're going to make money at the top end of the market you need to have class, or at least be Russian. And anyway my early ambition, to get into TV and show them all, remained.

'With Velicette's help, we thought up a really good plan. She'd got a college place and was studying Tourism and was living on campus – she was bright, even brighter than me – had taught herself Greek and Latin and could have done Classics if she wanted, but she didn't. It smacked too much of imperialist oppression and she tends to be chippy about her origins, which are West Indian out of the Gambia. She's one of those very beautiful and classy black girls with the long legs and the tight butt that men go wild for. But she didn't like men any more than I did. They were either all like my dad at heart, and bullies, or like her dad, and absentee. She lives in New York now and is married to a guy who helps run that modern art museum. MOMA. That's why I want to get transferred to the Arts sector, I guess. If Velicette can do it so can I. I hadn't thought of that until now.

'Anyway Velicette was mates with this computer nerd Jimmy – everyone needs a Jimmy in their life – who altered my results on the UCAS computer so at least I qualified for college and while he was at it wiped the stuff about my background. I didn't even have to do anything for it; he was so nuts about Velicette. Academic records and personal history are no real problem to access, but when it comes to money the firewalls tend to be solid. So money remained a problem. I was going to have to hand over real stuff in the end. I wasn't going to go the Student Loan route and leave college with massive debts – that was just too sad to contemplate. Velicette and I planned the solution like a military operation. She would take ten percent. You get at least £10,000 from the Criminal Injury Compensation Board, if you can prove a really nasty rape, sometimes more. Conviction rates are low, so it's a bit of a risk, but the lady lawyers are working on it, so it'll be easier to get money in future.

'I got myself on to the History of Art course and some remedial basic literacy courses and started my studies and smiled a lot and kept out of trouble: and just kept telling them the money was on the way. But it couldn't go on forever. I struck up an acquaintance with a young guy called Matthew, who was one of the Brethren. Witnesses don't have much time for Brethren – they're soppy, and believe everyone is born into a state of grace, not of sin. So you don't have to be saved, you're saved automatically. Brethren don't have to bother about going from door to door warning people about the end of times, and telling them to hurry to be saved before it's too late. They're just lazy, if you ask me, and want to save shoe leather, or so my father says. There's no kind of religious discipline in it, but there's enough of the same kind of language used and I could easily pass as Brethren. Which I did. Brethren, like Witnesses, are encouraged to keep their relationships within the group. In fact there's hell to pay if you try anything else. Matthew was a medical student. He didn't have friends outside the group that I could see, that he was likely to blab to. He was a bit older than me. Twenty-two.'

And Mira lent over to me and whispered, 'Rather worried about the past tense,' and she got glared at. We both shut up and paid attention.

'You tend not to get medical students amongst the Witnesses,' she went on, with the slight estuary drawl TV presenters favour, the edge of the nasal demotic which never rings quite true. 'Too much trouble with the doctrine of blood – but again, the Brethren aren't fussy that way. So I suppose I did rather despise Matthew – it can get irritating when people don't realize how hard a place the world is, and how you have to look after yourself – though he was pleasant enough. Just wet. He kept pictures of his father and mother and siblings on the table by his bed, and they lived in a nice big house with a proper garden and a couple of Labradors. Why couldn't I have had a background like that? I'd be a much nicer person if I had.

'I did my normal stuff, once I'd targeted him, and brushed up against him once or twice at prayer meetings – I was dressed very subdued, so no one would notice – asked his advice and so on, and stayed in bed with a sore throat at Velicette's pad, and got him to bring me medication so he got a glimpse of breast and thigh. And Velicette's presence somehow upped the ante: she walks around in a kind of fuck-me trance, which is somehow catching. It just seems sex is what she's *for*, and because she is, so is everyone around.

'He asked me out to the cinema twice, and I leaned into him, and startled him no end by kind of half accidentally rubbing his penis so he got an erection. He was delighted. You don't meet many Brethren girls looking as I do, let alone so available. But he had no doubt about my intentions, and his poor, good little mind was going off in all kind of directions, so when Velicette asked him over to supper with me there was no doubting he'd come. We had a good meal, curry, and drank rather a lot, or at any rate he did – I didn't; they do a breathalyser when you report in, and the higher your level is, the word is, the less compensation you get. Girls do the date rape scam quite a bit to pay off their credit cards and so on, but I was playing for higher stakes. I'd spent a lot of thought and planning on this and was having to give Velicette ten percent, which was beginning to seem unreasonable: five percent was more like it. If everything went wrong I'd be in prison not Matthew, but she'd be okay either way.

'So it was about midnight when I went back to Matthew's place

and we met a few people going in, and I seemed cheerful and
happy, sober and demure in a high-necked sweater and mid-calf
skirt and Bridget Jones knickers. And I got into bed with him and
we had unprotected sex and he was much too quick to get anything really going between us but he didn't notice. It was his first
time. He was just overjoyed. That was what was so beautiful:
knowing the way the look on his face was going to change. All
men are beasts: they deserve what they get. He went to sleep and
I unhooked his arms from round me and left at about one.

'I went straight back to Velicette's and she gave me a quick
blow to the side of my jaw which knocked me out, more or less,
and then bashed me up a bit and used this rather large
dildo without jelly both entrances, so I was thoroughly bruised
where it mattered. And then I staggered round to the Rape Crisis
Centre, making sure people saw me crying and half out of my
mind, and they took me round to the police station, and I
cried rape. They were at his place within the hour and hauled him
away.

'"You are a beast, a monster!" the Judge said to him. He had a
lousy lawyer. "This nice young girl, quiet, studious and religious,
going to your room in all innocence, and now she is damaged for
life, traumatized, too frightened to go out on her own. You have
destroyed her." His parents and sisters were in court. How they
carried on when he was led away. He didn't even meet their eyes.
It was spooky.'

'How long did he get?' asked the Judge, coldly. The Weather
Girl seemed triumphant in her answer. Now she wanted to tell.

'Eight years,' she said. She was proud.

'How much did you get?' asked the Trophy Wife,

'Twelve thousand pounds,' she replied, reverentially. 'I did well.'
We were all silent.

'I didn't have to live with it for long,' she said presently. 'Neither
did he. He hanged himself in his cell after about three months.'

More silence.

'I made good use of the money,' she volunteered. 'Education

isn't cheap. I did three years History of Art, one year Media Studies, got an internship at the BBC and the rest is history.'

She looked at her vulgar, expensive watch. 'I'm late,' she said. 'I'm never late. You've kept me late with your interruptions.'

'But why are you telling us all this?' asked the Surgeon. 'Isn't it rather unwise?'

'I don't know,' she wailed rather than spoke. 'I've no idea. Perhaps if I confess they'll take me back. It was just so horrible being disfellowshipped and my own father doing it.'

And the Weather Girl's watch wrist, which she'd rather nervously kept out of the water, just in case the proofing on the Rolex didn't work in spite of the price – you can never tell – dropped below the surface of the pool, as if she didn't care about anything any more, and her face swelled as she began to cry.

'I just want my mother,' she howled and got out of the pool and ran from the room.

Twenty minutes later there was the sound of acrimony from the lobby, between, presumably, Beverley and the Weather Girl, and then the revving of her silly little sports car as she fled from Castle Spa and I can't say anyone was sorry to see her go.

16

All the props – the ever present husband, the expected family get-
together, a bathroom floor fit to walk upon, had been snatched
away – perhaps it was only that. I felt pathetic and neurotic, and
the Weather Girl's tale had upset me.

Mira said she might get the paper to investigate: perhaps for the
sake of the family the boy's name could be exonerated – the
Weather Girl might just come forward and confess – but what
would it really benefit anyone to stir up the past? And perhaps she
was a fantasist – I said the story had a terrible ring of truth about
it and she agreed. It was a shock when what one accepted as
normal – the pain men could and did inflict upon women – was
reversed, and one had to remember it was a two-way street.

But I was brooding again. How had one got by in the days
without mobile phones? One could grasp that the lack of a mast
meant no signal: as much was obvious. I could well understand
Lady Caroline's refusal to have one, and even have some sympathy
with her belief that the old ways were the best. I had some friends
who still insisted on handwriting letters, having no e-mail, and my
heart sank when I received a handwritten letter, as once I would
have rejoiced. Handwriting was so difficult to decipher. And the
new technology was flawed. Even Mira's expensive satellite phone,
she told me, was on the blink. How did they work anyway? I had
little idea. Did different providers hire satellite space from the military, or were the issues purely commercial? Did satellites need
land-based computers to work? Or did they just circle the earth
without help and interminably?

'Perhaps the Chinese have shot your satellite down,' I suggested.

'They do that kind of thing when annoyed. Or perhaps they've shot a whole batch down and debris is flying around the outer atmosphere doing no end of damage.' I was joking.

'It may well be,' Mira said darkly, 'Murdoch is married to a Chinese woman.'

On the way back to our rooms for new gowns, Beverley having returned fresh laundry to each of us – I asked Mira if she had any better luck with her laptop than I had and she said no, there was no Wi-Fi connection, but I could try her phone again in the hope that some mysterious deal had been done between robots, and the satellite wonder was now working again. So we went to her room and I, who had hoped to have said over the air waves 'happy Christmas, Julian, and good night,' was thwarted. Supposing something untoward had indeed happened? Supposing the satellite to which I beamed my message had indeed been struck by a Chinese missile – or the debris left spinning in space forever by successive Chinese missiles? Supposing Sumatra flu was real and millions were to die? Struck dead by the raisins in their Christmas puddings? The children would all have had Christmas puddings if only for the sake of the brandy butter. Did people panic for nothing? The sign on the Hydrotherapy door had been real enough. 'Gone home'. If everyone was home watching the TV the grid would collapse; I'd read that somewhere. Two hours power black-out in our small town had brought it to a standstill: tills couldn't open, trade stopped. Supposing all the computers in the world crashed? It could happen, through a massed hacker attack on the thirteen root servers that form the internet's backbone – hadn't there already been a warning? In that very twenty-four-hour closure which Alec said no one took any notice of? Supposing all these things happened at once? What would become of Western civilization? I might never see Julian again. I sat down on the bed with a bump.

'What's the matter with you?' asked Mira. 'You've gone quite white.'

I told her. She laughed. 'You're projecting. End-of-the-world hysteria, internalized by a woman insecure in her relationships: translate it as end-of-marriage fear.'

What I'd done to her she now did to me. I had accused her of listening to Zelda's story with the ears of a woman unhappy in love: now she accused me of looking at the world as a woman insecure in love, vague fears triggered by Shimmer's story. Did not I earn more than my husband, much more?

'When exactly did the fever start?' asked Mira. 'Trace it back to that.'

I thought. I realized. 'In the car on the way to the station. When Julian said since I wasn't going to be home he might as well stay in Wichita.'

'Point proved,' said Mira.

'But I couldn't get through on the phone to Julian just now,' I said. 'Just because you think there's a plot against you doesn't mean there isn't.'

'Look,' Mira said, 'they've had ferocious ice storms in that part of the States. Lines are down all over the place. *Lex Parsimoniae.* Occam's razor. The simplest solution is the likeliest. Not the end of the world, just a local problem with communication.'

'What we seem to be saying to each other,' I said, 'is that there's no such thing as an outer reality, just the sum of one's experiences, and one's emotional responses?'

'Yeah,' she said. 'More or less. If you're a woman. Paying attention to the news is just diversionary activity. That's why Lady Caroline tries to keep it out. Where your Julian is in real terms makes no difference. The point is he isn't under your nose. I know well enough where Alistair is. At home. It's where in the home he is that matters. At this very moment he's probably in bed with his wife or worse, fucking her under the Christmas tree, having sent the children to bed early. And this is what he has chosen. What do you think that makes me feel like? It is with difficulty that I concentrate on the here and now.'

I was really good at denial, I could see that. It hadn't seriously occurred to me that Julian could indeed use our separation for sexual dalliance with another. Let me out that more plainly. Fuck someone else.

Out of the question, like the end of the world.

It was time for the Conspiracy Theorist's tale, which seemed fitting.

The Conspiracy Theorist came from a family who owned their own horizon, sent their male children to Eton and rode to hounds. She herself campaigned against fox hunting, which her family resigned themselves to with good grace. She was effortlessly pretty, and effortlessly clever, with good cheekbones, a peaches and cream complexion, and was I suppose in her midthirties. She had a degree in economics but stayed home to look after the children, keep a wing of the stately home open to visitors, do the flowers in the village church, and help out at a convalescent home for wounded soldiers just outside the village. She had won the seasonal break at Castle Spa in a charity raffle. Her husband, who searched for wrecks in the South Pacific, for some urgent reason to do with shifting sands ands changing currents, could not be home for Christmas. The grandparents liked the children to stay, so she had taken up the opportunity.

Perhaps the effort of so much conventional good behaviour had driven her a little mad. Her eyes were piercing and glittery, the pretty mouth a little twitchy. She should have avoided the rolling acres, marriage and the social obligations she was born to, and stayed an economist or better still been a lecturer in political science. She was too clever for her own good. Give her an audience and she expounded. Her hunting shooting fishing neighbours must have run when she approached; on open day the teachers must have dodged. Her foolish, obsessive husband preferred to spend Christmas with a marine wreck rather than with her. I liked her. I am sure her children loved her. Her motives were entirely good.

Now she warned a not entirely sympathetic audience, who would rather think about their toenails than the state of the world, about what was going to happen next and how it had come about. How the Reds under the bed which so obsessed her parents' generation had not gone away but simply underground, biding their time, unobserved; like a tangle of nettle roots in winter, sending shoots in all directions into a cold dark soil, just waiting for the spring, when its strong, green, stinging foliage could push up into a friendlier political sky.

Oh, she was a conspiracy theorist all right: she saw plots where others saw happenings. She made herself unpopular because of it. If you do not want to be bothered, like the Manicurist and the Vicar's Ex-wife, with a tale of Marx and Trotsky, Gramsci and Marcuse, simply skip this one, and carry on with the Manicurist's on page 167. This may well be more to your liking, being about true love, desert sheiks, and how a pale little girl from a sunless city ended up on the edge of our Jacuzzi, draped with jewels and with a bodyguard all to herself. Me, I'm sticking with the doomy stuff. But then I would, wouldn't I. I see the end of the world as accidental: she sees it as a plot, which is comforting, because at least it means that someone, somewhere, knows what they're doing.

17

The Conspiracy Theorist's Tale

We high-achieving ladies, or so the Spa brochure would have us be, sat on the edge of the marble Jacuzzi, drifting our legs in the scented water, and listened to the tale the Conspiracy Theorist had to tell. She spoke with the accents of the bourgeoisie, as so many radicals do.

'I am over forty, old enough to know the world is going to hell in a handcart. Under-forties, I notice, think everything's just fine. But my thesis is just this: of course they do; they have been brainwashed by the Gramsci Project. Me, I still have a dim memory of what the world was like once, when we had our institutions, our national boundaries, a common ethos, there were no credit cards and above all, no debt, by which our rulers have us on a fish hook. I was born into a happier world, believe me. Where there was no political correctness and we all rubbed along just fine. For those under forty, thanks to the Project, there is no history: the world began yesterday and has always been as it is to day.'

The Manicurist yawned.

'How old are you?' the Conspiracy Theorist asked her, taking mild offence.

'Twenty-two,' said the Manicurist. 'Though I don't see what fucking difference it is to you.' She swore without affect: fucking was just another word to her, and even in its usage, sometimes quite charming.

'That's what I mean,' said the Conspiracy Theorist. 'You are a young thing and it seems only reasonable to you to be antagonistic towards your elders. Why would you not? You have been reared by teachers who treat your parents with suspicion, seeing fathers as abusers and mothers as neglectful.'

'Too fucking right,' said the Manicurist. 'But I'm out of that now.'

'The younger you are the happier you will be with the world you live in,' continued the Conspiracy Theorist. 'You will see nothing to argue with. The Gramsci Project is alive and well and has been since 1967, the year the world turned upside down, and Marxism and its offshoots moved in to create a new Europe, and bring about the birth of a new world order. It has been a two-pronged attack: to hasten the end of capitalism by attacking its props and institutions – marriage, the family, the Church, the stratified society; and to create a new, biddable, correct-thinking citizen fit for the perfect society. It has done very well. The Gramsci Project speaks with a silver tongue, in glossy management speak; it talks of stakeholding and issues, targets and performance indicators. It soothes, it persuades, it offers us goodies. We all have iPods, plasma screens and mobiles, don't we? Aren't we endlessly entertained? Gramsci has had his way. In 1928 he wrote to a friend, "The revolution also presupposes the formation of a new set of standards, a new psychology, new ways of feeling, thinking and living." That has been achieved.'

She paused for breath. We were glad.

'There is a fall-out from the revolution: there are victims, in such number they threaten to overwhelm us. See them all around. Our druggy, unhappy lads and drunken lasses, who once were golden, exhausted mothers and rejected fathers, childless, neurotic singletons, the flight to the sperm bank as the family collapses and love goes out of fashion. The under-forties think it has always been like this, and accept it, or at best acknowledge there are "issues to be solved". But these are the very issues created by the Gramsci Project in its attempts to create the new world order.'

'Who was this Gramsci?' asked the Mortgage Broker. 'Why haven't I heard of him?'

'Because he is the unspoken secret of the left. He was an Italian hunchback with beautiful eyes and the gift of the gab who was put in prison by Mussolini in 1926, as a communist and a danger to the Fascist state. "We must stop this brain for twenty years," the prosecutor said. But prison wasn't enough. Gramsci smuggled his writings out of prison, where he died in 1937. Now his name is seldom spoken, but his thinking is there in every decision taken by the political and cultural elites of the West.'

'That's rather romantic,' said someone.

'It is,' said the Conspiracy Theorist grimly. 'A narrative always helps; a prison sentence too. Think of St Paul and the spread of Christianity. Gramsci's ideas were spread by the Frankfurt School, communism's version of St Paul.'

Now I am well up on the Frankfurt School because my great-great-uncle, Sigmund Lowenstein, had been one of them. Few were listening. They were drinking their coffee, or wandering off to find champagne. The story had lost its hold, other than for the few semi-converts who remained. I'd kept quiet so far. Let the Conspiracy Theorist take the flack of boring everyone.

But my distant relative Sigmund was a German Jew, philosopher, sociologist, man of letters, who was a member of the Institute of Social Research at Frankfurt University. I knew something of the subject. Perhaps I should speak up? This grouping of very bourgeois and well-heeled neo-Marxist intellectuals, assimilated Jews, had flourished in Frankfurt in the early thirties. 'Neo' – because it had become apparent that the original Marxist model no longer held water. The predicted working-class world revolution hadn't happened: Nazism was on the rise. In the Soviet Union Stalin had taken to slaughtering millions of his own people just to keep the show on the road. Some revision of the theory was required. The revolution had been delayed, but must be made to happen. The destruction of the current order was still required. How to hurry it up? The new discoveries of psychoanalysis were roped in. Freud and his 'pleasure principle' suddenly became very relevant: the growing child – and society can be seen in terms of an individual, can it not? – normally grows out of a destructive all-pervading eroticism into an adult state. But supposing you kept that society in its indulged pleasure-seeking state: surely then it would destroy itself pretty quickly?

And then being Jewish, and with Hitler in power, they were thrown out of the country they thought of as their own. Some went to New York, some went to Hollywood. Sigmund wrote to his daughter Anna, who chose to stay behind and who was to die in Auschwitz in 1943:

> I beg you to reconsider and join me when you can. On the
> journey here I heard Hitler's speech. His word reaches over the
> plains and the seas of the world. He speaks peace but means
> war. I have never felt so strongly that it is not a word but rather
> a force of nature. I am frightened for you. I would stay with
> you but there is work that has to be done if the force of
> Hitler's National Socialism, not the true Socialism, is not
> to sweep all before it. Besides that duty my own inclinations
> are nothing.

Poor Sigmund, he hated America: he felt the country was irredeemable in its vulgarity and died in New York in 1942. His fellow refugees – Marcuse, who became a power in the universities, as did Adorno in the field of the arts, Fromm in psychoanalysis – flourished in the alien air. Then came the publication in 1946 of Gramsci's *Letters from Prison*, and with it a new burst of energy, a validation of what this sect of neo-Marxists was trying to achieve. Gramsci was their martyr. The pleasure principle joined up with the idea of creating the new citizen, who would willingly embrace what became known as political correctness, in an increasingly infantilized culture, in which only popular thoughts could be openly expressed. Marcuse, by the way, invented the slogan 'Make love, not war'. And the summer of love began, and has never really gone away, just turned sleazy and sinister.

I did not say all this to the ladies around the Jacuzzi. I was cowardly. I hate to bore, and besides, the Conspiracy Theorist was under way again.

'Never accept defeat, only a change of tactics. So, Marx hadn't got it right, but the collapse of capitalism in Gramsci's view was still inevitable: it just had to be hurried along. It was increasingly urgent that all things counter-revolutionary must go. Bourgeois history becomes irrelevant. Best that the world began yesterday. A favourite revolutionary theme: it happened, literally, in France in 1789, in Cambodia in 1975, when the new eras started with Year Zero. The thinking permeates our culture today. Start anew! The psychotherapist urges the patient to cut the ties that bind, keep the children away from the grandparent, don't build on the old, start again afresh. All things being relative, there being no absolutes, history no longer relates to facts, but to a perceived reality.

'Dominoes start to fall. Loyalty and tradition are bad, you may still need a regiment, but at least change its name. Christianity is the great enemy: Christianity must go. Every church left to crumble, every mosque built, suits the Gramsci Project very well. Health and Safety puts an end to spontaneity. No more cake-baking for the village fete: someone might get food poisoning. No more gathering in pubs – so ban smoking and no live music without a licence. Thirty-one percent of us live in single house-holds and that figure's rising fast. Let the people go to their lonely homes, close the door, retreat into their bedrooms to smoke freely and watch porn. Porn saps the old order like nothing else. Sex replaces love: love is counter-revolutionary, it might lead to marriage.'

'Coffee anyone?' asked the Vicar's Ex-wife, brightly, and when hands went up went off to make it.

'The Project sees marriage as a plot by men to perpetuate an evil system in which men dominate over women and children: so do away with marriage. Remove the taxes that favour it: let anyone marry anyone; marriage is no longer about men, women and children. Gay or straight, no difference. Give housing to single mothers; penalize them if they have boyfriends. Do away with monogamy or the expectation of it: if people want love let them love the state.

'The family is depicted by the Gramsciists as counter-revolutionary, a dangerous institution based on violence and exploitation, so do away with the family, do away with parenthood. Take the babies from the mothers – women have no choice: they have to work. Put the babies in the nurseries from three months old: imprison any mother who keeps a child off school. Assume all fathers are potential child abusers. One man's wages no longer keeps a family anyway, who wants a father cluttering up the place? What woman these days has as many children as she would like? She can't afford it. The birth rate falls and falls. Good. The Project approves. The longer you spend in education the fewer children you have. So pile everyone into universities – we all have careers now: careers mean fewer babies. Only the poor on benefit can afford large families: and the children of the poor, made prosperous, are the biddable, dumbed-down citizens of tomorrow. Who is left to argue with the Project? The people are docile, busy recycling, hooked on the trash of *Big Brother*.'

'That's fucking crap,' said the Manicurist, but at last she was listening.

'Take your city, Liverpool,' said the Conspiracy Theorist. 'I know it. I run a charity up there'.

'How very kind,' said the Manicurist, genteelly.

'The streets are alive with the sound of gunfire. The Project loves crime and disorder, it means the end is nigh, the new order is nearly here. Do you think it is accidental that there are so few police on the streets?'

'I thought it was just muddle and incompetence,' remarked Shimmer. 'You mean it's a *plot*?'

'How else to explain it? Doesn't it all make sense? The extreme Christian Right has its own form of The Rapture: the taking up to heaven of believers only, any day now; the extreme left has its own version: the day the revolution comes, and the right-minded take over. If the old do not dare leave their homes, who cares? So, they've had their pasts and the significance of their lives, not to mention their pensions, stolen from them. They are exiles in their own land. They notice, but dare not even mention, that those who tote the guns are not white.'

'That's racist!' said the Vicar's Ex-wife. 'That's out of order.'

'How quick you are to say it: how those words, racist, sexist, preclude any proper discussion. Bet I'm less racist than you,' said the Conspiracy Theorist.

'Anyway in Liverpool gun crime is mostly white,' said the Manicurist, but no one took any notice.

'It's not skin colour that's important to me,' went on the Conspiracy Theorist. 'It's that these gun-toting children too have had their traditions stolen from them, in pursuance of the Project's demented theory that the sooner national boundaries go and everyone's mixed up together the better. The road to social hell is paved with the good intentions. And line your pockets while you're about it.'

'No rich man ever thinks he's evil,' said the Trophy Wife.

The Conspiracy Theorist had rashly paused for breath. Now she continued.

'In its pursuit of the theory of universal equivalence, the denial of difference, the insistence that all are born equal – when it is quite obvious to any parent, any child, that they are not – the Gramsci Project has brought us to our knees. Art and culture as we knew it is at an end.'

'Oh please,' said someone. 'Please!' But still she went on. The arts must have their day.

'The day of the artist, as set apart from the ordinary citizen, is over. High art is élitist, élitism is counter-revolutionary, so get rid of it: foster the cult of celebrity in its place. Push the artist off his perch. It's what you are that matters, not what you do. Anyone can be famous for being famous, no special talent required. If some of us seem to be better than others at drawing, fudge the issue: stop the art schools teaching skills. Let "art" become someone's bright idea: a sexy bed, a tortured sheep. Lo, it happens, the Turner Prize. In TV seek the lowest common denominator: prize quantity more than quality, ratings win. Dumb down. Change the definition of "good" to "popular". Let *Big Brother* rule. The BBC socially engineers for all its worth: teaches its announcers the muddy language of the streets. We can all learn creative writing and be novelists now. The writer is under siege: the literary midlist in publishing goes, only Jordan and footballers need apply. Someone high up in the Gramsci Project must like opera: it survives. "Art films" don't get funded: if they are, they aren't screened. YouTube, the people's art, takes its place.

'We are all as one, think as one – sorry, not think, feel – as one. Something missing, some vague yearning for some other manner of existence? Astrology will help you find your inner self. If you feel guilty, let the therapist take the place of the Pardoner, forgive your sins. Therapy has its own special place in the Gramsci Project. In the eyes of the therapist individuals are all nurture, no nature. We cannot help doing what we do: if we are unhappy, blame our mother. If we are fat, recover memories and blame our father for abusing us. The hegemony of a new improved inverted cultural revolution has arrived. Common sense has been turned on its head. The common sense of the culture now belongs to the people, not the bourgeoisie. Gramsci wins.'

Someone yawned. Someone else nearly slipped under the water and woke with a start.

'Our human and family misery is worse in this country than any other in Europe,' the Conspiracy Theorist went on, unabashed. She clearly had the confidence of the class she was born into. 'Why? Because the Gramsci revolution, the Gramsci Project is further advanced in this country than elsewhere in Europe. We obey rules which now seem common sense to us. We believe in Human Rights! We welcome our enemies – if we're nice to them, surely they'll be nice to us – practically place bombs in their hands. Other countries, where the old common sense is still entrenched, put up a fight, but soon their energy will run out. They too will collapse beneath the weight of their own empathy.'

'Tell me,' said Shimmer. 'Do you see a room somewhere, with Gramsciists plotting secretly, rubbing their hands with glee when the Human Rights Act is passed? Or is it more nebulous, almost metaphorical, the sum of human folly taken a certain turn, people just wanting a better world, legislating to get it? A cock-up, not a conspiracy?'

'I don't know,' admitted the Conspiracy Theorist, suddenly looking insecure, and about thirteen. 'Even I can see it's a bit far-fetched. But how else is one to make sense of it? If it's an actual plot everything falls into place.'

'But why would they do it?' asked Shimmer. 'If you end up with nothing but the rubble of a disintegrated society – then what?'

'Power,' said the Conspiracy Theorist. 'Ultimate power. The joy of being right. The thrill of success. The glory of achievement. Seventy-two virgins. God knows what people want when they destroy. I told you they were demented.'

'They did it to Iraq,' observed the Judge. 'Destroyed a society without worrying too much about what would happen next. They were only foreigners; they don't count. But Reds still lurking under the bed? Here at home? Really, darling! Time your husband came home.'

'You'd better be careful,' said Shimmer, dangerously. 'Your former gender is showing. What are you inferring? All she needs is a good shag?'

'And what has happened in your courts lately?' enquired the Conspiracy Theorist, ignoring the exchange. 'The courts lose power to the state, as do the doctors, as do the elected representatives of the people. MPs are demoted to glorified social workers. The state rules by dictat.'

The Judge said nothing and looked sulky.

'So far the state has been comparatively benign: but now the iron fist begins to show beneath the velvet glove. Prison is the fate of the holocaust denier, of the inefficient recycler, of the mother

who keeps her child at home. Thought crime is more severely punished than the crime itself. A simple mugging gets you three
months, a racially motivated mugging three years. It's your mind
they want, and your mind they've got. Gramsci saw two stages in
the revolutionary struggle: the first a hidden "war of position" as
the bourgeois hegemony was gradually destroyed – a kind of cultural trench warfare – which would, when the time was ripe, give
way to the "war of movement" – a frontal attack, like the storming of the Winter Palace. Well, the time is ripe. See how the prison
gates gape wide.'

'There are plots,' said the Trophy Wife, firmly, 'there are coups:
they do happen. The October Revolution: when the Bolsheviks
came to power. The storming of the Winter Palace in 1917 was no
great popular uprising, as those early Russian propaganda films
portray. Gramsci probably saw them too, and believed them.
People did come running, but because the handful of revolution-
aries who had simply walked in and taken over, without a shot
being fired – other than one blank shell from the cruiser *Aurora* –
were liberating casks of wine from the cellars, and the precious
stuff was running away down the gutters. Or so an Intourist guide
once told me.

'In 1947, according to my creaky old millionaire – but he was a
kind man, a nice man; he could afford to be, I daresay being so
rich, and I made him happy in spite of what his family said – the
Commies were poised to take over in the States. There had been
decades of civil unrest, strikes, violence. The Soviets had taken
half Europe – even Britain had turned socialist – there was a good
chance the US could be tipped. It didn't happen. Senator
McCarthy happened instead: the "witch-hunt", the rooting out of
Communist cells. They got there on the thirty-year anniversary
almost to the day of the Soviet's October Revolution.'

'Everyone knows McCarthy was one of the bad guys,' said the
Vicar's Ex-wife. 'Even me.'

'McCarthy fell foul of the Hollywood propaganda machine,'
said the Trophy Wife.

'Thereafter his name was mud. But the US was saved. That's what the old guy told me. But then he would, wouldn't he.'

'So the Project moved on to Europe, having refined its ideas,' said Shimmer, 'to create a Gramsciist version of the Soviet Union, another expansionist empire, another surveillance state, but nicer to live in, being based on consensus, not coercion.' She seemed quite taken with the idea.

'So far,' said the Conspiracy Theorist, 'but as I say the time is ripe, and the legislation is in place, and the prisons are already filling up.'

Finally I spoke. 'Just because there's a plot against you,' I said, 'doesn't mean the plotters are not gullible and naive. The Project has won in this country and may well do in Europe. But there are things it's too blinkered to notice. The way globalization now laughs all the way to the bank. You don't go to church on Sunday you go to a shopping mall instead. Every high street destroyed suits the supermarkets very well. Every marriage that splits, every home that breaks, means an extra car on the road, an extra bed, an extra dishcloth, extra profit for someone. The people choose to worship Mammon and forget the revolution. The enemy's at the gate, but the Project can't focus. Oh yes, armies! Armies are counter-revolutionary. Islam laughs, China laughs. There are more of them than there are of us. And they've never heard of Gramsci. As I'm sure you wish you hadn't.'

That was enough of that. We were tired. We stumbled off in our separate directions.

18

I lay in bed the next morning and wondered why I had intervened at that point in yesterday's tale: why I worried more about attack from outside than attack from within. It was like worrying a lorry would crash through the walls of your house, when it was far more likely – was it not? – that someone would let the bath overflow and bring a ceiling down. I wondered whether I had been an anxious child, or whether anxiety had only come with the arrival of my children, and decided it was the latter. With every bonding came an increased propensity to free-floating anxiety – a kind of malevolent butterfly that hovered here and hovered there, and settled randomly, feasting on whatever it could find.

I tried to treat an attack as someone had once advised – like an attack of flu – one kept quiet and tried to do as little as possible until it went away. But there was quite an acute episode hovering in the wings, I could tell, brought on no doubt by strange sur-roundings, the difficulty of communication with the outside world, and the consciousness of how very different other women's lives and preoccupations were from one's own. So much choice in a life and where had one ended up? Could one have played one's cards better in some way? Differently?

Mira reported to me that her satellite phone was on the blink. I'd have to face Beverley if I wanted to call out. I said it wasn't exactly that I felt Beverley had to be faced: it was just that she was so good at making one feel useless, a person without inner resources. And for some reason I didn't feel I had many.

'You are so insecure!' she complained. We were sitting in the Orangery, drinking black coffee. Coffee with milk would make one less jumpy but add more calories. 'Yes,' she said, 'exercises in the unlikely. And your husband may not have come home because at this very moment he's fucking the home help in his mother's house in Wichita.'

'Okay,' I said. 'You win.' I was not offended. I had made remarks to her she could very well take offence at and she had not. These kind of hot-house friendships – when would I see her again, or she me? – didn't follow normal rules. We were all of us around the pool doing the same: exposing ourselves both physically and emotionally – a few bikini tops had by now come off – taking short cuts to intimacy.

'At least,' she said, 'you have something to be fearful of losing, like a husband. I don't even have that. I have no husband, partner, children, no dog nor cat, just an elderly mother who doesn't have a clue, not even a proper home. I live in a service flat. I don't collect possessions.'

I bleated some conventional wisdom about how unnecessary partners were in the new age, and what a bind children were, and how desirable freedom was, and how good to have only your own self to please, your own money to earn, spend or save: a sense of achievement that belonged to you and you alone, and spared a thousand domestic irritations daily.

'Good God, and I thought you were panicking,' she said. 'So you'll be really glad when your Julian doesn't come home, and you'll be free at last. Oh yes.' Which put me in my place. 'I roll through life and nothing sticks to me, nothing. I don't know how it happened. I don't know where the time went.'

Her father had been a printer with a local newspaper in the Midlands, her mother in small ads. She'd been Daddy's girl. When she was seventeen the editor had offered her a job as a cub reporter, covering local weddings, school prizes and so on: soon she'd moved on to council meetings and local scandals. Yes, the editor was Alistair, yes, she'd slept with him. It had been her idea. He'd been engaged to the proprietor's daughter. She'd told him she didn't want to interfere with that. She'd always been just someone in his life he slept with every now and then. No, she didn't think she suffered from low self-esteem. There were always lots of men after her, she just wasn't interested. One day he'd get tired of messing around with the others and they'd be together.

He'd married his fiancée, gone to Fleet Street and had taken Mira along with him. She stepped sideways into television: he hadn't liked that. She'd done really well, was soon a familiar face on the small screen. People kept telling her she was wasting her time on Alistair, so she went off to Afghanistan and presently to Iraq as a war journalist. She met warlords and sheiks and ministers but none of them were worth the time of day. While she was away Alistair had got divorced and married for the second time and started a new family. Well, what did she expect? Men only cared about what was under their nose. But he had turned up in person with the money to pay her kidnappers. That time they'd spent four whole nights together in an hotel in Baghdad. Then he went back to the stay-at-home wife. He liked a domestic woman, he told her, but he loved her.

And she was working for him again: in features because this was, frankly, where she got to see him most, but her age was beginning to tell, and the backs of her hands were wrinkled and sometimes she felt lonely, because where was it leading? These days she could reckon on him sleeping with her once or twice a month when she was around, now it was down to every couple of months.

'He says it's because he's not as young as he was,' she said. 'In the past we've always managed one or two nights over Christmas and the New Year, but this year he just sent me up here.'

'You could try hypnotism,' I said. 'I've known people it's worked for. Obesity, smoking, unrequited love – what's the difference, one craving or another.'

'It's not exactly unrequited,' she protested. 'There was this one time he told me he loved me, and I know I'm part of his life. I must be; he is part of mine.'

The trouble with being stuck away up here, she complained,

knowing the world was rolling on outside and you weren't part of it, was that you began to think about yourself. And what you'd done and where your life was going, and if the answer was nothing and nowhere, what did you do?

'Worry about the Chinese blowing up the satellite that runs your phone,' I said and we laughed.

19

The Manicurist's Tale

I'm telling Dorleen's tale for her, since she's quite right, she's not all that good with words. Probably because, unlike the rest of us gathered in those days at Castle Spa, who for the most part have had to struggle for a living, and earn success, and still haven't qualified for our own personal bodyguard, she's never needed to develop the skills of language to get by. All she has to do is *be*, as delicate and exquisite as some rare Lalique piece, which you have to be extremely careful not to break. 'Fucking' may be her favourite adjective, but it is said in so mild a voice it's hard to object. The sweetness of the voice quite overwhelms the meaning, or lack of it, of the words she chooses. And that in itself is the odder since the accent is crude Liverpudlian and slightly nasal – and ought by rights to grate on the sensitive ear.

One's instinct was to look after her. Her eyes were large in proportion to her head, and I am told that's what triggers the caring response in the adult, so the kitten or the puppy doesn't get booted aside, but is stroked and cherished. It's why cats will nurse puppies, and wolves take in human infants, and we give alms to starving children: the larger the eye the more sympathy we feel.

She was very, very pale, almost to the point of being albino: her hair fair, thick and straight, cut short in a bob. She had the whitest and tenderest of skins, pale brows in a perfect arch pencilled in by a steady hand, the hands so small and fragile you could see the tinge of pink as the blood coursed through them. Slender feet, stretching long perfect toes into the bubbles of the Jacuzzi: enough to send any foot fetishist wild with desire. They say if nature's plan for the harmonious being fails at the very last hurdle, it will be with the toes. The big toe of the supermodel will be out of proportion, the little toe of the Greek god down to earth in some way deformed. But Dorleen's were just perfect. She had sprung from her mother's womb the epiphany of symmetry and grace. I thought of my own large hands and legs too short from knee to ankle and thought, *unfair! unfair!*, but when it comes to female looks what was ever fair?

But we were, I hope, nice to her: in the absence of men the edge of competition is dulled, and as I say, she had these wide, blue, young, trusting eyes.

'Go on, Dorleen,' we said. 'Tell us your tale!'

'Nothing much to say,' she said, in the seductive voice. 'Just fucking happened, dinnit.'

We craned: someone turned the bubble-rate down so we could hear better over the foaming waters. She had a sapphire navel stud, ruby earrings and two rings: white diamond and gold, neither on the third finger of her left hand. If she was a wife she wanted nobody to know it. 'And perhaps I'd better not say, come to think of it. Fahd mightn't like it. He can be quite nasty, Fahd, if you're out of fucking order.'

Her bodyguard hovered. Kimberley was to Dorleen as a wedge of hard Parmesan is to a sliver of Brie: it seems almost unreasonable to refer to them both as 'girls' as to call the latter 'cheeses' – the categories are too wide. For the most part Kimberley kept tactfully in the background: you would catch a glimpse of her neat dark trouser suit between the enamelled Doric columns of the room, as the scented steam curled and twisted through the fantasy that was Burges' Egyptian Room, but at Fahd's name she came closer. I didn't know if Kimberley was armed today – bodyguards aren't, necessarily, these days. Hands, legs, knives, and poison are the weapons of choice.

But she struck one as pleasant, well educated and tactful: she would need to be. The bodyguard holds the same ambiguous position in the household as a governess did a century back. Not quite family, not quite servant, expected to eat in the no-man's land somewhere between the banquet hall and the staff dining room: paid to keep an eye on her charges, yet not to make her presence felt. You knew your place, took the money, and shut up.

Dorleen agreed, though reluctantly, to answer questions. She had volunteered to give an account of herself. We had gathered here at her suggestion. In other words we softened her up by making her feel bad. It became apparent that she had no sense of life-narrative: she was not conscious of ever having taken a decision. She was in the still centre of a hurricane, while events swirled around her. 'Just happened, dinnit.'

'How do you come to be here, Dorleen? Tell us!'

'How do you mean?' She looked at us, puzzled, the great blue eyes unblinking. People blink, or so I am told, when they absorb a new idea or sensation; those recently subject to a conversion experience seldom blink at all: they're careful to allow no new idea to come into their heads. Well, that figured, with Dorleen. We had to be cunning. So we played a kind of Twenty Questions. We would get her life story out of her in that number of simple enquiries. As a jury appoints its foreman with very little problem, Mira was appointed adjudicator. The one who asked the most pertinent question would get the prize. There was some argument as to what the prize could be – the kitchens were empty of staff and unlocked: we had dined ourselves silly on Iranian caviar and chopped egg yolk and onions, and it was hard to think of an available treat. Chocolate melted in the steam of the Jacuzzi: we liked our clothes, not other people's clothes. The person who won would have to be content with gaining the respect of the others.

'Who booked you in?'

'Fahd did. Well, anyway, his people.'

'Fahd. That's a Saudi name, isn't it? So he'll be one of those Saudi princes. Is he your boyfriend?'

'No my boyfriend's Morrissey.'

'Morrissey the pop singer?' Hard to believe, but anything is possible. Though wouldn't she break? He so tough and she so tender.

'No, just his mother was a Morrissey fan. But now he's dead. He was so bubbly and full of fun. He was a trainee butcher and had his whole life before him.'

'What happened?'

'I texted him from the police station. He was up north and I was in Heathrow but he'd said he'd always be there for me.'

'Why were you in a police station?'

'I'd bitten this bitch of a customs officer on the hand. She slapped me: what was I fucking meant to do?'

Poor Morrissey, it transpired, had been on his way down from Liverpool to fetch her, and his bike was going at over a hundred on the M5 when he skidded. It was the police's fault; they shouldn't have chased him. She didn't see how anyone could blame her, not that that stopped them. By the time they let her out of customs and she got to the hospital he had breathed his last. The family tried to keep her away from the death bed. But she was the one he loved, she was the one he asked for in the end, the nurse told her. '*Leader of the pack*,' she sang softly in the entrancing voice. '*Leader of the pack.*'

We tried to assimilate this. Where did one begin?

'Why did the customs officer slap you?' That was the Mortgage Broker's question.

'Because I didn't want her to put her hand up my skirt. There was no call to search me. It was out of order. If you ask me she was a lezzie.'

We all felt concern for the various lesbians in the room, thus traduced, but no one seemed to hold it against Dorleen.

'I'd gone through all this crap to get a forged passport,' she said, 'so I could get out of Riyadh, and now this. They stopped me at customs to ask me for proof of purchase. I said I hadn't bought it, I'd been fucking given it. They made me take it off, and I said were they sure, and they said yes, so I took it off and it was all I was wearing. That was when she slapped me.'

'How did you get to Riyadh without a passport in the first place?' That was the Company Director.

She'd never been out of the country before. She didn't know what was meant to happen. She went with Fahd and his people had waved bits of paper about, that was all she knew. She'd ended up in the palace in Riyadh, and she wasn't allowed out without a minder, and nobody bothered to talk in English. There weren't even any proper shops, not what she'd call shops, not like Liverpool. She knew she just had to get out. They told her she couldn't leave because she didn't have a passport. She got a friend to forge one.

'And it worked?'

'It worked fine. Until the bitch phoned the palace and checked it was a gift. I begged and begged her not to because he'd only send his people after me and get me back, like I was a bit of prop-erty gone astray. Which he did.'

'Where did you meet Fahd?' A simple question, but telling.

She'd been selling perfume in Harrods. She was just seventeen. It was agency work. She had to stand there squirting scent at passers-by. It paid less than back home in the frozen chicken factory but it was nicer work. Fahd passed by with his minders, and stopped and looked at her and moved on. Then his people came back and bought a bumper bottle of the scent and invited her to his apartment in Park Lane. She declined. She explained she was true to her boyfriend.

'The Butcher's boy,' they laughed.

It really fucking pissed her off that they'd laughed. She might have said yes if they hadn't. Her grandfather had worked for Dewhurst all his life, and it was a fine, skilled trade. Mind you, times had moved on. Morrissey was training as a veal specialist and when he'd got his meat retailing qualification he hoped to get a job at Harrods and they could be together.

We had the picture now, a young girl of extreme translucence – the result of a poor diet and the lack of light in northern climes, I fear, rather than from association with the angels – slender, fragile, dressed, one envisaged, in palest pink, wandering among glass counters and gold-topped bottles, inhaling the many, many heady fragrances which war for the consumer's attention in these places – *'take me, take me: just a touch of me on wrist or ear and I will change your life, make you truly loved, desirable and sought after, don't worry about the price'* – and the sheik passes by and sees this bloom of pure delight and snatches her up, not robed and on horseback but the same Rudolph Valentino principle – top-of-the-range Armani and a Ferrari instead – and what chance does a girl have?

'What was the scent?' someone shrewdly asked. It seemed perfectly possible she was a fantasist. And Kimberley too. Why not? They could be a dual act. And the mink not real but one from Props. It was so long since anyone had seen a real mink. Who these days can tell the difference?

But quick as a flash she came back. 'Lacoste's "Touch of Pink". For dynamic women. You dress up like the bottle. A grey top and a pale pink skirt with a deeper red hem. I could have done Lacroix but the colours are too strong.'

His people had come back again and again and finally offered to buy her and Morrissey a mews cottage in South Kensington in exchange for a two-hour dinner in a private room in the presence of a chaperone.

'So did he buy you, Dorleen?' That was the Shimmer, the Brain Surgeon. 'Buy the bottle, buy you? As simple as that?'

'Of course it wasn't,' said Dorleen, indignant. 'I'm a good girl.' She was engaged to Morrissey. They'd taken the chastity pledge for purity. There was no going back on that. They'd even exchanged chastity rings: they would wait for each other. No, it was just Fahd had fallen in love with her. She'd come to him in a dream the night before he came across her in Harrods – an angelic vision. She liked him but she didn't fucking fancy him. Morrissey had said it was all right for her to have dinner with him if there was a chaperone and a house at the end of it.

'He did really crap things as well,' Dorleen went on, 'like send diamond necklaces, the kind old ladies wear, and hundreds of red roses which made me sneeze.' She'd sent them all back, but a house, well, that was different. She and Morrissey could walk to work. 'The only thing I ever took from him,' she said, 'was that fur coat, and that was because I wanted my own back. He'd dumped me in the desert naked and thrown the mink out after me. That's the same as giving it to me, don't you think?'

All agreed it certainly was.

'So did you end up in the desert with him?'

'Yes. He flew me out to meet his family in Riyadh.'

'What airline?' asked the Judge. Some of us were still trying to catch her out in an embellishment or a downright lie. Me, I was satisfied. If anything is stranger than fiction it's the truth.

'His own, of course,' she said. 'I suppose that's why I didn't need a passport.'

She hadn't liked the way his staff looked her up and down all the time and smirked. They'd showed her no respect. They took it for granted she was his latest squeeze. She didn't think that was right. There was some kind of trouble on the way, to do with her, she thought, but how could you tell if you didn't speak the language? All she knew was that nine men and she left the ground and eight men and she landed. And she might have counted wrong. Perhaps she had. But anyway after that they kept their eyes to themselves.

'Weren't you frightened?'

'No.' She'd told him about Morrissey and the ring of purity and he'd gone for that in a big way. He called her his vision of delight, his pearl of the West. He was quite old, in his late fifties, probably. He'd had other wives but they'd all run into accidents.

'Why did he dump you in the desert?'

'You know what men are like,' she said vaguely. If they didn't get their way they could turn nasty. She never got to meet his parents, either. That really fucking pissed her off. She'd given him a piece of her mind about that. So she'd just got shut in this palace while he waited for her to change her mind and say she loved him. But she wouldn't say anything that wasn't true. It was wicked to tell lies.

He had other girls anyway, she knew he did. She'd catch a glimpse of them sometimes, being ferried in. But she was kept apart, a great big palace all to herself and no friends, nothing. No telly and she hated reading books.

'How was the palace?'

'Okay as palaces go, all mirrors and glitz. Rather like Harrods cosmetic hall, and all these servants pad-pad-padding about.'

'How long were you there?'

'Three fucking months? I dunno. Couldn't read their stupid calendars, could I.'

But she must have put on four or five pounds at least: they didn't understand about salads: it was all nuts and honey and stuff, on a golden tray so heavy you could break your wrist, and carved so if you spilt anything you couldn't clean it up. Every evening at sundown this guy Amhed would turn up out of nowhere and ask if she'd changed her mind and every evening at sundown she said no.

'You'd think if it was that important to him he'd have come and asked me himself. But no such luck. Or I might have said yes, and saved myself a lot of trouble.'

She said she had a nickel allergy and the chastity ring was making her finger sore so she'd taken it off.

'They have this thing in Saudi about no one saying no to the prince,' Mira put in. 'So they have to send in emissaries.'

'Men are bad enough at home but when they're from abroad they can be fucking weird,' observed Dorleen. She said she hadn't been frightened for herself. If they thought you were a good girl they could be quite respectful: it's when you were a bad girl you had to look out. She'd reckoned it was safer anyway just to go on saying no. She did worry about Morrissey. The longer it went on, the more likely Fahd was to take it into his head to get the opposition out of the way. But there was no way she could warn him. There was no signal for her mobile.

We all knew what that felt like. Bad.

'Was it Ahmed who got you the forged passport and the fare home?' asked the Trophy Wife.

'How did you guess?' asked Dorleen, the great blue eyes only mildly surprised. You could see how a man could get obsessed, just to get some kind of reaction.

'What did you have to do to get it?'

'Not much. Considering.'

In other words – as his Bible Belt supporters said about Clinton – 'Eatin' Ain't Cheatin'. 'Only when it comes to spying they've all got eyes in the backs of their heads, not to mention fucking CCTV cameras everywhere. One day Ahmed didn't come any more, and his penis was served up to me on that stupid golden platter for breakfast.'

There was a short silence and then someone said, 'Are you sure that's what it was?'

She was pretty sure, though she could have imagined it. It didn't look like the Wall's sausages they flew in from Manchester for her Sunday morning fry-up. She'd scraped it down the loo. She felt sick so she went back to bed but she was hauled out and taken to the hospital to have a medical check-up. She knew the other girls had to have them, every week. She'd never been made to, before.

'I must have passed because I was still alive,' she said. But then she'd been driven out into the desert and was tipped out of the Land Cruiser with nothing but my fur coat, hot sand and a few birds hopping about – I reckon they were vultures. I knew Fahd was just punishing me: if he'd wanted me to die he wouldn't have given me the mink, or this one mingy bottle of water. It can get to forty-three by day, but it's really, really cold at night. So I just crawled under a stone, and waited and sure enough in twenty-four hours they came back for me.'

'What was the medical check-up for, Dorleen?'

'Why, to see if I was a virgin.' She thought Ahmed must have gone back and boasted. Men just couldn't resist, could they. She'd quite gone off fry-ups. But she might just be being paranoid.

'Have you had any other scary times, Dorleen?'

'There was the time I was thrown out of a taxi outside Hell's Waiting Room back in Liverpool, late at night with all the dykes on the prowl. That was worse.'

A few raised eyebrows but no protest.

'Why were you thrown out of the taxi?'

'Because the driver was going the long way round, and I took exception. I'm not soft in the head, the way people seem to think.'

So thanks to the wretched Ahmed she now had the passport. Things were hotting up on the Fahd front. She had to get out of there fast, and not just because of the lack of shops. Ahmed's replacement gave her the creeps: he was a eunuch but not a nice-natured one. She would have to give in soon and declare her love for the sheik. And then she'd really be in trouble.

'Why's that?' asked the Judge.

'Because once he'd had me he'd lose interest and girls vanish very easily out there. I only took the fur coat – I thought I deserved that after what I'd been through. I waited until dawn, put a niquab over everything and sneaked out of the palace – Ahmed had shown me a back way out through the gardens – and got a taxi off the street to the airport.'

'But airports won't take cash these days.' It was the Mortgage Broker, pleased to have found her out.

'You can get men to stretch a fucking point if you're me,' she said, and we could believe her. 'If that fat tosser behind the desk finds himself in a fry-up like Ahmed that's his funeral.' And she thought she was home free but then the police murdered Morrissey and she had no job, no work, and no house – that had been all talk – no documents, nothing. And Fahd's people looking for her, to get her back. Kidnap her.

She couldn't even go home to Liverpool. Morrissey's family had it in for her – when he heard she'd gone to Riyadh with Fahd he tried to hang himself but his mother had cut him down in time. It was only a cry for help, but she'd got the blame. Then the accident – she was blamed for that too. They said she'd got the evil eye. She'd been told by a girlfriend there was a contract out on her. Morrissey's mother was like that. Liverpool Irish Mafia. 'Sorrow will come to you in the end.'

'So what did you do, Dorleen?'

'Harrods saved me,' she said, simply. There'd been a poster in the staff room offering free help and advice for personal problems, so she made an appointment with Human Resources. They'd been really helpful.

'Bet they were,' said the Judge. 'They didn't want to be sued for failure to protect.'

They'd taken her back onto the staff and put her in Hair and Beauty on the fifth floor right at the back, doing manicures. Silence fell, except for the soft bubbling of the water around us.

'Nobody's asked a really brilliant question yet,' complained Mira. 'Somebody try to do it in one.'

'So did Fahd give up?' I asked. I thought that should do it. It did.

'Fucking didn't.' He'd sent his people after her. She'd been at Harrods for three months. She looked up from her lady's nail extensions and saw three bearded men in Armani suits running up the circular staircase to the nail salon. She nipped out the back – her lady got smudged, but what can you do? – and hid down in the powder room. There was a digression while Dorleen complained about the hideous nature of this room – painted purple and left unfurnished and a disgrace to the store. But they followed her and burst in even though it said 'Ladies' and she had thought she would be safe. One of them pinned her to the wall, hands above her head, and put his hand in his pocket and she thought it would be a gun and she would be dead. But all he pulled out was a bit of paper. He read from it in English, shouting in her ear. 'The prince says okay, will you marry him?' So I finally said yes, subject to negotiation.

'Men are like that,' said Dorleen. 'They only want what they can't have.' So now she was going to be a princess. She was to be married in Riyadh next month. It was going to be a big do, costing millions, so she was here with Kimberley while Lacroix made her dress. They really went for big white weddings in Saudi. She'd always wanted to make a difference, and now was her chance. Girls' education, all that kind of thing and she liked wearing a thobe, you didn't have to diet. And she knew about her kind of looks – they don't last. By the time you were twenty-five you were looking like your own mother, and frankly, her mother was nothing but a backstreet whore with a heart of ice.

'I've got to make something of myself while I fucking can,' Dorleen said, 'and me, I've always thought a girl's best friend was her virginity. It's worth hanging on to, until the last available moment, and besides, then you can be married in white and not even fucking cheat.'

20

I heard the card with my schedule on it being pushed under the door, and got out of bed reluctantly to see what was in store for me. But the appointments had been struck out and in their place was a handwritten request from Beverley to meet with the other guests at nine o'clock in the Orangery.

We were all there, mildly complaining. Euan had coffee and croissants laid out, and the apricot jam was in jars with big spoons plonked in it, not the usual little glass saucers which suggested frugality, delicacy and self-control. Our routine was upset; we needed comfort; I noticed that more jam was consumed than usual. We asked Euan what the matter was. He shrugged and rolled his eyes.

When Beverley arrived she was thin-lipped and determined and no one liked to protest about their appointments. I did not particularly mind missing holistic yoga, not that I was quite sure what it was. But I was pretty sure it would involve lying on rubber mats on the ground, always somewhat damp from the sweat of those who had gone before, and the obligation at the end of the session to relax completely, close one's eyes and turn the mind to pleasant experiences – lying sunbathing on a tropical beach in the warm sun is a favourite with yoga teachers. I really do try, but I have always hated sunbathing – and my mind pretty soon turns to giant sea monsters crawling over the sand to get me and I have to open my eyes and sit up to make sure they are not, and the session ends with me more agitated than when I began. So I for one was perfectly pleased with Beverley's summons.

She read from a prepared statement, saying in effect that eight out of a clinic staff of twelve had terminated their employment and had left the premises, as had nine out of twelve domestic staff. She, Beverley, had juggled appointments as best she could, but the best she could do was to provide guests with one treatment a day. This being the case if any guest wished to cut short the agreed period of stay they were at liberty to do so, and a full refund would be offered.

We were only three days into our stay, but we had relaxed: we were women who slopped around in towelling gowns, and looked to others for guidance, not at all the same as the fast-thinking, quick decision-makers who had arrived.

Eventually the Judge said, 'But why have they left? Is it this Sumatra flu? Is there something we don't know?'

At this Kimberley moved a little closer to the Manicurist, scenting danger. She would stand between her charge and a flu virus if she could, risking death, as she would stand between her and a hired assassin. I felt a chill run up my spine.

'What's Sumatra flu?' someone asked, and someone else replied, 'It's this nasty bug that's going round.'

'Could we keep to the point, please?' asked Beverley. 'How many of you will be staying?'

We all stared at her. She clearly hoped there would be a mass breakout of guests as well as staff.

'I'm staying,' I said. 'Though I'll ask for a rebate. Shouldn't Lady Caroline be here saying this to us herself? It seems unfair to leave it to you.'

There was a murmur of assent from the group.

'Lady Caroline has been unavoidably detained,' said Beverley. She was very pink in the face, and biting her lip. It would be sore later on. 'The helicopter has had to go in for repairs.'

There was some laughter at this.

'And the dog ate her homework,' said someone.

'It's too bad,' said the Trophy Wife. 'I was depending on leaving this place ready for the fray. I really deserved something good to happen to me.'

'I can do your fucking nails and face and stuff,' said the Manicurist. 'I know I'm not bright, compared to you lot, but I have got a diploma in beauty treatment.'

'That's so nice of you,' said the Trophy Wife, genuinely touched. 'It means a lot to me. I'm really happy here.'

'The chef's gone,' said Beverley, frustrated in a very clear ambition to be rid of us all. 'There'll only be cold food.'

'I can cook,' said the one who turned out to be a Vicar's Ex-wife, 'a lot better than whoever's been doing it. That lobster bisque we had on Christmas Eve – you couldn't taste it for the dill. It was a travesty.'

'Don't think any of you are going to get refunds,' said Beverley. 'You aren't. If I've had to work for nothing for the last three months what makes you think you'll be treated any better than me?'

There were clucks of sympathy and disapproval from round the room, and Beverley, emboldened, told us she'd already had to dip into the money she'd put aside for her fare home to New Zealand. She'd hoped to go back in March, now she'd be lucky if she made it by July. She couldn't wait. People back home didn't cheat you, bilk you or have their helicopters repossessed so they couldn't come over with the cash they'd promised you, week after week, because you were working without a visa and couldn't complain.

'So that's why the staff have walked out,' said the Mortgage Broker. 'They haven't been paid.'

'That's it,' said Beverley, flatly.

We took a little while to absorb this.

'The moment of praxis,' said the Conspiracy Theorist. 'When theory turns into practice. When the working class has had enough, the foreman says down tools, and everyone walks out.' She was shushed by the others.

Beverley said she had done what she could, tried to keep up appearances, she so hated it when things were messy, and everyone always blamed her when things went wrong, and could she have a list as soon as possible of those who were going to stay and those who weren't. She had to stay anyway because she had nowhere else to go.

'I don't have anywhere else either,' I said, seized by self-pity, and then told myself it must be worse for many of the others in the Orangery at that moment. At least I had a family, that bulwark against loneliness. You make plans and sure, plans fell through. Ceilings fell, husbands went missing on feeble excuses, your family was relieved not to have a family Christmas – but at least back in November I hadn't had to start worrying about where I was going for Christmas.

Beverley went back to her eyrie. The consensus round the room was that we would stay. One treatment a day would suffice – might even be a welcome. Many said they had work to get on with, reports to write: internet access had become patchy – but there was always a backlog to catch up with. They liked the friendly atmosphere and they looked forward to the next tale.

But the Jacuzzi Narratives, as Mira called them, had upset some. There were dissenters. Some declared they wished the Weather Girl's story had not been told at all. The Conspiracy Theorist's account had bored as many as it had fascinated others. Romantics among us had been a little shaken by the Manicurist and her account of the run-up to the biggest wedding of the desert season, though at least her need to have Kimberley standing by was made clear. The dissenters won. It was agreed we were storied-out for the day and what we needed now was food. Supper. The narratives would be resumed tomorrow. In the meanwhile we would eat. Few kept to their decision to go to their rooms and work.

Supper? Ah, but there was no chef. Mira and I went into the kitchens to forage. We found potatoes in good condition and set them on trays in the ovens to bake. Surely that would do us, with salad and grated cheese? There were great wheels of cheddar, neatly covered in cheesecloth, on marble slabs in one of the pantries. Salad in midwinter would be difficult to organize, Beverley being so against the air-mile footprints of out-of-season greenery. The more we thought about it the more we agreed we would certainly require a rebate, if only from the liquidators, if what Beverley claimed was true: Castle Spa was going bankrupt.

We considered our entitlements and upped our expectations. Someone found jars of real caviar and spooned it out lavishly onto oatcakes. Someone else found the key to the cupboard where the more expensive wine was stored. The older it was, the sooner we would drink it. The more sombre of us stuck to baked pota- toes and cheese. The Vicar's Ex-wife made sausage and mash and the judge found tomato sauce in the stores.

Kimberley heaved trestle tables and chairs into one of the larger pantries: the great hall and the Orangery, especially with the green mould now growing in its windows, could be intimidating. This was more like the kitchen eating of most of our childhoods. Beverley kept out of our way. Another two of the beauticians failed to turn up. Euan the young work-experience porter devel- oped a cough and a sniffle and I of course thought at once of Sumatra flu, and dismissed the thought. I was projecting my own insecurities. I did not take advantage of Mira's offer to let me use her satellite phone. It was working again: whatever trouble there had been in the heavens had sorted itself out. I was not going to chase Julian. I had my dignity. If he couldn't think of a way to get through to me – that was his misfortune. I didn't call Alec or any of the children, for the same kind of hurt-pride reason.

Mira too was upset. She had broken her rule and called Alistair at home to wish him seasonal greetings.

'You could have called on Christmas Day or even Boxing Day and got away with it,' I said. 'But today! He won't like that.'

'He didn't,' said Mira. 'He said to stop persecuting him.'

'The bastard,' I said.

'He was drunk,' she said, by way of excuse.

Down in the kitchens the cat's saucer sat on a newspaper dated Christmas Eve. I read upside down that talks at the TGWU had broken down. That was why Lady Caroline had had to use the helicopter. And another thing: it had been a great year for scented Xmas candles – shipped in by the million from China, sold mostly through garages and over the internet, but a small proportion were now reckoned to give off dangerously soporific fumes. Fortunately Health and Safety had been alerted in time and the product withdrawn.

And this triggered off another burst of anxiety. You lit a candle and it suffocated you? Supposing at this very moment deadly candles were guttering over my grandchildren's tea tables? I mentioned it to the Vicar's Ex-wife and she said I was being over-fearful, and I must look at things statistically. And I said yes, normally I did. But three years back on Boxing Day there was tidal wave in the Pacific, and Alec and his family were in Sri Lanka, I'd told myself the chances of them being involved was minuscule – and they had had to run for their lives. The Vicar's Ex-wife said then I was bound to be extra-nervous at this time of the year, and perhaps I was still suffering from post-traumatic stress disorder. I should try for an extra Reiki massage if the girl hadn't done a bunk.

Later I heard she'd trudged all the way up to the east wing to the office to get Beverley to arrange an extra Reiki session for me. And Beverley had obliged. I felt really warmed and cheered. I was amongst friends.

I changed the paper under the Spa cat's saucer, and threw it away. It was encrusted with sour milk and dried-up cat food. That was probably what had made me suddenly shivery: just the horror of it. The real horror, of course, and I would have to face it sooner or later, was what had happened to Eleanor and Belinda, which I had so carefully and successfully put from my mind. Knives cutting into flesh. Blood everywhere. Evil had brushed by me, leathery devil's wings flapped by much too near, and left all kinds of nasty things stirring in their wake. Fears and fancies heaving in the mud: why not? There were real things to be fearful of: nasty imaginings that came true. I tried to make my mind turn to it, though still it shied away.

I could smell joss sticks, a heavy, sweet fragrance. The Judge again? But this was not the Jacuzzi smell, which always had a tang of chlorine, it was none of the scents of Castle Spa: it came from somewhere else. I tried again. I must hold them in my mind. An acquaintance, Eleanor: a colleague, Belinda, once alive, now dead. Simply gone. So hard to accept I had simply not tried. And Nisha came to mind, poor mad Nisha, whom I'd never met, with her heavy, glossy hair which Pauline struggled so to dry. I tried to hold them all in my mind, as you do in prayer: enclose them, enfold them, mourn them. The smell of joss sticks grew stronger. And then I thought I heard Belinda's voice. *'Sorry about the phone call, Phoebe. You were right. I should have listened.'* And then another voice – Eleanor's? *'You never liked me, Phoebe, but then I wasn't very likeable. It's all right now. It's evened out with Belinda, we're friends. It all goes on.'* And then a little laugh – Nisha's? – and a new voice. *'Nothing ever stops.'* And then silence: just the wind getting up, and the smell was gone. Look, I am a novelist. It can be hard for me to tell the difference between the real and what I think is real. But I'll swear I heard them, and was comforted.

It is the living one should be sorry for, not the dead – Billy, Sam Klines. There is no such thing as death, a blanking-out, oblivion, no such luck, just more of the same. It's not too bad: probably just nearer the knuckle of existence. Who is to say where justice lay, or how they sorted it out, or what had led to disaster in other frames of experience?

And the dead do come visiting: that I've always known. They brush by dearest and nearest, touch them with their spirit, make their peace. After funerals you have to wait patiently: it can be hours, days, months – you never know what order of precedence you are. Then suddenly this clarity of understanding. Here I am, here I am, goodbye. All we owe to the dead is that we should enjoy our lives. But this had been something different. I'm sure they don't usually do the rounds in threes. But all you owe to the dead is that you should enjoy your life.

A sudden change in the weather can be disturbing, make you receptive to all kinds of things one usually prefers to ignore. At least and at last it felt like a proper winter. And we were warm and snug inside, and friendship abounded. No worries, as Beverley would say.

21

The next day few ladies surfaced before midday. We were here for a rest and rest we would have. We compared notes. Beverley had left our day's programmes under our doors as usual – but in neat handwriting, not the usual computer script – and beauty treatments were down to one a day, in some cases down to one every two days. She warned that the rail strike was spreading and those who hoped to travel by train would be well advised to make early arrangements for their return. Car drivers might find petrol in short supply, since the tanker drivers were threatening to come out in support of the TGWU. We were asked to make sure that all culinary surfaces were wiped clean before lights out since there had been a problem with rats in the past. That made us laugh.

'She just wants us to go,' said the Company Director. She said she wasn't surprised. Had we realized Beverley had been going round making the beds and cleaning the rooms with Hoover and scourer, there being only one maid left on duty? The fewer of us there were, the easier her life would be. We agreed Beverley had a well-developed superego, and were grateful to her for that. She had not just walked out and left us in the lurch, but stayed, like the captain on the bridge of a sinking ship, albeit complaining the whole. All the same, she should loosen up.

The Judge, who, as well as Mira, turned out to have a satellite phone, said she'd rung round various spas and found them either closed for the season or fully booked. She personally would just enjoy the rest, and go home at the time arranged. A few good nights' sleep would work better than any number of facials, and the diversion of stories, and a release from DVD or TV viewing, might be better for bags under the eyes than cucumber slices or whatever herbages they had been using on hers.

The Trophy Wife said now her hair was done and she'd had a manicure and a pedicure, and fitted in a few exfoliant skin treatments she was feeling a lot better about herself. Now all she needed was to meet a millionaire – but she wasn't likely to meet one before the holidays were over and she too was staying put. She really liked food being freely available. If you were hungry all you had to do was open one of the great fridges and choose.

The Judge asked if anyone wanted to use her phone and I said yes, I did. She might not stay in the room while I spoke, as Mira did. I did not want to be upbraided for paranoia, even though I'd started it, telling her she was too sensitive, she was imagining things. Nor did I want to use Beverley's phone and be found fault with. The Judge at least tactfully left the room while I talked, having first taken the trouble to explain to me how it worked.

So I ended up calling Alec and asked him if he had seen the piece about the Chinese candles, and he said yes he had, and I must try not to be an anxious mother because that made for jumpy children. I said I had never known less jumpy children than the ones I had borne, including him: on the contrary, they seemed to think themselves inviolable from any blows of fate. I refrained from mentioning the Sri Lanka holiday. I asked instead if he had heard from his father. He said he had, hadn't I? He was surprised at that. But there had been a series of ice-storms in Kansas: communications came and went. He'd been cut off in the middle of the call himself. But Dad was fine, Gran was mending fast, and your old friend Jenny had turned up to help with the nursing – remember Jenny: she was always very fond of Gran as he, Alec, remembered from when he was little. We exchanged pleasantries, I said I was using someone else's phone, asked him to send on love to his siblings, and put down the phone.

The Judge came in and asked me if I was all right. I said I was fine. She said I looked rather pale, did I want to talk about it, she had a feeling something was bothering me. I said I wasn't in the mood for sharing, some other time perhaps, and went into my room and sat down on the bed and stared into space.

I remembered Jenny very well. Just because you are paranoiac doesn't mean there isn't a plot against you.

And then it was time for the next tale, and I tried to put my troubles aside. We were joined that evening by the psychoanalyst, Linley Banes, part of a group who were cycling all the way up from Land's End to raise money for a prison charity. It had taken two weeks: the rest of the party – Dykes Behind Bars – was continuing on up to John o' Groats. We were suprised by her late arrival. Rumour was that she had a special relationship with Beverley. She was surprised to find the Spa bereft of proper staff and in the hands of a manic group of storytellers, and was understandably slightly put out – who wouldn't be, who had cycled an average of fifty-five miles a day for a fortnight through winter weather. She had been looking forward to steam baths, massages and yoga. But she soon recovered her good temper, after bread and cheese washed down by whisky, and joined us round the Jacuzzi. Hers was the next tale.

Linley was good-looking and vigorous, with an overall masculine air – as if there had once been some kind of internal gender conflict and testosterone had won hands down, but had now learned to live at peace with oestrogen. It was certainly not the exquisite beauty of the transgendered, but something solider and longer-lasting, more socially acceptable. She had a high colour, as one would expect in someone who had just spent days cycling through a wintry landscape. Her arms and legs seemed too long for her body, as if her trunk was an afterthought, and her neck was sinewy. Yet she hung together pretty well, in an athletic kind of way: strong, regular features and a long jaw which made her seem gloomy. When she smiled, her face lit into loveliness, and she was almost jolly. She did not quite belong to the rest of us round the pool – but perhaps that is always the fate of latecomers: they are forgiven, yet must always stay slightly apart. Her hair was black, short, plentiful and curly: uncontrollable, and her eyes dark and very bright, and the thick, dark brows above them un-plucked. She wore a black one-piece swimming costume, with the air of one who ran through Marks & Spencer on her way to an appointment and grabbed the first one she came across. She needed an AA-cup or at best an A, and wore a C.

Those who deal with the mind sciences do not usually excel at sport: it's as if the intensity and complexity of their study drains them of physical energy. If they enjoy any physical sport it is, I have noticed, usually tennis: perhaps the batting two and fro of the ball is like the batting to and fro of ideas. How about this, then, how about that? I must be right, so you can be wrong. Love all. Well, possibly. But it seemed Linley just loved the challenge of wet wind in her face, wet rain in her hair and burgeoning calf muscles – or perhaps, who is to say, she was in love with one of the members of the Dykes Behind Bars brigade. I have met one or two sailing women in my time who hate the sea, but love the sailor.

22

The Psychoanalyst's Tale

'I do a lot of work in prisons,' said Linley. 'I get called in to assess the mental state of prisoners on remand. I must tell you about a woman I saw just before I came up here.'

'We rather hoped,' said the Judge, 'that you would tell us about yourself. I cannot quite decide whether to be a lesbian or a heterosexual woman, and you might be able to give me a few pointers.'

'It is not a matter of decision,' said Linley, 'but of what is. Unless you want to claim to be a bisexual, which is a cop out.' She spoke a little briskly, I thought, and I remembered that neither true lesbians nor gays of intellectual bent think well of women who start out as men and make the switch. It seems like cheating. The struggle for social acceptance is too new, has claimed too many victims on the way, for the search for gender authenticity to be seen as more than a luxury. People may sneer, and stare, and not like to see you kissing – but they don't slam you in prison or tear off your balls. Drag is one thing, drag is witty, but the snipping and rearranging of reproductive assets is neither here nor there. The Judge decided not to pursue the matter and studied her pretty pink toes instead.

'I was talking to a good mother,' said Linley, 'so good a mother indeed that bad mothering seemed a lesser sin than murder. She had killed her husband, father of her two children. The law had caught up with her. I did not think she would be a risk to the general public, only to any man rash enough to have children by her. Some women are like this: they seek out men to father their children, and then get rid of them as soon as possible, keeping only the marital home, and child support. This seems to them perfectly reasonable. They have a low sex drive – or satisfy it with casual lovers, and avoid intimacy from the beginning. But they do not usually go as far as actually killing the father.'

'If a man sexually abused my children,' said the Manicurist, 'I'd kill him.'

'There was no question of sexual abuse,' said the Psychoanalyst. 'Nothing so simple or likely. No, in his own view, and that of society the poor man had done nothing wrong.'

'Then why?'

'Who is to say what goes on in the head of a murderess?' interjected the Judge. '"Why?" in criminal cases, is a question often asked, in the hope that there'll be a decent "because" to follow. But in my experience there is seldom a single, simple, motive to any act, just an accumulation of moods, actions and unintended consequences. Intention is actually rare. Most of those who plead "guilty" in my court seldom have any clear understanding of the word, having little grasp of the abstract. They say the word their lawyer tells them to say, if they can remember it for five seconds. But one has to go through the rituals.'

'That is very interesting,' said the Psychoanalyst, who was not easily going to forgive the Judge her gender shilly-shallying. 'Though one wishes you had more respect for the general public.' The Judge had sat down next to her, perhaps rather too close for her comfort. 'But I can assure you this murderess was intellectually competent. It was her emotional state I was interested in.'

'Personally I seldom ask for psychiatric reports,' said the Judge. 'I always think one can tell what people are just by looking at them.'

'Like whether they're male or female? And I suppose you can tell whether someone's gay just by looking at them?'

'Certainly I can,' said the Judge, 'I've had enough experience.'

'So easy to commit a murder,' said the Company Director, in a very quiet voice. Years spent bringing up a family had trained her in the arts of diplomacy. 'But so upsetting to friends and family. So why did she murder him? Do get on with the story.'

Linley huffed and puffed a little before continuing. The Judge gazed at her with open admiration.

'She told me her name was Patsy – just an ordinary name, she said, for a very ordinary person, a stay-at-home wife and mother. She wore her own clothes, not prison gear, as persons on remand do – actually very pleasant and discreet: a pleated skirt and a pink blouse with a tiny floral pattern buttoned at the wrist and high at the neck. Her hair was freshly washed and neat, and her nails clean and clipped short. Even simply sitting neatly as she was, on a prison-issue chair, she managed to give the impression of someone who would at any minute be up and busy, bustling about improving the world. She would have viewed askance, I am sure, the very idea of a group of women sitting idly around in a Jacuzzi swapping stories, and some of them gender switchers, too. Did they have nothing better to do? What about the germs? Surely they would multiply in the damp, warm air? Patsy's house, I had no doubt, would smell of air freshener and disinfectant.

'She could be quite aggressive, but I felt this was in defense of her children. She did not like the fact that I was a woman without them. "Only a mother, surely," she said, "can understand a mother."

'She said she saw no point in seeing me. She was not mad; it was the law who was mad. It was damaging to her children and demeaning for her that she should be subjected to psychiatric reports. Supposing her children found out and thought she was insane? The judge should have sent some properly qualified psychiatrist, not some proponent of the talking cure. People were too self-involved. They should pull themselves together. She apologized for the room – it was airless, and smelt of cabbage and old urine. She had asked for broom, soap, scrubbing brush, hot water and disinfectant to clean it out before she received visitors, but these had been denied her. She had been told to leave it to the cleaners, but the cleaners, from the look of them, and from the state of the place, had no idea that you were meant to sweep a room out before you swilled water over the floor and went away.

'"At least," she said, "they've allowed me to keep my own clothes. I don't have to wear their nasty dingy dresses. There isn't an iron available but I keep my skirt beneath my mattress at night, so the pleats stay in. I like to be smart. It's so important to set an example to the children, don't you think? But I don't suppose you know much about that. Too busy following a glittering career to be able to make way for children."

'Which to her mind was an insult, but to mine was the opposite. The notion that it would be prudent to keep on my good side if she wanted a favour did not occur to her. She told me again how important it was to stress to the judge that she was in her right mind when she eliminated him. It would do Janet and Harvey no good at all to believe their mother was insane, too great a burden for them to bear. They were already having to cope with the loss of their father and it was Janet's birthday the next day – she was going to be eight – and she would be unhappy enough that for the first occasion ever she would not have her mother to say "happy birthday, darling" when she woke. She might even begin to doubt what she had been told – that her mother had gone on holiday in Greece to recover from her father's death.'

'But that's crazy,' said the Mortgage Broker. 'I thought you were meant to tell children the truth.'

'That was my problem,' said the Psychoanalyst, 'was she crazy or wasn't she? Telling lies to get out of trouble may not be sensible, but it is not crazy. She said she meant to talk things through with the children as soon as she got out of prison, as soon as the silly and unnecessary fuss came to an end. The children were staying with her deceased husband's parents, and they were not as child-centred as she would like, though not bad for people of an older generation. They certainly had enough sense not to let Janet see the newspapers, and Harvey wasn't reading yet – possibly due to the shock of his father's death. An unexpected blessing.

'"*Crime Maternel* must be recognized in this country," she said.

"To kill for one's children is no crime: it is something for which a mother should be honoured. I did what it was my duty to do," she said. "I chose my children's interests over my husband's. Their lives are just beginning: the young, in matters of life and death, take precedence over the old. As soon as I'm acquitted we can get back to some kind of normality. It may mean moving house and changing names and schools afterwards, of course, but that is nothing to the avoidance of trauma."

'I refrained from saying that her children might already be quite traumatized, if their mother was accused of killing their father in cold blood, and asked her to give me the broad strokes of her life. She had been molested as a child by her father, she said, and her mother stood by and let it happen, but incest was surely such a regular occurrence in families it should be seen as normality, and not as it so often was these days, as an excuse for all sorts of bad behaviour. She was fostered when she was twelve by a kind and pleasant family against whom she had no complaints. She knew there was good as well as evil in the world. She had always wanted to have children and give them a perfect life. What could be more important in the world than this? She trained as a nurse and did well in her chosen profession, but always with the thought of her future role as a mother in mind. Men liked her, and several asked her to marry them.'

'Nurses are always very popular with men,' observed Shimmer, 'as we know.'

'Please don't interrupt,' said the Psychoanalyst. 'In my profession I am accustomed to just sitting and listening, and refraining from comment, which is hard enough, but now I am actually allowed to tell a story I wish you would just let me get on with it.'

'Sorry,' said Shimmer.

'In brief,' said the Psychoanalyst, 'each time she decided the man involved would not make a good enough father. Her standards were high. He would have to be loving, kind, gentle, patient, intelligent, sensitive to the children's needs, and able to provide the proper male authority within the family group.'

'You wouldn't get all that in the one man,' said the Judge. 'Believe me, I know men. She could have got the loving to sensitive range in some new man type, I suppose, but then she'd have had to forgo the male authority. She'd have done better to have a female partner and gone for a surrogacy.'

'Please!' said the Psychoanalyst, provoked, jabbing the Judge savagely in the ribs with her elbow, so she squealed and shut up. Cycling had given the Psychoanalyst good strong elbows, and I could see that the pain of the blow was bringing out the masochist in the Judge. The squeal was positively flirtatious: the Judge's admiration positively soppy. I found myself longing for the days when men were men and women were women and had segregated Jacuzzis.

'Patsy could settle, even happily, for less than perfection herself, but not for her unborn children. Then finally she met Peter, on an internet-dating site, asyetunborn.com. He fulfilled all her requirements, and she met his. She was looking for the perfect father, he for the perfect mother. They married and agreed to wait a year before starting a family so the children would be born into a settled and secure domestic framework. The year had been surprisingly happy. Peter had had much the same personal history as she, and both had felt that sex was not for them other than for the procreation of children. Now they discovered otherwise. The year was spent in an erotic haze. Then, according to plan, she became pregnant with Janet, and of course after she was born she lost interest in sex. "She could only sleep if she was in bed with us," Patsy told me, "and then only if she was at the breast, and I got an ulcer and you know how it is with small babies." I said I didn't, because I had no children. "You poor thing," she said. "You poor thing! Let me just say that Janet was a sensitive baby and cried a lot, and then when Harvey came along he turned out to be hyperactive and I'm sorry to say Peter's views on childrearing began to change: they simply did not coincide with mine. I would remove salt, sugar and wheat from their diets: Peter would advocate Ritalin. It was as bad as that."

'Peter was teaching and in Patsy's view beginning to spend far too much time away from home. She realized he had obligations to his pupils but surely he had greater obligations to his own children. Patsy insisted that he always be home for bath time: it was important that the little ones had the reassurance that a rock-solid routine provides. But sometimes he would fail to turn up. He'd call to say he had to supervise after-school detention, or some such excuse. Then she had to watch their little faces fall. Splashing about in the water, so important to the development of their tactile responses, just wasn't the same without their daddy.

'Peter and Patsy began to quarrel. The atmosphere in the house became tense, and Janet and Harvey began to look pale. Peter said that was because it was the middle of winter, but Patsy knew it was something deeper than that. The children were picking up vibes, and Peter was responsible.

'I asked her to go into the mechanisms of their quarrels and she replied thus: "Well, he'd say terrible, unkind things to me. Such as 'why do you always ask those kids questions? Why do you say, "Are you sleepy? Would you like to go in your cot?" Why don't you say "You feel so sleepy, darling. Now I'm putting you in your cot."' I'd reply 'Because I'm developing consciousness of self. Because children are not there for parents' convenience, to be shut up. Because the child knows how it feels: it is up to the parent who decipher those feelings and act upon them. I don't tell my child it's hungry: I require it to give me an accurate description of what is in its head. That way it learns who it is. And you should be doing the same.'

'"But by that time he'd have walked out of the room. And then the whole sex thing was such an embarrassment: after the children I didn't have orgasms: supposing they needed me and I wasn't paying attention? But he'd insist, and then he'd finish without me and that is unforgivable in a man, isn't it? So we stopped altogether. If we were out he'd shove ice-lollies in their mouths and they were already beginning to be addicted to sweet things. Janet actually shop-lifted a bag of sugar from the supermarket and emptied it out between the aisles and I found them both on the floor licking it up with their tongues. Sheer poison! Please don't think he was a bad father, he wasn't. He loved Janet and Harvey almost immoderately, and they loved him, which was why I had to do what I did."

'Try as she could to be brave and bright for the sake of the children she had failed. They would see her red-eyed and depressed, and hear their father shouting. Her trusted book on childcare explained that it was very damaging to overhear their parents rowing. For the children's sake she had to act. They would have to part. Between them, they would have to provide two loving and caring environments between which Janet and Harvey would travel, since they were incapable of making one. "Now I knew I would do my part in this, but I was not convinced Peter would do his. Already he was seeing another woman – a junk-food addict whose idea of an afternoon out with the children was not a museum or a gallery but to go to McDonald's on the way to the zoo – can you imagine – a zoo? – the torment of those poor wild caged animals. And Janet and Harvey were actually encouraged to gawp and throw peanuts."

'She said she was well aware that it was best for children to see their parents happy, and Peter's sex drive was such, apparently, that he could only be happy when it was more or less satisfied. She had no grudge whatsoever against his girlfriends, one or all of them; it was most definitely not a *crime passionnel*, but a *crime maternel*. "An act committed for the sake of the children which involved the death and/or disenabling of an incompetent and/or damaging parent."

'"It wasn't Peter's fault that he was what he was," she insisted. "Blame God if you must, blame anyone, for creating parents and children whose emotional needs overlap but do not coincide. But there it was. I could see no way out but the way I took. Statistics show that a paternal death has a less damaging effect on the children than a divorce, so long as the family home is maintained and family income does not fall. So he had to die."

'And this, so far as I can tell, and I believe she was telling the truth, is how it happened—'

'This is great,' interjected the Screenwriter. 'Let me take over. This is what I do for a living.' The Screenwriter, a lanky young woman with an agitated and impulsive manner, had not so far made an appearance round the pool. She had kept very much to her room; claiming she was only at Castle Spa because she had a script to finish: there were far too many stories in her head already to be able to cope with any more. But she had turned up for the occasional meal, and perhaps rather rashly, for we could see how it did indeed set her off, had turned up to listen to the Psychoanalyst's tale. Now she wanted nothing better than a re-write.

'How did she do it? Poison, gas, gunshot? Witchcraft? Let me guess. She poisoned him. Very Borgia, very female.'

'Yes she did,' said the Psychoanalyst, crossly. 'You are spoiling my story.'

'No I'm not,' said the Screenwriter. 'I don't want a credit. I am merely improving and amplifying yours. Making motivation clear, developing character and atmosphere. All she's been doing so far is sitting in a room talking, buttoned up to the neck. We've got to get out and about.'

'But I was in a room just talking to her. That was what happened. It's a true story.'

'Real life makes bad art,' said the Screenwriter. 'Peter's girl-friend needs developing. Just a mention so far. What does she look like? Is she sexy? Does she want him to marry her?'

'I've no idea,' said the Psychoanalyst. 'I can only go by what I've been told.'

'That's the difference between you and me,' said the Screenwriter. 'The trick is to invent, embellish, and embroider. So what sort of poison?'

'Mushroom,' said the Psychoanalyst. 'Death Cap.'

'Excellent,' said the Screenwriter. 'That takes us out of doors. Can't you see the scene? Autumn, warm and moist, oak trees, horses grazing, green fields, mushrooming weather, blustery, the family party, early morning. Dark clouds scudding in a blue sky. The mistress has come along too. We're on her side: she's nice, and cute, and loves the children. We know because she takes them to McDonald's. Renée Zelwegger plays her. Whereas Patsy is cold and calculating: Nicole Kidman, obviously: remember that early film of hers in which she's a weather girl who murders her husband? We need an earlier scene of course, in which Nicole persuades her husband to up the insurance. She seduces him: he stumbles from the bed to sit by the children's bedside – his mobile goes: it's Renée, she just has to tell him how much she loves him – she's outside the house and he goes down to her, and there's outdoor sex: they probably live on a beach so there's waves pounding on white sand – no, that's not good with mushrooms: I guess this is much more a Lady Chatterley sort of thing—'

'For fuck's sake,' said the Judge. 'Just let her get on.'

The Psychoanalyst looked gratefully at the Judge, and the Judge allowed a hand to stray towards her knee. She did not object.

'Patsy insured Peter's life,' the Psychoanalyst continued, 'and he and Patsy and his girlfriend and the children went on a country walk and they picked mushrooms, including a Death Cap, which she spied under a hedge.'

'Death Caps are very rare,' said the Mortgage Broker. 'I'm surprised by that.'

'She describes what she did as opportunistic. She knew he had to die, and then when they were out mushrooming early one morning she just happened to see the Death Cap growing under a hedge. They're almost indistinguishable from ordinary mushrooms except they grow under hedges and they have pink gills not brown. So she picks it along with the others and asks the girlfriend to join them for dinner. She prepares a beef casserole, using the Death Cap. She didn't like handling the meat – she is a vegetarian, as are the children: not that I imagine they'd have had much say in the matter – but put up with it for their sake.'

'I'm a vegetarian,' put in the Manicurist. 'I can't really feel sorry when carnivores die because they've been eating dead animals.'

'He died because he'd eaten a vegetable,' the Company Director pointed out, and a discussion arose as to whether a Death Cap was a vegetable or a fungus.

When the discussion had died down the Psychoanalyst continued.

'Patsy told me she usually asked Peter to keep his disgusting carnivorous habit out of the house: to her it was worse than smoking. So he had been surprised when she offered to make him and Alison a beef stew with dumplings, but when told it was a peace offering, and that she was prepared to do it for his sake, he had been grateful and seen it as a sign of their reconciliation. "Why should he not die happy?" Patsy asked me. "I wished him no ill. I just wished him dead." Her real purpose, of course, was to make sure that only he and Alison ate the meat stew. Patsy had made the ordinary mushrooms into a vegetable stew with soya, nuts, parsnips and potatoes for herself and the children, healthy, well balanced and nourishing, and they all sat down and ate together, and it did occur to Patsy as she watched her husband and his mistress eating with so much pleasure, that perhaps the situation could have been avoided. But then Alison had offered Janet a spoonful of the meat stew – which of course Janet, being loyal to her mother, had refused – saying a little first-class protein never did anyone any harm – so Patsy knew she had done the right thing. The woman was without principle: and Peter colluded with her. When Patsy first approached asyetunborn.com she should have been more careful and ticked the "definitely yes" box when it came to vegetarianism, not the "neutral" one in the middle. She hadn't wanted to cut down on her chances, but she should have stood out more for her principles. She only had herself to blame.

'The Death Cap proved as fatal as the books said. What seems like food poisoning for three or four days: then ten days later the liver fails and you die. She had done everything she could, got the pair into hospital as soon as the vomiting started, and set a trail running back to the butcher's from which she had bought the beef: a firm notorious for its scant regard for the food hygiene regulations, and had succeeded in getting it closed down, an unexpected bonus. After three days Peter and Alison had been sent home, only to collapse a week later. She had managed it so the children didn't get to see anything nasty. When tests showed that *amanita phalloides* poisoning had caused the deaths the authorities had questioned her further about the beef stew, and she'd explained she'd sliced one of the mushrooms straight into it and the others into the vegetarian mix. At no time had she uttered a single lie. So why they brought in the police and arrested her she could not think – though perhaps the recent million-pound life insurance had raised someone's suspicions. But surely they realized that she needed money to support the children in the absence of a husband? She was now a single person family and needed all the help the state could offer. It was outrageous that a mother should be separated from her children on account of a *crime maternel*. The meeting ended abruptly. She said she needed to go now to make the weekly permitted phone call to her children, and left, pink with indignation at the folly of the world, leaving me to make my report.'

'What did the report say?' I asked. 'Was she mad or was she not? She certainly showed no sign of remorse. Isn't that typical of a psychopath?'

'It took me some time to decide,' said the Psychoanalyst. 'What tipped the balance was the name of the mushroom. But I would say this: *amanita* is the genus of mushroom; *phalloides* its description. It means penis shaped. I think we can take it sexual jealousy was the motive, that this was indeed *un crime passionnel*, not *un crime maternel*. She had worked out an ingenious and all but convincing defence, in the hope that she'd get a light sentence, or even an acquittal. I advised the court that she was completely barking and not fit to stand trial, which meant she would be sent to a secure mental home. Part of my thinking was that you get out of a prison more quickly than you do from a mental home, where there are no fixed terms, and the longer she was shut up the better. Peter's parents sounded just fine to me, and I hoped the kids would get sausages and bacon for breakfast once their mother was out of the way. *Crime maternel*? I figure it's on its way on to the books. Whoever these day trusts a father?'

Silence fell upon the group.

'It's a lovely night,' said the Judge to the Psychoanalyst, disturbing the silence with her thrilling voice. 'Cold but bright. Shall we go for a walk in the grounds?' And the Psychoanalyst rose and off they went together, though I suspect, the night being blustery and not in the least lovely, they got no further than one of the bedrooms. But you never know. The Psychoanalyst was used to inclement weather, and the Judge, I am sure, would put up with anything for love.

23

I spent the night brooding. I could not sleep. I would not take sleeping pills. I chose pain over oblivion. I fell further into the black pit of madness, if this peaky, knowing, squinny-eyed obsession was how it was described. All became clear. Julian had let the bath overflow on purpose to bring the ceiling down, so Christmas would have to be cancelled, and he would be able to sneak off to Wichita to meet his long-lost love and even now they were staring into each other's eyes, in some hotel – surely, surely they would not copulate under his mother's roof – but then hadn't he once before done exactly that? While deciding he did not love me, had never really loved me, had put up with me at best, loathed me at worst, for years. Who cared if I was stranded in the wilds? Not he. He had managed to contact his son. He had not bothered to contact me.

They had arranged to meet, obviously. Of course he had not phoned me. How he must have blessed the ice storms. Was it possible that his mother and her new husband were in the plot too? Had they told him Jenny was coming? They had always preferred her to me. Or did I just see conspiracy everywhere I turned; Sumatra flu in every cough and snuffle?

Had there actually been a phone call from Julian's stepfather about his mother's fall? Or had Julian merely reported it to me? I was too distracted to remember. Had he checked that there were no seats available on the flight for me, or was this just what he had told me? Surely 'compassionate grounds' would stretch to me as well? Had he simply contrived, by lying and cheating, that he would get over to Wichita and there meet the one-time love of his life, Jenny? But even as one part of me cried almost joyously, yes, yes, I told you all men are bastards, and relished every shred of evidence as to my husband's depravity, another saner part said, hang on a moment, but this is mad.

Julian has never before shown signs of deviousness: it is not in his nature to plot. Shout, bang tables and remonstrate noisily, when one wishes he would be calm and think, perhaps: but he is not sly. Only the once, twenty-five years ago, when the children were little, when he told me he was going to the cinema alone, first checking it was a film I had not wished to see, had he been underhand. He'd taken someone else and not said. I found the ticket stubs. I asked who it was and he'd replied, 'Oh God, it was Jenny. Rumbled!' So there was indeed a precedent. Yes indeed, the very same precedent. After all these years, Jenny again!

Perhaps when I'd phoned him from Beverley's office, she had been lying beside him in the bed, and they were laughing and giggling together at me, making a fool of me for my naivety, my stupidity. For trusting, for suspecting nothing.

Jenny had been my best friend long ago when we were students in London. Julian lived down the road and we both fancied him, in an idle kind of way. When Jenny's parents split up and her home evaporated my mother offered to take her in. She lived with us as one of the family for a year. Then she left us and moved in with Julian and his family instead. Probably because Julian was coming round too often to see me. And thus Jenny nabbed him from under my nose. Soon she was his girlfriend, then his lover, then his fiancée. His mother – the one with the conveniently troublesome hip – thought she was the bee's knees; she didn't like me: I was three years older than her son and had 'too controlling a nature'. But then Julian saw it was mad, she had simply cornered him, broke with her and came to me. When we set up together Jenny stayed with Julian's mother and suffered long and publicly. He had broken her heart. I had always been over-sensitive when it came to Jenny, Julian told me. He could hardly never see his mother again just becasue Jenny was there. Let alone never see

Jenny again just because he was married to me. If he'd taken Jenny to the cinema it was because he wanted to restore things to normality, and he'd wanted to see the film and so did she, and he knew I did not. If he hadn't told me it was becasue he knew I'd make a fuss.

I gave in and took sleeping pills and once I was out of bed in the morning felt better, almost normal. I was not used to sleeping alone, I realized. You get accustomed to a sleeping body beside you, keeping night fears away; the warm solidity of normality. Without it you're vulnerable to all the fears and fantasies that stir in every drift and current of the night air.

The Spa ladies were in a good mood the next day. Treatment rooms were found unlocked and some of us took advantage of slimming pads and the water massage, and slapped black sea mud on one another with shrieks of joy. Mud fights broke out. The Vicar's Ex-wife took it upon herself to clean up. At tea time we gathered together in our white towelling gowns around the big central dining table in the medieval hall in the south wing – a vaulted ceiling, stone gargoyles, stuffed bears, suits of armour, an immense gilded buffet by Burges himself.

By tea time neurotic fears began to surface again, taking hold like a fever in a patient who spends the morning cool and happy, only to be poorly again by evening. Surely Julian would have found some way of contacting me if he wanted to? In a world dedicated to communication it could not be so difficult. If I had access to the internet I could check out the weather in Wichita, but I did not. I could have done with some contact from the children too. But then I supposed it was much the same for them as it was for me. Out of sight is out of mind, unless some crisis arises. I tried to concentrate on the admirable decorative eccentricities around me but failed. They had become cardboard sets within whose walls I played out some intense interior drama.

Euan coughed and spluttered into his tissue and then dropped it on the floor and didn't pick it up and I did not even care. I had a Reiki session and hardly registered it. A couple more beauty therapists had walked up from the village – the taxi drivers having retired into the bosom of their families on the grounds that there was no business about – one to a do a yoga class, one to do Pilates, and though we were all rather full from lunch the rest felt obliged to make their journey worthwhile, in the spirit of *noblesse oblige*.

And then it was time for the Company Director's Tale, but I couldn't focus; I was scarcely registering words. I handed over to Mira. Mira said kindly she'd type up an account of what went on in the session. And this is what she later delivered to me.

24

The Company Director's Tale

Her name was Eve and she was handsome: her body was perfectly sculpted, her features regular, her brow unwrinkled, and her hair was thick and glossy and I believed her own. There was no telling how old she was. Only the straight up-and-downness of her calves, as she dipped them into the bubbling water, suggested that she might no longer be actively young. Little old ladies tend to have legs like that – but then so do patients on heavy psychoactive drugs. But that was soon cured anyway – silicone implants could flesh them out if necessary, as they already had, I thought, both bosom and buttocks. And if there was a faint disordered look about her that reminded one of Michael Jackson, at least here a native beauty had been built upon the better to preserve it, not man's hand creating what God had not intended in the first place.

And she was sensuous enough, I noticed. She curled and re-curled her toes in the warm water, and ran her fingers almost joyously through the bubbles that swirled around her, pinching and snapping them like a child. Her voice was low, young, melodious, and lovely, and she was charming and accustomed to being liked – one can always tell.

'Well, then,' I, Mira, said to her, when we were all settled, 'your turn next!'

'But I'm not a very interesting person,' she said. 'I live an ordinary life.'

'Everyone thinks that,' I said. 'But very few do.'

'And I'm not good at telling stories. I can't get any kind of narrative flow. Nothing comes out in the right order.'

'But if you listen to other people's stories,' I said, 'it seems only fair that you should make a contribution.'

'But I'm really self-conscious,' she said, 'and rather shy. I'm just a wife and mother, an ordinary country Englishwoman.'

Frankly, all of us doubted it more and more.

'We'll try the twenty-question method,' I decided, 'as we did with Dorleen. Only this time we'll truly try to keep it to twenty. But in return for doing half your work for you, it would be really helpful if you undertook to tell the truth.'

'I always tell the truth,' she said. Personally, I thought that was unlikely. Her whole being was a lie; she was an artifice created by cosmetic surgery.

The Judge had threatened to introduce some essential oils – namely bergamot, ginger, lavender and rosemary – into the water source, the better to loosen our tongues and reduce performance stress, and I thought perhaps she had indeed sneaked in and done this earlier. Alas, like the marihuana which the Grateful Dead in their heyday used to feed into their stage air-conditioning systems, what is good for performance can drive all judgement from the mind, suffusing it instead with a kind of swoony, steamy stupor. Certainly the air we breathed was delicately scented and pleasurable, but I worried in case it undermined the discipline required to run a good twenty-question session. Questions have to be well thought out, and I wished the Judge had consulted with me first, instead of just going ahead. I would certainly have advised her to leave out the lavender, which tends to simply send one to sleep, and have gone for rosemary. Perhaps she was a little jealous that I had been appointed mistress of ceremonies, and thought she could do better?

But they were waiting for me to begin.

'How old are you?' I asked. That startled her: the wide eyes widened more. It's a trick question, actually: they ask it in lie-detector tests as a benchmark of veracity, on the grounds that it's an undeniable fact, though I'm sure I never speak the truth about it if I can help it, nor do most women. I daresay it wasn't a very well-thought-out question – I blame the lavender – but it was what I wanted to know.

'I don't usually tell people that,' she said, a little huffily. 'It's bad for business.'

'Don't worry about it,' I said. 'It's confidential.'

I was lying but then I had not undertaken to tell the truth, she had. It seemed fair enough to me. I had my mini recording device tucked into the underside of my bikini, and it was switched to on, because I was going to type the tale up and give it to Phoebe, who was using it no doubt for some writerly project of her own. Or indeed Alistair might be interested in this particular story: the Company Director's appeal to the European Court of Justice would make headlines for a week. I worried about Phoebe. She had seemed so calm and confident when we met on the train: now she was a mass of anxieties and fears. Perhaps she was just not good at being far from home without her familiar support structures.

Women with grown children, I find, tend to be like this. They are so accustomed to being needed that if there is no one to need them they go to pieces. They stop seeing themselves as individuals but as in their pre-feminist roles – someone's mother, wife, sister, daughter, their function to serve and support, and part of that support is anxiety – the talisman that keeps disaster away. If she worries enough about the fumes from Chinese candles everyone will be safe. Yet she pities me because I have no husband, no children. She must be joking. Though I must say to have a little Alistair running round my ankles might not be too bad. But it would probably be a girl and I could do without that.

Had Mira meant to include this last passage in her report back to me, to serve as a rebuke, or was it accidental, meant for her diary? Probably the former. But it was friendly enough. And I could see that what she said was true. Having children is a life sentence to anxiety. That is all bonding is – nature's way of ensuring that the mother protects the children from danger: that they fear the sabre-tooth tiger long after it is extinct.

*

I had looked up the Company Director in a register in the lobby: now unmanned and even growing a little dusty. Beverley presumably had enough to do with the bedrooms. Euan the teenager ran round with a can of polish from time to time, coughing and sneezing, but failed to dust first, so the place was beginning to look almost grimy. Her name was Eve Hambeldon, Company Director. The name rang a bell but I could not place it. I'd looked her up on Google but there was nothing. That in itself could be revealing. It can be quite difficult to avoid the attentions of Google, let alone Wikipedia. She might have had friends in high Google or Yahoo places. The citizen who fears observation from the state is barking up the wrong tree. The internet is the problem. I repeated my question.

'Go on, tell us how old you are.'

She gave her pretty little laugh. 'I'm seventy-seven,' she said.

There was a gasp around the pool, and even a little cry of horror. How could anyone be so old and still function?

'How come your voice is like it is?' That was the Manicurist, and a real waste of a question.

'Question Number Two,' she said. 'I've had my vocal chords tightened. They get loose with age but you can tune them like a guitar.'

'Why have you come to Castle Spa?' I asked, into the contemplative silence that ensued – perhaps we could all do with having our chords tightened. Another simple question from me but a useful one, I thought, which with most people would lead to a burst of communication – at this time of year mostly about work challenges ahead, but at other times accounts of emotional disturbance, dietary panic, lovers to be wooed, or husbands placated. But all she said was, 'My doctor said I needed a rest.'

I said that was not a sufficiently full or fair response, and she gave a little laugh and apologized and promised to do better. People who have had a lot of cosmetic surgery do tend to be self-centred and neurotic, it goes with the territory, but Eve was charming, and basically, I thought, friendly. It was just a question of getting through the barriers, and then everything would flow. Unless of course she had done something dreadful like a murder, or was wanted by the police, in which case no amount of bergamot and lavender would help.

'I have been involved with the European Court of Justice over a personal matter,' she said. 'And dealing with the bureaucracy can quite wear one out and affect the skin. Skin is the one thing surgery cannot improve. Will that do?'

Obvious to ask her what the 'personal matter' was, but I'd no doubt she'd skirt round that too. She was happy to admit to cosmetic surgery, but where to go from here? As for being nothing but a shy, properly brought-up Englishwoman, forget that. I would take another tack entirely. I came up with the right question, intuitively.

'Why did your parents call you Eve?'

And then the facts began to flow.

'My parents were old-fashioned romantics,' she said. 'I was their first child. They would probably have preferred a boy, people did in those days, but they did their best: they called me Eve in the hope that I would be essence of all women. And I think at first I was, born on New Year's Eve, 1932, a sweet, pretty, obliging little thing, and they loved me very much. But on New Year's Eve, 1935, a boy baby was born and they called him Adam, in the hope that he would be all man, essence of male. And so he was.'

'Sharing the same birthday,' said Shimmer, the Brain Surgeon. 'Like me and my twin Sparkle, but three years in between! That was the only thing I didn't like about being a twin; I wanted my own birthday. Did you feel like that?'

'That doesn't count as a question, Eve,' I interjected. 'That's more of a remark.'

'Very well,' said Eve, agreeably. 'Let me put it like this. I wanted my own birthday; I just didn't want my brother to have it too. My parents thought our being born on the same day was significant, meaningful: the coincidence impressed them. My mother was a follower of Madame Blavatsky and a theosophist: you young people think you have invented karma, but it featured large in my early life, to my detriment.'

'It's not really so much of a coincidence,' said the sex-change Judge. 'If the parents love each other and like a celebration, no one should be surprised at the appearance of a baby nine months after a wedding anniversary. You know what month your parents married?' Another question, down the drain.

'Question Number Five,' said Eve. She meant to go on counting; she would not let go. She would tell her story and reveal nothing, if I was not careful. 'Towards the end of March, I think.'

'If both of you were born on New Year's Eve,' said the Judge smugly, 'my reckoning is the 26th March – 274 days gestation.' Her gender might fluctuate with her hormones but she had a calculator for a brain.

'And it's not really so much of a coincidence,' said Shimmer the Surgeon. 'Statisticians tell us if you have twenty people in a room; odds are that at least two will share the same birthday.'

'All I know is that the night before my third birthday,' said Eve, 'when I was happily anticipating the very special present my parents had promised me, I was woken in the night by screams from my mother's bedroom and much running up and down of footsteps on the stairs, but went back to sleep easily enough. When one is small one believes that adults are capable of running their own world, though in sometimes mysterious ways. I went down to breakfast the next morning and found no one in the kitchen and no present, and was in a bad mood when finally my father came into the room, and took me upstairs to where my mother was sitting up in bed with a newborn baby in her arms.

'See, your present, darling!' she said. 'And he came in time for your birthday. Isn't that a simply joyous thing?'

'I don't like it,' I said. 'Take it back to the shop.'

'You must understand that in those days parents did not speak about pregnancy in front of the children. For decency's sake women stayed home once their bumps couldn't be hidden: they did not walk about the streets flaunting the results of their recent sexual activity. The less children knew about sex the better, and who is to say that is not the right way to go about these things? I think my mother, being a progressive, may have mistakenly tried to explain the coming event to me, but made such a hash of it I had confused sexual with excretory functions. So far as I was concerned what my mother was holding in her arms was a piece of shit.

'Indeed, so great was the wave of disgust and loathing I felt at that moment that it was to be a full seven decades and four years before I achieved closure. New Year's Eve, 2006, to be exact. By then my parents had long gone, wondering to the end why their daughter had turned out the way she had. When I bent to kiss my baby brother I bit him instead; I tipped him out of his cot if I could get into his nursery; sat the cat upon his face and stroked it till it stopped struggling and fell asleep; turned on the scalding hot tap when he was in his bath. He survived but only just. My parents marvelled at my ingenuity, while fearing for their son. Three nannies gave notice because they could not cope.

'As Adam grew he developed his own defences. If I entered the room he was in, he uttered a piercing yell loud enough to wake the street, so staff would have to come running. He soon learned to do it even when I wasn't in the room, just on a whim, and I would be blamed, and punished. Yet all I was doing was trying to protect my family from this interloper, this nauseous creature. I began to despise them for not seeing through his wiles, his sunny smiles, to the piece of shit within. Yet still I loved them. But for their part, I am afraid; they began to lose their affection for me.

'And it had all started out so well: two handsome healthy babies, a pigeon pair, boy and girl, born on the same day: how could they not love each other? Sharing a birthday, and that birthday New Year's Eve! The disappointment was great. They turned their attention to starting up and running the Hambeldon Printing Company, which was to blossom into a nationwide business and make the family rich, and thereafter concentrated on that.'

Of course. Eve Hambeldon, fifth wealthiest company director in the country. The Hambeldon chain of retail shops is so familiar one hardly registers it. She had always been beautiful, one knew that, but she didn't exactly look now as she had when she started out. If I hadn't recognized her at once it was hardly surprising.

'What happened on New Year's Eve, 2006?' asked the Mortgage Broker. I wish she hadn't spoken. It was endangering the flow.

'I shall ignore that question,' said Eve kindly, perhaps sensing my anxiety. 'If we have time I will get back to it later.' Cat and mouse, cat and mouse, which was which? 'Now you know who I am, Mira. I didn't mean to tell you but these things slip out. I hate the media: I go to great lengths and expense to protect my privacy.' Bet she did. How had she escaped Google's attentions? Or had I got her spelling wrong? It can happen.

'All the same,' she went on, 'when I was six, and lured my three-year-old brother up into the attic and shut him into a trunk, locked it and threw away the key, the drastic nature of the event caught their attention. Doctors had to be called in to resuscitate him.

'They consulted my mother's astrologer, Lola. Lola was a theosophist and also a follower of Mrs Blavatsky. I believe my father, rather the weaker character of the two, accompanied my mother to the session though he was no believer. Certainly he did nothing to protect me. Years later I asked Lola about the occasion. She was convinced she had done the right thing for me and my brother. My mother's sun was in Leo, she said, and Leo mothers are protective but can be competitive with their daughters. And I was a very pretty child.

'Be that as it may, Lola explained to my parents that although Adam and I had been born with our suns in Capricorn, I had Saturn, Venus and Mars clustered very powerfully in Aquarius in the second house, that of possessions.'

'Possessions include the love of the parents?' asked Shimmer.

'Question Number Six,' said Eve. 'Of course. Alas, not only

Adam's Mercury, also in the second house in Aquarius, was in acute opposition to my most influential planets, but both our Marses were at war.

'"What is to be done?" asked my mother, distressed at this news.

'"Separate the children,' said Lola. "The conflict will never be resolved, or not for many years. Saturn moves slowly. It has to be done, or neither will flourish. Send the girl to her relatives in Canada: she has her moon in the ninth, travel will suit her. There is a war on: she will be safer abroad in any case." And so I was sent by my mother into exile.'

'Is that why you said astrology was to your detriment?' asked the Manicurist. I was surprised she knew what the word meant. She was hot on cunning but not on vocabulary.

'Question Number Seven,' said Eve. It seemed she couldn't make up her mind whether she would rather tell her story or thwart me. I tucked the recorder further under my bikini top. I didn't think she could have seen it: perhaps she just sensed it. The old often seem to have an uncanny sense of what's going on behind their backs, and no matter what she looked like she was old, old, old.

'World War Two had begun,' she went on, 'and children were being shipped out of England at a great rate, to save their lives, and also sort out many a parental problem. I was to be the one to go. Adam, Adam the shit, was to stay, to face his country's danger like a man, take up his place at prep school, eventually to go on to Rugby. A good education was for boys. Finishing school, Constance Spry flower arrangements and a good marriage was the destiny of well-born girls.

'Well, my parents are long dead and gone. Too late now for anyone to apologize: my parents for muddling me so hopelessly about the facts of life, for sending me off to live with strangers while keeping my little brother with them. Lola, for interfering in others' lives. Myself, I daresay, for clinging to my wrongs, for the many murderous attempts on my sibling's life, for deliberately upsetting the family atmosphere. We can blame ourselves or we can blame our stars. I don't believe in them, what rational person does, but all the same...

'One of you asked me what happened on December 31st, 2006 to help me towards closure. It is only fair of me to tell you.' The Manicurist had her pale legs out of the bubbling water, and was attempting to touch up her toenails where they had chipped. Kimberley stood by with the little lacquer bottle in her large hands. All of us, I noticed, favoured scarlet for our feet. Fingernails these days can be any shade from green to black: toenails remain the colour of sin.

'The sun was in Capricorn, and my Mars and Mercury too, all conjunct, and for once doing nicely in relation to Adam's natal chart. My seventy-fifth birthday and Adam's seventy-second. We had been obliged, the pair of us, to host a combined birthday and New Year's Eve party. We did it to keep the shareholders at bay, certainly not because we wanted to. Profits had taken a dip lately and there were grumbles that these days togetherness and team spirit were an essential element in market success and rumoured rifts in top management was doing no one any good. Rumoured! That was putting it mildly.' I had been right. Now she had started there was no stopping her.

Eve was fifteen by the time she came back to England. Lola had been right. The child had flourished in the absence of her brother, to the extent that her Canadian uncles and aunts had been reluctant to let her go. She was pretty, smart and popular – her bile was reserved for her brother, far away and overseas – and was voted Junior Prom Queen in the eleventh grade – and had written proudly to her parents to tell them so. She received no reply. Either the letter had gone down with the ship – U-boats were active in the Atlantic that year – or they didn't know or care what a Junior Prom Queen was, other than that it smacked of vulgarity and Americanization – then seen as the same thing. She wrote to tell them she was studying economics, and there were jobs open to women in Canada. She might even get a job in banking. Still no reply. The war ended. The adults exchanged correspondence: she was not informed.

She sent photos. She was far too grown-up for her age. She had a figure, and showed it. English schoolgirls dressed to hide from male attention: Canadian ones went 'dating'. Instead of sensible lace-ups their daughter wore ankle socks and cork wedges. Her hair was not cut short and plain and kept out of her eyes by a proper kirbygrip, no, she had a 'page boy' and artificial curls curved round her face, topped by a scarlet bow. It was impossibly vulgar. There was even a boyfriend in one of the photos: they were holding hands. He was well over twenty and wearing an extraordinary floppy black and white striped garment called a zoot suit. That was 1947. The parents were horrified at what the relatives had allowed to happen and called her back home.

When they went to meet her off the boat at Tilbury it seemed unlikely, from her dress and demeanour, that the girl was even a virgin. Supposing she took it into her head to lead her brother astray? She was deported to a girls' boarding school within the week, and back in a gymslip. The school taught cooking, deportment and perhaps a little geography to girls of good family. She caught a glimpse of Adam as she passed through the portals of the new big house in Esher on her way to her new school. Her hair had been straightened, cut and kirbygripped: her pleated navy tunic hid her figure.

'Oh it's you,' he said. 'Back from the Colonies!'

Now one way to rile a Canadian is to call him or her a colonial and Adam was so cock-sure and confident, practising how to tie his new Rugby tie, that Eve spat at her brother – actually spat – in derision and contempt. This one spontaneous action was to influence the rest of her life, and her brother's too. Adam recoiled in horror, as well he might. This was not how his friends' sisters were or any female he had ever met. The tale of her murderous attempts on his young life had made good dinner-table conversation for many years, now it no longer seemed a joke.

Unfortunately the father was passing by as Adam came charging from the room. 'She spat at me! She spat at me!'

Adam, according to his sister, was in those days not quite the full hamper – perhaps as a result of being tipped out of his cot so often in infancy – but good-looking and sexually attractive (Venus in Scorpio works wonders) but unable to 'commit' – always thinking something better might be over the horizon. He never married. 'Couldn't possibly risk it,' he told her, when at some unavoidable family event she loudly taunted him with unfounded accusations of gayness – 'Supposing the babies turned out like you?'

Eve, defeated in her ambitions by her lack of education and the social needs of society, had been to finishing school, been presented at court as a debutante and had married 'well' – a pleasant if boring banker. 'If you can't beat 'em, join 'em' she'd said to Lola, whom occasionally she would go and consult. She had two handsome, clever sons, both Aquarians, Aquarius in the first house, Moon rising. Most auspicious.

When she was forty-five, to everyone's surprise – and shock, for she was well before her time in this, and women were meant to put up forever with the face God had allocated to them at birth – she had cosmetic surgery to straighten her nose, lift her chin, and widen her eyes. While Adam looked old before his time, balding young, becoming paunchy, losing his appeal to women, Eve looked more and more spectacular. She had an affair and lost her pleasant but dull husband, and took lovers. That was in the Seventies.

'And your brother?' asked the Almost Lady Judge.

'Question Number Eight,' said Eve. 'Remember you only have twenty. Adam had joined the family firm way back. In the eighties my father developed Alzheimer's. I'm sorry to say that Lola's response to the news – Lola had become quite a friend of mine over the years – was "how could they tell the difference?" So Adam slipped easily enough into his shoes. My mother had been the business head all along, and lately had been making all the major decisions. She put us on the stock exchange, while managing to keep executive power well within family control. Father took five years passing away, and then Mother unexpectedly died after a brief illness.'

'What did she die of?' asked the Manicurist.

'Question Number Nine,' observed Eve. 'She broke her hip and the shock killed her off. She changed her will on her deathbed, however. She left half the business to me: I'd been expecting the family silver if I was lucky. Perhaps she remembered those happy first three years of our life together, and was seized by remorse? How am I to know? Her sun in Leo was in the fifth house when she made the will and the fifth house is the house of daughters, and our Venuses were conjunct.'

Hambeldon's, it seemed, was now massively rich, thanks to the mother's gift – or perhaps it was Lola's – for staying ahead of the game. Hambeldon retail outlets had been the first to sell goods on credit, then to go into television rentals, then into computers. There was a great deal to leave. Adam challenged his mother's will in the courts but it was declared valid. Adam sulked and Eve gloated.

'All those wasted years at home,' sighed the Mortgage Broker, 'before you came into your own! Tied up with family, husband, children! Trapped. Unable to reach your potential. How did you put up with it?'

'Question Number Ten,' said Eve, and though I argued it was a rhetorical question, and did not require an answer, she would have none of it.

'I'll tell you exactly how I put up with it. I did what was in front of my nose, to the best of my ability, and preserved my energy. Children grow up. Husbands drift off. Lovers come and go. I read, I thought, I watched, I planned, *j'ai reculé pour mieux sauter*. When the time came, which it always does, I had stored-up energy to release.'

Adam hoped Eve would stay away and just take the money, but no, she came storming in to play her part, learning management-speak, cutting out the dead wood, streamlining business methods.

The brother and sister met only, and reluctantly, at monthly board meetings. Like the mother, the daughter was an innovator. Mobile phones, Eve predicted, were the way ahead. She demanded massive investment. Adam scoffed. She insisted. Eve wanted her sons – now both effective and qualified barristers – to join Hambeldon as directors but Adam would not have it. He gave no reason. He refused. He was entitled to refuse. Then Adam wanted to sell out, to take the offered millions and run: the corporate structure was changing, there was no room left for family businesses. Eve gave no reason. She refused. She was entitled to refuse. Now it was a battle as to who was to outlast the other. If Adam died first, his share of the firm went to Eve and then to her sons. If she died first Adam got the lot and charities inherited. Both became health freaks. Each would outlast the other if it was the last thing they did.

'And it's your birthday very soon,' pointed out Dorleen. 'It's nearly New Year's Eve. And you said you'd tell me what happened two years back. And you still fucking haven't.'

'Ah yes,' said Eve, 'the question that never was. This will be your eleventh. Are you sure you want that?' she asked me. 'There's a lot to tell still and you're using them up rather quickly.'

'You want to tell us,' I said. 'Nothing will stop you now.'

'Don't be so sure,' she said. 'But have it your own way. The invitations for the joint party went out in November 2006. The sun was in Scorpio but our Mercuries and our Venuses were for once friendly.

'"Adam and Eve Hambeldon", my brother Adam instructed the printer.

'"Eve and Adam Hambeldon," I snapped back.

'"Why?" asked Adam. "I was doing it alphabetically."

'"I was born first."

'"I suppose that's true," he acknowledged. "I'd never quite thought of it like that. You were always away. Canada, wasn't it?"

'He could have said "the Colonies". He didn't. Perhaps over the years some of his brain cells had repaired themselves. They take their time, but they can and do. I felt almost friendly towards him. Indeed, a surge of affection. And I think perhaps he felt the same. People say we have the same mouth: it curves upwards at the edges. I had to be careful when my lips were enhanced that that did not alter. But if you pay enough you get a good surgeon. I think on that occasion we almost smiled at one another.'

'Do you think Michael Jackson tried to cut costs?' asked Dorleen. 'Do you think that's what went wrong?'

'Questions Number Twelve and Thirteen,' said Eve. 'Yes and yes. We both had the same stubborn, Capricornian temperament, but he budged first.

'"Eve and Adam Hambeldon. Okay," said Adam. "You had it worst as a child. You can go first."

'And that somehow melted the first layer of ice; the elephant in the room had at least been acknowledged. When Adam picked me up in the Rolls on the evening of the party, I quite appreciated the feeling of being cared for.'

'Did he drive, or did you have a chauffeur?' asked the Vicar's Ex-wife. 'I've always wanted a chauffeur.' She spoke languidly. I think the fumes in the water were beginning to affect her.

'Question Number Fourteen,' said Eve, who, alas, seemed as alert as ever. 'Adam always drove himself. For all his wealth, he did not believe in wasting money. Two minutes into the ride I had to beg him to stop. I had forgotten my party shoes. I told him that we had to go back. "You're wearing shoes," he said.

'"But I need my party shoes," I said. "We have to go back for them."

'He stopped the car. No doubt the ones I was wearing looked okay to him. And I daresay he thought back to the impossible behaviour of all the other women he had ever known: nevertheless he did an elegant three-point turn without comment and we set back the way we had come. The husband I had thrown away would never have behaved so well, pleasant though he was reputed to be. But when we got back I had forgotten my keys. I had locked myself out of my own house.'

'You're making this bit up,' said the Trophy Wife. 'Surely you had staff?'

'Question Number Fifteen,' said Eve. 'It was late. I had sent them all home. There was no one in the house. And I told you I was no liar. I am telling you the truth, unexpurgated. My manner of life was such that I quite enjoyed privacy of an evening. Yes, even at my age. And a party is a party and you never know what is going to happen next. And Adam didn't even tell me I was a fool. No, he cased the joint and said, "There's an open window on the second floor." And so there was.

'"There's a ladder in the garage," I said, "and it's unlocked."'

'That doesn't ring true,' said the Mortgage Broker. 'Surely no one leaves ladders in unlocked garages?'

'Question Number Sixteen,' said Eve. 'I saw my brother's face in the street light as he stared at me. He gasped as if for air. I knew he was remembering the cat on his face, the stifling dark of the trunk in which he had nearly suffocated. The venom of my spit long ago still stayed with him. I was his born enemy.

'"Trust me," I said. "I'm your sister."'

'"That's the problem," he said. "Always was."'

'"I'll hold," I assured him. "You climb." Together we manoeuvred the ladder against the house.

'And climb he did. Steady as a rock I held the ladder. Brave as a mountain goat, Capricornian, he climbed. I did not try to kill him, though it would have been easy enough.'

There was a swelling of protest from around the pool.

'I don't believe it,' said the Mortgage Broker. 'Of course the end of the story is that you swung the ladder out and he fell off and was killed. You had your vengeance. Surely that's tidy, that makes sense?'

'Question Number Seventeen,' said Eve. 'It may make sense, but I am of an age where I know that what happens next is not necessarily expected or indeed sensible. I have surprises yet to come but you are running out of questions fast. In the old twenty-question game, may I remind you, only yes or no answers could be given. I have been very generous in my replies, but at the twentieth question I am getting out of here and going to bed.'

'You're lying,' said the Judge. 'I've seen enough liars in my time to know one when I see one. Everything about you is a lie, from the shape of your nose to your implanted hair. Not that I'm being judgemental about this. Takes one to know one. I am a woman but I began life looking to others like a man. I may even have spent as much money, time and pain turning from a phoney man to a true woman, as you have from an old one to a young one. You killed him, didn't you?'

'Question Number Eighteen,' said Eve. 'No. I did not.'

'I think you should admit it,' said Shimmer the Surgeon. 'We're all on your side here. You had a raw deal when you were small. And this was a repetition of a childhood compulsion: you could argue you were in a second childhood. Even if it went to court they'd let you down lightly. We have so little control over our impulses. You should see some of my patients before surgery.'

'I understand what it is to feel murderous,' said the Mortgage Broker. 'Aren't we all sisters under the skin?'

'Question Number Nineteen,' said Eve. 'A rhetorical question requiring no answer, but still a question. No, I did not murder him. It did occur to me: of course it did. But real life is not a story. It has no meaning in itself. Real life has no beginning, middle and end. Even death is not the end, I fear: no such luck. Do you think my mother is dead just because she is in her grave? She is there forever sending me away to the Colonies because she is jealous. I forever stand there in my ugly uniform spitting at my baby brother. Eve is evil, Adam is an innocent. Eve exists so can Adam stop? No. All our actions circle in infinity like the stars in their courses. Of course we look for patterns in the stars. We're desperate. One more question. Make it good.'

'Okay,' I said. 'What happened next?'

'I don't accept that as a proper question,' she said. 'It's cheating. Think again.'

I thought. 'Okay,' I said, 'you told us you had been to the

European Court of Justice. What was that about?'

She took her time replying. I wondered why I thought I was so much cleverer than other people, why I was so dismissive of others? I wished Phoebe had not trusted me to record the tale. I could have written it up from memory, and enhanced it in the telling. I understood why Alistair could never commit himself to me. I was a bully and a cheat and a liar. Who did I think I was, other than some cheap journalist after another woman's man, who had once been brave in the field of battle and picked up awards, and had given up the fight for truth and justice, and now sat in a Jacuzzi in a bankrupt Spa, with a mini recorder tucked under a bosom that had been, I must admit, surgically enhanced – although cunningly – so there was still sufficient fold of flesh between breast and bone to do the hiding. I had looked at the mote in the Company Director's eye and ignored the beam in my own. I'd had my breasts enhanced the week Alistair got married. The bride had great big fleshy tits of her own. I would seize the recorder from its wretched hiding place, I would throw it in the water, it would float and churn a little, like Frodo's ring in *Lord of the Rings*, and it would sink, and good would be brought back to Middle Earth. Then I would have my own round globes un-enhanced. What was the point of them? I had dug my own grave: I had called up to wish Alistair seasonal greetings and he had told me not to persecute him.

Eve spoke at last.

'Very good, Mira,' she said. 'The European Court was the clue. Now I can continue.'

She did not try to kill him, though it would have been easy enough. He eased through the window, went down the stairs, and when he opened the door she was waiting. They put their arms round each other.

'Brother,' she said.

'Sister,' he said.

'Well, that was a waste of life,' both said.

The shoes were a fabulous success – red Manolos, unreasonably high heels, silver strap, and red ribbon round the ankle – as was the party. The Hambeldon siblings beamed at one another. Not just the appearance but the actuality of family unity had been secured.

They even suddenly looked like each other: once they were smiling, it became apparent.

Both not only made New Year resolutions as the midnight bells tolled but, defying superstition in their elation, told them to each other. They would hereafter be friends. Adam might even move in with Eve: they could keep each other company through their declining years. There was so much time to make up, so much to talk about. How had he got on at Rugby? What had her divorce been like? Why hadn't he married? Perhaps only that if you can't accept a sister, you can't accept a bride? A remorseful visit to the graves of the parents, perhaps, was on the cards, not just to forgive those who had trespassed against them, but to ask for forgiveness themselves.

'And we were able to keep those resolutions,' she said, 'if only because those born between December 22nd and January 20th, under the sign of Capricorn, lead lives that get better as they get older, so the rift was bound to be healed. Or so our mother would have understood it, having first consulted Lola. And the European Court of Appeal? We want to be married. Nowadays anyone can marry anyone, and since we are both beyond reproductive age, there can be no possible case against it. We would love the approval of the world, and we love parties. What do you think?'

And she stood there with her perfectly sculptured figure and almost perfect face and the hair that might be a wig, with now only the faintest touch of Michael Jackson, and turned and went off to bed, leaving us to ponder the question. And I thought as she walked away that when the slightly too-straight-up-and-down calves were remedied, she could rival any woman there, at least in the soft, seductive light of Burges' Oriental Chamber, with the sleepy smell of lavender and the astringency of bergamot drifting through the humid air.

25

While Eve spoke and Mira wrote, I, Phoebe had gone to my room to take stock of myself. I was not doing as well as I thought I would. Even with the Eleanor/Belinda/Nisha business laid to rest in my mind, all was still not well. I had gone to a Spa in search of serenity and instead found mayhem, both inside and out. It is not necessarily a good thing to search for your inner self. You might find someone you don't like very much at all. I did as I normally do in times of stress, and consulted my mother's spirit. My mother was a very wise woman and when I'm in trouble I try to act as she would, think as she would. She too was capable of foolish action and reaction – for example, when moved by pity, she offered a home to Jenny without first consulting me. I could have told her it would have ended in disaster. It was Jenny's nature to hog the bathroom, hog my mother's time and attention, and any boyfriend I might happen to have, in particular Julian.

But my dear good mother, though in her grave now for five years, was happily internalized in me. Now I would follow her advice. When overcome with emotions that strike suddenly, over-whelmingly and irrationally, it is helpful go back in your mind to other occasions when you have felt the same, perhaps with better reason. What you are feeling now may be flash-back emotions that belong properly to that other time, some similar, lesser situation: they have lain dormant and unacknowledged until they suddenly rise up to get you. Like a tsunami retreating only to gain strength when it roars back. Try and sort out what belongs where. The next wave of the tsunami can do more damage than the first.

I thought.

Rage? At a teacher who rapped my knuckles when I made a spelling mistake: when a nurse was rude when I was giving birth. When Julian's mother wouldn't come to our wedding.

Yes, come to think of it. Rage is tempting: one is wronged: one reacts. It is orgasmic, leaping out of the blue, leaving one shivery but satiated. Julian had left my side: the status quo had altered. I had gained a degree of control over myself.

Jealousy? Of my younger sister who was pretty and neat and got all the attention. Who could read and write before I could.

That, come to think of it, was a kind of rumbling anger that underlay so much of what I thought and was. Jenny, pretty and neat and younger than me, fitted a bill very nicely. If she didn't exist I would have to invent her.

Rejection? When I was turned down by the school netball team, when I wasn't asked to a birthday party and everyone else was: when no one wanted to dance with me and I had to busy myself in the kitchen.

Humiliations, come to think of it, that still hurt, that were a loose tooth that one worried at forever with the tongue: and the greatest of these would be Julian preferring Jenny to me. It was bound to come, I deserved it.

Abandonment: misery? When my father walked out on us, me; I was seven. When my mother married again, and there was a baby yet younger than me. When my mother took Jenny into the house, and chattered away to her more than she chattered to me.

Yes, come to think of it, the same familiar feeling: the actual rising up of pain in the heart, the shortness of breath. Misery. I felt it now. I thought Julian caused it. But did he? And had I only wanted Julian because Jenny had him? And I thought my mother preferred her to me? In which case Jenny was wronged, not me. Now, there was a thought.

A pleasure at being wronged? Yes, it was there,

Every minor hurt endured, every slight overlooked, every biting-back of the tongue, the common compromises in any marriage – could now be avenged. If Julian deceived me, abandoned me, rejected me, loved and fucked another, I could cleanse and scour my life of the slights of the past and start again.

Sudden disasters: my life had been punctuated with them. You wake up one morning: your father isn't there. You share your mother's bed, and late one night she moves you out to make room for a stranger. Your sister is killed by a drunk driver on the eve of her wedding. You have a still-birth at seven months.

Come to think of it, there hasn't been a sudden disaster in your life for ages: twenty years if you don't count the Sri Lankan near miss. It's time for one. You're addicted. Eleanor/Belinda/Nisha set you off. You are a horrible creature. So you imagine the end of the world, by epidemic, general strike, internet collapse. You are almost disappointed when it doesn't happen. So you invent a real humdinger: your husband leaving you for your old enemy, Jenny, your sister reborn.

Come to think of it, come to think of it, all this was in my head. Yet there was a reality: Jenny was in Wichita; Julian's mother with her not so broken hip after all, was probably still planning my downfall – though with the first grandchild she had appeared to give up her antagonism to me, and we had become almost friends. It was not too bad a reality.

Julian would get through to me, when he could. If Jenny had indeed turned up at the house that was natural enough. She would be concerned. We were surely beyond the age for bed hopping. And so forth and so on. I had had a fit of madness. I had passed through it. Unlike Nisha, unlike Belinda. Thank you, Mother. I forgive you all the wrongs you ever did me. Like the rest of us, you were the best mother your nature and circumstances allowed you to be.

Jenny, I'm sorry, I apologize. I quite deliberately stole you away from Julian before I had even begun to love him, which I now do. I broke your heart, and your life, and relished doing it. If I fear your vengeance even now how can I be surprised? I wronged you. Come to think or it you were really nice, and probably still are: I just didn't like you being so chatty with my mother when she took you in.

Mira came in with the transcript of the Company Director's Tale. I settled down to read it, and thought how powerful sibling rivalry is in our lives, and so often overlooked, and sibling love as well. I hoped Adam and Eve would be allowed to marry: I am all for happy endings. Men can marry men, and women, women, and no sexual relationship need be involved. It was not like father and daughter or mother and son – no power relations were involved – why should they not? Though the Manicurist, according to Mira, had become quite hysterical at the thought. No doubt she felt an elderly brother-sister wedding somehow devalued the purity and whiteness of her own, and the majesty of the rituals and traditions involved, even though they were not her own.

And with the next morning, came the next story. The Mortgage Broker's Tale.

The Mortgage Broker had been seen stepping out of a local taxi dressed in a business-like knee-length red suit and a white blouse, as if for an important meeting at the office, and had apparently argued about the bill. She did not see why she should pay double fare simply because it was a public holiday. She was good-looking enough in a thin-faced sort of way but not exactly sexy – the female equivalent of the man you know will fold his underpants before getting into bed with you. Her dark hair was curly but suspiciously neat, as if she had had it in rollers the night before. She was wearing make-up: and more lipstick than is considered fashionable these days. She seemed anxious and jumpy, but perhaps this was her normal position of rest. I would have put her in her early thirties, but in ladies who frequent spas age can be difficult to get right.

She had helped herself rather over generously to caviar the day before, and had taken three sausages at lunch instead of the allotted two, and ate quickly and guardedly, with one arm curved round her plate, as children do when they are worried a sibling might steal a chip. She saw me watching and after that moved her arm away and ate like the others, as if hunger was the last thing on her mind. She was slim enough so I supposed she was bulimic.

As we settled round the Jacuzzi, waiting for latecomers, there was a disturbance. A mouse ran across the floor, pursued by the Spa cat. The mouse was small, lively, cheeky and fast: the cat was a great, fat, black, furry thing but fast enough. Its custom was to sneak out of the kitchens into the dining hall whenever it could, rub itself up and down the guests' shins until rewarded by a sliver of chicken or a scrap of tapas – it particularly enjoyed anything with olive oil – and stroll casually off when shouted at. The guests liked it – other than those who suffered from allergies – management less so. Hence no doubt the sorry state of its saucer. We were all startled now by this sudden display of animal energy, but the Mortgage Broker actually leapt to her feet, was unable to stifle a scream, had an anxiety attack, and had to be calmed by breathing into a brown paper bag which someone found in the ecologically-conscious kitchens.

'It's not the mouse,' she explained to us when she recovered, and both animals had long since disappeared, 'it's the cat. I can't stand cats.' She went into quite a catalogue of the evils cats heaped upon mankind – from helicobacter, toxoplasmosis, scratch fever, viral heartworm disease, to their propensity to breed fleas, shed hair, and kill songbirds. And then she shook herself as if to free herself from some other persona, and smiled quite brilliantly round the room, and I was reminded of the sun re-broadcasting itself from all available points earlier in the morning, and she was suddenly beautiful, and apologized, saying she was aware there must be cat lovers amongst us, it was just that she was particularly sensitive at the moment, and like a woman divorcing her husband, had to stress his bad points the better to justify her actions, the sooner to be free. And finally, finally, she told us her story, by way of explanation and excuse. And of course, of course, we forgave her everything. To know is to understand.

26

The Mortgage Broker's Tale

'I had it hard when I was a child,' she said. 'There was never enough to eat, and what there was, my brothers and sisters used to steal from my plate if they could. So I eat too fast and too hungrily, I know. I try not to, but when I am upset the tendency surfaces and I am a little upset at the moment. In the throes of a moral dilemma, in fact. I am the oldest of five children. My father was a poet and never made enough money to get a deposit together for a house. He loved us, and loved my mother, but had no idea how to support us. So it was a feature of my childhood that he and I would often find ourselves trudging the streets looking for accommodation, any accommodation, anywhere large enough to take us all in. I had a wistful look, he told me, and if he took me with him, hearts were more likely to melt and doors open.

'It is surprising how many kind people there are in the world, who would go out of their way to find us disused factories, empty warehouses, even if we were lucky actual empty family houses. But sure as eggs are eggs we would presently find ourselves on the streets again. My mother had a passion for sick animals, you see, and felt obliged to take them in, not just the normal dogs and cats, but hens, rabbits, foxes, badgers, and passing road kill that hadn't actually died. Even once a piglet. It is amazing how the countryside seeps into the city, as housing projects take over from green fields. Eventually the neighbours would complain, the smells become unbearable, our landlords would run out of patience and we would be evicted.

'My mother loved babies as well, of course – anything she could look after – though as we grew older and less helpless she would tend to lose interest.

'The royalties from any slim book of poetry my father managed to have published, or the small fees he received from poetry readings or TV appearances – he was a good-looking man, slender, lots of black, curly hair large poetic eyes, and a sensuous voice – she would spend on vets' bills. Mostly we lived on our children's allowance, and though my father often pleaded with the authorities to house us they declined, because of my mother's passion for animals. Many estate families keep pets in defiance of their rental agreements, and the housing office will overlook the odd dog or cat but my mother would not lie. By going out of her way to declare the truth she put the authorities in an impossible position. We were on the books as "a problem family", although heaven knows we were well mannered enough, drug- and alcohol-free, literate, clean and responsible – other than in my father's determination never to "sell out", by which he meant earning enough to keep us in comfort – and the lame dogs, bald hens, mangy cats and lethargic rabbits who urgently needed to be taken to the vet, which came with us wherever we went.

'If I am always at my most nervy around Christmas and the New Year it is not surprising. Those early festive seasons left their mark. The child you hope you left behind never truly is left behind; still she waits for disaster to fall, for the dog to savage the temporary postman, for herself to be apprehended stealing sandwiches from the supermarket for the family Christmas. If the police came round about the dog, or my delinquency, it would be the last straw for the neighbours. The eviction would follow as night follows day, and my father and I would find ourselves knocking on doors once more down the long, silent, hung-over streets. "You don't by any chance have a place to rent?"

'When I was thirteen my mother, alas, contracted encephalitis – some low-grade viral fever travelled to her brain. Undulant fever, perhaps, caught from the dogs, or something nastier than usual in the cats' litter tray. She lived, but lost much of both her long- and short-term memory. She could no longer recognize my father, or her children, though she could still distinguish well enough between the animals, and call even our three sickly angora rabbits – they had some respiratory disorder – by their right names. We humans of lesser account simply vanished from the screen of her mind, deleted. A virus had got into her computer, and it had crashed.

'The poor woman was hospitalized, perforce, on a permanent basis, and two months later my father hanged himself in the shed behind the housing office. He could not live without her and left us to look after ourselves – or perhaps he thought I was old enough to do it. I was not. Or perhaps I just would not.

'I tell you this not so that you will feel sorry for me, but so you will understand why I behave as I do. One knows, but can do nothing about it. One's obsessions and compulsions remain.

The authorities, finally, moved in to help. Most of the animals were put down by the RSPCA. We five children were taken into care by the NSPCC. They did what they could to keep us together as a family, but the scale of the task proved beyond them. The two youngest children, Guinevere and Gawain, went to a pleasant enough family where they would join a couple of Labradors and a cat, and Morgana and Peregrine went to the Bartons, who had three dachshunds. I was able to reassure social services that I would be quite happy on my own with an elderly couple with a budgerigar, and that is what they found for me. Thus I was able to shrug off my past, and without the accompaniment of babies wailing, dogs barking, rabbits wheezing, cats yowling, hens coughing, poetry droning in the background, I did well at school, passed exams, went to college and am now a mortgage broker. Nothing is more important to me than helping people acquire stable and permanent homes.

'In good time all my siblings came to me to help buy their houses, and I was able to do so. All are now well and securely housed with manageable mortgages, and live stable family lives.

I like to feel I have achieved at least this much. But nothing is for nothing. It has been at a cost.

'I own a very nice property myself, mock-Tudor, three-bed, three-bath, in a well-thought-of suburb with good schools and easy access to motorway and public transport. I live in it on my own, being unmarried and without children. Just as my grand-mother, brought up in the war when butter was rationed, could never get enough of it in later life, so I can never get enough space and solitude. I like my lovers to go before breakfast: I must drink my coffee and eat my yoghurt on my own. Sometimes at night I am woken by someone else's cat howling in my garden and my heart begins to pound and I sweat, and must get up at once and go to check in case a cat flap has mysteriously appeared in one of the doors and it can get in.

'No, one does not escape such childhoods unscathed, and I am left, it is true, with quite a few problems. You have already seen what a cat chasing a mouse can do to me. My love of solitude is balanced by a craving for the company of strangers. I have a com-pulsion to steal food rather than buy it. But I have found a not too anti-social way of dealing with these two obsessions. I attend the weddings and funerals of strangers, and eat greedily at the wedding feast or funeral wake. I wear smart suits and little hats for the weddings, and deep black with a touch of purple for funeral wakes. The food at weddings is always better than the food at funerals – people have months, years to prepare – with funerals it is often only days. But then the sense of theft I require is more easily assuaged at funerals: people give so gladly at weddings it seems like a kindness to accept what is on offer; funerals are usually tense affairs, because the will is yet to be read, and the chil-dren will almost inevitably have quarrelled, about the ceremony itself, or who gets what, as sibling rivalry surfaces, and funeral expenses come out of the estate. Nobody is feeling generous.

'Weddings are easy to find. On any Saturday afternoon in the prosperous suburbs, you are bound to come across a church with a bride in a wedding gown on the steps outside, and a wedding party posed for the photographs. Then park your car and join the guests on the steps, and look helpless, and a little wistful, and someone is sure to give you a lift to the venue, and if any questions are asked, which they seldom are, to the bride's friends you are of the groom's party, and vice versa. And you can eat all you want. And such variety! Canapés and vol-au-vents, little triangular sandwiches and sausages on sticks if they're old-fashioned, salad dips and flax crackers if they're New Age, mango-and-brie filo and quails' eggs and very occasionally caviar if they're posh. I take what I can home: so much gets thrown away normally it's a wicked waste not to. The fashion for big designer bags has really suited me: most people need them for their stilettos at parties but they're good for food zip-locks too. Once I found myself popping a piece of cheese on the end of a stick into the bride's mouth – for a moment I'd thought she was Morgana my little sister: they had the same blonde hair. Morgana was always so hungry. As indeed, was I.

'June's the peak season: very few people get married between Christmas and the New Year.

'Funerals are different. I take them more seriously and they need more research. *The Times* is good when it comes to serious people. I like to go to the service: it shows respect, and you are more likely to be given a lift. People ask fewer questions: for all anyone knows you might well be a secret lover or lesbian partner out of the past. I drive a black Bentley so if I happen to come across a funeral cortege I can just slip in and follow it to its destination. Also, after funerals, there is a strong desire to have sex; the instinct is there to create new life. A lift of the eyebrow, an inclination of the head, and a man will follow you where you lead. They are better than supermarkets as a place for picking up men, though not necessarily for keeping them. Which suits me just fine.

'The ethical dilemma I was referring to? Yes, it worries me. I feel guilty. It concerns a cat.

'I so dislike household pets. They ruined my childhood, reduced my mother to little more than a vegetable, as good as murdered my father. And yet is not my duty here on earth to forgive, as I hope to be forgiven? Will the Almighty forgive me if I murder one of his creatures? For that is what it amounts to. A plump, self-satisfied tabby, which tried to jump from its garden wall to its kitchen window and missed, and fell into a concrete pit from which, because of an overlay, it has no hope of escape. I know. I saw it happen. If I did nothing it would simply starve to death. I decided on the instant to do nothing, so great was the joy of revenge, the sense of justice finally achieved. That was just before I came up here.

'I am amazed at myself, being able to sit here in such close company with others and talk and talk as I never have done before. Perhaps I feel I am amongst friends. And perhaps I am changing a little. During my stay here at Castle Spa I have missed two good funerals and not minded. Funerals peak at the end of December and the first two weeks of January – the season is too much for some: hearts tend to burst. I surprised myself by booking in for these particular two weeks, but for some reason I did.

'The cat? I try to forget about the cat. It's obviously the best thing to do. I should never have told you. You're all just a bunch of cat lovers. You wanted that cat to catch that mouse: you were on the cat's side, I could tell. No wonder I freaked out. The cat is not interesting: as I say, forget it, the cat is as good as dead. What happened was this. I was driving through the Hampstead Garden suburb just last week. I do a lot of business in the Jewish ortho-dox community, and it's always a pleasure. People keep their word and their gardens tidy and honour their contracts. Yes, my mother is Jewish, which makes me technically Jewish too, but she married out and under my father's influence became a staunch atheist.

'This is a really nice area I'm talking about, some way from the Heath – which can get quite rabid, these days – almost no crime, substantial family houses, high birth rate, excellent schools and nurseries. I happened to be driving towards the Hoop Lane, think-ing perhaps I might pick up a cortege, when I passed a house with its front door open. An open door in the area usually means someone has died and just been buried and the near relatives are sitting Shiva. They'll all have gathered together in the house for seven days to receive visitors. It's considered an act of loving kindness and compassion to pay a home visit to the mourners. You bring food and leave it, so there's usually lots about. You don't exchange greetings and the mourners initiate the conversation. Then you can talk about the deceased and it's easy enough, whether you know them or not, like telling someone's fortune. You just make what you say all-purpose, as astrologers do. "Mercury is retrograde so expect to make mistakes this week." Who is likely to argue with that?

'Best to find out first whether the departed was a man or a woman – you can tell from the condolence cards – and then just say what a wonderful person they were, how strong their personality, how much they will be missed, we were all so fond of him, her, mind you, they had their little ways! And that latter always lifts the atmosphere because nobody's perfect and it's as well someone says it, without going into particulars. The family probably assumed I was someone from his office: when you are recently bereaved one kind and concerned face looks much like another. You're not meant to distract the mourner from their loss so it's okay to slip away pretty soon. I was the youngest person there so there was not going to be any sex involved. I know when I'm beaten.

'I was helping myself to smoked salmon sandwiches in the kitchen on my way out when I saw the cat fall from the window. No, I didn't tell anyone, I had to get on, I had to catch the train up here at two o'clock and no, I don't think anyone would necessarily notice its absence, in the circumstances. Or hear its cries, because of the double-glazing. It's a very well-appointed house, worth well over a million, I'd say. How long do cats last without food? It had water: there was a trickle from a drain. Water would be no problem.

'I can hardly be expected to leave here, catch a train if there are any running, which is doubtful because of this stupid strike, and go all the way back to Hampstead Garden suburb just because of some stupid cat, so overfed it can't even get from a wall to a window!'

But even as she spoke she was getting up from the table, and smiled at us so radiantly we knew that was exactly what she was going to do – she was going to make amends. She would go all the way back to make sure the cat was okay, and by saving the cat she would save herself. She might even be relieved of her compulsions, so her rather unusual eating disorders would be cured, and the only weddings and funerals she would go to in future would be ones to which she had been properly invited, or indeed to her own. Well, there is always hope.

'The thing is,' she said as she left the room, 'in the end we all turn into our own mothers, no matter how we struggle against it.'

The Brain Surgeon gave the Mortgage Broker a lift to the station. By good luck there was a skeleton train service still running to London. She would not get there until the early hours of the morning, and taxis at the other end would be few and far between, but still she took it.

27

And soon it was time for the Screenwriter's Tale. She had only occasionally joined us at the Jacuzzi. She had surfaced on occasion to eat, had been at the meeting with Beverley, seemed uninterested in the fate of the Spa, or its staff, and had certainly no intention of leaving, having planned the ten days for peace and quiet in order to finish a script – a political thriller. She now wanted to try it out on us. So far we had had life histories but we supposed we could put up with being pitched a script, Hollywood style.

She could do with a few beauty treatments, we thought, though with every day that passed she seemed less and less likely to get one. Her interest in her appearance was minimal. Her rather muddy skin spoke of late nights and cigarettes. Her shaggy brows needed plucking. She was wide-shouldered and slim-hipped, had a broad brow and a tapered chin, and large feet at the end of long legs. Her fierce, proud, grey eyes were her best feature. She was proud and defiant in gesture and movement: she was accustomed to argument, to staring her opponents out. Mira had looked her up on Google and been impressed. Rosa Anchor. She was British, had started out in advertising, won a prize or two there, moved into film and before she was twenty-five had scripted a small art film which had won a Palme d'Or at Cannes. She'd crossed over into Hollywood, presumably lured by big money, and been nominated twice for best script at the Oscars, one for an action/ adventure movie, another for a crime/drama/thriller. This was some going, even in a world where the writer is devalued, and a main writing credit normally goes to the one who has the mouse in their hand when the movie is closed, the cycle of rewrites is over, and the production manager says 'go'. It became apparent why she looked as she did – the attempt to make the unreal real, to turn idea into form the idea can act like a radiation blast and quite drain the life out of you. And the bigger the budget the stronger the blast. The fashion industry does the same to those who serve it. If films are to take off, if new fashions are to bounce around the world, sacrifice is required.

Like the rest of us, damp and sodden, white-gowned and anonymous, bereft of the normal tools of self-presentation, the subtle signals by which women normally impress one another – hair styles, make-up, clothes, jewellery – we had only our life stories and our histories to offer. But Rosa was dealing with something else: an outpouring of inventiveness that overwhelmed her. No sooner had she taken her place by the pool than she was in a trance state. If I hadn't known better I would have said she was channelling, simply letting the spirits move through her. It was spooky. Plots flowed like water. Scenes formed in front of her eyes and she pitched them to us.

28

The Screenwriter's Tale

'Okay,' she started. 'I am a man.'

'Then you have no place round this pool,' the Trophy Wife said. 'Even the Judge here does her best to be a woman.'

The Judge waved her pretty hands around and lilted her reproach. 'But I am a woman! How can you read me as anything else?' Nobody took up the challenge.

'I live my life in fiction,' the Screenwriter retorted. 'I can be a man if I want. That's my point.

'I am sitting waiting. Something is going to happen. The audience is expectant. What? Where am I sitting? That's the first clue. A luxury hotel in Hollywood? Why not? No, not the Four Seasons, that's too quirky. Somewhere more ordinary like the Beverley Wilshire: can you see the Hollywood sign from there? Would it be easier to move the hotel or the Hollywood sign, or just start in another location? Get my researchers on to that.'

Her voice is a low monotone: she stares at her feet as she speaks, not seeing them.

'I could be sipping my martini or mango juice in the lush hotel oasis. Trees actually grow here and flowers. Surely you'd get a view of the Hollywood sign from here? Early establishment of city identity essential. Skylines do it or number-plates. I can do LA better than say Chicago or New England so yes, keep it Hollywood. But oasis is good. Oasis is green. Green is good. Yes, make me nature boy. Backstory, my last pic hit a seven mil release high, romantic comedy, young disabled parking lot attendant, and bitter, butch girl angel with a broken wing. Sandra Bullock? Of course. I end up handing out peace apples to world leaders: is there a merchandising op in there? What's a peace apple? I don't know yet, but I'll get there. Green is good but green apples can be sour. Avoid GM crops though, too contentious. Peace butterflies? A possibility. Leave the backstory be, we're here and now, in the lobby, let's settle for that. I'm mean to a black lad who wants my autograph. Am I an anti-hero or a wounded hero? Wounded, I reckon. Yes, I'm troubled, troubled. I have to be redeemed at the end of my journey. But what is the journey? We're in Hollywood. So is it sex, celebrity, or pride goes before a fall? Yeah, that's it, I'm a troubled celebrity: I am waiting to meet my nemesis in a garden.

'Nemesis comes towards me in the shape of a beautiful woman. But this is an action film, so someone comes out of the door after her. I'm out of my chair going to meet her. Bang crash explosion and she's dead. Flames everywhere. I am rolled over and over in the blast. Singed and blackened oasis. That's good. It was me they were after, not her. Villain's last words tell us. What did I know that I shouldn't? What have I done? I'm shocked, wounded – my girlfriend comes running towards me. She's Puerto Rican. Good arse. Not too good or we can't have her killed off early. She's adopting a baby from Malawi. My, are her credentials good. Or perhaps she's pregnant? The shock makes her lose the baby. Yes, that's good. Part Two is simple: tracing the villains. I have a friend who'll put in the action sequences: I'll do the jokes. A death squad from Iran, no, that's over, film-wise – an extremist Bible Belt squad trying to root out sin and I've sinned. My saintly pastor explains yes, I am guilty. Redemption never fails.'

She seemed to strike an obstacle, and sighed, and remembered where she was.

'I'm sorry. Are you bored already? Not very interesting really. Nothing new, startling, on the pulse. Yes, it's a rotten film. I suppose I could turn out to be a Federal Agent, black, doomed to relive a certain day over and over and this is it. That might work. Oh, forget it. My mind takes off into the alternative realities, that's all. I write them in my sleep and sometimes go to sleep to write them. I've reworked too many other people's scripts too many times, looked out of too many other eyes to remember who I am anyway. Everyone wants to be creative but there are drawbacks to being the way I am. I am a bad, nervous, slow driver. My mind is so full of scenarios of disaster: the brow of a hill can only mean a pile-up the other side.'

'If you'd had him sitting in the lounge not the oasis,' asked the Mortgage Broker, 'would it be a different film?'

'Totally. I think the problem lay there. A basic inconsistency of setting. Action movies don't start in hotel grounds, but in lobbies. Breaking glass and searing heat not singed avocado plants. Unless of course blessed by one-winged Sandra Bullock and sprouting all over the place. I may rewrite, I may abandon, I haven't made up my mind.'

'Scenes from your own life, please,' said Shimmer. 'As a woman. We'll have no evasion here.'

'I can't put them in order,' said the Screenwriter. 'I need an editor to do that. But there are good scenes. Yes, I am confident there are good, workable scenes which could be used and worked on.

'I am in Concorde, I am in the toilet, I am becoming a member of the Mile High Club. I am certainly in Concorde, flying into New York. I cannot quite be sure about the Mile High part but the basis of all art is certainly sex. We circle round that centre secret. Now that centre secret is available on the net there can be no more art. What is its point? We have arrived. We are there. Now we have no art, only commerce, and a few dull French movies for critics to worry over and get their salaries. My Mile High companion was young, good-looking, slim though I think he had had pubic hair implanted in his scalp. It was a time back and they weren't as good at transplants as they are now.

'Yes, I am pretty sure that happened, though again, fact and fiction get difficult to sort out. I looked at him, he looked at me across the aisle, we were in hyper space, or super sound or ultra speed, whatever it's called, Mach 2, which is stirring to blood and

sex, so high, so fast, so beautiful, this soaring bird, one feels the
need to contribute to the experience in the best way one knows
how, and as one we moved from our seats, slipped in together, did
our anxious, impetuous thing, wedged between basin and loo, me
leaning back, him thrusting upwards; and then hardly two
minutes later we were out again, first him, then me, in time for our
trays to arrive. The caviar and the lobster and the free gift pack of
cards in their real leather wallet. I left mine behind, and the
luxury poker set. I was needed at a meeting down Fifth Avenue at
11 a.m. Concorde got in to Kennedy at 9.30: takes at least an hour
to get in. The regular flights don't get in till half-ten so Concorde
it had to be.

'I smiled at him as we went out through customs and I never got
his name. In those disease-free days this kind of thing happened.
I expect he was temporary-rich like me: I had just done a film deal
and again, in those days, that meant big money. I got to the
meeting in good time, but it had been postponed until 2 p.m. Fog
on the Hudson River.

'So I went down Fifth Avenue and bought a fur coat. It was
cold. It was just after fur became a no-no. I only got to wear it
once. I gave it to my sister. She wears it to feed the animals when
the weather's cold: best mink. Light but hardy. $22,000 way back
then. My sister's a country girl. I go mad with boredom in the
country. All that patient virtuous growing foliage. I reckon there's
something there in that scene: when the bomb explodes and
Nemesis is killed. The tragedy is that growing nature has been
harmed, forget the women. Humans replaceable, nature not.
Global warming. Think round that. Why did I bring Nemesis in,
in the first place? She must be there for a reason. A triangle? Hero,
pregnant girlfriend, beautiful woman? I gave the girlfriend an
arse; I didn't give Nemesis a face. Beautiful means stereotype:
okay in an action film but this one is turning into something else.
Perhaps she has a scar? Out of the past? His guilt? What is he,
what am I, so fucking guilty about?'

'Rosa,' said the Judge, warningly. 'Your life, please.'

'Sorry,' she said. 'I took acid once with coke and I reckon it did something to my brain. Guilt? Casual sex? Perhaps sex is never casual. Perhaps the man whose name I never took had a wife, and he confessed to her, and they had a row and he threw acid, and now she is Nemesis and comes to confront me across the oasis, and I have to stop her somehow and I am the hit squad. I myself am the villain that has to be stopped.

'I gave birth to a child once but it was brain-damaged – perhaps that was the acid and the coke, I was pregnant at the time – the hospital kept it alive when left to itself it would have mercifully died, so I refused to take it home with me. Bonding seemed unnecessary in the circumstances, but they wanted me to feel the whole pain of my failure, my guilt. But why? To what end? Real life is so unmalleable: the screenplay so wonderfully open to change. The action hero becomes a gardener, a planter of oases. Perhaps he is in the desert, not an LA hotel? What was that film, *The English Patient*? Oh yes, sorry, the child. I could not bear to produce anything less than perfect. It died within the month, anyway. I had a husband once but he was unfaithful. I sent him away. He was sorry then. He said it was because I was so successful and he was not, but I think he was just weak and useless and without resolution. He was a good driver, I'll say that for him, but that was because he had no imagination. I can always hire a chauffeur.

'Oh yes, okay. My life as a screenwriter. I had another meeting on that trip: a big-time New York producer, out of TV into films. He was in his fifties, I suppose, rubicund, Jewish, and charismatic, with a wide American face and a lot of smiles. He seemed the kindliest of men. He took me to a production meeting. He was setting up some big-budget thriller. His people were there, seven or eight hungry young men. He was pack leader: he took advantage of them. He humiliated them, tore them to bits and flung the shreds of flesh about, and set others to devour them. They were an ignorant lot, true: asked for casting suggestions all they could utter in their terror were the name of box office stars in descending order of importance while he shouted. It seemed an absurd way to set up a film. I told him so. He asked me out to dinner. He collected me from my hotel, and I was flustered. We went out through the revolving doors and I misjudged and got into the same slot as him and fell out the other end. It was awkward, but he seemed to like it. He gave me a lesson on how to cope with revolving doors. "Never, never, follow on anyone's heels. Make a space."

'A Bridget Jonesy, Sandra Bullocky kind of moment. But not right for this film, not so far, nothing sweetly comic. Put it on hold, somewhere in the Final Draft file. Bed was fine, he was the tenderest thing, and he worshipped at a shrine, reverent: American men do that – though he complained of my silence.

'"Why do you say nothing?" he asked, but what is there to say? "*So good, so good, ooh,*" as in the porn films? It is a debasement.

'But he had a big family and Hanukkah celebrations to go to and some celebrity wife he'd just married and already seemed to hate and fear. And I had my Concorde ticket home. We kept in touch for a bit but then he had a heart attack, I heard, and I didn't hear from him again. I read in the papers that he died. Alpha male, anger and outrage. That was as near to love as I ever got. Lost opportunities. It would never have worked. A Christian English girl with big feet she fell over: best to be Jewish in the film business anyway, smarter, quicker, tougher. English tough, as I am, is so different from Jewish tough. But we have the ideas, for us they're two a penny: we throw them about, they sweep us away. For them, ideas come hard. A lot of stealing of ideas goes on over there, if only because of their rarity value.

'Alpha male, anger and outrage. My hero is not troubled, not a gardener, not a grower of love apples, not a proposer of world peace. My hero would not look after an angel with a broken wing; my hero would like to rid the world of imperfection. My hero is a terrorist, leader of the pack: ruthless, he tears his inferiors to shreds. My hero does not have a partner who is adopting a Malawian baby. He has a wife he loathes, rightly, who is a worse villain than he. And yes, he has her killed. And the audience must feel sympathy. He is Tony Soprano and his wife is talking to the CIA and he must kill her. The scarred wife as Nemesis, the one who turns men's blood to ice. Archetypes. When drifting off fictionally get back to the archetypes.'

'A little less fictional drift,' said the Judge, severely. 'And a little more you.'

'Okay. On the way back to Kennedy and Concorde, the hotel called me a yellow cab off the street. It was a beaten-up rusty mess, and the bearded driver looked like a man from the mountain tribes. An NY version of the London one that public speaker woman had. I should have said no but one's instinct for fair play got in the way. He needed the fare, and besides I was in a hurry. The six-lane Kennedy Freeway was packed. We were in the outside lane going at sixty when we had a blowout. Somehow the driver managed to get us across the six lanes to the verge without dying. Horns blared and brakes squealed. The driver trembled and wept: he spoke no English, he had no spare tyre, I looked. It was pre cellphone days. I got my luggage out of the trunk and hitchhiked. No one stopped for me. I prayed. An empty cab came by. His fare had had a heart attack and died. Paramedics had removed him. Now the driver, furious, had to continue towards Kennedy without a fare because there is no turning back once you are on that road. I caught Concorde.

'I tried to tell a few of my fellow passengers about my adventure but they could not hear. If you were in the back section of Concorde the noise was terrible because the sound caught up with you. Only in the front section was it sublimely, surreally quiet, demanding the stillness of pure, indifferent sexual encounter. I had not known that. They do not tell you. Someone had to occupy those unpopular seats, but the staff despise you if you do. You know nothing. My luggage came to pieces on the carousel at Heathrow, and my belongings were strewn around for everyone to see. I had bought the cases at Wal-Mart: why pay more, I asked myself, guilty about the fur coat, and other insane purchases which had to be brought home. Nobody demanded proof of purchase, as they did with you, Dorleen, because I was in the Concorde queue. Should I feel social guilt because of this?

'It occurs to me that this might relate to the *"what do I know that I shouldn't, what have I done?"* solution. A man's cases burst open on the carousel. Some truth is inadvertently made public, some guilt made known. Who then is the scarred woman? It is me. Of course it is me. My own nemesis. I killed myself off very near the front of the film: no sooner on screen than off. Really I couldn't bear to live with my doppelgänger. I flew off to New York while my baby was still in hospital, when I got back she had died. My little imperfect, hopeless alter ego. But what can one do? The producer calls, the writer jumps!'

'You're making it up,' said the Mortgage Broker. 'Yellow cabs always carry spares. They have to.'

'He hadn't read the by-laws,' said the screenwriter. 'The taxi ride to Kennedy is true, though the death from heart attack of the previous fare in the cab I was fortunate enough to pick up is an invention. I wondered why a cab would be driving empty in that direction at that time of the morning and thought of an obvious reason, pre-empting your questions, subduing your doubts. That is what film writing is about: getting in first with an explanation so the question can never arise. The bit you took for granted was false: the bit you doubted was true. That's how it goes in the world of the screenwriter. We snatch elements out of real life and tone it down and shape it up to make fiction. I surf my real life, like a sea bird, unsure of even that reality, I dip down into the ocean of uncertain memory and pick up morsels of fictional nourishment. That's a nice image; the sea bird dipping over the sea. An opening shot – no, or better still a closing one. Off into the sunset, happy ever after.

'I am the lady screenwriter, scarred. Guilt. Dead babies. Aborted screenplays. Boom! Crash! Gone. Nemesis. Behind me, lining up for grievance, tens of thousands of wasted scenes. There in the back of my mind, fingering it, never giving up, still nudging for acknowledgement, the aborted scenes, the wasted lines. In yellowing typescripts, printouts, corroded tapes, computer archives: *remember me, you let me go. Int. The Lobby Evening: Ext. Round the Pool. Day. Cut.* Too late, too late, the world's moved on. No-one will ever want you now: bring you back to life. *Your fault, your fault, you failed us, and we were good, my, how good we were!* Yet I fought, oh children of my fevered brow, line by line I defended you: I fought, struggled and argued to keep you in the world, risked shame, contempt, derision, weariness, exhaustion of the spirit – cold-eyed, your enemies and mine set out to destroy you, and they did. Draft two, draft three, draft four and still not "right". My poor dying baby, my script, my scene, my line, don't kill my child: you say it is deformed: *why are you so silent? What is there to be said? So much, so much, and still the right words do not come.* My poor, poor half-aborted child, don't fillet it, please let it live, but no, I weaken – changes please, or shall we find another writer? Forgo the fee? I rewrite, lose the plot, and down the plughole goes the child, rewritten into nothingness. Scenes struggle and die. Another project lies abandoned. *You have worn your mother out: she has no strength or nourishment left for you, she must feed the others.* Well, well, brightly, on, forward, recreate the universe in a reasonable manner, what is this commission now I see before me, sign here please on the dotted line? Lose not a moment: regret treads hotly on the heels. One must always be one step ahead.

'New page, new scene, new line, *Int. The famous marble Jacuzzi at Castle Spa. Night.*

'The water bubbles like a thousand ideas before bursting. My head, my poor head. Did I tell you about my time in India? The lady screenwriter in Bombay? She'd been hired just as she was divorcing her husband: he wanted reconciliation but she didn't have time for it. The producer, once a NY dilettante, heir to a vast fortune, now dressed in white robes, drugged out, sitting cross-legged in Bombay, consulting the I Ching, the book of Chinese Oracles. More Confucian than Buddhist, but never mind. His wife, a Buddhist monk of Russian origin and jet-set fame, had found peace and died up a Himalayan mountain. Now she was safely dead and no longer claiming alimony he loved her and nothing would do but that the lady screenwriter of note would write the film of her life. He'd cast the yarrow sticks, and threw Kun-Kun, Kun-Kun, the receptive, the female: this confirmed his choice. She must fly out, now, now. She flew, the hired hack, but her agents demanded first-class fare. The filmmaker resented it, and let her know it. Away from home in a strange land, in a villa out on Chowpatti beach, like Rapunzel imprisoned in her tower, she wrote. Visions came to her: she was visited by the irate deceased, not so peaceful now, who gave her messages, seized her hand and wrote with it.

'A scene she still remembers, the helicopter, circling, searching, between the Himalayan peaks: the voices of the pilots, laying down the plot. That was fiction. The sound of the big jets out of Chatrapati International Airport five miles away, every seven minutes, roaring into, over, the room so she'd duck and tremble, so sure was she that death was coming. That was fact. The visions; the elegant white hand that wrote: the smell of lilac that came with them, they were surely dreams?

'The script delivered, silence fell. He called her down, white-robed, bleary, cross-legged, to the druggy, humid air: *changes, there must be changes*. What sort of changes? *The I Ching says changes*. The I Ching is the Book of Changes, she said; it says so on the cover: be more precise. He couldn't be. She panicked: she forswore her calling. She made changes, any changes. He hid her ticket home. He called her in again. *How did you know all that? You are a witch: you are a grave robber; you have stolen the thoughts from my head. I will take back what is mine: now go.* The noise is fearful – it's the flight from LA – surely the pilot has got the flight path wrong: he's coming in too low, they will all die. *Go, go!* She goes, gladly, but the haunted helicopter circles forever in her head. The blue sky, the white peaks, the majestic beauty, the silent plane – the helicopter has changed into a glider (a good change, that: quiet is essential) – broken by the casual voices of the searchers after who knows what? But all in vain. The film is never made. When she gets back she is divorced.

'Secretly she'd made another copy of the script – paranoia is catching – she hides it in the bottom of her suitcase, smuggles it out. That comes to nothing too. She should save her breath to cool her porridge. Things may come to you from the other side of the grave, but this is the world of film, and not even ghosts can break through.'

'You're always in the third person present,' the Judge complained.

'That is the language of film,' says the Screenwriter, 'that is how it is done. How else could it be? Things play out in front of you. No past or future, only the invented present, no overview allowed.'

She fell silent. I almost think she slept, relieved at last from the visions tearing at the inside of her head. At any rate the wide, grey eyes closed – though I feared the hectic movements of the eyeballs beneath them did not – and I was happy for her.

As for us, we lingered by the pool, glad of the rest. But then the Stepmother came up to me and asked if she could have a word with me. She was going to ask me if I would read her manuscript for her: I could tell. It took courage to ask. She had stayed very quiet until now and indeed, like the Screenwriter, had been less interested in treatments than peace and quiet to write. Personally I prefer chaos and mayhem around me, and to write over difficulties, pressured by deadlines, but all writers are different, and many subscribe to the notion that time must be set aside in which their 'creativity' can flourish. Personally, I just do what I do, in the time I can find. I said of course I would. I liked the look of her. She was in her late thirties, I imagined, approaching forty, and had an air of pleasant integrity, confidence, intelligence and accomplishment, and the kind of even-featured, clear-complexioned good looks that go with those attributes. She spoke in the accents of the English educated classes: her voice was musical and friendly, but accustomed to command. She worked, as I discovered, in radio, where people are slower on their feet than in, say, TV or the press, but are more socially conscious and have better judgement. She would be pleasant to her subordinates and courteous to her superiors, and never at a loss for conversation. She would take a meeting, one thought, without undue fuss, ease and charm, never doubting her own competence, and get everyone home in time for tea. She described herself not as wife, mother, or high-powered executive, but as a stepmother. I asked her if her book was about being one such, and she said yes. She had a little tidying up to do, and then she would show it to me.

It was only a novella, she said, but she'd been to creative writing classes, and a publisher had been interested, and had gone ahead to proof stage, but then she had withdrawn. Her stepdaughter Eliza had objected, and her husband too. But she'd heard a few of the other stories and now she thought she just might go ahead after all. The tale needed to be told for the sake of stepmothers everywhere. 'If I could make it illegal for a woman to marry a man who already had children, I would,' she said.

She spoke bitterly and drew the attention of the others. The Vicar's Ex-wife pointed out that this being the age of second marriages it would cut down the marriage rate considerably, and the Stepmother admitted it was a counsel of perfection.

The Psychoanalyst, now snuggling up to the Judge, said there was a lot of truth in the archetype of the wicked stepmother: the father very rapidly forgets the wife he once had, whether he has put her aside for her inadequacy, or she dies. The wife currently in the bed and the kitchen, providing him with sex and food, is the only one he notices. Likewise the youngest child, the one under his nose, is the one to get the full blast of his protective instincts. These were Darwinian rather than Freudian truths, but tallied. While the stepmother, for her part tries to push the rival wife's children out of the nest, to provide better sustenance for her own. So stepchild, beware!

The Judge nodded approval, and the Stepmother, surprisingly, and quite losing her cool, clambered out of the water, and stood on the marble edge of the Jacuzzi, tapping her plump little foot nervously, flaring her nostrils.

'Good Lord!' said the Stepmother. 'In my case it was pity the poor stepmother.' And then, controlling herself, 'Forgive me, everyone. I have been under a lot of strain lately.'

'With a little intelligence and understanding,' said the Psychoanalyst smugly, 'even these complex relationship problems can normally be happily resolved.'

'Quite right,' said the Judge, happily clapping her plump hands together. 'Well said!'

At which the Stepmother tossed her head about and practically snorted, and then head held high, walked off, in what can only be described as a huff, a hissy-fit. So she too could lose her composure. It was quite consoling to know. We decided not to go after her. The Jacuzzi was rich in jasmine oils, no doubt introduced by the Judge while in seductive mode. It had the effect of making us all agreeably languid.

29

Mira and I repaired to the kitchen to talk. Some went to play Scrabble: some went to their rooms.

But she and I were restless. I felt elated because I had resolved so much, so simply. I was not fighting myself any more. Perhaps I disliked Eleanor because I saw myself in her. But the Eleanor/Nisha/Belinda story had to be left out of the equation. It was too extreme. Jenny's story had no pools of blood, no sliced flesh. I had behaved badly to her once upon a time: that was all. I could see it and put up with it. Vague fears of punishment from fate, which had focused so strongly and unexpectedly, had dissipated with the acknowledgement of my guilt, my acceptance of responsibility. Sumatra flu had vanished with its paranoiac blogs. Mira's satellite phone had come to life again. Beverley's computer was working. Julian, equally, was not going to be having an affair and was not going to choose Jenny over me. And yet I had the strangest feeling that it could have all gone the other way: that some cosmic decision had rested upon what happened to me. That in the last few days I had served as a fulcrum for some balance between good and evil, as it tilted first one way, then the other.

Had I failed to resolve my own crisis to good end, nothing in the outer world would have resolved itself well either. Things had been dangerously hotting up, like the planet itself. It had been a near shave. All the fears and angers of the world were massed outside the walls – just a shove and they'd have given. Pandemic would have struck, nuclear weapons been unleashed, the virtual world been brought to book: global warming boiled the seas and an asteroid strike finished us all off anyway. And then the enemy had drawn back – the video had rewound, back to the beginning, because of me. We could start again. Mad! My solipsism, I could see, knew no bounds.

But how do we manage to live at all, attend to our own small lives with such passion, in the face of so many dangers? That's the marvel. Mira stopped grating cheese for yet more baked potatoes and looked up at the window.

'Look at that!' she said. Flakes of thick white snow had begun to fall. We went to the window and looked out, but there was nothing to be seen but a gently moving, particulated white wall. I had never seen snow fall so determinedly and solidly.

'We're going to be stuck here, like it or not,' said Mira. 'A few hours of this and the roads will be impassable.'

Beverley put in an appearance. 'I hope you ladies remember to wrap the cheese in a damp cloth before you put it back in the pantry,' she said. 'It can dry out and that's a wicked waste of money. My parents keep a dairy farm outside Hamilton so I know about these things.'

We promised to remember.

She said she hoped the snow didn't bring the power lines down: the telephone was already out.

'A lot of the ladies may be sorry they didn't take my advice and leave a lot earlier,' she said. 'It's going to be hard to get out of here now the weather had closed in.'

Lady Caroline's cash flow problem had been resolved, and the staff were now up to date with their wages, including hers. But now of course there was no way she could get through to the staff to tell them to come in, no way they could get in anyway because the road was blocked. She seemed quite pleased to relate this. She said she'd had a couple of phone calls earlier, both for me, just before the phone line went.

I asked why she hadn't told me at once and she said it was a long way down from the top of the East Tower, and she had been very busy. She was keeping the place running almost single-handedly and doing her best for everyone. She consulted her notes. One message had been from someone called Julian to say he was flying home on New Year's Day. Someone called Jenny had turned up unexpectedly with her new husband Pete, and the house had become too crowded for comfort. Not unlike this one, Beverley remarked aside, with no staff to keep it running. There had been a message from someone called Alec who when she wanted to write it down said it wasn't important. If it wasn't important, why did they bother to ring?

I remarked that having her wages paid hadn't seemed to have improved her temper, which took her aback, but also made her giggle rather charmingly. She had her moments, and she had been making our beds: in my present mood I forgave her. Beverley admitted it was true. Now she had to start making up her mind again whether to go home to New Zealand or not; the dreadful indecision struck again. This country was not so bad. Oh, and there was a message for Mira. She knew there was something. It was from someone called Alistair, who said he was flying up to Glasgow and would be touching down on the way.

Mira also wanted to know why she hadn't been informed immediately. Beverley said there hadn't been much point, since touching down was rather unlikely; in New Zealand helicopters were fitted with skis but it wasn't going to happen here in a hurry, and the pad was a snowdrift.

'Oh yes,' Beverley went on, 'there were another couple of calls for you, Phoebe, but I couldn't make head nor tail of them so there didn't seem much point in writing them down, let alone going all the way down to fetch you. Just a lot of children saying they missed you and where were you. Kiwi kids know how to behave and don't all shout at once.'

I said I was only ever coming back to Castle Spa if there was a proper telephone system installed and a mobile mast.

'All the ladies say that,' said Beverley, 'but more than enough come back. Lady Caroline plays to full houses as it is, why should she bother?' She helped herself to grated cheese.

'I'm not surprised she has cash flow problems,' I said.

'They're nothing to do with this place,' said Beverly. 'It makes a fortune and doubles it with phone calls and bottled water.' The debts, apparently, were because of Lady Caroline's gambling habit. She, Beverley, didn't approve of gambling. The occasional flutter on the races was okay, but anything else was decadent.

The Judge came in to say the Vicar's Ex-wife was waiting to start her story at the pool, and we should come quick. So we went and Beverley actually came too. And Mira took a hop, a skip and a jump on the way.

'He loves me,' she whispered in my ear. 'He loves me, he loves me, and he wants to be with me.' I groaned. And she a grown woman.

30

The Vicar's Ex-wife's Tale

'Ghosts can always break through,' said Tess, the Vicar's Ex-wife, 'at least in my experience.'

We were installed again around the pool. Rosa still slept, or partly slept, and we left her unconscious. It seemed merciful.

'Whether there are or there aren't,' said the Trophy Wife, 'it's best not to acknowledge them. In case they come rushing in, whirl round the room in a gust of air and out again, snatching our souls as they go.'

'That's what I always think,' agreed the Vicar's Ex-wife. 'We had ghosts in our house the way other people have mice, but it was ages before I'd acknowledge it. And I don't think my husband ever quite did. You pretend if you don't see the mice you don't have a problem, but in the end one cute mouse in the cupboard is a hundred mice in your path, and you bring in the rat catcher.'

We were ready for a ghost story and demanded her tale. She demurred. She said ghosts liked nothing better than to be talked about, and she didn't want to gratify them. She said they caught wind of fear and came clustering like sharks round a bleeding man. This wasn't the time or the place for ghost stories. She said, as it was, she spent a lot of time with her fingers crossed to stop the ghosts from stealing her soul, let alone give them a story to feed upon.

It was true. The long, pale middle fingers of the Vicar's Ex-wife crossed on both hands even as I watched. It's the sign children make when they are asking the fates to forgive them a lie. She was pale – not translucent like the Manicurist – but with a kind of thick, marbly pallor of skin: her neck was long, rising out of shoulders so sloping that her bikini straps kept drifting down to smooth elbows: a long neck, and a brow wide and smooth, with a high hair-line – from which burst a mass of pale, curly hair, which ringleted itself in the steam. She looked like the illustration of a fine lady in some medieval manuscript, a falcon on her arm. I wouldn't say she had pop-eyes, but the eyeballs were certainly prominent, and her lids hooded – which gave her an air of being over-cautious – yet ready on the instant to take flight. She was fine lady and falcon all in one. She was certainly nervy.

'Yet I have ghosts to thank for what I am today,' she said. 'Without them I would still be the vicar's wife, not in charge of an investment bank, with an annual bonus which frightens even me. But I don't think their purpose was to help me: their purpose was – well, I don't know what. To frighten and torment the living? If so, it worked. They frightened me out of my old skin into a new one. I imagine this place is haunted, wouldn't you?'

And most looked sceptical but one or two shivered around the pool.

'I saw the Devil once,' the Judge ventured. 'You see him where you least expect him. I woke up out of some minor medical procedure to see him by the bed. He was wearing a white gown and pretending to be a doctor. His head was shaven and you could see the bumps under the skull, but they were in the wrong place. Everything about him was wrong, but it was hard to put your finger on. When he opened his mouth the red sinews went across the mouth vertically not horizontally; I thought he was going to bite my balls off – I had them, in those days, poor me – so I screamed. The next time I looked he was a perfectly ordinary medic.'

'People see all kinds of things when they're waking from anaesthetic,' said Shimmer. 'A lot of projection goes on. In this case I would think quite unnecessary guilt about gender change. Personally I'd think angels were more likely to be present, not devils, when you had your balls cut off. Don't worry about it.'

'I don't believe in the Devil,' said the Vicar's Ex-wife, piously.

'How come you don't believe in the Devil but you do believe in ghosts?' someone asked.

'The Devil is religion and ghosts are superstition,' said the Vicar's Ex-wife. 'I can live with ghosts in the room but not the Devil.'

'I don't like the shadows down there in that row of obsidian pillars. Why are those peculiar lamps swinging if there's no wind?'

'It's a clockwork mechanism,' said the Trophy Wife, 'installed by Burges more than 150 years ago, and still working. Originally the lanterns – which are not peculiar, merely oriental – would have contained incense: I switched the mechanism on just now: I love the way the light moves.'

'All the same,' said the Vicar's Ex-wife, 'would you mind if we didn't talk about ghosts? I'd rather tell you about my divorce.'

But the Judge would have none of it, and her sweet, newly female voice was persuasive. 'Most people have divorces,' she said. 'They're two a penny. Not so many experience ghosts.' So Tess began.

'Strange things happen in houses, we all know that. Whether we notice them or not is a different matter. Letters that should be on tables vanish and reappear somewhere else; pictures fall off walls for no reason; the scissors disappear; a mug falls off a hook; keys go missing. If the events are sufficiently random, or sufficiently far apart, they are overlooked. They don't make "sense" so we don't try. As the scientist whose experiment comes up with a bizarre answer, we simply try again until it makes sense. Anything rather than believe that the laws of nature are mutable. Only when the pace hots up, or makes a pattern, do we have to face facts.

'I refrained from facing facts for years, until one Sunday evening in the fifteenth year of my marriage, the thirteenth I had spent in the Vicarage. My husband, a curate when I married him, was twenty-one years older than me, and would now be labelled as a borderline Asperger's or perhaps OCD – obsessional compulsive disorder. The Vicarage had been added as a late Victorian after-thought to a rather handsome Norman church, the original having burned down in a fire set by an arsonist. The house was large, ramshackle, dark and draughty, and prey to wet rot, dry rot, woodworm and beetle. It leaned up against the church and by some trick of acoustics when you were sitting in the kitchen you could hear what was going on in the church next door, particularly the base notes of the organ. We had no children, which was a source of disappointment to both of us, and indeed to the parish. It is always pleasant in a small, stable and increasingly elderly community, to watch other people's children grow up.

'There was no reason the doctors could find that made me infertile; Tim did not have himself tested. Men have their pride and Tim had a great deal of it. He did not like doctors, nor trust them, and the indignity of what such examinations entailed put it out of the question. If God wanted us to have children, He would see to it. Otherwise there was enough work in the parish to be getting on with.

'I come from a good, steady, church-going family – my own father was a bishop – and was studying classics at Oxford when I met Tim. He was a member of the Prayer Book Society and came to give a lecture on the 39 articles of the Anglican way. He was astonishingly good-looking – beautiful, even – as those not given to empathy often are. I do some charity work amongst autistic children, and I sometimes think the label "handsome" could almost be one of the main diagnostic symptoms. If "handsome" can be equated with symmetry of feature, why then these implaca-ble children grew perfectly in the womb, unlike the rest of us. They noticed nothing of what was going on. Perhaps the normal foetus is more vulnerable to maternal mood change, hormonal swings, than we think: this is why so many of us emerge asymmetrical into the world, with noses too long and foreheads too high.'

'Please,' said the Manicurist. 'I thought you were telling us a ghost story. Let's just accept the husband was a fucking monster and get on with it.'

'Very well,' said the Vicar's Ex-wife, quite mildly. 'One could see she had good people-management skills. She would have made a good vicar's wife, which explained why the not-so-young curate would have snapped her up, and a bishop's daughter to boot. Anyway I fell in love with him. I had been reading *Jane Eyre*, and had always thought Jane should have gone off with St John Rivers the preacher and not listened to Rochester when he called to her through the aether. I found Tim most romantic and he found me most alluring and we married within the month and set about doing good works together. Our sex life never failed, and never varied, during the years we were together. Tim attended to the spiritual welfare of his parishioners; I presided over the Mothers' Union, the Women's Institute and ran the amateur dramatic society. It was a traditional way of life, and one I thought suited me. I had artistic skills, and did several courses in ceramic restoration at the art school in the local town, and was able to start workshops in the village, which brought in a little extra money for some of our poorer parishioners. It was unfortunate our Bishop was all the things that Tim was not – a modernizer, keen on the ordination of women to the priesthood, with no sense of language or church aesthetics – and so Tim's way ahead in his calling was blocked. He became bitter. He spoke rancorously and dismissively of our Bishop, of new style bongo-drum-and-therapy services, and made matters worse for himself.

'It would have been sensible for Tim to have moved over to Catholicism at this time, but he would not. He was married: Catholic clergy don't marry, but forswear the flesh and focus on the spirit. At the time of the women priest issue, when many Anglicans did convert, concessions were made so that married Anglican clergy could keep their wives and continue to officiate, but Tim felt this was no more than a self-interested move at the time of a dramatic drop in the numbers applying for the Catholic priesthood – who, these days, wants to declare themselves celibate? – and no doubt he was right. But it is in the nature of man to blame his spouse for anything that goes wrong, and I suspect Tim preferred to stay wronged and blame me, because he had the misfortune to be married to me, rather than adjust to the new world order. I had begun to go round with a kind of cloud of apology over my head. *My fault, my fault!*

'I realized things were not going as well within the marriage as I had hoped when I found myself addressing a Coronation mug. Next door evensong was ending. I could hear the faint sounds of 'Immortal, Invisible' through the walls. My favourite.

We blossom and flourish
As leaves on a tree,
And wither and perish,
But nought changeth Thee.

'But today I had a sudden fear that I, who was meant to be a young woman, was almost no longer one: that the withering and perishing business had begun. I was sitting at the kitchen table working on a pitted but pretty Dutch tile – circa 1840, I would have thought – treating it with silicic acid, and should by rights have followed through with silocane, a sub-surface repellent, but that has a distinctive smell – a rather lovely sweet orange smell, I always think, but still a smell, and Tim might have noticed. So I refrained. The service next door did not have long to go. I put away the tile paraphernalia and took out my darning, and I must admit I was brooding, as women will, upon the injustices of my life – darning whoever darned socks these days! – when the Coronation mug began to show signs of life.

'"Oh no, please," I said to it. It was a rare piece, produced in anticipation of an event which had never occurred, the Coronation of Edward VIII in 1937. The mug was, so far, uncracked and unchipped, and worth some £700, but had just moved to the very edge of its shelf, not smoothly and purposefully, but with an uneven rocking motion which made me hope an entreaty from me might yet calm it, and save it from itself. And indeed, after I spoke, the mug was quiet again, and lapsed into the ordinary stillness I had once always associated with inanimate objects.

Immortal, invisible, God only wise,
In light inaccessible—

'I joined in the hymn, singing gently and soothingly, and trying to feel happy, for the happier I felt the fewer breakages there would be, and perhaps one day they would stop altogether and Tom would stop blaming me because a) he was not an Anglican bishop, and b) not a Catholic priest. And perhaps he would never, ever find out that one by one the ornaments and possessions he most loved and valued were leaping off shelves and shattering, to be secretly mended by me, with varying degrees of skill, and with superglue?

'Long ago and far away. Once I had had an ambition to work as a restorer for antiquities in the Victoria and Albert and know more about the subject, theoretically and practically, than anyone in the world. Then I had met Tim. Now I darned. Tim's feet were sensitive to anything other than pure, fine wool. Not for him the tough nylon or carba mixes that other men wore.

'I thought my entreaty had worked, but now the movement began again. The mug rocked its way to the very edge of the dresser, where it paused, its base a third of the way over the shelf edge.

'"Stop there," I said sternly. Sometimes an appearance of indignation on my part was enough. I was lucky: the mug stayed where it was; the gentle king that never was, haloed in gold enamel, staring impassively at me, waiting for his fate. Just a fraction further and he would have fallen. I unpicked the last few stitches. I was in danger of cobbling the darn in my inattention and there is nothing more uncomfortable to a sensitive skin than a cobbled darn. Though not many these days know this.

'"You do it on purpose," Tim would complain, not without

reason. My faults were the ones he found most difficult to bear. I was careless, lost socks, left lids unscrewed, taps running, doors open, saucepans burning; I bought fresh bread when yesterday's at half price would do. And because there was some truth in his accusations – had I been as bad as this before I married him? Surely not! – they were the harder to bear. She loved him, and he loved her, or so he said. Why should either of them want to sabotage the other?

'No sooner thought, than the Coronation mug leapt off the edge of the shelf, arched through the air and fell and broke in two pieces at my feet. I put the pieces at the very back of the drawer beneath the sink. I couldn't attend to it now, even with the very crudest of a superglue join. It would have to wait until the morning when Tim would be out parish visiting, in houses freshly dusted and brightened for his arrival. Fortunately Tim scarcely ever inspected this particular drawer. It smelt, when opened, of dry rot, and reminded him of the large sums of money which needed to be spent in the repair of the Vicarage, which he did not have, and the Church Commissioners managed not to either. Also, fortunately, Tim now spent so much energy looking inwards to his grievances he spent less time noticing what was happening on the dresser shelves. Yet it was all understandable, and I was on his side in life's battles, I really was.

'Tim's mother died when he was four; his father went bankrupt when he was eight; relatives had reared him and sent him off to boarding school where he had, I suspected, been sexually abused. If he looked to inanimate objects for his security it was hardly surprising. I wanted to make his past up to him. I understood him, forgave him, loved him and tried not to argue.

'The hymn stopped. Time for the blessing. I put the socks away in the mending bag. It was a larger pile than usual today. Socks had recently taken to disappearing, not in pairs, but one by one. Lately Tim had found a whole pillowcase stuffed full of them, pushed to the back of the wardrobe. He'd read this as a sign that I was deceiving him – hiding socks! Yet what a pointless thing to do! Not just deceit, but the sheer careless waste of it all. Had I been buying new instead of mending the old? Socks weren't cheap.

'He'd tipped the bag out in front of me, onto the kitchen table. "What are these? What have you been doing?" Odd socks are strange things at the best of times; they seem denatured by the loss of their companion, limp, washed-out and undecipherable. One odd navy sock with a long elasticized top? How has that got into the house? Tim never wore socks with tops which gripped his ankles: never wore navy, stuck to brown or black. Just there it was, the sock of the phantom lover, looking innocent, for all it must be a sock drifted in from outer space. In other words I had no explanation to offer, other than that I was going mad, which Tim did not seem inclined to disagree with.

'Thereafter I made a real effort: I took to tying the pairs together when Tim discarded them. He'd change his socks once or twice during the day – his skin is prone to allergy and athlete's foot – and just a week back I'd even admired them and my own forethought as I put them in the machine. Thirty degrees delicate. In the morning I'd found the socks in one great monstrous knot, but each sock oddly long, as if stretched by a hand too angry to know what it was doing. Rinsing had quickly restored them to a proper state, including even the sock traceable to no known man, but I had been obliged to put a whole bunch in the mending bag: the stretching had worn the already thin fabric into holes.

'But it had, lately, been ever thus: difficult, always upsetting. Tim's possessions were under attack, as if the monstrous hand was on my side: yet it was I who had to repair the damage, follow the source as it mobbed around the house, mending what it broke, wiping tomato purée from the ceiling, toothpaste from the lavatory bowl, replanting Tim's uprooted seedlings, rescrewing lids, refolding linen, turning off lights that came on by themselves for no reason. Sometimes I scarcely dared leave the house for fear of what might happen in my absence. Tim interpreted my reluctance to a lack of interest in the parish. It was disloyalty to God and to husband. And so it was, in a way. Yet still we loved each other.

'I realized my finger was bleeding. Was that from a fine thread, or had I cut it open on the pieces of Coronation mug. I thought I had been so careful. The poor non-king's face had been split in two. I opened the drawer where I kept my sewing things and took out the first piece of cloth I came across and wrapped my finger to stem the bleeding. It had really got going now. The tap, as if to help me, started running of its own accord, but I did not reproach it. I simply used the water it provided. The blood spread vigorously on the cloth but presently, fortunately, it stopped. I daresay it was possible to die from a small cut in the finger, if there was sufficient loss of blood, though the coroner might think it strange.

'Tim would be back any minute: he would have to drink up the communion wine – I was pretty sure it had been a Eucharist service – and have a word with the verger and no doubt foist off approaches from Mary Leverton, who was in love with him, poor soul. No sooner thought than the invisible hand swept the entire dresser shelf, knocking all sorts of treasures sideways but breaking nothing. It had never touched the dresser before, but simply managed to animate pieces one by one. It was showing off what it could do, not quite daring to do its worst. Perhaps it was awed, as I was, by the ever-increasing value of the dresser's contents – rare blue and white pieces, frog mugs, barber's bowls, luster cups, a debatably Ming bowl, which a valuer had said could well fetch £7000. Enough to paint the Vicarage inside, and install central heating and replaster the walls, buy a new vacuum cleaner. The whole dresser rattled and shook and I could have sworn the whole thing bent down towards me from its waist.

'Tim did not give me a housekeeping allowance. I asked for money when I needed it and listed what I needed. Tim was out of sympathy with what I saw as necessities. He saw no point in things like washing-up liquid, sugar, scourers, and toilet paper. Once or twice I had stolen money from his pocket while he slept or taken a coin from the offertory on Sunday morning – but now people put money and notes in little brown envelopes so that route was closed. These days there were a number of wealthy incomers into the village – week-enders – barristers and surgeons and so on – and they supported the church – never to the extent of a new roof for the Vicarage – but enough to make the little brown tax-relief envelopes a practical development.

'A woman who stole from her husband, from the Church? How had I come to it, why did I stoop to it? A bad wife, a barren wife, and a poor sort of person.

'Tim came through the door. The house fell quiet, as always. The dresser straightened itself, like a child told to sit up straight. Taps stopped running and china rattling. As quick as I could I set the dresser to rights. The space left by the Coronation mug gaped like a missing front tooth.

'"Tess," asked Tim, "what have you wrapped round your finger?" I was curious myself as I inspected the cloth. I'd used a very good lace and cotton handkerchief, which I'd left in the drawer for mending and never got round to, the current crisis being what it was. It had once belonged to Tim's grandmother. It was sodden and bright, bright red.

'"I cut my finger," I said, inadequately, but rather glad he had not asked how I had hurt myself. I lied frequently these days but never liked doing it. Tim took the handkerchief and pointedly began rinsing and squeezing the fabric to clean it. His grandmother's! I put my finger in my mouth and licked that clean. The blood tasted as ever salty and exciting.

'"Couldn't you just for once have used something that didn't matter?" he asked. "A tissue, say?"

'I didn't retort that he was the one who thought tissues a waste of money – they hadn't been used in his youth, why should they be used now, in his middle age? It was important to keep the peace. I should have looked before I wrapped. I said I was sorry. He took the handkerchief upstairs to the bathroom in search of soap and a nailbrush.

'"What kind of wife are you, Tess?" he asked as he went.

'A barren wife, a fig tree, struck by God's ill temper. In the beginning we had shared a luminous God, rather bleak and plain and sensible by some standards, but holy, transfiguring. But now Tim had his own God, I realized, and didn't want me sharing. Tim's God was jealous and punitive, and needed wooing with ritual and richness, incense and images, at which I always rather raised my eyebrows. These days Tim changed his vestments during services, rang little bells to announce the presence of the Lord, swung incense, and the parishioners – such few as had opinions – began to feel he might as well just become Catholic and be done with it.

'The water pipes in the kitchen shrieked and groaned as Tim turned on the taps upstairs. But that could be bad plumbing not ghostly causes. It was hard to know where one stopped and the other began.

'When the phenomena first started – as I had thought of them at first – or at least leapt from the normal scale of ordinary domestic carelessness to something more extreme, I went to the doctor. "Doctor," I asked, "do mumps in childhood make men infertile?"

'"It depends," he said, proving nothing. "If the gonads are affected it well might. Why? Did Tim have mumps as a child?"

'"As an adolescent boy" I said. "He was in the school sanatorium when he was sixteen."

'"Then it might well have affected his fertility," he said. "However, since your husband will not have his sperm tested we will never know." The doctor quite liked me and rather disliked Tim. Men are like that, aren't they, always locking horns.

'I asked him about psychic phenomena and he offered me tranquillizers and suggested I get a job in town before I went mad. I said I was not depressed, I saw things falling. If they broke I knew they had fallen, but sometimes they just bounced and all I had to do was put them back, and that was really disturbing because I could just have imagined the whole thing. He asked if Tim saw them too. I told him Tim was never there when it happened.

'He suggested hormone replacement therapy and that I found

myself a lover. I think he was suggesting himself, though one can never be sure, and declined politely. As I say, I loved my husband. But the doctor was an attractive man, even though he didn't wear a tie and wore navy socks with brown shoes, which Tim greatly disapproved of.

'We decided I probably just released too much kinetic energy – the kind that poltergeists use – and since there was no known pill for that I would just have to live with it. But these spirits can make living side by side really difficult. They want an audience: they crave response. They listen in and up the ante, I'm sure of it. My visit to the doctor aggravated it. When I got home whatever it was had churned up the lawn and torn the gate off its hinges. Perhaps "whatever it was" was an expression of "the other me"? I told Tim a child must have done it, and he accepted that, although it would have taken a forty-stone giant to have twisted the gate off its hinges in the way it had happened. I raked and smoothed, and called in the local metalworkers, who put things more or less to rights. Tim did not argue about the cost, for once: he knew instinctively that in some regards the less some things are faced up to the better.

'As I say, I would rather think about my divorce, than ghosts.

'However, now the moment of the lace handkerchief and Tim's pointed rinsing and rubbing away of bloodstains away had arrived. The wound on my finger gaped open as the kitchen pipes gurgled. I thought I could see the white bone at the bottom of the cut. This could not have been done by a darning thread or a sliver of ceramic. I went upstairs and found Tim in the bathroom.

'"Do you think I should get a stitch in this?" I asked.

'Tim had a tooth mug in his hand. His jaw was open, his eyes wide with shock. He had somehow smeared toothpaste on his black lapel.

'"My toothmug has been broken," he said. "How did that happen? Why was I not told? And someone has tried to mend it, very badly, with ordinary superglue."

'The toothmug dated from the late eighteenth century and was worn, cracked and chipped, but Tim loved it. It had been one of the first things to go, rocking wilfully to its destruction across the bathroom basin. I had not mended it with my usual care, thinking, mistakenly, that one more crack amongst so many would hardly be noticed.

'"I am horrified," said Tim.

'"Sorry," I said, and so I was.

'"Why is it that you always break my things, never your own?"

'"I thought when people got married," I said, "things stopped being mine and yours and became ours."

'He was looking round the room carefully, seeking out change and imperfection. He would probably now go on a tour of inspection and all would be discovered. The wound in my finger was really beginning to hurt.

'"Tim!" I beseeched him, but my entreaties had as little effect on him as they had on the Coronation mug. "Try and see it like this. Ours, not yours and mine. We're a family."

'"Family!" Tim said, with some bitterness. "What sort of family have you given me? I wanted a warm happy house, with music and laughter. I wanted children. And all I have is deceit, ruin and breakages."

'I could see it was difficult for him. He did want children, and in his head I could not give them to him. I thought briefly of the doctor and the possibility of asking him to make me pregnant and not telling Tim what I had done. But that was too much to contemplate: although my happiness had become dependent on Tim's, which I suppose is the case with most marriages, there was too great a danger of the plan misfiring. There came the crash of breaking china from downstairs; Tim ran down the stairs to where the noise came from. I followed on behind. But when he got into the kitchen everything was still and normal. "You've shattered my life," said Tim. "We have nothing in common."

'"I suppose," I said to him, aggravated, because my wound still went unattended, "you're now going to say that my not having children is God's punishment for my sins."

"'Yes," said Tim.

"'It could be to do with you having mumps when you were an adolescent."

"'How do you know about that?" he asked. "I never told you about that." Which was an odd thing to say, if he had forgotten, or didn't know. One's economies with the truth normally flow quickly into forgetfulness.

"'You are a sadistic person, Tess," he went on, before I could respond. "Even the pains and humiliations of long ago aren't safe from you. You must revive them."

"'Well," I said, "I know it isn't me. Before we were married I became pregnant and had a termination. I was fourteen. My mother and my doctor arranged it."

'That was very foolish of me. One should avoid the temptation of being right at any cost. Tim fell silent, but I could almost see his brain going click, click, click, beneath his balding scalp, as realizations to his advantage fell into place. The beautiful brown shiny hair which had been his glory and my delight was thinning. My finger throbbed.

"'You killed a Christian baby," he said, flatly.

"'I killed my uncle's baby," I said.

"'What kind of family—" Out of the corner of my eye I saw the Ming vase begin to rock to the edge of the dresser. Quickly I moved to push it back but it was too quick for me. It fell and broke. Not just broke but exploded across the floor as very good porcelain will: tiny sharp flakes of white, blue, red and gold everywhere. Tim cried out in pain and rage.

"'You did that on purpose," he wept. "You hate me. What have I ever done to make you hate me?"

"'I didn't do it," I said. "The ghost did it. Or the ghosts. There may be several."

"'What ghosts?" Tim said. "There are no ghosts, there is only you."

'I went upstairs to the bedroom and started to pack. There was no point in living in this house any more, where the very walls rose up against me. I would think of somewhere to go: there must be a way.

'Tim came up and watched me. I was indifferent now to the pain in my finger. Or perhaps I would just go to a hospital and throw myself on their mercy.

'"There are no ghosts," he said, "just the souls of unborn children knocking at the door."'

The Vicar's Ex-wife paused and sighed. Her large eyes were sad. 'The children we didn't have, and should've!' she said. There was a kind of exhalation of breath, a moan of air, from around the pool. I daresay there was not a woman there who had not had an abortion, to save her sanity, or her career, or out of love of other children, or to keep some man. Women have the number of children they can afford, and sometimes, and more and more these days, that means none – but for many of us the ones we wilfully kept out of existence never quite go away: they keep tapping on the doors of common sense and reason. '*Let me in, let me in,*' they murmur, '*remember us, we should have lived.*' They break things if they can.

'It is true,' I said, 'and we have to face it. Wherever women are gathered together, the souls of the unborn come knocking at the door.'

'That's absurd, Mira,' said the Surgeon. 'Tess is just telling a ghost story to while away the time. Do go on, Tess. So what happened next?'

'So I left Tim and went to the hospital and they admitted me: my blood pressure was so low they worried for me. The spirits drain energy out of you. Once I was gone Tim moved through the house weeping, not for loss of me, but for his treasures. I have the admittance from him. Well, he was understandably very angry and upset: I had lied to him, misled him, trapped him into a marriage on false pretences, and my family had colluded. What respect could he have now for them or me? He took a wicker basket and laid an altar cloth in it and in it laid tenderly – as if they were the bodies of children – the many broken and mended ornaments and dishes he found pushed to the backs of cupboards and drawers; amongst my sewing, my knitting, my odd-sock bag. Sometimes the joins were skilful and barely detectable to his moving forefinger; sometimes careless. But everything to his mind was spoilt. What had been perfect was now second art and without value. The finds in junk shops, the gifts and inheritances from old ladies, the few small knick-knacks which had come to him from his dead mother – his whole life spoilt by the single-minded malice and cunning of his wife. And how had he not noticed? What dreadful sexual wiles had she employed?

'He went down to the kitchen and sat with his head in his hands. I had gone. Out of the door, through the broken garden gate, into the night, through the churchyard, where the locals never went if they could help it, and even Tim was reluctant, though he never let it show. It could only seem to Tim that the powers of the dead disturbed me less than the powers of the living. I understood that.

'He told me he began to smell dry rot; it became strong enough to make him lift his head. It was coming from the drawer beneath the sink. He got up and opened it and a barrage of foul odour came out at him. The cold tap began to run. A faulty washer, he concluded. He moved to turn it off, but the valve was already closed. Still, the tap ran. He called out to me, although I was not in the house.

'"Tess, what have you done now?"

'And this to all accounts is how it went then. The whole top of the dresser fell forward to the ground. Porcelain shattered and earthenware powdered. Oddly he could hear the little pings from the church next door, announcing the presence of God at the Eucharist, although so far as he knew the church was shut, and closed. He thought perhaps there must have been an earthquake but the central light hung still and quiet. Upstairs heavy feet bumped to and fro, dragging, wrenching and banging. His instinct was to run from the house but outside the black trees rocked so fiercely he thought he would be safer in than out. He could hear that the gas taps of the cooker were on and he could smell gas, mixed with fumes from the coal fire; he saw socks writhing in my sewing basket. All his senses were assailed by error: he was not frightened. He knew that he saw, heard and felt these things but that they had no substance in the real world. They were a distortion of the facts, as water becomes wine at the communion service and bread becomes flesh, though on an altogether more significant level.

'He prayed and when next he opened his eyes the dresser was restored and the socks lay still in the mending basket. Hallucination, brought about by the shock of revelation. He wondered if the uncle had been on the mother's side, or the bishop father's. He went upstairs to bed but found the bedroom door locked. Why had I done that? I was full of malice. He went to the spare room and slept peacefully without the irritant and temptation of my warmth beside him.

'In the morning, he told me, he missed me, and when I reappeared in the kitchen in time to make his breakfast tea as if in reply to his unspoken request he was glad.

'"I spent the night in the hospital," I told him. My arm was in a sling. "I went there for a stitch in my finger but I fainted and they kept me in."

'"I'm sorry," he said to me. "You should have told me it was a bad cut and I'd have been more sympathetic. Where did you put the bedroom key?"

'I denied all knowledge of it and the teapot fell off the table and there were tea-leaves and hot water everywhere, and one-armed, I bungled the business of wiping it up.

'"I tell you," I said, trying to lighten the atmosphere, "we have ghosts as other people have mice."

'"We have the soul of an unborn child," he replied.'

Around the pool faces were intent, shocked and frightened. The Vicar's Ex-wife was so pale herself she too might have been a ghost. The marble-like thickness and stillness of the skin which I had remarked on earlier was one I had seen many times on corpses. But that was absurd. She talked, she even laughed; she told a good story. We waited for her to continue, but even she seemed nervous of what she was to say next. The water bubbled: we waited.

But then a crashing of glass came from the misty end of the great hall down where the enamelled Doric pillars stretched into invisibility. A gust of cold air drove in and sped across the bubbles of the pool and made us shiver and some cry out. What could be approaching out of the night, what monstrous thing? But it was only Kimberley, Dorleen's bodyguard, easing down towards us in her running shoes.

'Sorry, you guys,' she said. 'It was the cat again. I tried to catch it and I slipped.'

We all relaxed. Random conversation started.

'I do have to be careful,' said Dorleen. 'Cats give me asthma, and I don't want to be sneezing all through the wedding, do I?'

'Poor cat,' said the Trophy Wife. 'I hope you didn't frighten it; perhaps the poor thing is hungry,' and she got out of the pool and went off towards the kitchens, as if to find the cat and feed it, but I think she wanted to get away from the story, and from the souls of the unborn dead, of which I reckoned she'd created quite a few in her time.

Presently a little colour came back to Tess's face and she was ready to start again.

'Again Tim asked me what I had done with key and again I denied any knowledge of it. He went up the ladder to the bedroom window – he had put on clerical garb that morning, although he did not have a service that day, as if to demonstrate the sheer seriousness of my confession, and subsequent flight. He perched halfway up the house like some white-ruffed crow. He looked down at me where I held the ladder steady—'

'But this is my story,' interjected the Company Director. 'I am the one with the ladder and the man I may or may not murder—'

'Many women hold many ladders steady for many men,' said the Vicar's Ex-wife, 'in their time, and I sincerely hope thoughts of murder do not come instantly to mind – I am sure it did not occur to me at all, not even when he turned down to me and said "I've never seen a room in such a mess!"

'He climbed in the window and I heard him cry out, so I scuttled up after him. The heavy wardrobe was on its side, wedged against the door, the bed was upside down, the bedclothes were knotted and twisted and had the same stretched and worn appearance as the drier-load of socks I had once decanted, and the carpet had been wrenched up, tossing furniture as it lifted, and wrung out like a dishcloth.

'Tim went down the ladder to fetch the verger. "God knows what I'll tell him," he said to me.

'"God knows," I said.

'I waited in the room: the air felt sullen and heavy at first, and I saw the carpet ripple and heave a bit but I stood my ground and it subsided again, and by the time Tim and the verger got back the air felt soft and sweet again, as if washed by a storm. I felt it had done its worst, made its rage undeniable by either of us.

'The verger was an old man. He came up the ladder, looked inside, and said, "I saw something like this before. The woman had just had a miscarriage. Just as well, I always thought, that baby didn't get born."

'And we set to work, the three of us, to restore order. We moved the wardrobe back into its place, heaved the carpet and the bedclothes out the window, and patiently and peacefully unwrung them.

'We had to go on living there. There was no option. The door was found to be locked from the inside, and the key inside the chimneybreast, but never mind. We just didn't go there in our minds.

'"I'm sorry," was all I said to Tim. "I was really very angry, what with one thing and another."

'"I can tell that," he said shortly. "I was angry too, as it happens. You took the mumps so lightly. It was one of the worst times of my life. I itched so badly Matron tied my hands together to stop me from scratching. My friends saw, I was humiliated. I don't like to think about it."

'"You don't scratch with mumps," I said. "You're sure it wasn't chicken pox?"

'"I can't remember," he said, "Probably. Is there a difference? And the baby. You should have told me. That was still a mortal sin, it was still murder, but God forgives where man does not."

'And so peace, of a sort, was made. The marks of the wringing stayed on the carpet, reminding us to keep it. I had the Ming vase mended by experts – it's amazing what they can do these days – and Tim actually agreed to sell it and we installed central heating, and had the washer on the kitchen tap mended, and the dry rot beneath the sink cleared out, and the wobbly floorboard beneath the dresser replaced. The acoustics in the kitchen changed so I couldn't hear what was happening in the church.'

'And you lived happily every after?' asked the lady Judge.

'Hardly,' said the Vicar's Ex-wife. 'After we made peace the impetus to have sex left us. There seemed no point in it other than as a step in negotiations, and our goal had been achieved. No, I went off with the doctor, who left his wife for me. And then I was a doctor's wife and that is almost as bad as being a vicar's wife, so I left our baby with him and went into banking. Tim married again and asked my father the bishop to exorcize the Vicarage, because it was sill troubled with spirits. It didn't work. I could have told them that, if either of them had been speaking to me.

'Whatever was there is deeply rooted, and I don't think had anything to do with unborn souls, and was certainly not the spirit of my father's nephew – though I can see that confusion of the generations might have made a soul child angry. After I left the two of them became good friends, my father and my ex-husband, united in indignation at my behaviour.

'My mother wrote to me that before the exorcism my father had consulted the diocese records, and a pregnant maid servant had hanged herself from a yew tree in the churchyard, a century back, distraught after being fined £4 19s she hadn't got for "breakages". That must have been an awful lot of china for one girl to break. So I reckon it went back even further than that. Do I believe in ghosts? Not really. I can't afford to, it is all too disconcerting. But I believe in the power of rage if you try to deny it. And now can we leave the subject, please?'

There was silence, and then a strange sound, as if the wind was carrying the noise of a hundred murmuring, conspiring, complaining, whispering women through the broken glass that Kimberley had somehow managed to contrive: it was the sound of nuns pacing, praying, spinning; it was the soft voices of endearment and cosseting, *my lady this, my lady that*; it was shot through with raucous laughter and oaths, like darker strands in a pale cloth – that was the WAACS, I thought, who'd lived here during the war – and with the sound came a cold, cold breeze as the wind got up.

'It's only the bubble machine,' said the Surgeon. 'It's turned itself off. It's the water in the pipes.' And so it was of course: our ears had been playing tricks. We went back to our rooms, first walking stoically, and with dignity, then many of us running – even Kimberley – turning on as many lights as could be found as we went. The moon was just past full and the castle turrets black against a windy sky, and hoar frost already forming on the ground. Everything seemed suddenly very beautiful and very dangerous.

31

Mira sat on the end of my bed and complained: it was a dirge for her life, a threnody played by a slightly out-of-tune bagpipe. Well, I have done the same for other women, many a time, and they have done the same for me: there is nothing to it. You murmur, you listen with a sympathetic air. You say 'all things will pass', and 'yes, you're right, he is a bastard', 'yes, you did the only thing you could', and wait for the fit to pass. If you listen too hard and respond and say 'yes, but surely, if you did that you can expect that', or 'but he's done that so many times before, what's different?' she will 'yes but' until the cows come home, and the end of the divorce, or the affair, or whatever it is that has collapsed her life into misery.

But I was in the most benign of moods, as you will imagine, Julian was coming home, Jenny had a new husband: I had been paranoiac and mad and now was cured, and we might be being cut off by a snowstorm but what did I care? The news that Alistair was 'touching down' or had hoped to, had caused Mira only passing joy. It seemed to have exacerbated her self-pity: indeed, set her off. She had decided he called through to Castle Spa and said he would be touching down only after he'd read the weather forecasts and knew snow was on the way. She reminded me of myself. And I thought how strange it was, and how often it happened, that such seemingly, strong, cheerful, independent women, a credit to themselves, their families, indeed to the nation, should so often end up in this sorry masochistic state, crumbled crying on a bed.

It wasn't fair, she lamented, like a child. Though why the child should expect fairness in a world so evidently unfair from the moment of conception I have never understood: nevertheless the child does. I daresay it is some survival-friendly Darwinian streak; otherwise I can only explain it by reference to God or the existence of some Platonic ideal, but Mira was hardly open at the moment to such theoretical discussion. Nothing was fair. Why did she fail to command Alistair's concentrated attention? What was the matter with her? Other people thought she was okay; an easy conversationalist: people would switch place names to sit next to her at dinner. Her face was ravaged by wind and weather, but her body was still spectacular and always had been. She did not have to bother to dress it up much. She could be at ease in the Jacuzzi with women ten years younger than her. And you should see Alistair, the same age as she was and a monster of flab, with red veins round his nose, spreading now into his cheeks and black pits on his face where the hairs sprouted. He had lost a lot of hair: he grew what he had on the side and combed it over the bald bit. It was pathetic.

'Then forget him,' I said. 'Find someone else with a better skin and more hair. Try internet dating.'

'I don't want anyone else,' she moaned. 'You don't understand a thing.'

She just didn't want him to tell her any more lies. She wanted him to stop saying he loved her when they were in bed, promising that they'd be together one day, just not yet, that he'd break it to his wife when the children went to nursery, then primary school, then A levels – now they were at college and he had started a new family and the same thing was happening again. Why couldn't he just fuck her every now and then and leave it like that?

'Some men feel so guilty,' I pointed out, 'that they can only get it up if they're talking about love.'

She said that was sick, but I think it came as a shock to her. I suggested she gave him Viagra to see if it still happened. There'd been much less talk of true love since that came on the scene, only of good sex. She thought I was joking but I wasn't. She gasped and gulped on. It was intolerable: he had ruined her life, owned her and disposed of her. Soon she'd be feeling so low she'd be reduced to picking up minicab drivers. She despised herself as a whiny, feeble, over-emotional masochist, and I was a star to put up with her. She was going to Skype Alistair now to break it off, to tell him he could touch down as much as he liked, but if he touched her again she'd cut it off.

'Mira,' I said, 'calm down. I have some sleeping pills. You're welcome to them. It's the middle of the night.'

But she was at her laptop, and the devil was in the detail, she had borrowed a spare battery from the Judge, and had found a Wi-Fi connection, feeble but there – it could only be the atmospheric pressure – and was through on Skype to Alistair. The little formal man shape appeared in the panel, the bell trilled, the connection was opened, the webcam was on. A second or so and a man's echoey voice and a rough janitorial hand loomed large as the connection was closed. 'Ah, shut the fuck up. It's the middle of the night!' But in those few seconds before the hand intervened there was a glimpse in the panel of what I supposed was Alistair's office: a big window in the background, a vast old leather chair with a grease stain where a head would rest, and a coffee mug on a splendid editor-style desk. 'It turns my heart over,' said Mira, 'just to see it. He takes that chair with him from job to job, office to office. It's where I lost my virginity. He takes it with him because of me, because it *is* me.'

I thought: 'No, he takes it with him because it's comfortable, because he's superstitious and sentimental, and because he forgot the incident long ago,' but I knew better than to say so.

'I shagged him in that chair I can't tell you how many times: you see the mark where his head leans against the back?' It was hopeless.

And Mira closed the connection and started dialling another number.

'Mira, what are you doing?'

'Skyping Alistair at home.'

'Mira, don't do that. It will end in tears.'

She took no notice. Again the formal man shape: the trilling. Again the connection was made. This time it was a child's face filling the square in the panel: a little boy, around three years old, he'd been crying: there was snot round his nose. He moved away: he was in his pyjamas.

'Mu-um!' he shouted. He was a very bad-tempered little boy, and not very appealing. But I expected his father loved him. 'There's a lady.'

'Mark, is that you?' It was a sudden eagle squawk, the mother as bad-tempered as the child, but these microphones can distort badly. 'Leave the computer alone. Go back to bed at once!' And then the child's face was gone from the screen, but we could hear noisy protest, a mixture of maternal chiding and cooing, now quite gentle, and talk of drinks of water, fading into the distance. We were left looking at another chair, this one of designer plastic, clean and neutral, and without any sense of shagging just of polishing, and I felt a sudden sympathy with Alistair. What had he come to? Perhaps Mira was right. Twice he had married and twice married the wrong person, in his flight from true love. We gazed.

'I hate her,' said Mira. 'And how can he put up with that voice?'

And then the square in the panel was filled with a woman's face, distorted by the camera: an enormous jaw and a madly receding forehead.

'It's you, isn't it?' she shrieked. 'You bitch. You slag, you marriage-breaker. You journo scum. If you want him you can have him: he's shit, he's rubbish. I've thrown him out. You tell him I've changed the locks. I'm not to be treated like this. He'll pay and so will you—' and a jewelled hand came forward and the panel went blank, and the screeching stopped.

We were silent for a little.

'Well,' I said, 'that's a turn up for the books. He's left her. He's coming to you.'

The strange thing was Mira did not look entirely pleased. 'It'll only be to bend my ear,' she said. 'That's how it was the last time he walked out on a wife. And what's the point of a husband nobody else wants?'

I remembered how Pauline and I had talked about Eleanor at the very beginning of that terrible tale, when we did not know how it would all end, of the witch bitches who only ever wanted men that other women had, and once they had stolen them, moved on to the next, and I wished I had not remembered, because perhaps Mira was one of these. A scavenger, stealing the choicest morsel on the plate, and then spitting it out, complaining it was leftovers.

Mira left. I could not sleep. I did not want sleeping pills. I liked being awake, savouring my own escape from sin, Mira's descent into it, the saving of the world, the possibility of ghosts, of tangled socks and so much else. I thought I saw a moving glimmer of yellow by the window – could they be the flowers on Eleanor's coat? – but that was all over. I looked again. Nothing. I heard a sound which was real enough: someone was tapping on my door. It was the Mortgage Broker.

She had been down to London, located the cat's presence, found it still alive, disturbed Shiva to have it rescued, left it fed, rested and purring on a cushion, hired a private aircraft, flown back from Elstree to RAF Crosby-on-Eden two miles from Spa Castle, walked the difference, and here she was, back again. Journalists think they have influence, but it is nothing compared to what those who provide other people with their dwellings can have. She told me she was tired, but at peace with herself, said good night, and left, closing the door behind her. No sooner had she gone than I heard another knock on the door. I went to open it. It was the Stepmother.

'You said you'd read my novella,' she said, and handed it to me. It was a proof-copy, softly bound, called *Step-step-stepping On My Dreams* – in a pretty pink and gold jacket – by Janice Clarence. They must have forgotten to tell her at her creative writing classes that you are meant to change names in a novel, even if you are writing fairly observably about yourself, if only because otherwise people might sue you. I am not surprised her stepdaughter Eliza tried to stop publication. I thought I would suggest to the Psychoanalyst that perhaps a new archetype had been born: along with the fairy princesses of yore, the wicked witches, the kindly kings and so forth, now came, in response to popular need, the angry stepchild.

It was New Year's Eve, as I had quite forgotten. Janice went down to join the celebrations but I stayed in my room and read her novella. I have never liked New Year's Eve. The clock ticks on: midnight strikes, nothing has changed, other than that a hangover looms. People get maudlin and sentimental and holding hands and singing *Auld Lang Syne* to me is just embarrassing. I let them get on with it.

32

Step-step-stepping On My Dreams

From the age of nine Janice had always dreamt of perfect love. She had the very man in her mind. He was a wounded hero: he was Kirk Douglas in *Lonely Are the Brave*. He was a man out of his time, a cowboy in a modern age, tragic, romantic, and misunderstood. He was tall and handsome and had a cleft chin, wide thin lips and narrow, meaningful eyes. Her mother took her to see the film when she was nine. In the film Kirk plays a fugitive on the run, sacrificing himself out of loyalty to a friend, pursued to a sorry end by Walter Matthau – the honest and kindly cop who came to understand and admire him.

'That policeman looks like Daddy,' she said to her mother when they came out into the air.

'I agree with you there,' said her mother. 'Your father was born with a rumpled look.'

'I'm going to marry a man like the cowboy,' said Janice, 'and live happily ever after.'

'You could do worse,' said her mother. But because it was the Seventies she added: 'Of course you don't have to marry anyone if you don't want to, and I hope you look beyond marriage and see yourself as a doctor or an engineer who happens to have a happy home life,' and Janice said yes, yes, but she was already lost in a romantic dream: she would have made Kirk Douglas happy; she would have rescued him from his fate. She realized she could never have Kirk Douglas exactly, he being of another generation, but someone just like him would come along for her. She was sure of it. Everything had always gone right for Janice: it would surely do so when it came to love and marriage.

And she wanted to be married: when her friends declared they never would, that all men were selfish beasts and a girl could do better in life without them, she would speak up bravely and say no, the thought of sharing a bed with a man forever thrilled her: always to have someone, to be with one, to go through life hand in hand with a man she loved seemed to her beautiful, and brave, and romantic. Her parents loved each other, and shared a big bed and she felt lonely in her small one.

When little, the single child of Paul and Alice, the only trouble she had ever been to them was her passion to be in bed with them, and not stay quietly in her cot. She was secure in her love for and trust in them, and they returned the love and trust.

Janice was pretty and clever and nice, popular and good at netball. She was honourable, and fun, and never told lies or tried to get anyone into trouble. Had fairy godmothers gathered for her christening, she could not have hoped for a better start in life. Boys were interested in her from an early age, but only the best of the bunch dared come forward, so she liked them and got on with them even while she said 'no, let's just be friends'. And they would consent to that as better than nothing. She was looking for a man with a dimple in his chin whom her rumpled father admired: one day the knight in shiny armour would turn up and whisk her away to the next stage of her life, when she would have a nice house, an interesting job and six children.

A rather disconcerting thing happened when she was sixteen. Janice had a weekend job helping out in an art gallery. The owner was in his forties, had a beard, wore sandals, and wrote poetry. Something Janice said alerted the parents and they enquired closely into the relationship. They decided the pair were becoming too involved. Janice was forbidden to go on working with him: she argued his good qualities: he was sensitive, understanding, a genius, age was no barrier to love. Love? That had not been mentioned before. They stood firm. She chafed and protested but her father had the bastard checked out by private detectives. He was married but his wife had left him because he was too fond of his teenage daughter, though no charges had been brought.

'I know all about that,' said Janice, defensively. 'It was just a lawyer's trick to get more alimony.'

But now it had been brought out into the light of day, Janice was shaken into sense. She left the job and worked instead as a waitress in the café of the National Gallery. In a month or two the gallery closed down: it had never made money anyway. When all was safely over, Paul showed the detective's dossier to Alice. Alice studied the photographs. 'Well, he's good-looking,' she said, 'the bastard. Who does he remind me of? I know, Kirk Douglas. It's the hint of a cleft chin and the thin lips and the meaningful smile. The opposite of you. You're Walter Matthau, with a crinkled face and a mouth that smiles when it's at rest. What was that film I once took Janice to see? *Lonely Are the Brave*?' But she thought no more of it than that.

Paul had done well in the antique business. He had a shop in Bond Street, and sold only the best, to the richest, at home and abroad, and was an honest man, which is unusual in a trade dominated by those who know, who buy cheap and sell dear to those who don't know. But he was a man of enthusiasms for history, for all things beautiful and old, and for the craftsmen of former times, and the wood and metal they worked and could tell one from another just by looking, and somehow managed to translate the gift into money. Alice sat in the converted woodshed and painted pictures, which sold for not very much but hung in people's dining rooms and were liked. Janice came of good stock, though couldn't draw for toffee. She liked business, and selling, and was serious, and quite religious, and took business studies at A level.

Now around the time Alice and Janice were watching *Lonely Are the Brave* a young couple, Waldo James and Josephine Cutler, got married. Like Kirk Douglas Waldo just so happened to have a slightly cleft chin, a wide mouth and narrow lips, and eyes that girls found very meaningful. The similarity to the film actor was much remarked upon and was one of the reasons that Josephine, Jo for short, married him. The other reason, perhaps more pressing, was that she was pregnant by him, and also she loved him, probably rather more than he loved her. Once they were married, she revealed that she had lost the baby and Waldo always wondered whether the pregnancy had been wishful thinking rather than the real thing. But it was a mean and petty thing to think and Waldo was not mean and petty. He was honourable, just and true.

Waldo was an artist, a good painter, had been to art school and had an eye for higher things. Jo was beautiful, in a slightly flouncy, moody, talkative kind of way, and neurotic, self-centred and frankly, not very bright, though good at her job, which was picture restoration. She wore flowers in her hair and arty skirts and low-cut peasant blouses, and believed you were as old as you felt. Jo wanted to have a baby straight away but it was nine years before they did. It was a girl and they named her Eliza. She was a November baby and a little Scorpio.

When Eliza was born Janice was twenty-five and still looking for a man who looked like Kirk Douglas, with a cleft chin and thin lips. Eliza was to end up as Janice's stepdaughter. It was not to be a fortunate relationship. Eliza loved her father but not her mother: and Scorpios, when they hate, hate with a venom, and when they love, love with passion and a steely determination. Most small children fortunate enough to be born into a home with two natural parents switch affections between mother and father as they grow, first adhering to one, then to the other. First it's all mummy, mummy, mummy, I don't like you daddy, go away: then it's all daddy, daddy, daddy, go away mummy. That's normal. With Eliza it was always daddy, daddy, daddy, I love you; mummy, go away, I hate you. This was a little unusual, and distressed her mother, but made her love the child even more, that being in her nature too – to love where she was not loved.

Eliza was born with a tooth and bit her mother's breast so badly she had to be bottle fed: she held out her tiny arms for Daddy but never for the flowers in Mummy's hair. She cried a lot and would be comforted only by her daddy: she had tantrums in the shops and Daddy complained once that Mummy didn't know how to mange the child – better to lower the voice than raise it: if you shout the child shouts back – so Eliza, sensing a rift between the parents, had more and more tantrums, which could be soothed only by her daddy.

Eliza seemed to know when sex was in the air between the parents and would choose the time to come screaming into the bedroom after a nightmare and demand to be taken into the bed. Sex between the two of them fell into disrepair and disarray. Sometimes Jo would catch the secret smile of satisfaction from Eliza, a little flicker of the tongue, out of the mouth fast and in again, when a cross word between the parents was exchanged, and tried to say something about it to Waldo but he didn't want to hear. Eliza was his precious, Daddy's girl. She sat on his lap whenever she could and charmed him and wooed him, while Mummy aged fast from the strain of being disliked by her own child. By the time Eliza was ten Jo had silver hairs amongst the grey, which Eliza loved to point out over breakfast.

'Look, Daddy, Mummy's got a bit of white hair just there! See! And there's a great bit tough one coming out under her chin. Can women have beards?'

'She doesn't love me,' Jo complained to Waldo. 'She only loves you.'

'Of course she loves you,' he'd say loyally, but since he liked and cared for Jo, but had never really loved her, not with the tender passionate love you read about in books, he could understand where Eliza was coming from. She was a decorative person, and the flowers in Jo's hair were pretty, but she was both frivolous and always needed reassuring that he loved her and the more she asked the less certain he became. He was a serious artist and understood the relationship between form and content, and was beginning to be asked to smart dinner parties, as his gallery asked for more and more for his paintings. He suspected that the more popular you were the less good you were as a painter, and worried about this, but it was no use trying to discuss it with Jo, because she had no idea what he was talking about.

'Silly old fuddy-duddy,' she would say, affectionately. 'They like it, they buy it, what on earth's the matter with that? Anyway, darling, to me you are the best painter in the world! Let's have another gin, to celebrate!' And she would, and he wouldn't. She wasn't an alcoholic but dealing with Eliza sometimes made her feel that a stiff drink was the only answer to her problems. At the dinner parties she'd drink too much and be an embarrassment.

They lived in a big, comfortable house in Notting Hill, not smart or grand – though later it was to be worth millions – but comfortable, and Jo loved it, and was happy with her life, and didn't want to give dinner parties anyway. Frankly, she found Waldo's friends rather pretentious, and it was this, as much as the drink, that made her giggle.

Eliza was good at schoolwork, and ambitious, and not exactly popular, but always had a circle around her of children who felt it was probably safer to be her friend than her enemy. There was no shifting mid-way point. She was captain of hockey, and her opponents' ankles were always black and blue, and sometimes those of her own team too, if they hadn't run fast enough, or driven home enough goals.

When she was eleven, and discovered stealing from other girls' lockers, the school, feeling perhaps bad mothering was at the heart of the problem, suggested the child saw a therapist. Drink had been smelt on the mother's breath one sports day, and the flowers plaited into Jo's greying hair, but often a little awry, disturbed them. The family was artistic and they liked that, creativity being something the school encouraged, but they also liked it when parents turned up at the school looking like everyone else – as indeed did Eliza. So Jo had a quite undeserved reputation as a non-caring, alcoholic mother.

If Eliza fell sleep in class, which she did quite often, since she would use the internet chat rooms until the early hours – a fact unbeknown to either parent – she would explain it away by saying her mother had been out to all hours and come home with an uncle, and she hadn't been able to get to sleep for worrying, or that her mother never got up to give her breakfast. The opposite was true: Eliza would push aside her plate of delectable and perfectly cooked scrambled eggs, and demand poached, since scrambled was fattening, and claiming Jo was so jealous of her she was trying to make her ugly. She never said things like this in her father's hearing, and when Jo reported them to Waldo, he would doubt her, and there would be an argument. And Jo would see the smile of glee that hovered round Eliza's mouth and the little flicker of the tongue, and would want to cry and sometimes did. It is terrible to love a child and know it doesn't love you in return.

The therapist, noticing that Eliza was good in all subjects other than maths, thought with the school the mother might be the problem. Children who have a problem with sums often have a problem with family numbers, and can be paralysingly jealous of their siblings: Eliza being an only child, the problem must lie with one of the parents, and a few questions swiftly elicited the fact that Eliza wanted to drive out her mother and have her father to herself. The stealing was the attempt to steal the father. The therapist sent for the parents. She traced Eliza's problems back to the sudden withdrawal of breastfeeding in infancy: Jo should have persisted.

'But she bit me!' cried poor Jo, but the therapist was a breast-feeding fanatic and said Jo would have to compensate by being less critical and more supportive, and then perhaps the stealing would stop.

Eliza, secretly rifling through her parent's correspondence, as was her custom, discovered the reports and blamed her mother the more.

'Why didn't you breastfeed me?' she would ask. 'Breastfed babies get better results at school and never get fat.'

'But you pass all your exams and you're not at all fat,' her mother would reply, mildly.

'You just didn't care, did you! Why did you have me in the first place if you weren't going to love me? You thought if you breast-fed you would lose your figure, I know what you're like.'

The stealing didn't stop but Eliza's ability to blame others improved and what happened was that she was simply never caught again. Another girl, one whom Eliza particularly didn't like, got expelled in her place.

When Eliza was twelve, Janice was thirty-three and still waiting for Mr Right to come along. Mr Wright, unbeknown to her, and aged forty-eight, was living down the road with Jo, and knew her father quite well. They appeared on TV arts pro-grammes together: Paul, who knew about the price of things; Waldo, who knew about what it was to be an artist. Jo had tried to have another child but it just never happened and, frankly, she was not all that sorry. She knew she was clinging on to Waldo by the skin of her teeth: he seemed to prefer Eliza's company to his wife's. He even took Eliza to the cinema once and simply left Jo behind – it was an 'art film': he knew Jo would hate it. Jo would want to clean his brushes but she'd find Eliza had already done them. And Eliza grew prettier and prettier and Jo grew older and older. Her friends took their daughters shopping and had fun together: Eliza was just not a fun person, at least with her mother. Could it be her fault, as everyone now assumed, and about breastfeeding? Surely not! Wasn't it possible for people to be born just *not nice*?

Eliza got taken to social events in Jo's place.

'You don't really want to go, do you, darling?' Waldo asked Jo. 'It's good for Eliza to learn to socialize.' And she didn't, and she could see it was. Sometimes there were tickets for three, and then Jo would go along.

'Did you see the way that lady last night looked at Daddy?' Eliza asked after one such function.

'I can't say I did,' said Jo, who didn't notice very much, if truth be told. Waldo had been elected to the Royal Academy. Women threw themselves at him. He was all but a celebrity: he had been declared a genius, a true artist. He wasn't rich, because he painted what he saw and not what people wanted him to see. But he was famous for his integrity.

'And the way Daddy looked at her! Wow!'

'Don't talk about your father like that.'

'He is a man. He's not a block of wood. And you and he don't have it off much, do you? Well, you are older than him I suppose. You're going to be fifty soon. Much older than the other mothers. Do you think he's having an affair with her?'

'Don't be absurd, Eliza, and don't talk about things you don't understand.'

'Mum, this is the twenty-first century and I'm twelve. You go around looking like an old bean bag the dog's sat in. Couldn't you go blonde or something?'

Meanwhile Janice had a good career in radio, both as a journalist and increasingly on the management front. She was asked to join a TV company but she preferred the company of the quieter more reflective people who worked in sound and left vision out of it. She moved into programming. She had a gift for it. She earned a good deal, bought share options, saved, bought a flat, had good friends, went out with men, turned them down after a while, politely, if it all became too intense, saving their face when she could. Nothing personal, just not the man of the dreams. The man with the cleft chin. Colleagues peeled off, got married, had kids, Janice didn't. Alice got worried about grandchildren.

'Lots of time,' said Janice: the man with the meaningful eyes had not come along. She would know him when she saw him.

'What about my grandchildren?' asked Alice. 'Eggs get old.'

Janice, ever obliging, internet dated, and speed dated, but it got depressing and she stopped. Men who were fine in theory did less than nothing for you when you met them face to face.

'You're too picky,' Alice said.

'Oh leave the girl alone,' said Paul. 'There's lots of time.' He found the thought of Janice married to someone else rather uncomfortable. He was now buying antique furniture for royalty:

furnishing a new wing of Windsor Castle, on permanent display to the public. *500 years of royalty – a European perspective*. He and Alice built themselves a grand new house. His friendship with Waldo and Jo got closer. He assumed Waldo had affairs. Artists were not famous for being family men, and a wife in her fifties with flowers in her hair might not be enough to keep a man at home. And still Waldo and Janice had not met.

This was how it came about, finally, at a Royal Academy dinner. It was a very posh do, with royalty at the top table. Jo wanted to go, so Waldo asked for three tickets, not without some reservation. Paul and Alice contrived a third ticket for Janice. Since both men now counted as TV personalities, special privileges were allowed. Waldo was seated next to Janice: Jo sat opposite and wore a dress cut too low and drank too much and the pink satin rose in her hair fell over her ear.

Janice, by contrast, sat demurely and politely and spoke well and interestingly about this and that. She was recently back from Laos, where she had been setting up community radio. The light caught Waldo's chin. There was a slight cleft in it, his lips were thin, and his eyes looked at her meaningfully: she fell in love with him. Did she remember Kirk Douglas? No, though later he was to resurface in her dreams.

He thought she was the most beautiful, most desirable woman he had ever seen. He looked across the table at Jo and was sorry for her but knew he had no choice. He was going to make Janice his own. He looked at Eliza and thought perhaps after all she was rather spoilt and conceited and Jo had not made a good mother. Janice, with her sweet, intelligent, thoughtful brow, would give the child the emotional depth she lacked, and would never get from her mother; it was for Eliza's sake that he had to leave Jo, and he was sure Jo would understand. They had never been really suited, and Jo had tricked him into marriage in the first place. Now he must have a real wife, a proper wife. Waldo's hand, the painter's hand, that gave so much pleasure to so many, covered hers and Janice felt the total thrill of it and let it lie. With that touch she was in tune with destiny. In an instant both lives had changed. And that is how it ought to be, surely. The White Knight gallops over the hill and that is that. He had taken his time but now he was here. Venus had moved into the ninth house.

He gave her his card. Eliza was sitting one down from her father and noticed and a frisson of horror ran through her. She had finally defeated her mother: she was not going to be sidelined now by some dull bitch with tits and a big bum. Eliza was on the anorexic side: the problem for girls who hate their mothers is that they hate themselves as well. She pushed a bit of salad round her plate and waited for her father to lean over and say in the stern, loving voice of his 'Eliza, EAT!' but he didn't. He was too busy with the bitch.

Jo did not notice: she was giggling and bending over the plate of the man next to her and cutting his meat with a knife and fork. She thought it was a rather charming thing to do. A flower fell out of her hair and fell into his gravy. Together they fished it out. The man, a Count Sakovski from somewhere abroad, thought the English were strange but he liked this foolish, untidy woman who didn't know how to behave and was probably very unhappy. He thought perhaps she was anyone's and it might as well be him.

Alice and Paul both noticed the looks that passed between Waldo and their daughter and turned to each other, troubled and amazed. But Alice thought instantly of grandchildren – the inheritance would be just fine. A pity about the wife and daughter but if you left it to so late, as Janice had, you weren't likely to find someone unencumbered by the baggage of the past. Paul thought, well, I could bear to lose her to Waldo. He respected Waldo, as Walter Matthau all that time ago had respected Kirk Douglas in *Lonely Are the Brave*. The Waldo marriage was evidently on the rocks. And the daughter looked sweet.

More wine was poured. Janice felt light-headed. Sometimes social events seem to have been set up by the deity so that life stories can switch, and their characters go off in different and unexpected directions. These are the parties at which alliances are made and broken, love affairs started and ended, children conceived, jobs found and lost. The dinner at the Royal Academy was one such.

After dinner coffee was served in the Fine Rooms and guests repaired to wander around the Summer Exhibition in which three of Waldo's paintings were hung; the company he kept on the walls was not necessarily the finest in the land, but he was a democrat and did what he could to help aspirants. Janice asked if he would show his work to her, and he was happy to do so. Jo for once noticed the way Waldo took her smooth young elbow to show Janice round, and was filled with sudden outrage. The Count asked her why she was so unhappy, and she felt inclined to tell him. He took her to a dark corner behind a massive sculpture and some new architectural conceit which hid them from passers-by and there partially disrobed and embraced her, to make her less unhappy. They had both gone round the table when the others were drinking coffee and had drained the dregs of the rather too sweet dessert wine which others had left in their glasses. It seemed funny at the time.

Eliza followed her mother the better to be able to mock her for her alcoholism in the future – 'remember that time when your hair flower dropped in that poor man's gravy: you are so embarrassing!' – and was genuinely shocked to see what was going on. She went to find her father and told him he must come at once, and led him to the spot. Janice went too. Jo looked up from the floor past the Count's elbow and saw the grim faces looking down at her.

'Nobody loves me,' she said, to which I am afraid Waldo's reply was, 'No. They don't.'

Waldo took Eliza home to friends for the night and went home to Janice's little flat and spent a glorious night in her bed, justified and guilt-free, but nevertheless furious with Jo for thus having embarrassed, shamed and betrayed him. And he dreaded to think of the effect of his wife's behaviour on poor Eliza.

It had of course been Janice's determination never to go with a married man. She despised people who did. But a wife such as Jo, immoral, drunk and dissolute, hardly counted. And his poor child! Eliza, what a pretty name! Janice would have to make it up to her, give her the mother's love she had obviously never had. Janice had so much love, stored up and ready to go, now the man she had been waiting for, with the clean-cut face, the wide mouth with the thin lips, and the dimple in the chin had arrived. His hair was perhaps more thinned and receding than that a hero's should be: there was quite an age difference, but love was love, and does not alter when it alteration finds.

Paul and Alice had left before coffee in the summer exhibition. 'Nothing can happen,' said Alice to Paul. 'The wife was sitting opposite, the daughter just a couple of seats away.'

She felt the power of family to restrain and control. Paul was less impressed.

'Oh no,' he said. 'He'll be after her all right, but she'll have the sense to send him packing. She wants a man of her own, her own age and background, not a family man and someone else's family at that.'

When she called the next morning to say she was in love they were alarmed.

'But he has a wife and a daughter,' said Alice. 'What are you doing?'

'The wife is useless,' said Janice, 'and a tramp. And I can look after the daughter better than she can.'

'Step-children are difficult,' said her mother.

'But I'll love her as I love her father. She is his flesh and blood.'

'She might hate you,' said Paul.

'Why should she?' asked Janice. 'I'm not a hateful person. If you give love it's returned. Poor little girl, she's had an alcoholic mother to cope with.'

Waldo texted Eliza in class and arranged to meet her after school. He told her he was moving in with a dear friend and she must remember that he loved her more than anything. She must go on living with her mother for a little but as soon as things were sorted out he would send for her. He had made sure she would have the best stepmother in the world.

'I see,' said Eliza pleasantly. 'And yes, I will remember that. You love me more than anything.' If there was irony in her voice he did not notice it.

She went home and up to his studio and drove a knife into some of his paintings, and some of them she just kicked and hurled about the room. Then she called her dad on the phone and said her mother had gone mad and broken up the studio and what should she do? When the police came Jo denied having done it, and Waldo said he wouldn't press charges, though obviously it would go in the divorce petition. Fortunately most of the works currently in the studio were rejects brought out of storage to get rid of them. Nevertheless it was upsetting.

'Eliza,' said Jo, emerging from tears of grief, shock and rage. 'There's only one person who could have done that to Daddy's paintings and it was you.'

'The police don't think it was,' said Eliza. 'They think it was you. I said you might be getting Alzheimer's. Or perhaps you drink so much you just blank out. You're down on my school notes as query alcoholic.'

Jo tore the flowers from her hair and retreated again into tears of grief, shock and rage. She couldn't remember much, it was true. Her brain cells seemed to have been shaken up and reassembled. When she closed her eyes at night she saw zig-zags of light which were feeding up from her heart. The Count didn't get in touch. Very few people did: they were all on Waldo's side. He was famous and Janice was liked, but not enough. Eliza was actually quite sweet for a bit and brought her mother cups of tea, into which she'd crumbled valium.

Paul and Alice went round to visit their daughter to find out what was going on and found Waldo in the kitchen clearing out her fridge for her. Janice was busy: a full-time job which often involved staying late at the office, various charity commitments, an active and cheerful social life – if she had a fault it was that she let the fridge fur up and ate out of the microwave. Waldo was used to home cooking.

'I'm stealing your daughter,' he said to Paul. Paul rather liked that: it was true enough, but it was upfront. At least it acknowledged prior entitlement and was a pack leader kind of thing to say. Paul thought Janice would be safe.

'We'll give you fine grandchildren,' Waldo said to Alice. 'And high time too.'

Alice was a little more difficult to persuade.

'I'm sure you will,' she said. 'But you have a wife and a child already.'

'A divorce petition is already on its way to my ex-wife,' he said. 'And I will sue for custody of the child.'

'But the courts favour the mother,' said Alice.

'I hardly think in this case,' said Waldo. 'And Eliza's fifteen. She'll make up her own mind.'

'Stop worrying,' said Janice. 'I know what I'm doing. I know there's an age gap but he's young for his age and I'm old for mine.' And both mother and daughter knew she was all too fertile, though neither mentioned it.

'What will happen to Jo?'

'She can stay in the matrimonial home,' said Janice, loftily. 'We're not going to be mean about it.'

If Waldo felt rather doubtful about this he did not say so. What about his studio? The north light was important. And supposing Jo used it to entertain her lovers? She didn't need so big a place. Eliza would be living with him, and he and Janice would be having the real family and deserved the real family home. But there was no point in bringing up these matters now. For the moment living with Janice was a delight. He was between commissions and could do with a rest: Janice was currently working from home. They had all the time in the world for each other.

That seemed to the parents if not wholly satisfactory not nearly so bad as it could have been, and Waldo and Janice glowed with such happiness that very few gave a thought for Jo.

Of course there was trouble. Jo's mother paid for a good lawyer: it would use up nearly all Jo's expected inheritance and one way and another most of her capital had gone – Waldo lived well in spite of being so publicly poor. Jo threatened to commit suicide, and Janice found herself thinking one of the most uncharitable thoughts she had ever had – if only Jo would. But they stomach-pumped her in time.

When it became apparent that Waldo was trying to get back into the matrimonial home, Janice did not now object. He was becoming restive, wanting to get back to his easel. He needed familiar things around him. He had spent twenty years getting his studio just right. He had an artist's eye and was acutely conscious of the rightness or otherwise of his surroundings. Jo had never had particularly good taste. Eliza said she would only come and live with her father in the matrimonial home so that settled it. Meanwhile she went on living with Jo.

Eliza went into full anorexia, and refused to come to Janice's house, though she'd see her father at the Savoy for tea, where she'd only drink jasmine tea and under pressure, a little ham from the middle of the delicate sandwiches, which she'd promptly throw up in the grand halls of the marble Ladies, though Waldo didn't realize this.

Janice found herself rather resenting these outings: she hadn't yet even met Eliza. Waldo said it wasn't time. These things had to be done little by little. He was firmly and profoundly out of love and even liking, with Jo, who had done the terrible, shaming, cuckolding thing at the Academician's dinner, but Eliza seemed to take up a larger chunk of his heart than she had reckoned a daughter would. She could see what her mother had meant about marrying a man with no baggage. But there it was: love was love, and the sex life was out of this world.

Waldo couldn't stand packaged or frozen food so Janice cooked: which meant a new freezer and a proper cooker and even an Aga because that's the only way to get proper slow-cooked casseroles. Something about the way heat convected: Janice had always thought heat was heat but no. The wine she bought doubled in price. He wasn't one for Chilean wine and preferred Californian. She found she was paying. But money talk was sordid.

He didn't like the idea of having a cleaner, and though Janice had managed well enough without one when it was only her and the microwave, cleaning, not to mention cooking, took up time and strength. Waldo was perfectly right: it was not fair to use another person to clean up after one – in Sweden household help was more or less banned. The prime minister had all but been unseated because his wife, a lawyer, was found to be employing a maid. But this was not Sweden. And Waldo had high standards. He couldn't stand a mucky fridge or dirt behind the cooker. Janice wondered if perhaps she should work part-time but Waldo said one of the things that had gone wrong between him and Jo was that she was at home too much, distracting him, and he liked to work in an empty house. So Janice scrapped that idea.

Things calmed down. The divorce went through. Jo found herself described in court as an alcoholic – with police and school reports to back the allegations – and, by implication, a nymphomaniac. Her plea that she had been faithful all her married life sounded oddly old-fashioned and irrelevant. Waldo kept the house beacuse it was his place of work and because it was Eliza's home. The fact that Jo employed one of the top divorce lawyers in the country went against her. Her pleas of poverty didn't add up to much. Waldo used a more modest Human Rights lawyer, but one who wrote a weekly column in a newspaper. Waldo bought Jo out of the house and now she lived in a two-bedroomed flat in Earls Court, just right for a fifty-year-old divorcee with a liking for pubs and foreign Counts, Janice and Waldo agreed, laughing. Paul and Alice rather wondered what was happening to Janice, the bright-eyed lass. She seemed able to laugh at, these days, rather than laugh with.

Waldo prepared the house for Janice. He sent Eliza to stay with friends for a week, and disposed of all Jo's things. Those she did not collect in time he put in black sacks and took down to the Council goods exchange. Sack after sack of silk and velvet flowers went that way – Jo no longer wore them. He very decently let Jo take the bed and the mattress, though when it came to it the movers could not get it through her front door – it was a rather small flat in a rather small new house – so she told them to take it down to the dump. (One of the movers took it home and he and his male partner slept happily on it thereafter, which was something. It brought them luck if no one else.) Jo slept on the sofa for quite a while. Waldo bought a new bed and a new mattress. He got in professional cleaners – they seemed more acceptable morally than ordinary domestic ones – and scrubbed out the old and brought in the new.

Janice went to John Lewis and bought bedding and had them send it round to Waldo's house. She put her own house on the market and within a couple of days a buyer was on the doorstep. He wanted the carpets and furniture too and would give her a good price: china, crockery, bedding, everything. Eminently sensible – she was moving to one already fully furnished. She suddenly got cold feet.

'It's all gone so fast,' she said. 'Am I doing the right thing?' She found herself crying. She couldn't remember crying since her cat had run out in the street and been killed.

Waldo got his lawyer to hurry up the decree nisi so they could be married absolutely as soon as possible, and her feet were once again warm as hot-buttered toast and the tears dried. What was all that about?

'It's a woman thing,' said Waldo. 'I love you for it.'

The cleft in his chin caught the light whenever she looked and when he moved towards her she felt her body melt towards his. And then it was done. The new house and the new life was waiting.

He told her to come round at four on Saturday afternoon.

They'd have tea and then they'd go with the car and bring in the first of her things from her house. He needed the morning for last-minute touches. At four she arrived and knocked on the door of the house that was hers. Waldo would need to get a new key cut.

Waldo didn't open the door, Eliza did. At fifteen she was almost as tall as Janice: thin to the point of gauntness but beautiful: large blue eyes in a luminous face, long blonde ironed hair. Ironed jeans: spotless white T-shirt, long sleeves. Janice hadn't seen her since the night of the dinner: but she had been talked about incessantly – *what about Eliza? What's to be done?* – and the reality took her aback. She seemed so very much at home. Well, thought, Janice, that figures. It is her home. We have planned and plotted to make this her home. Nevertheless she felt a little freaked.

'How do you do,' said Eliza politely. 'You'll be Janice. Do come in.'

And she showed Janice into the living room, and said, 'Do sit down. I'll call Daddy. Not in that chair, that's Mummy's.' Janice sat down as instructed. Then Eliza called upstairs, 'Daddy, Janice is here.'

And after a rather awkward interval of silence Waldo came bounding downstairs from the attic where he painted, and said, 'Sorry, darling, I was softening up my brushes in turps. Great to be back at the old easel again. I'll need to get my hand in at portraiture again. New life, new style. So you two have finally met!'

'Yes we have,' said Eliza.

'Your new stepmother,' said Janice.

'Not yet,' said Eliza.

Janice was conscious of some vague implied threat but Waldo did not notice. He burbled on about portrait painting and how he'd love the first painting he did in his new life be a portrait of Janice. Janice, ever practical, said but that would take up ever so many woman-hours just sitting, wouldn't it, or could he work from photographs?

'Daddy never works from photographs,' said Eliza.

'I daresay we could make an exception for Janice,' said Waldo.

'But you always said that was cheating,' said Eliza. 'Have you changed, or something?'

'Of course I haven't changed,' said Waldo. 'Eliza's right, as ever. Eliza's my artistic conscience. No photographs. Natural light.'

'I've been suspended from school,' said Eliza. 'I can sit for you, Daddy. I've got lots of time.'

By the time the explanations about the suspension had been gone through – she'd been wrongly accused – it was somehow settled that Waldo's first portrait would be of his daughter, not his new wife-to-be. Tea was served, made by Eliza, whom Waldo praised for this sudden influx of domestic virtues.

'Now Mummy isn't here,' said Eliza, 'someone has to take care of you. The great artist!'

Janice kept quiet. She was being laughed at. So was Waldo, but in a different way, like a naughty boy being lovingly scolded.

'Are you staying for supper?' Eliza asked Janice.

Janice waited for Waldo to answer. He said nothing. She would have to take charge.

'I'm moving in,' Janice said, with head-girl confidence and determination. 'And I'm cooking supper.'

Eliza looked from one to the other of them as if this was the first she'd heard of it. 'Moving in with Daddy? But you're not married.'

'We will be soon, Eliza,' said Waldo. 'This is the twenty-first century.'

'And what's more you will eat the supper I make,' said Janice, pressing home her advantage. 'You are much too thin.'

'I don't believe this!' Eliza gave a great wail and pulled up the sleeve of her T-shirt and stared at it as if it was the solution to all problems and Janice saw that the thin but graceful arm was traced by scars. Then Eliza ran from the room.

'That wasn't very tactfully done,' said Waldo to Janice, before he ran after her. 'Now she'll be in a state for days. She's very sensitive.'

Supper was not cooked, but a run to the hospital had to be made for stitches and bandages: the white bone was showing through where the razor had cut. There was so little flesh between skin and bone, Janice could see, that the effect would be quite easy to achieve. There was quite a thick file in A&E on Eliza. Janice felt bad: had she precipitated this self-harm in the child? She was rather relieved to find it had been going on for some two years. She could not be blamed.

'I thought she was cured,' mourned Waldo. 'I really thought she was. Now this. Poor little chicken!'

They agreed Janice would go back to her place for the night so as not to aggravate the situation, and allow Eliza to settle. Janice left by taxi, with Eliza cooking supper at the Aga and humming, while Waldo laid the table for two.

The sale of Janice's house was proceeding apace. There was still time to stop it. She consulted her mother. Her mother said marriage went on a long time, and Eliza would be off their hands soon: she'd calm down. No girl of that age was going to actually welcome a stepmother and the divorce had been public and acrimonious, and if you were the Other Woman, what did you expect?

'But the marriage had broken down already!' protested Janice, but her mother just raised her eyebrows quizzically, and this unexpected censure quite upset Janice. She was accustomed to approval. It occurred to her that all her mother now wanted was that her daughter should provide her with grandchildren: the maternal concern she was used to had suddenly shifted a generation down. She felt betrayed. When Waldo called by with the car to move her belongings to Studio House she was the more grateful to see him. He's what I have in the world, she thought. Enduring love. We will have children and start a family and Eliza will come round. Of course she will. She signed the deed of sale and put it in the post.

Eliza was there to help her unpack. Her arm was bandaged but she did it with a good grace. She even ate a biscuit with her cup of tea and smiled a wonderfully pretty smile. It's all going to be all right, thought Janice. Waldo went up to the studio to prepare a canvas for the first portrait of the new life with the right wife.

Janice thought, oh, if it means so much to Eliza, let her be the one to sit for it. The one thing she must not do would be to be appear to be in competition for Waldo's favours with her own stepchild, or about-to-be stepchild.

When it came to hanging up her clothes in the bedroom closet she rather hoped Eliza would stay away. But Eliza didn't. Janice was accustomed to living alone and unobserved: everything, she could see, would be different now. Not just Waldo to admire her, which could be difficult enough when you were tired and just wanted to sink into an armchair, scratch your armpits and go to sleep in front of the TV, but Eliza too, always there to scrutinize and judge her? Would Eliza be going home for the weekends? Surely! If Eliza had really been suspended from school – perhaps she made things up? A girl who cut herself might well be some sort of fantasist – wouldn't a different school be sensible: perhaps one in Earls Court? Nothing had been really settled; nothing talked through. If she tried to take command, she could see, it might well mean another trip to the hospital. And Waldo would have nothing said against his daughter.

Meanwhile Eliza was taking out Janice's garments one by one, shaking them out, studying them, before putting them on hangers in what had once been Jo's closet.

'You're the same size as my mother,' she said. 'But your bum's bigger.' She spoke amiably, but she licked her lips as a snake does: a little flicker of the tongue came darting out on the mouth as if to enjoy the taste of cruelty and as quickly went in again. Her own hips were painful in their narrowness.

'Mummy wears a dress like this when she wants to be smart,' she said, shaking out a little black dress. She looked at the label. 'It *is* the same dress. M & S. My God, the dowdiness. Well, same taste in dress, same taste in men, I suppose.'

'I can do this on my own,' said Janice. 'But thank you for helping.'

Eliza sat down on the end of the bed and bounced on it a bit. 'New mattress,' she said. 'Expensive too. Bet Daddy made you pay for it. Mummy always paid for everything and now she's got nothing. But she isn't very bright. I expect you're a lot brighter than her. Daddy's moved up in the world. He wanted a newer classier model. I don't know why he didn't just make do with me. I was willing. I don't see anything wrong in incest, do you?'

'It creates confusion in the generations,' said Janice. 'Really, I can do this on my own.'

But Eliza didn't seem to hear. She was sliding open drawers in the chest that Waldo had decided was too nice to get rid of. The drawers were deep and slid easily.

'Mummy used to keep her nighties in this one and her under things in this one. I'd do the opposite if I were you or you might turn into her. Ooh look—' And she pulled from the back of the bottom drawer a pretty if voluminous green silk nightie, lace at the top and sexy, and held it up and shook it. 'Mummy must have left this. Shall I take it back to her or would you like to wear it? I don't suppose it's much use to her now. No one's going to look at her again, are they? She won't miss it. It might rather suit you. You could get three of me into it, I guess,' and then it seemed too much for her to handle, and her mouth turned down and she whimpered as if she was six and said, 'I'm sorry, I don't want to be like this,' and cried. So Janice put her arms round her and said, 'There, there, I understand.' But she still had the feeling she was being worked upon. It was not genuine. Eliza was resting, working out her next move.

Janice went up to the studio and reported the conversation and all Waldo said was, 'But I cleared everything out of that drawer, I swear I did. Poor girl, she's bound to be upset. Be charitable! Perhaps tact isn't your greatest virtue. I want more than anything for my two women to get on.' Waldo put his arms round Janice and before she could react bore her down onto the sofa: they made love. A cry of alarm halted them in their throes: it was Eliza, breaking in upon the primal scene.

'Janice,' cried Waldo, 'didn't you even think to lock the door!' And he ran after Eliza, first rearranging his clothing, but by then it was too late.

Weeping, Eliza ran out into the night, called a taxi on her father's account, which she had been asked not to do and went to live with her mother, until she disturbed her mother too in the midst of a primal scene with someone she brought home from the pub. Then she went back weeping to her father again, giving him information about Jo which though unpleasant to hear proved useful in his ongoing arguments with his ex-wife about alimony. Jo had used up all her inheritance on legal fees, and was now defending her own case, so Waldo was able to bring the payments down considerably.

Janice took the afternoon off work and welcomed Eliza home with cups of tea and tiny little bite-size cucumber sandwiches to tempt the anorexic appetite, which Janice made herself, first finely slicing and sweating the cucumber with salt, pouring on boiling water, then cold, until the slivers were all but transparent, and placing between thinly sliced white organic bread and even removing the crusts. But Eliza refused the sandwiches – she couldn't stand cucumber: so phallic! – and drank only water.

'Well,' said Waldo, generously, 'no one can say you don't try!'

They were sitting by the fire that evening listening to *The Rite of Spring*, and Eliza had gone to her rather splendid attic room, there to brood, when Janice heard the noise of furniture moving in the spare room, which was next to the master bedroom where she and Waldo slept. She went upstairs to see what was going on, though Waldo said, 'Oh, leave the girl alone' – and found Eliza lugging her bits and pieces down the stairs from the attic room and piling them into the spare room.

'What are you doing?' she asked, taken by surprise. She had learned not to ask Eliza a direct question, because the girl was likely to assume there was some sinister plot behind whatever was enquired upon, and wax paranoiac. But Eliza for once seemed quite easy.

'Moving down from the attic,' said Eliza. 'I hate being so lonely and away from everyone up there. I feel relegated. This room isn't so big but it's friendlier. I'll just finish this and then I'll come down and eat some of your little pale green sandwiches if you and Daddy haven't scoffed the lot.'

'Good idea,' said Janice, and went down to Waldo.

'Janice is moving into the spare room,' she said.

'That's good,' said Waldo. 'She always was rather stuck away up there. It was Jo's idea.'

'But the walls are so thin,' said Janice.

'So?' asked Waldo.

'Sex,' said Janice.

'Oh,' said Waldo, realizing. And Eliza came in and ate four little sandwiches straight off and said, 'Those are really nice, Janice,' and then went back upstairs and they could hear her singing. The walls really were quite thin, for an old house.

'We'll just have to be quiet,' said Waldo.

It transpired that Eliza had burned her boats so drastically she was not to be allowed back into school – she had been found smoking drugs, quite openly, and had, worse, then refused to sign a required contract with the school undertaking not to do so again.

'For God's sake,' said Waldo. 'A contract? I thought a school was meant to be a place of education, but no. Our schools have turned into institutions devoted to the coercing of children into right thinking! Good for Eliza!'

'But she has to get some qualifications,' said Janice. 'Or her life will narrow down dreadfully.' At least if Eliza was away some of the day, she and Waldo might manage some decent sex in her absence. No doubt the same idea occurred to Waldo: at any rate he suggested a family visit to the head, to persuade the school to take Janice back. It was arranged. But when it came to it Waldo was at a tricky stage of his portrait of Eliza, and needed her to sit for him while he got the hands right, so Eliza couldn't come along either. Janice went alone.

'She had settled down so nicely too,' said the head, who was sympathetic, but clearly thought everything that ever went wrong with the children was the parents' fault. 'Though there was some initial trouble in the early days. A very bright girl indeed. But then there was a divorce, wasn't there. Well, if often happens with these artistic families. But children do tend to react badly. We see it all the time.'

'But you would be prepared to take her back?' asked Eliza.

'If she will sign the contract, and take it seriously,' said the head. There was some kind of disturbance in the school, and the headmistress had to call the police because of a knifing – it was a state school, well thought of academically, but even the best-run schools have their troubles.

When the head returned, in some twenty minutes, she found Janice looking at her watch. Janice was meant to be at a meeting with UNESCO to do with the setting-up of a chain of radio stations to promote healthy living in Laos, and was already late.

'We're all very short of time these days,' said the head. 'If all the mothers were at home mothering, we'd have a lot less trouble from the kids.'

'I'm a stepmother,' said Janice. She suddenly felt like crying, but there was to be no sympathy from the head, who made a little *mou* of indifference.

'Well, there we have it!' the other woman said, dismissing her. 'Family breakdown! Bring Eliza in and if she'll sign the contract we'll think about it. That was Eliza I saw in the paper the other day with her father? She could yet be an asset to this school.'

Waldo had just been given a CBE by the Queen for services to art, and his picture and Eliza's had been in the paper. Janice wasn't able to go to the ceremony because of a meeting.

But Eliza wouldn't sign the contract. 'They don't want to teach us,' she said. 'They just want to be able to tick boxes. If I sign their fucking contract they get extra money from the state.'

'I wish you wouldn't swear,' said Janice and Eliza flew into a mood and said she had her own mother, thank you, and Janice was a sanctimonious bitch.

'Good Lord,' said Janice. 'Five syllables!' She couldn't resist it. She should have.

'I don't know what you're fucking talking about,' said Eliza, who hadn't heard of syllables. 'You do it on purpose to make me feel bad.'

It was Eliza herself who suggested she go to a private school. The classes were smaller and she'd be happier there. They were sitting at the dinner table, the three of them, and Eliza was pushing a lettuce leaf and a tomato around her plate. She was, she said, sick of not knowing anything.

'But where would we get the money from?' asked Waldo. His income was sporadic: he was with a leading gallery, his paintings were selling around the seven thousand mark, and rising, but the gallery was taking forty percent, the government another forty percent, and though he was teaching one day a week, and working as an arts journalist too, he resented the time spent away from actual painting.

'Janice could pay,' said Eliza. 'She's so clever she makes a fortune telling other countries how to behave. And her family's rich as Croesus, and I'm the only grandchild.'

'It is a thought,' said Waldo, and Eliza beamed and actually leant over and took a slice of flan from her father's plate, and began to eat it, carbohydrate, fats and all. When she smiled she was astonishingly pretty. When Janice brought out the *boeuf en daube* she'd had in the slow oven since before work, Eliza had a spoonful of that too. Everything might yet be all right, thought Janice, and felt a pang of actual affection for her stepchild.

And so it was arranged. Eliza went to school and Janice dipped in to her capital to pay.

Eliza left the house at eight. Janice moved her office hours – though her bosses did not like it there was little they could do about it – and left the house at nine. Between eight and nine Janice could join Waldo in bed, and they indulged their passion for each other, at any rate in term time. He was just a little older, just a little thinner: the cleft in his chin was more defined than ever. The painting of Eliza was finished, and was bought by a royal. It is always hard to let a painting go but the thought of a palace wall eases the strain. Waldo relented about the cleaning since the doctor, visiting Janice when she had an attack of bronchitis, suggested she might be doing too much. A cleaner came twice a week. She was a quiet, clean, hardworking Polish girl.

'Let's hope Daddy doesn't fancy her,' said Eliza. 'Another masochist!'

Janice saw the little cruel flicker of Eliza's tongue, gritted her teeth, and did not respond.

Waldo now helped out by doing the food shopping, albeit on Janice's store card. He went for the most expensive stuff in the shop, not the cheapest. And Eliza rewarded them by occasionally eating. Sometimes then Janice had the feeling they were puppets dancing at the end of her string, but not often. Eliza liked her new school, grew a little more rounded, a little happier. Janice felt she was achieving something. Jo was keeping company with another alcoholic from the pub and Eliza seldom visited her.

Janice had a phone call from Jo once. 'You bitch, you home-breaker, child-stealer, woman-hater! I hope you die of cancer soon!' She was drunk, and mad. Janice told Waldo.

'I am so sorry, darling. Don't be upset. Why do you think I divorced her? She was an alcoholic and insane. A wretched, wretched first marriage. You've done marvels with Eliza.'

'So when are you going to get married?' asked her father.

'As soon as the divorce is through,' said Janice.

'You're sure you want to?' asked her father. 'Take no notice of your mother. She's hooked on grandchildren, and no, a step-grandchild's fine, and we're happy to help with the school fees, but according to your mother it isn't the same. It's the genes that count.'

'Of course I want to marry him,' said Janice. How could there be any doubt? She was the envy of so many, and one year in still went round in an erotic haze, and if she fell asleep in meetings, she rather liked the quizzical regard of the others round the board table. She knew she looked lovelier than ever, Waldo's young wife: she was in her prime, loved and properly loved. She had waited for the man with the cleft jaw and it had worked.

The divorce was finally through. Time to get married. Eliza to be thought of. Janice would have loved a real marriage, an expensive marriage, crossed swords or paintbrushes or whatever the art community did, and the kind her mother wanted, but Waldo thought it might upset Eliza. So they went for a quiet register office ceremony: the kind you tell people about casually later. 'Oh, by the way, we're married now. Yes, did the deed a couple of weeks back.' It would certainly save money, as Waldo pointed out, and Paul's business was going through a bad patch as the bottom fell out of the antiques market – and school fees were soaring. Eliza was quite a spendthrift, too. She must have got that from her mother, as Janice realized: she certainly didn't get it from Waldo. Though when it came to her store cards he seemed lavish enough: the money she had saved in her single days was almost all gone. Every electronic equipment available on the market ended up in the spare room, now Eliza's room, and the beat, beat, beat of digitalization would keep Janice awake late into the night. Eliza's clothes were plentiful, changed many times daily and had recognizable labels. Janice tried to restrict her spending and a week before the marriage ceremony – not much point in calling it a wedding, Janice thought, with a flicker of resentment – Eliza responded by stealing and using Janice's store cards to the tune of £700.

Waldo just laughed when he was told and observed that they were getting off easily. And it was true – it was in the news – one of Janice's own school friends had tried to sell her left kidney for £3000 to get money for a designer jacket. A week to the wedding, as he pointed out, and Eliza was bound to get upset.

'Not exactly a wedding,' said Janice, 'my poor parents aren't even invited,' and Waldo bore her off to the studio and to bed, and the resentment evaporated.

Eliza said she was sorry about the cards, which was something, but she'd just wanted something special to wear to celebrate the occasion of Janice becoming her formal stepmother. The day of Janice's wedding arrived and Eliza came into the bedroom early without knocking and handed Janice a pink silk rose on a clip: the kind you wear in your hair.

'It's for you to wear for the wedding. Mummy always looked so pretty in them,' she said. 'Before she'd taken to drink, before you came along.'

And she went away again.

'That's a nice accepting gesture,' said Waldo.

'No it's not,' said Janice. 'She's ill wishing me.'

'Now why on earth should she do that?' asked Waldo.

Janice wore the pink rose in her hair at the register wedding. Really there seemed to be no option.

'You're too old to have children,' said Eliza to Janice at the Chinese restaurant where they all repaired for lunch after the ceremony. 'That's something!'

'Excuse me,' said Janice. 'You have that altogether wrong.'

'I suppose you could physically,' said Eliza, 'just about, but it would hardly be fair to the child. It would probably be born with Down's. And who would support Daddy if you weren't working? Anyway, men over fifty who have children are pathetic.'

'Eliza,' said Janice boldly, 'face up to it. Your father and I are going to have children just as soon and as many as we can.'

Eliza pushed away her plate after staring at its contents – she had taken a spring roll – and said, 'Yuk! That is so disgusting. You can see the fat glistening, and it's kind of withered, like old skin. Fine sort of marriage feast this is! Well, happy days—' and walked out of the restaurant. These days men's heads turned as she went. Janice rather hoped Eliza was going off to stay with her mother, but she didn't.

'You could have put it more tactfully,' said Waldo. 'And that rose has fallen over your ear.' So much for the wedding day.

But in fact more than a year had gone by and Janice, in spite of taking no contraceptive precautions, had not yet got pregnant. Her mother Alice said she had better take the matter seriously. Conventional wisdom was to wait two years before seeking fertility treatment but there was no real reason, as Alice pointed out, not to push ahead at once, just to check out that all was well: Alice would pay any medical bills. Times were tight, but not as tight as all that. Waldo already had a child, and so was fertile, which was something.

'I suppose Eliza is Waldo's child,' said Janice, succumbing to a rare burst of spite. 'I reckon she's a changeling, one of the mischievous creatures elves will leave behind in the cradle when they have stolen the real child. Or perhaps Jo cheated. She was the type.'

'I hope you haven't said as much to Waldo,' said Alice.

'Of course I haven't,' said Janice. 'And again, she might not even *be* Waldo's.'

But her mother just laughed and said, 'I'm sorry, my dear: wishful thinking! Of course she's Waldo's. She's got a cleft chin. What was that film you and I saw together when you were a child? *Lonely Are the Brave*? Kirk Douglas! The only film star I ever fancied, apart from Walter Matthau, in an altogether different kind of way.'

Janice couldn't remember the film, to Alice's disappointment, but that night she dreamt of Kirk Douglas, who was beckoning her up a mountain, and she kept slipping back, and back, into the void, and Eliza was clutching her ankles and she couldn't free herself to follow Kirk. She told Waldo about the dream and he said, 'People used to say I looked like Kirk Douglas. It's the chin, I suppose. But I never felt like him, certainly not in that film, what was it? *Lonely Are the Brave*? I always rather liked the here and now.'

'Funny,' she said, 'my mum was talking about that film just now: I can't remember it at all, except to have that strange dream.'

Janice went privately to see a fertility specialist and he suggested she lead a less stressful and active life. She turned down promotion and moved sideways to work in Features. Six months more and still nothing. The passage of time worried Janice more and more. Every month her mother rang up and said, 'Well?' And

Janice would have to report back, 'No, nothing.' She, who was so used to everything going well, so used to success, faced the possibility of failure.

'Honeybunch,' said her father, 'if you don't have a baby it's not the end of the world. I know your mother thinks it is but it's not. There are far too many children in the world as it is.' To which Janice responded darkly, 'Depends on what kind of child.'

She went back to the specialist who did tests, and when they came back he called her in and asked her if she was taking a contraceptive pill of some kind, perhaps inadvertently, because the tests suggested she was. She said she definitely was not, and he must have thought she was some kind of nutter, because he said he couldn't help her and perhaps she should find another specialist, which she did. She reported back to Waldo.

'You don't think perhaps Eliza has been feeding me contraceptives during all this last year?' she asked.

Waldo said she was being totally paranoiac, poor Eliza. Bad enough for her to be having to face the prospect of the arrival of a half-brother and sister, but to be blamed for her stepmother's failure to conceive! A bit rich! Janice really must stop behaving like a wicked stepmother. Perhaps she should go back to working full-time: there were mortgage payments to keep up – he had had to borrow more on the house.

This was the first she had heard of it. How could he have borrowed without her knowing? She realized the house had never been put in both their names after he had bought out Jo. Waldo seemed genuinely surprised when she brought the matter up – and said that had been sheer forgetfulness on his part and they went down together to the mortgage broker and within the month the house was in half her name. She was ashamed of herself for doubting him. He was right. She was getting paranoiac.

It occurred to her that Eliza could be putting contraceptive pills in the breakfast coffee. Eliza was the first one up in the morning, and she was the one who always put on the coffee percolator. It had always seemed rather odd to Janice that Eliza got up so early in term time and out of it. That she never had sleepovers like the other girls did. That every single morning Eliza was up and busy before anyone else. Busy at what? Grinding up pills, perhaps? Determined to be her father's only child?

She could not say this to Waldo, so she said it to Paul.

'Possible,' he said. 'But she's a bright girl. Eliza knows she'll find herself sent back to her mother at the first sign of bad behaviour.'

'You're too cynical,' said Janice. 'Too reductionist. Waldo won't be like that.' But she rather hoped he would be.

She rose early to spy on Eliza but the girl simply ground the coffee, and put on the percolator and left the room. Janice was ashamed of herself and tried to get her full-time job back before she went totally mad. But it was no longer available. Company policy had changed. The battle was to the young, the quick, and those unlikely to claim paid maternity leave. She should be grateful not to lose the part-time job. She was too easily replaceable as it was. All the same she switched from coffee to tea, and made it herself, with a tea bag and boiling water fresh from the kettle. She'd even empty the existing water out and use fresh from the tap, just to be on the safe side. Then she'd feel bad and mad all over again.

She went to creative writing classes to give herself something to do, in the hope of writing some of it out of her system. It didn't do much good. She could feel the paranoia burning away inside her. Eliza had taken to wearing red: she was convinced that Eliza was doing it on purpose to provoke her: *a red rag to a bull*. How mad was that?

For by and large Eliza was now behaving herself. She went to school, kept out of trouble, and ate simply but adequately. She had discovered a real talent for maths, been accepted at an Oxford college, and planned to go away for a gap year. She still treated Janice with a mixture of derision and contempt, at least when Waldo wasn't looking – what Janice wore, what she ate, what she said – but it seemed born out of habit, rather than something given fresh vigour every day that passed. She was seen as a credit to Janice. And still Janice did not get pregnant. Internal examinations came and went. Nothing wrong that anyone could see, and how they looked!

'Of course I want a baby with you,' said Waldo, astonished. 'I love you. It's just we know I'm fertile, so there's no point in my being tested. I don't want you getting obsessive about this, as you tend to be about poor Eliza.'

Mad and bad, that's me, thought Janice, that's what I am.

An extraordinary thing happened. Her mother split up with her father, and ran off with a younger man with three children under five. Janice blamed herself and her infertility. If she'd had children it would never have happened. Her father said as much, too. After a couple of months upset her father shacked up with Helen, a colleague of Janice's and roughly the same age. Janice wept in the kitchen.

'Face it,' said Waldo, 'your father is better off with Helen than he ever was with your mother. At least she has an intellect. He's been having an affair with her for years.'

'Why didn't you tell me?' She was outraged.

'I didn't want to upset you,' said Waldo. 'You don't have much appetite for reality.'

'Now you know what it's like,' said Eliza. 'But I bet you react by eating: you won't not eat, the way I did.'

She was right: Janice put on two stone in six months, comfort eating, and had to be asked to lose weight by the doctors to optimize their treatments. She was taking twelve tablets a day of drugs and hormones which wreaked havoc with her moods and metabolism. When they had her hormone levels right they'd start taking her eggs away for IVF.

IVF! So it had come to this. Waldo was alarmed by the idea of ejaculating into a bottle and suggested she went to a sperm bank. Younger fathers had better sperm than older fathers. Eliza, listening to these conversations as ever, interjected that she thought this was a great idea.

'You would, wouldn't you,' said Janice to herself, and to Waldo, 'No, I don't think so. Those who have husbands don't need sperm banks.'

She was not quite sure which she wanted more. To get rid of Eliza or to have a baby.

At breakfast the next morning Waldo said to Janice, 'We have to raise more money on the house: now we can include your salary in the joint income we're in a better position to do so.'

'Was that why you put the house in my name?' she asked.

'Janice, what is the matter with you? You are getting really boring. Eliza has to go to college, your parents are too wrapped up in their own affairs to help us out any more, and your fertility treatments are unbelievably expensive; we have no option.'

He took her upstairs to the studio to make love and she realized his penis was the weapon he used to soothe away doubt and keep her docile and content. Today the light somehow missed the cleft chin, or perhaps he'd grown fatter and older: at any rate he seemed to have a chin like anyone else's. Kirk Douglas struggling with his horse up the hillside came to mind and she finally remembered going with her mother to see *Lonely Are the Brave*, but this man wasn't like Kirk Douglas at all. She signed the documents he asked. She didn't think she had the energy to leave, and besides, she wanted a baby.

What had she done to deserve all this? Wasn't she, Janice, nice, kind, good? Perhaps Jo had cursed her? She saw, with shock, that it was not unlikely, and even what she, Janice, deserved.

That day Janice did what both Eliza and Waldo forbade. She went into Eliza's room uninvited. Eliza was sitting her Maths Special exam, and could not come back unexpectedly and disturb her. The room was tidy and clean though all the furniture had been painted red. She opened her drawers. Hidden underneath her scarves – Versace, Fendi, Dolce&Gabbana: again, lots of red: *red rag to a bull* – Janice discovered a shoe box into which were packed foil packets of the medications she herself took daily, piles of presumably forged prescriptions, envelopes of assorted and apparently random pills, bottles of white over-the-counter pills, and the razors which Eliza had used to cut herself. It became apparent that Eliza had been controlling her stepmother's medication. Delicately, with her young, thin, pretty, Saturn-in-Scorpio fingers, she would razor-slit the silver foil, extract the tablets, replace with ones of similar appearance, but containing God knew what, press fast the foil once more and switch the packets in the bathroom cabinet. And Janice, blunt, nice, trusting Taurus, noticed nothing.

Janice sat on the Eliza's virginal bed and wailed aloud and Waldo came running.

'What are you doing in Eliza's room?' asked Waldo. 'Peeking and prying is the worst thing you can do.'

'I've peeked and I've pried,' said Janice, 'and just as well. No wonder I haven't got pregnant. Eliza has seen to that.' She put the box under Waldo's nose but he didn't seem to see it.

'You'll blame anyone but yourself,' he said.

'You have to choose,' she said. 'Between me and a baby, or Eliza and no baby.'

He stared at her for a long time, weighing up his reply. She could see he thought he could do better than her, just as once he thought he could do better than Jo. She could see Eliza had won.

She moved out that day. There was no point in hanging about.

The End

33

I, Phoebe, had been lying on the bed reading the Stepmother's manuscript late into the night. Janice had described it as a novella, but so far as I could see it was simple autobiography. She hadn't even bothered to change the names. I knew Waldo: or at any rate had seen him often enough on TV. She would probably be sued to hell and back.

New Year's Day dawned to a thaw and a power cut. Later in the morning, when she and I were wrestling with the emergency generator, and trying to start it into life before the Jacuzzi waters cooled right down, I asked Janice if that was her real name and she said of course. *Step-step-stepping On My Dreams* was the story of her life. Why lie?

I asked her what happened next in her life and she said, 'Oh, I'm with someone now: a younger man with no baggage. He's like my father: he's not neurotic and has a Walter Matthau sort of face, crumpled but kind. And I'm pregnant, but that's by the by. And I applied for the Controller of Programming job and I got it, and will be the biggest cheese around. That's why I came up to Castle Spa, getting myself ready for the fray. And my father has split up with the cow and has asked my mother to go back to him, and he thinks now I am pregnant she may well. My mother is the kind of woman who can't stand an empty pram in the hall, even though she's long past childbearing age herself. My pram, or at any rate my Carry-Tot, will do instead. The pram in the hall is the enemy of promise, as we all know, but the Carry-Tot takes up much less room.'

The generator kicked obediently into life. She had a magic

touch, I thought, with everything, just so long as she didn't marry. Euan the pimply lad was helping, usefully, because like so many of the young he had the knack of knowing one lead from another. We were sloshing round in wellington boots. The thaw had followed as suddenly as the snow had arrived – but alas, not in time to save the power lines, which I could see from my window strewn across the damp hillside like untidy tram lines. Castle Spa was now without power or telephone lines. Euan had trudged around Limmus spreading the word that the staff should stay home on full pay until further notice. Lady Caroline's win at the gambling tables had apparently been spectacular. The cold brisk air had done Euan's cold a power of good.

The fates were indeed in convulsion. Bad luck swept out with the tide, good fortune swept back in. I dismissed the suspicion that at just about the time I was wrestling with my nature and winning, Lady Caroline had been at the blackjack table playing for impossible stakes, and fate had smiled on her. It was just a coincidence.

When the lights went off, as we were having breakfast and wishing one another Happy New Year, Beverley had come down from the East Tower torch in hand to plead with us. The sky outside was still lowering and there was little natural light. Our anxious faces were lit by candles, not to mention mobile phones, cigarette lighters and other forbidden accessories. The thaw might have come but the castle was growing colder by the minute.

'Please go home now,' she begged. 'There is no point in your staying. It will be days before they get the power back on. We are very low priority up here. There is no heating and no way of keeping the Jacuzzi water warm.'

'But I haven't told my story yet,' I said. 'Everyone one else has, just not me.'

There were murmurs of assent, which I found flattering. Somebody said couldn't we boil kettles, just to hear me out, but as someone else pointed out, there was no way of bringing kettles to the boil. Beverley said there was a generator out in one of sheds;

if anyone knew how to fit it up they were welcome. There was only a gallon or so of diesel. We could bring the castle back to life for an hour or so, long enough for one more story, and then please, please—

Beverley's argument suddenly sounded quite convincing. First the story, then departure. Beverley added she was sure Lady Caroline would refund the cost of missed treatments and so on. We hesitated.

'We've been considerably put out,' said the Mortgage Broker. 'I hope Lady Caroline will see her way to more than just missed treatments.'

Beverley said she was sure that would be the case.

The Manicurist asked why Beverley was so keen to get fucking rid of us, and Beverley said she hadn't been employed to clean fucking loos and make beds, thank you very much, and frankly she found it humiliating, and one more fucking day would be the end of her. We murmured our general appreciation.

The Company Director said if anyone was short of a bed until the world began again in the New Year, she had lots of bedrooms, all underused, in her London home, and she would be glad of the company. Adam was all very well and she loved him dearly, but he was quite deaf. There was an exhalation of relief among the assembled company. Many, it turned out, would be short of a bed, and the Hambeldon home would at least be comfortable. There would be lights, baths, showers, hot food, ordinary home comforts which Castle Spa could no longer provide. Kimberley was already busy on her satellite phone, sorting out the matter of the Manicurist's security.

So it was arranged. It seemed trains were running normally again: the Psychoanalyst and the Judge cycled giggling into Limmus to arrange for taxis for the early evening train. Euan, the Stepmother and I put on our boots and sloshed through half-melted snow to the generator shed, to get the Jacuzzi show on the road again, one last time. Mira sat in the Orangery, in a warm nest of medieval tapestries she had torn down from the wall of the

Oriental Room, drinking whisky, and babbling of Alistair. She was soon red-eyed and tearfully drunk. Beverley had helped her take down the tapestries: they were nylon reproductions, she said, and not in the least delicate. Now Beverley knew we were going, she was helpfulness itself. She just seemed frightened we might change our group mind.

With the restoration of power the castle began to warm up again, and the Jacuzzi soon bubbled at its normal temperature. I was to deliver my story after lunch. Until the diesel ran out we were safe. The ladies went to pack.

And I of course had no idea what story I would tell. I went to my room to think about it. Nothing came. My mind was numb. I tapped on the Screenwriter's door and asked her advice. What was left to startle and amaze? We had been in a Greek prison, held Adam's ladder and not murdered him, picked a Death Cap mushroom and stewed it, argued with a Coronation mug, changed gender, rescued a cat and God knows what else. She offered me some amphetamines but I have tried those in the past and they deaden my brain. I declined. And then she pointed out of the window and said, 'Lo, the deus ex machina! Always on cue. Saved!'

And saved I was. A roaring sound filled the skies. A helicopter was landing on the Castle Spa pad; not a little clattering mosquito like the one that had brought in Lady Caroline but a great big threatening beast, the troop-carrying kind they use in Afghanistan and the landing pad was inadequate. It hovered as if deciding and then went for it. Muddy water spattered up as far as our windows; when it cleared we saw the iron man-slayer settled and its rotors slowing.

I went to the Oriental Room, the scene of so many life histories, and found Mira coiled in her faux mediaeval nest. I didn't exactly kick her awake, but I think I battered her a little. When she sat up she looked dreadful. Her mouth was slack with drink, her eyes were bleary and not focusing properly and she had dribbled on the white shirt.

'He's come to get you,' I said. 'Alistair has come to join your life to his.'

'Tell him to go back to his wife,' she said.

And then Alistair strode into the room. I will say this for him; he had a presence, as people who are used to doing what they please at the expense of others often do. Mind you, or so Mira was to tell me, and going by her experience in desert lands, it was nothing to the presence people have if they've killed others with their bare hands. Those who have used the language of the state to get rid of others – *Terminate with extreme prejudice*, or *who will rid me of this turbulent priest?* – gets you eight out of ten. But for ten out of ten, Mira claimed, you need to have done it in person. Then you carry the souls of dispatched others around with you, like it or not. They're there for the duration. Firing people, the little murder, gets you a little way, and Alistair had obviously, from his demeanour, done a lot of that. Give him a six and a half. (After six months she was already dismissive of him.) He was not particularly good-looking, flabby, soft-mouthed, going bald, the absurd piece of hair combed across his bare pate, but most women would have gone with him for the asking. Status and power, status and power.

He yanked Mira to her feet. 'God, you look awful,' he said. 'I've come to get you. I've left the family. I can put up with her but I can't stand the kids. Promise you'll never have any.'

Others had gathered. There was a faint hiss of outrage.

'I have a family already,' she said. 'I've found a family here. Who needs men?'

But he wasn't listening. He said he could give a lift to anyone else who wanted to come to London. There was room. But they'd have to hurry. More snow was forecast.

By common consent – including mine – there was to be no story from me. We just had to get out of there. The taxis would probably never come. The Writer's Tale would have to wait, or perhaps I had already just lived it out, which was why a new one was so elusive. We had no choice: we must leave while we could in search of hot water, hot food, and back-lit mirrors to put on our make-up. We took off our towelling gowns and put on skirts with hooks at the waist, and shoes with high heels, so we were formed, no longer formless. We gathered in the Oriental Room and I ceremoniously turned off the Jacuzzi and we waited until the buzz of bubbles faded and died. And then we filed out to the landing pad, each so different yet so at one, ready for what happened next, and brave in the face of the future, I felt as proud of them as if I had created them, and glad to be of their number. The Psychoanalyst and the Judge held hands. The Manicurist was the last one in. She did not travel light. Kimberley had to make three trips to get in all her bags. Beverley helped, then stood back to watch us go.

As we waited on the pad for the pilot to do whatever pilots did, the lights of Castle Spa faded and died. The diesel had run out. Poor Beverley. We'd offered to take her with us but she said she had to stay. It was her duty. She was a Kiwi; she couldn't let Lady Caroline down. Now as she waited for our departure she wrapped her arms round herself and shivered. The spattering rain was already turning to snow. The Manicurist went to the open door and after a minor tussle with Kimberley, who was trying to restrain her, threw something out. It was the white mink coat.

'You'll fucking need it,' the Manicurist called.

'I'll do without,' replied Beverley, though I'm sure I couldn't have heard her, for the door was already closing and the rotors beginning to turn, so it must have been her mind I read. *'I don't believe in wearing dead animals.'*